P9-DWI-664

DAVID J. SCHOW
The Kill Riff

DAVID J. SCHOW
The Kill Riff

TOR

This is a work of fiction. All the characters and events portrayed in this book are fictional, and any resemblance to real people or incidents is purely coincidental.

THE KILL RIFF

First printing: May 1988

A TOR Book

Published by Tom Doherty Associates, Inc.
49 West 24 Street
New York, N.Y. 10010

ISBN: 0-312-93065-8

Library of Congress Catalog Card Number: 87-51396

Printed in the United States of America

0 9 8 7 6 5 4 3 2 1

To wine in your glass
The song in your eyes
And a dance in your garden

for

PEGGY

with love

The stuff that happens in *The Kill Riff* is made up. It is NOT REAL. The people are not real people. This is what is meant when you read "any resemblance to real people or incidents is purely coincidental." If you claim this book has made you do weird things, you should be locked away where you cannot hurt anyone. Repeat: I made it all up. That's why it's called fiction.

—DJS

1

THIS TIME HE WOULD PULL the trigger without blinking.

Training permitted him to lock his eyes open so he could watch the face in the crosshairs. As it imploded, blood would flush, brains would splatter wetly backward, two ice-blue eyes would fly violently away from each other. And the equity most people ascribed to an indifferent universe would be demonstrated. Balance would be restored.

That was how it should have gone.

Kristen's eyes are glittering.

He was sliding into the nightmare again, reliving her death for the thousandth time. His slumbering mind acknowledged that the recurrent dream was purely a product of his brain, neural impulses with nothing to do but spin their wheels, revving aimlessly, juxtaposing bits of data—always the same information, endlessly repeated.

His hair is white blond, floating dreamily.

The dreamer's knowledge that this *was* a dream did

nothing to dispel or dilute it; he was transfixed, a tiny desert animal trapped and hypnotized by the nova glow of oncoming headlights. There was nothing anyone could do about what was going to happen . . . except live through the whole terrible sequence one more time.

Encore: one more time!

Behind closed lids, the rapid eye movements characteristic of the dream state tracked avidly along to follow the actions in the sleeper's mind.

Kristen's eyes are glittering. It's encore time.

He had not been there. The expression on his daughter's face was what his brain deemed correct for the circumstance. Reflected in her upward gaze were equal parts awe, joy, apprehension, confusion . . . and yes, let's admit it now, shall we? A taste of lust. Or what passed for lust, in the sixteen-year-old hive mind. She was surrounded by acolytes experiencing the same emotions, swaying as one with the group. Her peers, the sleeper supposed. All their lust was directed at the man on the stage, the one with the power over them. The aggregate desire was as sheer and clean and blameless as honed steel.

His perfect mane of white-blond hair floating dreamily, the man onstage exhorts his congregation, teasing and beckoning. He makes a flailing, wildman leap and lands precisely on one knee, triceps jumping boldly as he brandishes his cordless radio microphone. It is scepterlike, of gleaming chrome. Sweat has popped forth to decorate his face in animal dots. His pupils are tiny, stopped down and aimed like sniper sights. He genuflects to his people. And they gobble it up. It is a spectacle in the true Roman sense, an onslaught of macho posturing, tribal rhythms and down 'n' dirty sexual amplitude, motive energy to spot-weld the musicians into their role as the ultimate Party Band.

Upstage, subordinately placed, the men with the instruments contort through a repertoire of the expected poses, forcing sounds out of their equipment as though in intense pain, white-knuckled, grimacing, all dead black leather and cinder-block chords in four-four time, pushing and reshaping enormous masses of air within the bowl of the arena—sculpting the very atmosphere so that the thump of the bass guitar is a physical thing that punches the diaphragm, and flesh is electrified by the tingle of the guitar solo, keening and soaring.

The percussionist is invisible behind his barricade of drums. His tom-tom lies face flat so that when he strikes it, his accumulated sweat flies up from the taut plastic in a spray. He is battling his drum kit, pummeling his sticks to shards, snatching up replacements without missing a strike, tossing the dead sticks into the imploring, grasping hands of the audience. Fistfights erupt over possession of the blessed splinters, pieces of the true cross of heavy metal. The fights flare and die like the flame of a sulfur match. The pieces are tasted by the crowd, digested, and found to be good. Hands in fingerless gloves and studded wristbands are clenched and raised. Finger symbols entreat the next offering.

Kristen glances to her left as a doubled fist lands hard on a kid's head. The impact drops his jaw. His eyes vanish into shock wrinkles; his lank yellow hair jerks upward as he is sucked under. The chunk of drumstick wrested from his grasp is held high. Kristen thinks of Neanderthals pounding each other over stinking tidbits from some half-charred prehistoric bird—hey, I want the drumstick, brontosaurus breath! Once again she has the fleeting thought that perhaps she is getting too old for the concert scene. Too often, she winds up next to hippie flotsam whose last bath was at Woodstock or gets vomited on by some thirteen-year-old who ate too many Quaaludes with his Cheerios that morning. She hates festival seating. Open arena floor, no seats, also called "dance concert" seating, seating that isn't seating at all. How fucking stupid. No room to breathe, let alone dance. As the music and crowd fervor intensify, so does the elbow room vanish. But she is a veteran at these things by now. She can handle not seeing a restroom for the duration of a four-hour, three-act show. From where she stands she can reach forward and touch the wooden security barricade, just two yards distant from the heroes onstage. That is her compensation. Shoulder to shoulder with the die-hard fans, she dismisses the fight (too gross to bother with) and keeps her attention on the show. Enraptured, she watches.

Too old at sixteen—now there's a giggle. . . .

The show is so pat that it could offend nobody but a fundamentalist. Bad boys doing the reform school strut, grunting primal lyrics, cranking out the moves as smoothly as millionaire bikers with platinum drive chains. It is harmlessly evil showbiz, a high-volume urban diversion, audience pleasing, good box office. The sleeper knew this. He liked rock, good and loud, an aural assault that could cleanse away tensions and allow you to boogie off the dead ass that came from sitting and working for hours. The music was blameless.

But the crescendo was coming. His body knew it and did not bother arguing with his brain.

The rollicking gusher of music vibrates through their bones and prompts frantic clapping, in cadence. A hand slides up between Kristen's legs from behind, squeezes, and is gone. The usual crap. She doesn't even bother to turn around. She is submerged, getting off on the sheer sound. And then—

Whores in Saigon. They did not care what you filled your hand with, as long as you had American money.

And then he looks directly at her, all shimmering white-blond curls and hooded adder eyes, the icepick stab of a come-hither glance, his glowing ice-blue irises locking on to her brown-green ones. She feels heat at her temples, a surging at her groin. Yum. She imagines his hand filling up with her. The masses feel her up with their closeness, their lemminglike forward momentum. Though she no longer sees them, she is pulled along by their riptide. Her eyes are captured. Green spikes of color in them flare and become prominent, as they do whenever she is excited or happy. Her feet shuffle forward. One step. One more. Two rows of crushed-together people, two thicknesses of human corpus, separate her from the plywood barricade.

He thought of taking those damnable nameless hills at night, a foot at a time. Six hours of fighting to gain a few yards of distance. Toting up the yardage in the gallons of blood you used to buy it. It was never worth it. The flame pots a lot of bands now used in their concert shows shot up columns of fire, like plumes of napalm. One such had fried off Michael Jackson's hair during the filming of a Pepsi commercial. A trench of gasoline could do a hell of a job.

God, she thinks, he must work out two hours every day, just like Doc Savage. He peels off his sequined gold vest to bare a professionally conditioned physique that is granite hard and as flowingly smooth as dry ice. She watches his pecs pump as he wheels the winking vest around and around overhead, lasso style. The crowd is more vocal now, the herd pressure escalating, a banzai charge in slow motion.

I think he's going to throw it. Oh, god. He's going to throw it at me. She has never had a rock star look *at her before. Oh, my god. . . .*

Rock god. Like the toadish, squatting stone idols in the jungle. Abandoned, forgotten gods, who evaporate for lack of followers. Gods need sacrifices. They rather insist on them. Gods always do. They are immovable in that respect. Like rocks.

Sinews snap into tight relief as the vest is hooked into a flat spin. Kristen's eyes do not follow it. The crowd breaks with fearsome suddenness, a tidal wave hitting a sand castle.

Despite the floodtide of articles in psychological journals, there is no simple sociological explanation for why such things happen. There is no pinpointed cause for the effect beyond presumed catalysts for the hive mind. These things happen spontaneously. Sometimes fires start the same way.

As in battle, some hazards come with the territory. A simple release clause on tickets for festival-style concerts could solve potential problems. Remittance of purchase price could constitute an agreement to waive one's right to police protection during a show. Every fan for themself. The core truth was this: As a solution, all such measures could do was cover asses, not heal fractures, not bring back the dead. Sometimes concerts erupted. Sometimes not. Reasonable predictions could be assigned to a particular band's appeal.

Whip Hand was an extremely popular heavy metal group.

Concert security is a bad joke. They're big, and they're bad, but they're also outnumbered. They are highly visible in yellow bodybuilding jerseys with broad black horizontal stripes bordered by studs. They want deeply to bull it out from behind the wooden partition, but once they see the charge, they break for the stage level. This is misinterpreted as free license to jump the stage, become one with the performers. The tidal wave backswells, for thrust, then surges forward. The center of the barricade bows inward with an unheard groan; the sides collapse and are stomped down. On his knees at the lip of the stage, one bouncer reaches into the front rank of rock 'n' roll commandos, grabs a face, and bangs it into the metal superstructure of the prefab stage. Blood spatters his jersey. The victim goes down and is seen no more. Like army ants, the crowd turns its brief but lethal attention to the bouncer, who is overwhelmed. His backstage pass is snatched as twenty arms pull him from the stage. His tattered shirt flies into the air. Maybe it was the blood that was the catalyst.

Over one hundred strong for the Civic Auditorium show, the sheriffs are up in the aisles, totally impotent. Bashing with batons toward the center of the arena floor will only reap them a full-scale riot. They are already at the limit of their competence trying to restrain the concertgoers seated at the periphery of the open floor from joining in the melee. Commotion is always a good excuse for working off aggravation against the minions of law enforcement. They represent authority and retribution and are untouchable —except in moments like this. One deputy turns his back to the stage, and a swinging fist crushes his rimless glasses into his face, mashing his nose flat. Blood spurts. Two more badges lay into the assailant with truncheons, and mace mist fills the air. One kid gets his eyes pasted shut from the whack of a baton. The blood dribbling from his nostrils makes him look as though he has a real mustache for the first time in his life.

Whip Hand was a seasoned combat team. They had a preplanned escape contingency for just such a situation as this. By the time the bouncer had been yanked off the stage and devoured by the crowd, the music had stopped and the band was gone, vanished into the labyrinthine convolutions of the Civic Auditorium's tunnel maze. In an underground garage, they piled into a Datsun station wagon with reflectorized; sun-screened windows. A radio cue dispatched two decoy limousines, diverting the gullible. Back at their hotel, the band could play the game of defeating their own security by sneaking through their chosen sex partners and other privileged hangers-on. There was security, after all, and there was SECURITY.

The audience had gotten rowdy; no problem. Party animals, all. A little healthy teenage catharsis. Three days later the band would be in a new state, on a new leg of the tour.

The heel of someone's hand smacked into Kristen's brow, scattering sparks across her vision. She was rudely shoved from behind and stumbled sideways between the two people in front of her. She went down on one knee, in a clumsy mimic of the genuflecting rock star. Her hand found the support of the barricade, now caved in at a forty-five-degree angle to the stage. Abrupt, numbing pain shot through her; people were walking on her legs. Heels dug into her calves. The panic roar of the crowd had drowned out the music. She could not even hear herself scream. Heavy weight bulldogged in on her from behind, and she felt the plywood crack beneath her stomach. She collected splinters in her chest as she slid down, clawing for purchase as the wooden partition collapsed.

Viet Cong regulars would scramble over the barbed wire of American encampments by using the corpses of their dead buddies hung up in the wire as miniature bridges. The barbed wire had been manufactured in Philadelphia; the dog soldiers were constantly admonished not to waste it. All it took to defeat this feeble shield was one dead Cong. It seemed like such a monumental waste, in both directions.

Kristen's spine stretched, then cracked apart like the slatting of an orange crate as a motorcycle boot stomped into the small of her back. Her breath whooshed *out as though she were deflating.*

Gas from a balloon, she thought. My life hissing out.

Then came the waterfall of arms and legs and weighty bodies, the crunch point of herd chaos.

Maybe if I yelled fire—

"Your mom's always hollering 'fire,'" he had said to Kristen following the divorce. He shrugged.

"The girl who cried wolf," Kristen had said. "The original. I think she just feels deprived of her flaming youth—y'know, the sowing of wild oats, all that great crap she thought she was supposed to have done before twenty-five? You guys just . . . I dunno . . . used each other up. Time to move on." She had shrugged, groping for clarity. During the entire acrimonious split-up, everyone had done a great deal of very important shrugging.

"We outgrew each other in different directions." He had stuffed his hands into his topcoat pockets.

"Let's see if we can scare up some lunch."

Kristen paced him, linking arms. She wore bright red woolen mittens. "Don't want to talk about it, huh?" Her words had puffed out into the December air in chilly white clouds.

"Daughters are supposed to look like assholes when they learn from their mistakes in life. Not daddies. Daddies should know better."

"Christ, don't be so sensitive." Then she had pounced on the straight line: "You're my favorite asshole, Dad."

He had made a face at her choice of words. Limousines whispered past them in an endless, taxpayer-funded procession. There were more limousines in this tiny city than at the Academy Awards.

Kristen kept wearing her mischievous grin, working to distract his mind and counter his glum mood. She could be frighteningly wise and manipulative—traits of her mother's—but she lacked Cory's meanness of spirit.

He forced a wan smile. "Lunch, huh." He was staring at the Capitol dome in the hazy distance.

"Yep. We can venture forth into the great primordial stone swamp."

"Interesting return address."

She puckered up her face. "Better than writing *Washington, D.C.*, on your letters. Like you live in a city that's gay or something."

"Whoa." He was mocking her now. "You're not supposed to be conversant in that stuff, yet."

"Next you'll tell me I'm too young for a gigolo."

Teasing each other, they strolled on, blending with the cold. Eventually they scared up some seafood. Nine weeks later, Cory, Kristen's mother, died of a barbiturate overdose. The whole time she was going down, down, she had lain in a hotel room bed, staring at her reflection in the desk mirror. She had left a note that concluded DIE AND ROT IN HELL YOU FUCKER THIS IS ALL YOUR FAULT.

Shriek of feedback. A kid with a magenta mohawk and a torn green leather coat achieves the stage and manages to grab an unmanned mike stand. He catches a shock from the coaxial connector and springs back. The stand tips over and THUNKS *on the stage. Amplified feedback loud enough to shatter teeth reverberates from the back wall of the arena.*

Bloodied now, Kristen attempts to turn her head to stare up through the assaulting chaos of bodies. Her double string of crystal beads, her dad's most recent Christmas gift, is cinched tight, cutting off her wind, strangling her. Another stomping foot crunches into the hollow of her neck, at the place where her ear and neck blend delicately together. The force pushes her through the remnants of the barricade. She sees sparks and tastes floor dirt. There is no sound beyond a medium-pitch roar—perhaps her own rushing, oxygen-starved blood, still pumping.

A final thought: Is this what dying feels li—

Kristen had left him a note, too.

DADDY—OFF TO SEE "WHIP HAND" (OBSCENE, NO?) WITH MARTA AND SUKI. PROMISE TO BE BACK BY NEXT THURSDAY (HA HA). LOVE YOU. K.

His life, summed up by two scraps of paper.

His mind almost craved the pain of playing it all back again. It was important not to forget a single detail. Seeing Kristen on the brink of her death, over and over, was better than never seeing her at all. The dream never changed. Things were shaded differently sometimes, but she always died. Twelve other concertgoers had died with her; the goddamned disaster had even made the cover of *Time*. He wondered whether a less notorious group than Whip Hand would have rated a cover spread. The band's lead singer, the iron-pumping blond with the Grecian profile, had made the *Wall Street Journal* a year previously, when Lloyds of London decided to cover him for $1.5 million in paternity suit insurance.

The hospital-sterile sheets were dumbed up with

sleep sweat; the man groped them in the wide, retarded motions of deep yet troubled slumber. His breath began to hitch. He was almost gasping.

What he needed was the ability to change the dream, to alter the configuration of the past.

The rock god strips away his golden vest like a carapace. The new vantage point is distant, higher, providing a godlike overview of the arena. At this distance the vest resembles a sheath of a thousand gold doubloons, polished, metallic. From here, Kristen cannot be seen. He can see the rockshow, but not his daughter.

He sees his feet, realizes he is standing in a spotlighting nest or on a girder high above the broad crescent of stage. Too far away to grab the singer, or save his daughter, or prevent the whole sequence from happening one more time.

I'm packed, he thinks.

He feels weight in his hands. Looks down, resenting the necessity to tear his vision from the imminent tableau below. He would miss the horror of Kristen's death. He saw in his grasp an abbreviated, foul-looking machine gun, a nasty, ventilated thing reminiscent of a Russian AK-47, with a curved banana clip.

And he thinks, Thirty slugs should take the bastard down all right.

He sockets the weapon into the hollow of his shoulder. His index finger brushes the trigger. Squeeze, don't snap. Be ready for the gun's tendency to kick toward the sky.

Write a jerk-off wet-dream child-molesting love ditty about this, *you overpaid baboon. . . .*

He cut loose.

(Don't fritter away your ammo. When you see the lead goon drop, chop the reinforcements. Fire selectively to generate panic and confusion. Make sure you've maximized disorder by the time you have to reload —you may need the extra two seconds.)

He was holding a longer, lighter weapon now. A rifle

with a powerful Leupold stretch target scope. Better. His marksmanship medals were no joke.

Light flooded in, spoiling his aim, startling him, making him wince.

Blood dribbled from the rock god's head. Spatters of it despoiled his gray three-piece suit. His palms were skinned from his abrupt tumble down the rough-cast stone of the courthouse steps. He is surrounded by bodyguards. Just like Reagan. Guns materialize from nowhere.

The gentle gush of unconscious orgasm warmed the sleeping man's belly.

He is standing on the courthouse steps below the rock god and his throng. He drops the pistol he has brandished. It is plastic. It cracks apart on the stone. He smiles a bitter smile of loss. Then they swarm over him.

Lucas Ellington huffed mightily and woke up.

"Do you want the candle?"

"Yes," he said. The candle was a bit of mumbo-jumbo he had requested. It helped him focus his thoughts.

"The same dream again?"

"I did it again, Sara. More explicit. Jumbled details. Scary, like a roller coaster. Almost a helplessness—as though I had no say, no control."

He stared at the wavering flame of the strawberry-scented votive candle. Near the desk, Sara fired up one of her filtered Salem 100s. He could smell it. The leather of the Stressless recliner crunched as he shifted around, eyes on the candle flame, riffling mental indexes to recapture the salient emotional high points of last night's hellish internal videotape replay.

"I'm afraid that while I was wielding all that phallic firepower in the dream, I came all over myself." He noted this unselfconsciously. Sara understood.

He heard her get out of her chair while he talked. Now she was behind him somewhere, near the office door. He heard her hose swish together as she moved. She was adorned with some light, spicy scent that was easy to pick out in the dark. She had a unique insight into his clockwork, he thought. Or, at least, she was convinced of that.

Clink. Her coffee mug on the glass desktop. The dark, the candle, seemed to open up all of his senses.

"You ready for tomorrow?"

"Ready for tomorrow . . ." He sounded almost wistful. "Yes. It's time I got back in the world. That was what we used to say. The place where the bad stuff was going down was not the world. And I think I can successfully leave the bad stuff here." It was his speech from yesterday and the day before.

"The nightmares?" She was interested. In more ways than one.

"Those, too, Sara. I really think I can do it. And you've done all you can for me here. It's time for me to prove myself to the world." He sensed she was waiting, so he added, "Besides, I can't invite my shrink to dinner while I'm still a patient, can I?" It was a good diversionary wedge.

"Mmm-hm."

On her desk was a small stand-up calendar, courtesy of Mission Street Flowers. The next Monday was circled in green felt tip. That was the day Lucas had decided to become normal again.

"This'll be the acid test of your ministrations," he opined lightly. "Technically, how am I?"

"Good. Not self-destructive. Not suicidal. The extreme fits of depression are no more. There's just the nightmares to worry about. This place focuses your attention on them. I think you just need to get back to work." In a more conversational, personal tone, she said, "I'll have you know I've pored over your files for hours coming up with this brilliant summary, sir. And I think this place has done all it can for you."

"And I've managed to develop a good healthy lech for my doctor, as well."

Lucas did not know how important a factor that had been in his progress. His death wish, the product of the suicide of his wife and the death of his daughter, had finally been elbowed aside by something more life embracing.

Sara had felt the attraction, too, a reciprocal force that manifested itself in a thousand little flirtatious gestures. One reason she wanted to get Lucas back in the world had nothing to do with his files and charts.

"Like, I had this other dream. I was getting gobbled up by a big green iguana with a name tag that read 'Sara' on it. Mean anything, doctor?"

"Ho, ho, ho," she said, deadpan. "That does not deserve the satisfaction of a retort."

"Is it time for lunch yet?" It seemed Sara had been satisfied. Or adroitly misdirected. It was all the same to him.

Papers rustled at the desk. The orange coal of the cigarette swooped from mouth level to light on the edge of a clunky geode ashtray.

"We're done. You've given me everything you can on the dream. It fits with all preceding. Hie yourself hence."

Lucas smiled to himself in the dark. It was time to stop dreaming. And start doing, at last.

2

THE NORTH HOLLYWOOD OFFICES OF Kroeger Concepts, Limited, had maintained an unchanged facade since the completion of its construction, some seven years past. On Vineland Avenue, a stone's lob from the Black Tower of Universal Studios, Kroeger had flourished with Lucas Ellington on their squad. Without him for the past year, it had fared comfortably enough. Or that was how it seemed. The facade leaked no secrets.

Lucas stood on the curb of the Vineland crosswalk through four changes of the traffic light, watching the building. Nothing had altered unduly here. At least nothing obvious enough to hurt him.

Kroeger Concepts had been born in 1970 as Burton Kroeger's ticket to the movie industry. Burt was a film buff, mesmerized, like many, by the idea of actually dipping into the filmmaking mainstream. Then he discovered the truth about his fourth favorite thing (after sex, spicy food, and sports cars). By daylight, the industry was a fetid cesspool of graft and lowball deals, a sausage factory run by soulless accountants and bankers who chewed and spit out creative talent like old chaw. In Burt's deathless, impassioned words, the business "spent all its time whoring with starlets and snorting dream dust and fellating the unions and bending over for the Mafia." Upon acknowledging this Great Truth, Burt had opted to make the giants approach him, rather than go begging to people he despised. He founded his own company, a publicity and promotional outfit, and things were bone lean through 1974, when two fundamental changes were implemented. The company got mixed up with three promising movies. Burt hit the technical journals hard, with a series of creative advertisements that built on reader familiarity with the previous ad. The spots were aimed not at the public, but at the professionals. Kroeger's ads for film stocks and new camera lenses tripled the company's revenue in eight months. How to induce executives to seriously consider recruitment drives from other studios? How to prove that saving the imbibition Technicolor process could be made cost-effective, so current color films would not fade to red within the decade? Then the promising movies carted off a number of minor Academy Awards. All that was the first thing that happened to the company. The second thing was Lucas Ellington.

By 1978, Lucas' drafting table served more for strategizing and less for drawing. By 1978, Kroeger Concepts commanded industry respect in the only way that counts in Hollywood—they were making money fist over pocket with high-quality, deftly targeted promotions. By 1978, Burt Kroeger was telling the studios how to go about their business, and he was happy. Disillusioned, but gruffly happy. Lucas remembered a sweltering August afternoon when he and Burt had bellowed laughter at a trade article detailing Kroeger's "meteoric rise" to prosperity.

"I thought meteors fell down, not up." Burt clinked his glass with Lucas'. Perrier-Jouët.

"Yeah, and they flame out on the way." Kroeger had founded its reputation on beheading clichés like "meteoric rise."

Lucas took time off to function as an independent contractor, redesigning Kroeger's offices for renovation. On a boulevard of eyesores, the new Kroeger building caught the eye the way a snappy commercial is intended to. It rose from a man-made hummock of real greenery that was landscaped to blend with the planes of the structure. The reflectorized wall of windows was either ahead of its time or still a mistake. The structure was flat and efficient without being a crackerbox. The rectangular, high-tech, soft-lit sign had anticipated the new billboard ordinances. Kroeger's self-proclamation did not despoil what remained of the city's skyline. It was mounted on a sandstone planter base next to the red-brick front walk and was modest enough to hint quietly at the company's true level of success. It prompted a tiny pang in Lucas now.

The receptionist's switchboard rig was new, too, and no larger than an electric typewriter had been in the olden days. The office decor had been logically reconsidered. In the beginning it had been a riot of paneling and hanging plants. There seemed to be an unspoken office pact around Hollywood that required the maintenance of a lush indoor jungle in every building. Maybe it was to counteract the smog level in the valley. The jungle wearied Burt quickly. It too readily reminded him of the jungle of paperwork cluttering up his office. In sober tones the employees later recited as a sort of company punch line, Burt bustled into the foyer one afternoon and made his pronouncement.

"The Black Lagoon has got to *go*."

Today there were still decorative plants to be seen. But each one drew the eye to it. They were more individualized. Burt's instinct for arrangement and subtle dramatics had prevailed. Now, the reception area left on visitors the impression that here was a company lacking even an ounce of fat.

Burt himself left a similar impression. He was a compact, honed man topping off at a neat five feet eight. His eyes were hawklike and direct, oiled ball bearings of intensity, a soft gray that accommodated a variety of moods and complemented the iron-colored thundercloud of fluffy hair that seemed to float around, rather than issue from, his head. Around the office, his voice always preceded his entrance. It was his advance guard now, booming from the corridor leading back to the office maze. Lucas knew he did not need to be announced.

"Emma, is he here yet? It's ten after, and the son of a bitch hasn't—"

"The son of a bitch beat you to the punch, Burt," called Lucas, feeling light-headed and happy.

Burton Kroeger burst into the reception area just behind his own pleased blurt of laughter. He was wearing a big, stupid country grin, and his eyes were alight with welcome. "Lucas! Goddamn my eyeballs, son, it's great to see you!"

Lucas executed a modest bow. He couldn't chase the smile off his own face.

"Emma, Lucas and I are out to lunch for the rest of the day." He clapped his hands around Lucas's shoulders; big, facile hands that could smother a grapefruit. "This is one of them extravagant business lunches you've heard so much about, Lucas." He was genuinely charged up by getting his cohort back.

"You mean you're going to spring for real food?" Lucas asked this with arched eyebrows, mostly for Emma's benefit. She was still trying to puzzle him out. She was new, and he was an unknown sum to her. All she would have heard was that *this* was the guy who'd spent time in the psychiatric hospital. Her expression was unruffled, amused, interested. Lucas trusted that she was sharp. After all, she had to put up with Burt on a day-to-day basis.

"Real food?" said Burt. "Hell, no! It's Dos Equis and Mexican chow from Ernie's for you!"

"Should I alert the police?" Emma put in. Lucas snickered while Burt flushed a brief red.

"The touch is yours," Burt allowed her grandly. After a precise beat, he continued: "That proves people who work here are touched. *Touché*!"

"Gasp." Emma rolled her eyes. They were brown, heavy-lidded, sensual. "It was nice meeting you, Mr. Ellington."

"Oh, yeah," Burt said. "Emma, this here is Mr. Lucas Ellington, my partner. Lucas, Emma. Now can we dispense with this amenities crap and please haul ass outta here? I need to discover some food! God *damn*, it's good to see you!" Another hearty whack on the shoulder staggered Lucas. Then Burt had his aviator shades on and was out the tinted-glass doors.

Lucas tossed Emma a little salute and chased the whirlwind.

Every third booth at Ernie's Taco House was occupied with fallout from the lunch-special crowd. Burt steered Lucas as far away from the jabbering TV sets at the bar as was feasible. The first uncapped round of beers with salted glasses came, and it took no time for Burt to boil their conversation down to a lean series of questions and answers. Lucas was prepared for it.

"Hope you understand about the . . . visits." For this, Burt had toned down the volume of his usually brash public persona.

"Don't think about that." Lucas tilted his glass and watched the dark beer form a thin diagonal head. "There aren't many pleasant, euphemistic ways you can tell people you're visiting a friend in the psycho school."

For Burt, one or two such visits to Olive Grove would be all his sense of loyalty and friendship could stand. Burt hated situations he lacked the power to grab in both hands and amend. Lucas had decided long ago that Burt did not need to be slapped in the face or hammerlocked into unproductive guilt. The choice of Olive Grove, over a hundred miles north of Los Angeles, had neatly abetted his decision to absolve most of the people he knew. The drive was just far enough to be inconvenient. This guaranteed a measure of privacy, without an overt edict demanding that no one was to see him. Lucas had not committed himself so that his friends could see him in a stimulating new environment.

"I'd prefer that everybody just continue with the gentle fantasy that I was on an unspecified, extended leave of absence," he said, "not squirreled away for my own good because a lot of bad publicity and bad events had inspired me to do myself in." He spoke calmly, rationally. Now it was Burt who had to be convinced, won over. He had to see that the topic was not taboo. Discussion would upset no fragile latticework of sanity. There was no insanity here. That was something all the folks in smocks had insisted upon. Even Sara, bless her heart.

Burt surfaced from his Dos Equis. It had always been his contention that conventional beer bottles were not designed to hold enough. The food came too fast; it always did at Ernie's. The mustachioed waiter bade them to enjoy. Burt's eyes bored into the man's back as he zipped away. The waiter stiffened, as if stung by a bolt of psychic energy, then returned with two more beers.

"Do I have to be nice to you?"

Lucas was slightly taken aback by this. "No, Burt, of course not. Fire away."

"Just between you and me. As buddies and vets and partners. If it was me, my daughter, I'd've blown that fucker away." He dug into a mess of green chile enchiladas and rellenos stuffed with beef as he spoke. His grave delivery had no perceptible influence on his appetite.

"Those times I did see you, I was afraid to talk about stuff like that. Or mention how the papers seemed to ignore everything that happened. Let some homo actor croak from AIDS, or some director get caught dipping a kindergartner, and it's page one, lots of embarrassing tape on *Hollywood Weekend Wrapup*. Thirteen kids dead at that concert, and they treat it like a plane crash. One mention, and onward to the happy news." He bolted a vast gulp of beer, to clear his pipes. "Ridiculous. No investigation. No nothing."

"I heard the band broke up," Lucas said. His voice was very quiet, without irony.

"Hm. And I repeat—if it'd been me at that courthouse, I'd have blown the fucker away. I don't think I could've controlled myself the way you did."

A ghost of a smile made a brief visitation on Lucas's face. He sawed into one side of a deep-fried chimichanga, and steam perked out. "What would that have accomplished? It would have made me the heavy. Big bad distraught daddy blows away rock star in fit of passion. Very sordid, Burt. Unclean. I had the effect I wanted, I think."

He chewed food as his mind chewed memory, and he saw it all happen again: Gabriel Stannard, Whip Hand's top gun, was striding down the steps of the Beverly Hills Courthouse, flanked by his attorneys, gofers, munchkins, and teeny-boppers. He was wearing a severely cut European suit with a plain shirt and tie, all business. But his vest was a metallic LSD paisley, and on his feet were bright red cowboy boots with wiggly gray snakes stitched across the tops. The snakes had emerald eyes.

The tragedy at the concert of April 18 had translated into a staggering amount of baksheesh to be paid out to local law enforcement. The concert should have been Whip Hand's last, but there was no way the flacks working for the band were going to ignore the drawing power of death. After a respectful hiatus, Whip Hand continued with its American tour. Every show was packed. No festival seating, as there had been at the disastrous L.A. show. No further L.A. dates. The deaths brought out the news media, yes, but their function became that of unwitting publicity. The first concert of the renewed tour recouped most of the cost of getting out of L.A. alive, and the band completed their cross-country schedule as very rich men. A few token appearances in court amounted to minutiae, a quick and noiseless sweeping up. End of narrative.

Except for Lucas. Representatives from band management had expressed weighty and meaningless condolences. He remembered the schmuck attorney. Woodberry. Or Washburn. The guy's name was a blur, like his face. Only his bit part mattered. Lucas's inspiration had come at the moment he'd chased Woodburn-or-Washberry out of his office at Kroeger.

There were fewer cameras in attendance at Beverly Hills than Lucas had expected. More groupies than reporters. It didn't matter. What mattered was the expression on Gabriel Stannard's face when he glanced up and saw Lucas waiting for him on the courthouse steps. There was a hint of familiarity behind the mirrored sunglasses—the heartbeat of time that precedes actual recognition. It was enough.

Lucas had spoken the band leader's name clearly enough to shut everyone else up for a second. Time took a snapshot. Lucas drew the gun, pointed it at Stannard's face, and said, "Bang. You're dead."

But no one had heard him. They were too busy falling all over each other, scrambling to evade the line of fire. Lucas recalled an enormous bald black man, Stannard's watchdog, jumping to shield, with killer's eyes. A girl with purple hair and spangles shrieked and went rolling down the stairs. She was wearing a cartridge belt. It clinked on the concrete.

Lucas dropped his gun before Stannard's bodyguard could do real damage. It hit the steps and broke. It was plastic, a toy.

Stannard had hit the deck with too much panic and broken his mirrored shades. A silver sliver protruded from a gash on his forehead, and blood was coursing from burst scalp veins. It was messy but superficial. It accomplished what Lucas had desired.

Stannard's PR elves and attorneys knew the positive value of *not* prosecuting Lucas. They did, however, recommend psychiatric treatment, "in his own interest."

That was when Lucas had gotten a second inspiration.

"And then there's all that crap about suicide," said Burt around another mouthful. "Jesus, Lucas—you're the last guy in the world who'd try to off himself. A guy like you and suicide don't blend. Sorry. You confront problems. You're the solution man. That's why we interface so well." He gestured with his fork, point making.

"No, Burt. Grief can overload anybody's circuits. And I didn't actually try to kill myself. But I did think about it, and that scared me. So I checked in at Olive Grove. Even the dummies working for Whip Hand were pleased; they thought *they'd* done it. I admit it wasn't in character. I never believed in therapy."

"Hashing over your fuck-ups with somebody who went bananas themselves to snare a sheepskin."

"Sara used to say it didn't matter what side of the food slot you were on. If you weren't nuts before you went in, you'd certainly be nuts by the time you came out . . . or your money back."

Burt chuckled. It was going well. But he did not look at Lucas's eyes when he said, "And were you? Nuts, I mean?"

"Cory's suicide, then Kristen's death," he said gently. "Yeah, Burt. I guess you could say I was a little bit nuts."

"Stronger guys have killed themselves over far less. If it was me, and I lost Diana, I might just swerve off an overpass on a whim."

"She's a terrific lady. Can't wait to get together with her."

"I'm sure she'd drop everything to see you now," Burt said. "I can give her a call—"

"Not just yet," Lucas overrode him. "I have plans. We'll get to them in a minute." He saw in his friend the eager need for everything to be okay, to be normal again.

Burt slid his Dos Equis bottle to the edge of the table. Another dead soldier. His plate was scraped bare. "Tell me about this Sara person."

"She's the one, Burt. She grabbed my lapels and yanked me up out of that suicidal depression. It's her fault. No group sessions baring my soul to loonies, none of that pro forma psychiatric bullshit like gaming or primal screaming or any of your garden-variety southern California cult craziness. Just understanding. My doctor and my friend."

"A whole *year,* though . . ." Burt clearly disapproved of what he saw as a waste of time.

"What do you want me to say, Burt? It took a year. It might take more. In sum, not even enough time to pay for a new car. Definitely an investment. I got the rest of my life back." His palms were open in entreaty, the sort of gesture one might use to assure a policeman that one was not packing any artillery. "I have returned. I'm okay. Past that it gets pretty dull."

"I'm no analyst," said Burt cautiously. "But like you, I was never patient with group anything."

"All the more reason to seek help when I finally smashed into a problem I couldn't resolve by myself. Everybody eventually hits one they can't take on alone.

Cory did. It ate her alive. And I don't blame myself anymore for what she did. My feelings on that cancel out to zero. She was a very disturbed person. If she could've known somebody like Sara, gotten help . . . she might still be around." Half his chimichanga grew cold on the plate. It was cheap but good.

"Do I detect a note of interest in this Sara person? I mean, beyond her professional wonderfulness?"

"More than a note. More like a whole goddamned symphony. She redeemed me. She didn't have to do it. Now Olive Grove is behind me. We've arranged to get together after a few weeks. In a nonprofessional capacity. And then we'll see if there's anything to exploit."

"Good for you."

"Hell, we're *already* more compatible than Cory and I ever were."

"You mean she hasn't tried to stave in your head with an ashtray or cut off your balls with a butcher knife?"

They both knew how violent and unstable Cory had been toward the end. No apology needed to be made for Cory. Lucas tried anyway. "She changed, Burt. After she had Kristen, she changed. I really think motherhood doomed her. She watched herself get old while Kristen got young, and it was too much for her." She'd watched herself right up until the end. Her last sight had been herself in the hotel room mirror, dying.

Burt cleared his throat.

"So," Lucas said, to break away from the topic.

"So what?"

"So do I still have a job at Kroeger, or what?"

"Oh." Burt jerked abruptly as though hit. "Oh! Of course! Jesus, Lucas, I thought that was a given." He looked embarrassedly before him and saw no plate, no beer, and nothing to fiddle with. He immediately signaled the waiter again.

"Nothing is as it seems," said Lucas. "Venerable old

ad-pub rule. And you're still looking at me as though you vaguely suspect I might suck babies' blood or something." His smile stole any sting his words might have imparted.

Burt sent the grin right back. "Fuck you very much."

The waiter looked nervously from man to man until Burt pointed at his empty Dos Equis bottle. Then he fled.

"Thanks." Lucas nodded. "Now we move on."

"As we get older," Burt grumbled. He pawed around in a coat pocket until he fished up a nicotine-colored prescription vial. It took him half the ice water in his glass to get the tiny pill down.

"What the hell is that?" Lucas said. His eyes went stark at the thought of information not shared between friends.

"Nothing. Blood pressure's too goddamned high, so the jerks at Cedars Sinai informed me. They cited studies on stress, as if those would change the way I do things. So here I am—not even fifty and putting down pills. Shit."

Lucas's eyes stayed on the vial until it was stashed. The pills Cory was full of when she died were fat Seconals. Different pills, similar container. Autopsy noted she'd swallowed at least seventy-five of them.

"I don't like the idea of taking any kind of medication," he said.

"At least God created alcohol to wash it down with. These chalky little things remind me what pigeon shit must taste like." He put away a huge draft of the newly arrived beer, settled back, and eased out a belch. Except for two other couples, they were the only people left in the restaurant. The hazy color set above the bar burbled sports trivia.

"What do I need to know?"

"Hm. Well, I've converted your office into the executive powder room. . . ." Burt laughed at his own joke. "Nah—it's just as you left it, dusty and encased in plastic until your return."

"Divine," Lucas hummed. The beer was making him stupid. Beer wasn't on the menu at Olive Grove. He'd never exactly been a beer fan, just an occasional glassful of something dark and thick and imported. Now he had developed a positive lust for the taste. It was delicious. What the hell, his imp of conscience told him. If he wasn't entitled to get a bit saturated now, then when?

Burt picked up the threads of update quickly. "Emma, the princess of the switchboard, you met. She's been in Monica's berth since . . . well, she was pregnant when you left, right?"

"I swear, Burt, we were just good friends."

"Not to worry. She had twins, and neither of them is as ugly as you. Then her husband got a job working on the space shuttle. Engineering. Trying to find a way to keep the damned thing from blowing up." Lucas watched a dozen space shuttle jokes of the gallows-humor variety flash through Burt's memory, behind his eyes. "But you know," he said, suddenly thoughtful, "if they gave me a chance to go up in the thing and do stuff in space, and told me it would blow up on the way back to Earth . . . who knows? I'd probably go anyway."

Lucas did not ask him what that meant.

"We overhauled the drafting section. Figured you wouldn't mind."

"I'm tangentially interested. Like to keep a hand in." Bingo—another bottle of beer was gone in no time. His newfound thirst was definitely intriguing.

"Tower and Barrington are designing shopping malls now. The wave of the future. You know they're calling it 'Southern Californiaization'? Fuckheads. May they be crushed in the elevator shafts in the malls those two'll design for the video drones."

Barry Tower and Stanley Barrington had amicably

parted company with Kroeger Concepts just over a year back. Lucas scanned backward for a second. "How's Sean?"

"He's not here, either. He's off discovering Europe on a budget, and to hell with the terrorists, he says. Probably becoming sexually notorious throughout Scandinavia while you and I sit warming this booth and getting smashed."

"That's good. Sean Markesson was the worst workaholic I've ever seen. What stopped him?"

"Me. He was embarrassing us all, making us look bad." Burt often exercised his prerogative as a self-made success to ignore all the rules of bossdom. Now he and Lucas shared the laugh. It was partly the beer, partly the release of pressure. Lucas was reassuming his place in the order of things. So far, the fit was smooth.

"When Sean first moved to L.A., he was the most self-effacing man you'd ever meet," said Lucas. "A really nice guy. Then he hit Hollywood and bam! He became a slavering monster. Mister Tinseltown. Whoo."

Burt continued laughing. "Yeah, he got wound pretty tight. Much longer, and we might've had to book him a bed next to yours in the—" The happiness on his face curdled. He actually winced. "Ah—sorry?"

"Stop being so goddamn *careful*. Funny-farm jokes are okay by me. My sanity is not an egg in a paint mixer. I'm not going to fracture and rape the barmaid before your disbelieving eyeballs. Trust me."

Burt cast a glance toward the bar. "He's not your type, anyhow." He let go a beery sigh. "Just let me acclimate. You can scare up a lot of misconceptions about mental health, even in a short time."

"Stop apologizing. You're a friend, you don't need to apologize to me. Now get up off your knees and tell me what's become of our ad pool."

The ad pool was the profit nucleus of Kroeger Concepts, the conceptual salad bowl where budgets and brainstorms were combined to yield profits and please the bankbook honchos of Hollywood. When the department was first formed, Burt and Lucas were two-fifths of the combine.

"Charisse and Evelyn are as you remember them. Only better. Evelyn had herself a showdown with a muckety-muck at Universal over violent sexist advertising."

"For or against?"

"Against. But it wasn't what you think—not that censorship rap, not the bible belt's definition of pornography. The VP she had it out with was Derek Windhover."

"Oh, jesus . . ." Lucas recalled an earlier run-in with the estimable Mr. Windhover, an executive infamous for forcing oral sex on demand from actresses who came in to read for bit parts. Mr. Windhover was history, Universal was blameless, but the stench of memory lingered. "What a guy. Winner of Mister Congeniality, three years running."

"Evelyn shouted him down. Oh, boy, it was embarrassing. We lost the account. We got it back after Windhover left. Guess who marched into Universal and sold it?"

"Here's to Evelyn. The sprite with the sword." They clinked mostly empty glasses. Evelyn stood five five in extreme heels. She had always been painfully polite to Lucas and everyone in the office, as though straining not to offend. She was the facet of the ad pool that never understood Burt's grotesque jokes. But it seemed she had found a cause and erupted from her chrysalis. Good old Evelyn, at the advanced age of thirty-three, had finally loosened up.

"Charisse concocted the campaigns for *The Nam* and *The Interloper*."

"I saw the papers," affirmed Lucas. "Yes, indeed."

The Nam was a surrealistic film about the Vietnam

War—not the real war, but the fantasy version presented to the American viewing public throughout the 1960s and 1970s on television. It walked off with a wagonload of Oscars. *The Interloper* had been a science-fiction thrill ride about a horny alien trapped aboard an interstellar freighter. The creature spent ninety percent of the film's running time raping the female crew members and eating the males. The kicker was that once the ship was completely subjugated, it charted a course for Earth, piloted by a new crew of insectile alien monsters . . . and the final woman survivor turned hunter and bumped off the aliens, ten-little-Indians style. What made *The Interloper* notable was, largely, the promotion cooked up by Charisse Hope. The film grossed $3 million every two days during its first three weeks of release and secured a prime position on *Variety*'s "Top Ten Moneymakers for the Year."

The fifth member of the pool was Gustavo de la Luces. Gustavo of the Lights, as he often signed his name—an energetic and volatile man Burt had signed on after incorporating as Kroeger Concepts, Ltd. Lucas had expected him to burst forth at the office, with his dark, twinkling eyes and generous, fraternal smile. Burt was obviously holding the news on Gustavo back for last. He and Lucas had been close co-workers and fair social buddies . . . before.

"Gustavo's out there in the smogscape, ramrodding with the Randell and Kochner boys."

Lucas whistled. "The billboard mafia?" Randell and Kochner owned half the billboard space in Los Angeles County. Kroeger Concepts dealt with them not through choice, but through necessity. "I take it from your tone that Gustavo is not absent from this party because he is dickering over cost per foot on ad space."

"Nope. He's in court with a platoon of lawyers from Marina del Rey. Randell and Kochner pulled a little game of hide the financial salami with us. Gustavo found out, and he's sinking some fingerholds into about a quarter of a million bucks that should be ours."

"When you want to claw something out of the hole, you send in a badger. Those suckers haven't got a chance. But like I said, I saw the papers. How'd I miss that one?"

"Ha, ha—are you serious? You'll never see this case covered in any paper." Burt let it hang until Lucas caught on.

Lucas banged his temple with the heel of his hand. "Right. I got it now. They got deep hooks in newspaper advertising. Right."

"You can bet the *Times* is gonna look for something else to cover, rather posthaste." He picked out a cold nacho chip from the appetizer basket and nibbled, more out of frustration than culinary interest. His hands needed something to do beside hoist his pilsener glass. He'd tried tracing patterns on its foggy surface, but that was unfulfilling. "You want anything else?"

"A Coke, maybe. All that beer makes me thirsty—it's the alcohol, dehydrating away."

"Caffeine will do the same thing."

"Don't chide me or I'll tell you you're too old to play my dad."

Burt beamed crookedly. "Me, I think I'll have a straight shot and blast it down with another brew. You?"

Lucas shook his head. The thought of swallowing a shot of Black Jack (which was what Burt would demand, he knew) was chased by the unexpected thought of vomit. "No hard booze for me. I'm such a sicko that liquor unleashes my bête noire. One whiff of booze turns me into an instant werewolf."

"Smartass. Knock that shit off." Pause. "Beta what?"

"Bête noire. The 'black beast' that croucheth behind the revolving hotel door, or some such biblical hoohah. Kind of like a rampant force of id. Your basic, uh, primitive hostility, as opposed to your rational, civilized mind. Well . . . *mine*, anyway."

Burt repeated "Smartass" in a low, sardonic growl. "Just the same. You sure you're any different?"

"Just being an asshole, at your expense. You react so readily; it's hard to resist. At least you've stopped apologizing. But, Burton my lad, I can read your deceitful eyes. I tell you again not to worry. Your reaction to me is cautious. It is natural. I've got several centuries of clichés to buck against, and yes, it's made me a little sullen."

"Cliché busting is our business."

"I *am* the guy who's just gotten out of what you normal folks call the 'fruit bin,' after all. . . ."

"You mean the nut hatch," amended Burt, deadpan. "Now *you're* apologizing."

After Lucas got his fizzy Coke inside himself and Burt chased his shot, Lucas said with mock astonishment, "What? We're not staying for coffee?"

"Urp. No way. I'm sloshing as it is. And the coffee here would take the paint off a tank. They make one pot at ten A.M. and keep it at the boiling point all day." He looked around at the nearly empty interior of the restaurant, as if seeking someone to blame.

"I'm supposed to break the news to you," said Lucas.

Burt's eyebrows went up. "What news?"

"That you will not see me bright and early tomorrow morning, on the job. I'm not dashing back to my desk to get gung ho with the new dawn. My first official act is going to be taking time off."

"A characteristic Los Angeles affliction." Burt's words indicated mild surprise, but no objections. "Where, when? You have ETA and coordinates?"

"Remember my cabin?"

Burt furrowed his brow. "Cabin . . ." Then his eyes lit. "I didn't think you were serious about buying that cabin. Geez, Lucas—that's going back a ways."

"Oh, I bought it all right, and the plot of land under it. I was serious about investing some money because the IRS was serious about taking it away if I didn't."

Burt inspected his empty shot glass. "I don't even remember where . . ." His voice trailed away. Losing this memory clearly upset him. Or maybe his emotions had been exaggerated by the drinks.

"It's up around Point Pitt, below San Francisco. It's backed up into a mountainside, and there's a half-hour stroll down to a natural rock jetty. It's very pleasant; isolated and nice. Very private." His gaze defocused as he imagined the setting.

"You sure it's still there? That it wasn't razed or turned into an unofficial hog farm by squatters?" Burt placed his American Express Gold Card on the check tray.

"I'll know when I get there. The rangers visit periodically and are supposed to report violations. The property is posted. If anything was awry, they would've phoned Randy the Accountant and I'd've heard by now."

"How is the financial sorcerer? Seen him yet?" Burt knew of Lucas' habit of christening his fellows in odd ways. Randy Carpenter was Randy the Accountant. He made a complete set when added to Simon the Broker, Ace the Legal Chickenhawk (Rolff A. Nikol, Lucas's attorney), and Stephen Zallinger, the Duke of Liability.

"I'm happy to report that my stock portfolio juggled well, and there's interest as icing. I've got a formidable nut now. Besides, Burt, you know I wouldn't take time off unless I could afford it three times over. And there's only me to support." An eyeblink-quick memory of Cory's outrageous alimony dashed painlessly past. He did not stop to reminisce about money spent on Kristen.

"My man. The compleat capitalist. Uh—" Burt seemed hesitant, as though dancing around an unsavory topic, trying to figure out a direct attack line.

"Um . . . so where is it, exactly, I mean. Your cabin. In case I have to get in touch." He petered out, lamely.

"Nearest phones are north, in Half Moon Bay. Don't worry, Burt, I'll be in touch." He tipped a wedge of melting ice from his glass into his mouth and sucked coolness from it.

Now Burt looked positively uncomfortable. "Well. Uh . . . I guess you don't want to go back to the office, then, or . . ." He held up his hands helplessly. "Or . . . ?"

"*Au contraire*. I need to blow the decay off everything in my corner. Say a few more hellos. Run an inspection on my desk. I'd like to borrow some of the equipment, too. One of the portable videotape rigs, if you don't mind."

It was a tiny favor. "We got a whole closet full. You want VHS or Beta? We traded some of the bulkier stuff for self-contained porta-packs no bigger than a phone book. With cameras—everything's built in."

"Don't need the camera. Just playback."

"No prob. Say—are you meeting, uh, Sara at this secluded mountain eyrie of yours? That why you don't want to tell me where it is?"

"Now, don't pry. You're not my mommy." Lucas shook his head. "Sara I'll deal with once I reengage with the real *urban* world. This is just for me." He laughed. "What do you think I'm up to, you old fart? I'm going to get bagged and watch pornies."

"Very funny," Burt snorted. "Watch that 'old fart' crap or you'll get fed your teeth. Listen, Lucas, if you—"

"I know, don't tell me," he cut in. "If there's anything you can do, doo-dah, doo-dah, and so on and etcetera and so forth. You've already done plenty, my pal. And you've got my sincere thanks for everything you've done, now and during my absence. Hey, you want blood? Or worse, a percentage?"

"Lucas, you know the thanks are as unnecessary as the apologies." To Burt, loyalty was fundamental, automatic. He did not know just how rare he was. "You need a car?"

"That's taken care of. I've been shopping. Simon the Broker told me it was okay. But I am glad you saved me the social discomfiture of climbing out the restroom window to avoid picking up the tab."

"They have iron bars for people like that." Recalling his entrance at the Kroeger Building, he added, "You crafty son of a bitch."

"Probably. Cheers." Lucas drank down slushy ice water.

They sauntered out in good spirits. Burt felt his duty had been done and was out of touchy questions. Several times, though, Lucas had caught him peeking, regarding him as if he might be an imposter hiding behind Lucas Ellington's name, a fake or clever surrogate. The sensation was mildly irritating, but not wholly unjustified, given the circumstances.

He would just have to prove to everyone how sane he really was.

But that would be after he got back from the mountains, the beach, the quiet.

3

TO THE WEST, THE PACIFIC Ocean shone a weighty, industrial steel color—massy, substantial, permanent. The road ahead of Lucas unwound in smooth gray curves, following the close topography dictated by the sea.

Again Lucas thought of the crate. It was buried, like a casket holding ghosts from the past sealed within. Whatever the condition of his cabin, the crate would be intact, protected by the embrace of the soil.

Around him, the vehicle, a dense mechanical buffalo some Detroit genius had decided to call a Bronco, all indestructible chassis and knobby tires and flagrantly shitty gas mileage, thrummed to the tune of a steady eighty-five miles per hour, northbound, a solitary locomotive of bronze-finished power highballing up the Pacific Coast Highway with no competition. The last real traffic Lucas had noticed was a flock of roller-skate-sized Nipponese deathtraps, trickling down toward Malibu. The sunspray on the calm ocean was magnificent, hot on the back of his neck. He cracked the pilot's window, and the sharp salt tang flared his nostrils and trued up his sinuses. The showroom smell of the brand-new Bronco blew out in a rush of sea air.

The vinyl slipcover on the portable video gear reflected a white gash of sunlight in the rearview. It had taken audiocassette recorders a decade to hit a state-of-the-art stride; home video technology had taken about half that time. Things were accelerating geometrically. Who would have thought that painters and writers and rock stars would one day be writing the damned things off as business tax deductions? A reference tool for the creative. Lucas thought it was a nice sentiment, but probably hogwash in most cases; most purchasers probably had a motive no more complex than the desire to suck up movies nine hours per day. Then came home computers. The brilliance of the home computer boom was that people bought them without any real knowledge of what they were going to do with them. Cable TV had wired the country together in a little less than a decade. And now everyone was so terrified of venturing out into the city streets that it made perfect survival sense to hole up in front of the glowing altar screen, processing words rather than writing them, communicating via modem, switching to twenty-four-hour sports and religion channels when the all-day, all-night movies paled, handing off from those to moronic video games. Firms like Kroeger Concepts had abetted the manufacturers of each of these new toys and would soon be responsible for insuring there was an endless flow of "product" to keep the video zombies in sopor and out of mischief on a long-term basis. A lifetime basis. True video acolytes could be talked into anything. Their attention spans could be molded, their lives programmed via advertising. MTV had managed the mind-numbing feat of convincing viewers to watch programming that was all commercials.

Lucas wondered whether he was a neophobe, bitching into his beer at Progress. On the other hand, any hive mind that could be gulled into believing there was no difference between seeing a film in a movie theater, in seventy-millimeter Super-Panavision with six-track Dolby sound, rolling off a $10,000 projection system and through a $12,000 audio system, and seeing the same film on a crappy beam-screen blowup with half the picture cropped away for TV aspect ratio, and calling both of these experiences "seeing movies" . . . why, such a mind could be conned into buying anything.

And what of the people who could not afford all this glittery, hypnotic hardware and software? Not that welfare families had ever lacked for television sets. Burt had come up with an intriguing answer for that, sometime between lunch and the bow-in back at Kroeger.

"Most people, I think, believe if *they* stay flush during a given business year, then nobody really gives a good goddamn what the unemployment stats are or aren't," Burt had said. "Not if they're working. And honest. So, what of the unemployed? Who the hell are they? A lot of nerds who believed that college would hand them a career. Ex-housewives, seeking life beyond marriage. Ditch-digger types. Peter principle dummies who were shocked when somebody wised up and laid them off. Career industrial workers who find it beyond their capacity to believe that there is no longer a need for what they've been doing for forty years straight. A vast workpool has been driven to welfare, unemployment, loss of dignity. Now, consider this in light of the current administration."

Uh-oh, Lucas thought. Burt rarely refused an opportunity to pontificate on matters political. Time to grit the teeth.

"It's so big, so obvious, that no one sees it. A huge number of the unemployed are unskilled, urban minorities and poor white trash. They're on TV every time some politicians or celebrities do a fund-raiser, like that Hands Across America thing. 'Give us jobs, not food,' they say. And what happens when they get frustrated enough at not having jobs?"

Lucas took the bait. There was no other way out. He was not normally a political person. "They liberate a few K-Marts, break bank windows, open fire hydrants, and kill a cop or two."

"And the government is sitting back with folded hands, waiting for that day, waiting for the riots to commence. Because when they do, the Guard can be rolled in with plenty of justification. In one fell swoop, our urban centers can be put under martial law. That freezes the country. Without the connection between the cities and the manufacturing locuses, we're pretty goddamn helpless, aren't we? Then we'll just have to wait for our orders."

During his tour, Lucas had spent several days in Qui Nhon, watching the aluminum capsules full of dead Americans come and go. Waiting for orders. It was not pleasant. The orders were too long in coming.

"I almost said that was pretty farfetched, Burt. But then I stopped and thought about it. Nuts. But not so nuts."

"You're dealing here with major-league lunatics. Guys for whom wars are fiscal solutions, manufactured to pull us out of equally manufactured economic 'depressions.' They're locked into the 1940s and can't escape. They hew to this good-guy-versus-bad-guy mentality, and if they point their fingers at their chosen bad guys long enough, with enough propaganda, they'll find they've got a whole country full of unemployed, largely illiterate cannon fodder—people who are just pissed and frustrated and emasculated enough to go for a violent cure-all."

"I never pegged you as a sociologist."

"I dropped out of college, remember? By the time the idiots in business administration had their degrees, I had a business."

"And you were hurting." Burt's dedication had ultimately reversed that snag, however. "Maybe violence is the only solution—sometimes. Not TV violence; not a baseball bat in the face as a responsible editorial reply, not a contest of firepower and escalation. I mean violence as a final, horrible last resort. When no avenue yields satisfaction. When the drones and robots and nine-to-five mannequins lurch through one more day of colorless life by fucking *you* over."

"Aha—go bomb the phone company. Bomb the phone company of your choice, that is." Burt laughed. "But who's to judge? Who decides?"

"You do, when you know it in your heart. Can you buy something as nebulous as that?"

"Depends. Maybe Rambo knew in his heart that he was right. If so, we're all in deep shit. You're a romantic, Lucas. That's not a slur; Jefferson, Franklin, Adams—those guys were all romantics. Idealists. So what the hell are you, a romantic, doing in the publicity business?"

They paused, then recited the joke's answer in chorus: "*Making a living, boy!*" Commercial irony at its finest.

"Those masonite doors on my office closet?" said Burt. "I always get masonite, so I can continue punching in the doors without breaking my hand when I get angry. I get angry a lot these days. I rarely try to check it anymore. It's a steam valve."

"It's therapeutic," said Lucas.

"Fucking-A. Vent thy anger, O mad one."

"The shrinks have reversed themselves on that one, too. Now they say venting your anger does no good. That while you do express it by, say, punching your door, you never actually rid yourself of it. Which was what punching the door was supposed to have achieved in the first place. The anger stays with you, always. Kind of like herpes. Once you've got it, you've got it."

"Are you telling me that you aren't cured?" Were they not friends, Burt would not have pushed it this far. "Do you hold that kind of anger inside? About Kristen, I mean."

"Sure, I'm still angry. Useless death should anger any sane man. Cory took a ride on a big red roller coaster and fell off. She knew what she was doing, and did it to 'get' me. And it worked. Case closed. Kristen's death was . . . insane. Five hundred police there, and they were totally impotent. In an evening's entertainment, thirteen people get trampled to death. Thousands are bruised, lacerated, bloodied, their bones broken. The band is called Whip Hand. Yet nobody anticipates the break point between stage violence—which is sanitized, like TV fight scenes—and the real thing. What's the difference between a disaster like that and the riot mentality you predict, Burt? No, I haven't lost that anger. You never lose it. You deaden it, anesthetize it. We have to take refuge in knowing we're right. In your heart, like I said."

"The ancient Christians felt the same way," said Burt. "A lot of folks with fish on their chests got eaten by lions. But even they got pissed off enough to lash out, the way Billy Budd did. *Pow*. The end."

Pow.

Lucas reached into the cooler on the Bronco's suicide seat and cracked open a can of cold Pepsi. He nestled the can in his crotch as he drove. He was thinking of Buddy Holly.

Holly had gotten chastised by the descendants of those Christians Burt had cited, for playing the devil's music, inciting young people to lewdness. Then came Elvis the Pelvis. God, how Presley had hated that epithet! They framed him from the waist down on *The Ed*

Sullivan Show, so that the children of America would not be possessed by sexual demons. Black performers were a hideous racial threat to the same minds. Janis Joplin unveiled a lesbian bent . . . bye-bye, Janis. The music of the Doors had been on Lucas's stereo throughout Kristen's infancy. Then Jim Morrison shouted "Ain't anybody out there gonna *love my ass*" in Miami one preternaturally black night, and they busted him for dropping trou. Then Alice Cooper (AKA Vincent Somebody-or-other in real life) cavorted with his snakes, hissed his lyrics about fucking the dead, was hung and decapitated onstage. This was after Black Sabbath had every pulpit pounder in the country up in arms. Ten years after Alice, good old Ozzy Osbourne took the rap for chomping the head off a dove. Gene Simmons of Kiss spit forth blood and fire. The sonic assault of punk juggernauted in and offended everyone. Explosions, raw butcher-shop entrails, skanking and slam dancing, and anything that could get a rise out of an increasingly jaded audience were dutifully noted by the watchers with unblinking lizard eyes. The kids didn't see the threat. All they saw were new invocations, new congregations, good clean fun, the *music*, with trappings that were an E-ticket attraction, a slide ride fraught with lots of disposable badness and terror. But Holly and Presley, Joplin and Morrison, and Keith Moon and John Bonham and Bon Scott and Sid Vicious were dead, dead for real. The audiences did not seem to understand that part. Kristen was dead. For real. To them it had all been part of the stage show. Another cheap thrill, another special effect. To read the hideously bland articles in the newspapers was to go *oh, wow* . . . and feel nothing.

Lucas enjoyed the music. He preferred it loud. But the boom-box audio network wired throughout the cabin shell of the Bronco was silent as the vehicle gorged itself on the highway. It was not the music that fueled the anger inside him.

Whip Hand's stylishly dangerous reputation was as pointed as a live grenade. It had preceded the band to the Civic Auditorium by months. Any moron could have seen disaster coming, if a mote of attention had been paid. And that was the problem: the shakers putting on this concert were *not* morons. They were consummate businessmen who knew that the profit margin for a party band like Whip Hand was in direct ratio to the number of warm bodies that could be packed into the arena. A standing-room-only floor would prove lucrative. Reserved seating alone would not have netted the promoters a sell-out show. Too boring; not enough window for action. Festival seating offered a fatter turnover. Just open the main floor to whoever can get there first, and they'll line up a hundred deep for the chance to rush the stage. Until the accident with Whip Hand, festival seating had been economical. Two dozen similar accidents spanned the country, but it took an even bigger name band—the Who—to nearly shut down the phenomenon entirely. When eleven concertgoers were crushed to death in Cincinnati, festival seating became a pariah gambit. The promoters could comprehend bad publicity, even as Lucas was sensitized to it by his occupation. To cover asses and provide the illusion of social responsibility, festival seating was banned. For a while, until the furor dissipated. But money talked; you could never shut it up for very long, and already selected events were backsliding. Now they called it "dance concert" seating.

Lucas raced the sun along the coastline, into twilight. There had been no victory. More people would get killed. The anger never really left you.

Then had come the toe-parade of Whip Hand's attorneys and the inevitable settlement offer. And the schmuck, Woodberry-or-Washburn, whatever his name had been.

"I'm sure, Mr. Ellington, that you can appreciate the fact that the individual members of Whip Hand cannot in any way be considered culpable for this horrible tragedy." He was ten years Lucas's junior. His suit was dark blue, in accordance with *Dress for Success.* There was bogus sympathy in his dead eyes. "Off the record, I hate this . . . this sterile write-off whenever someone . . . uh, loses their life."

"You talk like this happens all the time," Lucas said. He was not looking at Woodberry-or-Washburn and had said it through clenched teeth.

"I have a daughter." He said it as though leaking a state secret.

"How old?"

"Sixteen months. Nevertheless, I hate to think—"

"Think what you like, Mr. . . . whatever." Lucas's convictions were as unstoppable as the tides of the ocean. "The real reason you are cluttering up my office today is not because you feel *simpatico* in the matter of my dead daughter. You are here in a misguided attempt to prevent me from appealing my case, because it would inconvenience you. You have come to offer me a financial incentive persuant to my withdrawal." He warred with something inside himself, almost won, and continued. "I am quite close, as we speak, to shoving those stupid designer wire rims up your ass, folded double."

Lucas had already unnerved Woodberry-or-Washburn with his icy manner, and now that things were thawing the younger man got flustered and scrambled to save face. "Really, Mr. Ellington, I don't see how *threats* . . . " He detested dealing with such emotional nincompoops. He resented the amount he had been authorized to offer Lucas. It was obscenely high. "In the matter of compensation, my clients—"

Lucas stood bolt upright behind his desk. His chair was propelled violently backward and crashed into the wall. All commotion in the outer office ceased. His hands gripped the lip of the desk whitely.

The lawyer jumped up involuntarily, fumbling his

briefcase and nearly falling over the divan behind him. Papers scattered like huge snowflakes across the floor. His face was red. There was raw sweat on his upper lip.

"My buddy Ace, the Legal Chickenhawk, was kicking the shit out of recalcitrant insurance companies when you were still pissing your didies. Rolff got meaner with age. You just got stupider. Rolff has advised me not to appeal for reasons that seem sane to me. I have no use for your filthy fucking money. It has my daughter's blood on it. But Rolff is going to cost you guys more than you can comprehend. Much more than your prepared ceiling. And that's fine with me, too. Now get your ass out of my office before I spoil your promising young career."

Exit the schmuck.

Woodberry-or-Washburn never heard Lucas repeat the single word to himself: "Compensation."

Now Lucas was rolling up fast on a laggard Datsun long-bed pickup with a racy camper shell. He let it grow in his windshield. Montana plates, a CB whip antenna dawdling in the slipstream of air. It was laden with camping gear, straining along. The tailgate was brown with road dirt. Lucas blinked his headlights once, then blew past at a hundred per. They ate his dust, not blinking back. He thought he saw the driver give him the finger in the purple dusk.

He had purchased the Bronco outright, for cash on the tabletop. Fully equipped, winch and all. There was cash to burn. So much for the rioting minorities Burt had droned on about. Locally, it was a fat time. Nothing else mattered. He could loan money to friends in need. Wasn't that one of the purposes of life, to keep one's friends from harm?

Yeah, and wasn't another purpose of life to destroy one's enemies? After staying fed and paying the rent? And seeking out beauty in the world? Even if one was called a romantic by a Visigoth like Burt Kroeger?

The Datsun dwindled in the semidarkness, shrinking to twin dots of light in the rearview.

Highway 101 would have cut two hours off the northward haul, but Lucas had chosen the Pacific Coast road out of Los Angeles. He had never before taken the scenic route. Now the sun was fizzling out into the sea, and the ocean's uninterrupted surface began to resemble a trackless black desert. A wasteland. Out there, beyond a certain point, one would drop right off the curvature of the Earth. Lucas was pleased he had driven this way, pleased he had done something for the sheer pleasure of it.

It was compensation.

Miles to the north, the crate waited, like buried treasure.

He was doing the right thing. If not, he had Burt, his ally, to worry about him and steer him right if he needed steering. Past him was Sara. Problem dealt with and filed.

Lucas tooled into the night, toward home base.

4

THE BALD BLACK MAN STOOD an enormous six five, and his shoulders seemed a yard from end to end.

He strode down the long, carpeted hallway on broad bare feet thick with calluses. His toes gathered against the shag as he walked with feline grace, barely disturbing the still air as he cut through it. He was wearing a fighting costume tunic and trousers of black silk. It was not a karate *ghi*, nor did it feature a belt. The business of colored belts was for faggots. You could be strangled with your own belt in a close fight.

Workout sweat glistened on the man's shaved pate. On the right ear, gold studs traversed the fossa of the helix; the lobe was pierced by matching golden rings. A perfect two-carat blood ruby decorated his left ear. His lower jaw was massive, almost prognathous. His teeth were huge and perfectly aligned, except for a pair of large canines that looked like fangs and had displaced the bicuspids behind them. His eyelids seemed thick, and he did not blink often. His eyes were the color of strong, steaming coffee, liquid and unrippled. They drew in everything.

From the open door at the far end of the hall, a television set burbled. He recognized Eva Gabor's mangling of the English language and guessed that a *Green Acres* rerun was on.

The man also heard the creak of a bowstring being drawn back, the *pung* of release, the hiss of the triple-edged deer arrow, the *thunk* of the strike. Like Heimdall, the Norse god who stood sentry over the Bifrost and whose senses were so acute that he could hear grass growing and see the wool as it emerged from the flesh of sheep, the black man clad in black silk was especially receptive on all sensory levels. He heard the archer release his breath. From the sound of the exhalation, he knew the arrow had found the intended target. It was not a sound of disappointment. He stepped forward.

"Horus." Gabriel Stannard knew who had entered the room behind him. "How goes the sparring?"

"I am pleased," said the huge black man. His voice was gorgeously deep and mellifluous. "In another twenty years, perhaps fifteen, I may achieve a glimpse of the total balance I seek." Then, as an afterthought, he added, "As is, I can tear ass outta any ten white guys. Especially the mindless ones, the iron pumpers, the artificial body inflaters. They know not what they do."

"Cut some slack, Horus. Hoisting is good for the bod. Makes the teenies cream." Stannard drew another deer arrow from the leather quiver strapped to his naked back and slotted it into the custom bow. "Spare me the speech on how it's all fruitless labor, lifting to no end, huh? Check out these triceps, man. Eat your heart out."

Stannard pointed the bow and arrow toward the sky, pulled the string slowly parallel to his right cheek, and tilted down to sight. He bulged in all the right places. His golden, artificially curled hair bounced in sweaty loops. He was bare-chested, clad in skintight red leather pants, belted with silver conchos so large they resembled wrestling awards. His feet were installed in a worn pair of felony fliers—black Converse All-Stars. His sculpted physique glistened. Horus heard the languorous, nasal intake of air as Stannard aimed and froze.

He held the pose, muscles rigid in isometric competition, for several long moments. Then he released.

The shaft sliced the air at top speed and ate up sixty feet of distance in the blink of an eye. At the far end of the oblong chamber, it embedded itself square in the groin of a straw-backed, life-sized cardboard cutout of a policeman waving his hand. Officer Mort, the Friendly Cop, already had arrows sticking out of his face and chest. An arrow hole pierced the palm of his upraised hand.

"The dick shot. End of the line." Stannard propped the bow against a leather director's chair and drank from a quart tumbler of sun tea full of ice and sliced limes. "Go for it," he said to Horus, who watched with folded arms and a Bhudda-like impenetrability of expression. "Plug one through the badge on his cap, I dare ya."

Horus hefted the bow, notched an arrow, and did just that. Stannard applauded. Horus just shrugged.

"Joshua called," Horus said. "Your friend with the plastic gun has been discharged from Olive Grove."

Stannard's glass hesitated halfway to his mouth. "Is that so?" He had to consciously avoid touching his right eyebrow. The fine hairs there were neatly bisected by a shining diagonal strip of scar tissue. Having photographers favor his left side had become second nature after all this time.

Horus' gaze found the hairless scar.

"Do you have any special instructions for Joshua?"

Stannard took another slug of tea. "Let's be magnanimous. Bygones are bygones, right? Tell Joshua to report any unusual movement. Beyond that, I ain't interested in the fucker as long as he stays the hell away from me."

The radio phone extension on the director's chair twittered. Stannard looked at Horus. Horus made a face. "Pick it up yourself," he said.

Stannard smeared perspiration away with the crook of his muscular arm and telescoped out the unit's antenna. One Katrina van der Leewon, she of the perfume inheritance, long, long legs and energetic Swedish body, had debarked from her limousine and awaited his pleasure in the swimming pool wing.

Horus noted the way Stannard's ice-blue eyes smoldered with memory. It was his job to keep track of such things. "Are you positive you want nothing done?"

"Nothing yet," muttered Stannard, almost subaurally.

"You will notify me immediately if you—"

"Yeah, yeah. Don't fret it, Horus old chum. I'm cool."

Horus nodded solemnly, wheeled about, and was gone.

As he walked down the hall, reflecting on what a marvelous body Ms. van der Leewon possessed (Stannard had invited Horus to watch a videotape of them making love in the Playboy bed he'd had installed in 1982), he heard a crash, followed by a sizzling, popping noise, and knew that his employer had just put an arrow through the TV set.

The little hardware store bag was of very thick brown paper. Inside it was a brand-new heavy-duty padlock and a pre-stressed, case-hardened steel hasp. Lucas dropped it on top of the pile of supplies and groceries he'd hauled into the cabin from the Bronco.

He had sneezed almost instantly upon forcing the stuck door open. There was quite a lot of dust.

The cabin's walls were of split logs. It had a brick

fireplace. A large central room branched off into a tiny kitchen area with about two feet of counter space. In the opposite corner was a tiny five-by-five room with a wooden door. The cabin stood above the hillside on concrete pillars and had a good board floor and a hurricane-proof roof. The roof was currently supporting about two tons of leaves and pine needles.

Sometime, perhaps last summer, a tree branch had blown through the north window on the uphill side. It still hung above a scatter of dusty glass shards. Lucas was glad he'd brought a boxful of domestic cleanup gear.

The outhouse, twenty-five paces to the southeast of the rear door, was a spectacular mess. The wooden seat had warped and split and was totally unserviceable.

Lucas began enumerating a list of things to bring down from San Francisco.

The first night, by firelight, after he'd done a general cleanup and installed the industrial-strength hasp on the door of the tiny room, he'd unscrewed the collar nut of his folding army spade and reversed the blade, using the tip to pry up five of the central floorboards in the main room.

Digging down three feet, he uncovered the crate.

He heaved it out of the earth, shoveled the dirt back into the hole, and nailed the floor planking back into place. The exterior of the crate was no different from that of a recently exhumed coffin. The wood was moldering, corrupted. The long-rusted nails protested removal with grating screeches; their heads, once levered up, broke off in the claw of Lucas' hammer. He split the wood along the grain and pried it away like a sculptor chipping away everything that doesn't look like an elephant.

The footlocker was filthy, but less corrupt. The hasps and metalwork were corroded and dull. He brushed away free dirt. The lock was a loss, and he used the hammer and a screwdriver to break it.

The hinges gave way and crumbled apart when he opened the lid, which fell back and crashed to the floor.

Inside, the ten-mil plastic insulator was yielding to the touch, like a fresh mushroom. Styrofoam peanuts charged with static clung to it. When Lucas used his Buck knife to slit the sleeve open, he fancied he could hear a vacuum hiss. The packing material had remained fresh and crepitant.

He cut the sleeve wider and pulled it open. Demons flooded out of the footlocker to wrap him up in their embrace.

5

GARRIS WAS BUMMED.

He could see his reflection, minuscule and distorted, in the tiny blue plastic window of the computerized cash register. He had just keyed in and turned it on; it hummed accusingly at him. Next to an incomprehensible numeral code in neon blue, his abbreviated image looked harried. As the manager of On the Brink, one of the Bay City's most self-important rock shops, he had a lot to answer for.

Releases This Week had been taped to the top of the register. New Stones—not a compilation or tour album. Sting single. Pat Benatar. New live Slayer, from Metal Blade Records. Maybe new Prince. New Peer Gynt, for upstairs. None of them were in yet. A cursory examination of the A&M order proved that Flash had fucked up. The stock numbers were in the wrong columns. The amounts were wrong. Everything was wrong.

"Okay, new rule," Garris sighed to the empty store. "No more dope smoking in the stockroom while we're doing record orders."

The cash drop had been short for two days running, and some coin rolls had mysteriously evaporated. Garris suspected Diamond Ed had been dipping the till to (a) upholster his mad money stash for cocaine or (b) meet his rent because he'd blown his wad on blow already.

Last Thursday Garris had strolled into the stockroom after returning early from a crosstown shipment pickup. There he had discovered Charity kneeling in front of Ronnie Colvin with her mouth full. Ronnie's Jordache jeans were pooled around his ankles. The expression of torpid bliss on his face shifted to stark, bug-eyed terror at Garris' unannounced entrance. He fainted before Garris could fire him. Charity had licked her lips like a cat, and Garris knew he held only the ashes of what passed for a relationship. In retrospect, the worst part was that now Garris would have to fill in for Ronnie in the classical music department until a new warm body could be hired.

On the floor behind the counter, leaning against the videotape shelf, were three teetering columns of priced records waiting to go into the bins. That was supposed to have been done on Saturday, Garris' only day off.

Wrong.

Two minutes past opening, and On the Brink already seemed too glaring and bright by half. Garris was in a state his mom always termed "cross-eyed with bad anger."

Fucking cretins, was that all he was capable of hiring? First order: Burn the oil. Recheck the books. Redo the orders. Screw severance for Charity; she could keep the Human League promotional stuff she'd appropriated. Tomorrow afternoon could be spent bartering comp albums and deejay pressings in return for reliable emergency help—Mitchell from the Broadway store, Bianca, who could really rise to a crisis, and for sure Mickey, who wanted everybody to call him Slitboy but was a bonafide stocking and checking fool. Mickey would hold out for drugs but would settle for weed, and Garris always had a bribe lid or two stashed in eternal readiness.

Garris fought not to plod as he trudged up the wide, Christmas-tree-lit stairway to the Classical Music Nest and fired up the lights. Banners bearing the dour visages of Perlman, Ax, and Pavarotti wafted in the breeze from the air-conditioning vents. Lined up behind the counter were posters featuring famous composers. Garris had pet names for all of them. Mahler was the Mad Doktor. Franz Liszt was Son of Lovecraft. Mendelssohn was Santa Claus Meets the Hell's Angels. Beethoven was the High School Principal. Waist high on the counter was a blowup of Charles Ives with the eyes cut out. Ronnie Colvin had liked to kneel and peer out through the eyeholes like a Chinese manservant in some Victorian murder mystery. There was also a chaotic handwritten chart, much annotated, listing the film scores of John Williams and the classical music from which each score had been plagiarized. Ronnie really had a hard-on to berate Williams. Garris thought that the chart would go, but Peeping Charles could stay. So much for Ronnie's contribution. Let Charity try to blow him full of minimum wage.

He shut down the cooler. It was nearly forty-five degrees inside the store. He'd turned it on automatically, without thinking. Winter was hanging on too long. It should, by rights, be balmier.

Garris ascended from the Classical Music Nest and brought the store's third level to life. This was the potpourri section encompassing all recordings not covered by designations like SOUL/R&B, JAZZ/BLOOZE, FUNK/RAP, REGGAE/SKA, THRASH, SPEED METAL, NEO-RAGE, POST-PUNK, NUEVO WAVO, SPRINGSTEEN, MOLDIES, ROCK-ROCK-ROCK, and the challengingly eclectic IMP, the import bins. Up there were sound tracks, and Broadway shows, and spoken word, and foreign language, and three-for-a-buck discs.

Murphy's Law of Record Stores was in force today, he thought. No sooner did he get up on the third floor than the first customer of the day blew into the apparently abandoned store downstairs.

"Mornin'," he said loudly, jaunting down with his easy, lanky, sort of loping stride. "I was beginning to think there was no sentient life in the outside world today."

"The weekday curse," answered the customer, aimiably enough to make Garris feel relief. First customers were traditionally whacked out. They were either the eternally browsing unemployed, who never bought anything but always walked out with the free music papers and whatever else they could shoplift, or older folks —the seniors who rose with the mushroom-cloud blast of dawn just to ask for records Garris could not possibly get for them in a century.

This man fit Garris' loose definition of normal. His hiking boots were splashed with thin, tan mud, maybe clay, but not clodded with shit that would come off on the store's carpeting. He was tall and rangy, with a healthy backsweep of amber-gold hair just starting to streak with silver. No male-pattern baldness. A broad, pleasant face with character crags around the eyes. A Marlboro man, for sure. He was dressed in stiff new Levi's and a chambray workshirt that had, happily, seen real work. The sleeves were rolled up and the top buttons freed to reveal gray insulated longjohns. Garris' first blush was that this guy had come for some Willie Nelson or maybe the sound track to *Honkytonk Man*.

The customer surprised him by requesting Whip Hand. It was turning out to be an interesting day after all.

"Ah—ancient history," he said. "Your basic three-song band." On seeing the man's questioning expression, Garris elaborated: "Ahem—any of the multifarious, one-note, mostly faceless bands cluttering up our airwaves in phases."

"Sounds like you have a theory," said Lucas.

"I'm proud of it, too." Garris leaned on the counter. "A band required to pull one FM hit every six months . . . or they get the bargain-bin torture. Whip Hand had more than three countable hits. But their musicianship and compositional ability are summed up in three songs. That's as far as they grow. Grew."

"You're pretty good at this, aren't you?" Lucas was already amused by the performance.

"You have come to the source, my friend. Let's see if I can do this from memory. Whip Hand's big three were . . ." Garris paused and squinted. "'Riptide' was the first hit single, the image establisher. Your basic head-banger in four-four time. Lots of chunka-chunka guitar riffs. More flash than skill. What Frank Zappa called wank-wank music for hockey rinks. Chord bashing."

Lucas riffled some albums in bins. No telling where Whip Hand would be hiding, in this place.

"Song number two has gotta reinforce the first hit, right? It's in the same style. Or antistyle, if you prefer. 'Attack Dog.' The lyrics went beyond monosyllables in this one, just barely, and Whip Hand began to embrace the death-and-destruction fix of most basic metal. Um —*'Fangs'll shred ya / Teeth'll tear ya / Blood and thunder / My attack'll scare ya . . .'* The harmony line was devolved blues, but of course nobody gave a crap about that."

"You mean there's a line of descension from the Fleetwoods to Whip Hand?"

Garris broke into an a cappella rendition of "You Mean Everything to Me," then continued: "Then cometh number three. The compulsory ballad. 'Love Mutant.' Real gooey stuff. A lot of double-entendre sexual suggestion, garbage designed to make the readership of *Tiger*

Beat slide outta their seats. Everything else Whip Hand ever did was in the mode of those three. They did way too many covers for my taste."

"Covers?" Lucas was still reeling from Garris' monologue.

"Y'know, remakes of old songs. If it was a hit once, it can be a hit again. Beats creativity. Or thinking. They did . . . christ, everything. 'Changing All Those Changes.' "

"Buddy Holly."

"Righto. They did 'Turn Around' by Dick and Dee Dee, and another version of Edwin Starr's 'War.' They weren't the first. They did 'Out of Limits.' They did 'Big Girls Don't Cry,' a heavy metal version, with Jackson Knox's lead guitar substituting for Frankie Valli's falsetto. It was pretty strange."

" 'Out of Limits' was by the Marketts," said Lucas, trapped in a detour on Nostalgia Lane. "The song was called 'Outer Limits' until the TV show threatened suit."

"Yeah. Hey, you're pretty good at this yourself."

"And I'm not a sixties relic, either. I just need to catch up on the last couple of years."

"Seventies sucked, didn't they?"

"Beyond prog-rock, Roxy Music and Talking Heads and King Crimson, I'd agree with you."

"Hah." Garris grinned. It was a very huge grin. "You're my man. You want the most representative Whip Hand album, I'd say get *Overkill*. Aptly named. It was overkill for Jackson Knox to have six strings on his guitar for the type of crud Whip Hand churned out. Amazingly, he's become a respectable solo act, now."

"I want to back-trace the history of the group to their breakup. Delineate where each group member ended up. If you've got any videos, particularly concert stuff, I'm interested in that, too. Knox has gone solo?"

Garris had already slipped a copy of *Overkill* from the maze of bins. "Yep. Two albums. The first one, *High*

Dive, you can have for two ninety-nine, since nobody wanted it for list." It had been remaindered but had not yet made it to On the Brink's top floor. It had been stocked together with the newer album in hopes of some crossover sales. "*Panic Stop* is new. But you can get it for six ninety-nine if you buy any other nonspecial list-priced album. Which you just did, with *Overkill*."

"Tell me about the breakup."

"Whip Hand disbanded . . . um, December of 1984. Knox became a solo act. He's touring right now. Brion Hardin took his keyboards through a couple of groups, all losers, before moving in with a band called Electroshock. I think he might've been with Uriah Heep for one album—everybody else was—then Limey Iron, then maybe backed up Johnny Scepter on a tour. That stuff is pedestrian. You a completist?"

"Not that much of one. Give me what's current."

"The battle cry of most of my customers. If it's older than six months, they're not interested. Here's Electroshock: Two albums so far. *Force Me* and *The Crash of '86*. They'll vanish after their next album, mark my words."

"Another three-song band?"

"Only if they're lucky. Now." Garris struck a sort of rockologist's pose. "The rhythm section of Whip Hand was transplanted intact into a more hardcore band called 'Gasm. Your classic black-leather nonsense. 'Gasm started out as a glitter band in seventy-eight, did three albums everybody forgot, and reemerged in 1982 as a sort of biker act—motorcycle chains, bondage gear, special effects, flame pots, hot poses, the works. Chording right out of *Learn to Play Electric Bass with the Ventures*. Dry-ice smoke, strobe lights, gimmicks out the wazoo. They're so regressive I think they're the only live act that still destroys their instruments. I dunno. Is Ritchie Blackmore dead yet?"

Lucas laughed as Garris wound his way to the appropriate bins.

"Right here in the 'has bin,'" he cracked. "Here ya go—meet 'Gasm. Hold your nose." He handed Lucas two albums, *Pain Threshold* and *Primal Scream*, the latter a two-record live set.

"I don't know how to thank you," said Lucas, shaking his head with comic bewilderment.

"This music will scare the tread right off a snow tire. The fundamentalists were burning *Pain Threshold* last year; it was supposed to have Satanist propaganda backward-masked into the grooves. This was when Judas Priest canceled their Palladium show and Ozzy Osbourne got sued for allegedly prompting some kid's suicide. Sales went through the ceiling. The bible thumpers are the best thing to happen to the record business since Paul McCartney's phony death. Or John Lennon's real one, come to think of it. *Double Fantasy* would've died if poor John hadn't."

Lucas pored over the discs and nodded sagely. "Dangerous stuff, huh?"

"You betcha. When the Mad Mommies started raising hell about record labeling, the PMRC and all that crap? 'Gasm was one of the first to put a warning label on their record."

Lucas saw the sticker on the shrink-wrap of *Pain Threshold*.

> WARNING! This record contains music that has been SCIENTIFICALLY PROVEN to pollute your precious bodily fluids, grow hair on your hands, kill your goldfish, and cause mass starvation in the Third World. If you subject yourself to this music, your soul will fry in hell forever, world without end, PLAY IT LOUD!!!

"I mean, mommies across the country have got to protect their young'uns from stuff like 'Doncha Want To,' which is getting a lot of airplay. Very complex."

Garris contorted his face and twisted his hands into arthritic claws, growling, *"Want-cha*—**HUH!** *Need'ja* —**HUH!** *Gonna* **GETCHA!** *Oomph! Ack!"* Then he faded back to normal. "This is timeless music for our age. 'Gasm moved from power pop to a grunt phase. Kind of like crossbreeding Black Sabbath with Ted Nugent. Godzilla meets Con Edison."

"Jackal Reichmann," read Lucas from the personnel notes on the rear cover. "Percussion, assault and battery, machine gun. Tim Fozzetto, bass guitar and vegetables."

"Videos on 'Gasm we've got. They stole a riff from the Plasmatics—nuking stuff for the cameras. Backing up their latest song by dynamiting a high school or flying a plane into a cliff. A cliff by the ocean, let's not forget art, now. They did a film, interspersing concert footage with shots of good old American boys blowing away Vietcong and El Salvadorans. It was released theatrically. *Throw Down Your Arms.* It isn't out on video yet." He winked at Lucas. "Except on bootleg."

"What are you waiting for, a straight line?"

Garris grinned his economy-sized grin again. "Forty-nine ninety-five. Go for it? I thought so. Now, after all the dust clears, we're left with Mr. Whip Hand himself. Gabriel Stannard, the incredibly photogenic rock and roll vocalist. The poor man's Robert Plant. That would be Plant in his Zep phase, of course."

"Of course."

—the vest is hooked into a flat spin. Kristen's eyes do not follow it—

"Gabriel Stannard." Lucas' mouth tasted the name, tested it.

"When he went solo, most of Whip Hand's audience went with him. He's set up a Rod Stewart-like personality subcult. An album per year, each album with a different backup band, each band with enough superstar cameos to guarantee it works. He gets billing under his own name only; it's in his contract. He even hired Electroshock to open for him on his last tour. Pass a little butter back to his old buddies, right?"

"Just the keyboardist. Hardin." Another name.

"Yeah. But he's tossed scraps to all his old band members since his split-off. There are plenty of videos on him, plus two albums. *Pleased to Meet You in the Alley* and *Caught Unawares*. Say, if you don't mind my asking, what's all your research for?"

"Article," said Lucas without pausing. "One version goes to *Parents* magazine. The other goes to *Gallery*. The research also goes into a longer piece, middle-of-the-road, MOR, that'll get into *Time*, if I luck out."

"A good version and a bad version. Pro and con. *Time*, huh?"

"My title for *Parents* is 'Rock Corrupting Our Children—Myth, Cliché, or Reality?' For *Gallery*, it's 'Group Sex in Large Arenas.'"

"And for *Time*?"

"I don't know. Something *Time*-like and bland." Lucas knew his answers did not have to be complex. Just convincing.

"How about 'Rock's Bastard Family Trees'?" said Garris. "Or 'Music to Kill Yuppies By'?"

"Not bad." Lucas made a big deal out of whipping out an index card and scribbling down titles. "If I use it, you'll get the thrill of seeing your name in itty-bitty letters where your family'll never spot it."

"That's *great*," Garris said, sounding like Tony the Tiger.

"You got a first name?"

"C-h-i-c, pronounced *chick*, and no jokes, please."

"Right. Well, Chic, what does this mess come to?" They stacked the records and tapes on the counter next to the ever-ready register, which sat there humming. Lucas noticed an X-shaped wooden dump loaded with rolled-up posters, racked like skinny wine bottles. "Got any good shots of Stannard in there?"

Garris withdrew a white cylinder. "Your standard-issue wet-dream pose." He unreeled it for appraisal.

Gabriel Stannard was frozen amid defocused, saturated primary colors and bleary circles of diffused spotlights. He was in focus, they were not. His mike glinted a mean chromium. One fist was upthrust in a power salute. He was wearing the glittering golden vest on his otherwise naked, sweat-sheened chest. Perhaps he had a whole closetful of them to toss out to the hungry faithful. He was not looking at the camera . . . and by extension, his dead poster image could not be aware of who evaluated it.

"I'll take that, too," said Lucas.

"You can just rent the videos, if you want. Buying them outright can get expensive. Dupe it at home."

"No, I'll buy 'em. There're deductible, you know."

"Oh, right, for the article. In that case, I'll give you an itemized receipt. Two hundred and sixty-three seventy-two, with tax."

When Lucas peeled off cash, Garris' eyes bugged only a little bit.

"You said Jackson Knox is touring right now?" Lucas said as Garris recounted the money. "I'd really like to catch him."

"He does clubs now. Strictly under-two hundred capacity. Unless it's local, I wouldn't know about him; he's kinda small league. There's a copy of *Realer Dealer* in that stack over there; it'll have the club lineups for all of May, and if it's not in there, you'll find it in *The Rag* or the weekend section of the *Chronicle*."

Lucas paged through the pseudo-underground tabloid. Undergrounds, born of the 1960s and rebellion, had been co-opted. *The Freep* was dead, dead, dead. Now the "alternative press" wore suits and ties and used credit cards. Newswise, they were an alternative to nothing, except perhaps boredom at some bus stop. He turned to a section mastheaded *Hot Dates* and scanned for Knox's name. He was not disappointed.

> *The* ROCKHOUND*—formerly the Black Cat Bone, this recently refurbished club showcases quality small acts on weekends and local talent on weekdays. Full bar, 21 & over, upstairs lounge, dance floor, sandwich and munchie menu. Table seating for 100. Cover charge on weekends. 5/12: Bates Motel; 5/13: punk night; 5/14 Slim Slick & His Slick Dicks plus Urban Wreckage; 5/15: Yuppie Chow; 5/16–17: Jackson Knox & Friends; 5/18: The Hangovers. (415) 747-4414 after noon daily.*

Lucas began to dig out change for the paper, but Garris waved his hand at it. "No charge. You've bought enough to warrant a ton of freebies in any decent rock shop. Which, by the way, is why I threw in *Overkill* for free, too."

Lucas slid the tabloid into the On the Brink bag, one of those sturdy brown jobs with handles and an imprinted logo on both faces. "Thanks again. You don't know how much help you've been, and I'm grateful."

"My pleasure." Garris beamed, looking for all the world like this year's big winner of the Nice Guy Award. His shitty morning had been handily reversed. He stood there, rocking back and forth on his heels, his hands thrust into his pockets, his hair drooping into his eyes. "I'll watch for the article. The *Gallery* version, I mean."

When Lucas walked out of On the Brink with his purchases, Jackson Knox's date at the Rockhound was five days away.

6

NOBODY WANTED TO FUCK WITH a semi. Those who dared, thought Gunther Lubin, were flirting with superior trouble.

Red lights and traffic, therefore, became even less than annoyances. Backing the truck up the narrow alley inlet behind the Rockhound had proven too much picayune hassle, so Gunther had floored it in reverse, gracing an asshole Honda Civic with a door ding as penance for parking too far from the curb. He barreled the top-heavy truck around the block and through an intersection without watching the traffic lights. Horns howled. Tires striped the pavement. Gunther spat out the wooden match he had been chewing and pulled his rig into the alley from the opposite end. The wing mirrors cleared phone poles by about an inch on each side as he skinnied the truck in skillfully. Once he made it, crawling out through the cab window was no biggie. Halfway out, he snatched his roadie pass, still on its waxed-paper backing to preserve the stickum, from the clip on the pilot-side visor.

The label was color-coded for Friday and read ROCKHOUND—CREW. There was a stamped and code-numbered bit of intrigue beneath that, a cryptic okay from Rockhound management. Gunther slapped the pass onto the crotch of his jeans. He was expected, but early. He had debated stopping for lunch before unloading Jackson Knox's gear, but prime among the endorsements for Gunther as a primo roadie was his unflinching sense of self-sacrifice. The show must go on and on. About anything peripheral, Gunther really didn't give a gilded shit.

He dropped the lift gate, and the chain latches clinked. Musical footlockers and cases were padded and stacked and backed up to the inner edge of the door track. Nobody could pack a truck like Gunther Lubin.

He turned to press the red button that would summon the Rockhound's munchkins to open the back door and get the lifting started. But his finger never made it. The sudden, flat jolt of pain felt as though a lead meteor had bulleted down from deep space to crash-land right behind his left ear. Maybe it had homed in on his silver skull earring. . . .

Lightning jumped whitely across his vision, and he went completely numb. Dirty pavement rushed to fill up his view. He felt no sensation of falling except air on his eyeballs; did not hear the sound of his body colliding with the chuckholed alley surface. He could see abrasions on the palms of his hands. He could see the blood. He thought, *Bushwhack . . . goddamn . . . must've snuck under the truck ouch,* before his sight blanked out.

He expected to feel his wallet being pulled, and he did. He had been sapped, expertly, and could not depend on what he thought he felt in any case. He thought he felt the wallet being replaced. *Hallucination,* he thought. Strong hands crimped under his armpits and hoisted him. His legs lolled uselessly as he was dragged. Gunther Lubin, boss roadie, had just faded to black.

He thought he felt the all-important stage pass being peeled from his pants.

"All right, all right, goddamn it to hell, I'm coming, I'm coming already! Jesus!"

Ralph "Sandjock" Trope hurried to the loading platform door wearing his irritated-executive face and sucking on a Tums. He had just taken twenty milligrams of Valium to come down off the coke, and his mouth tasted like an armadillo had taken a dump in it. His face was intended to intimidate underlings out of his path. Lifters and swampers could be satiated with free tickets. If a return favor was of sufficient magnitude, Ralph granted special dispensation to sneak backstage and gamble for the chance to mate with a female backup singer or hump a thumbs-down groupie. But roadies, like the asshole trying to buzz himself through the dock door by osmosis or some goddamn thing . . . god! They were always surly toward Ralph. They never called him "Sandjock." To them, he was just a promotional underling, in no way connected with the almighty music, and to be held in that brand of sneering contempt that reminded Ralph that there were some clubs he could not join, period. And roadies could only be bribed with drugs. Expensive drugs, which were an executive hassle. So much harder to bury in the budget.

He cranked over the locking levers and rolled the door up on its counterbalanced rails. The roadie waiting outside was a dusty dude encamped behind three days of beard stubble, a leather eyepatch with a rhinestone in the center, a battered cowboy hat, and an unfiltered Camel.

Ralph asked the dude if he was Gunther Lubin and felt stupid at once.

The cowboy sucked slowly on his smoke, wearied, and cocked a thumb at the ROCKHOUND—CREW sticker pasted to his roughout jacket. His eyes—eye, rather—never left Ralph's.

"Just show me where you want it." His voice was a whiskey growl tinged with traces of an Atlanta accent. As he spoke, cigarette smoke puffed into Ralph's face. It tortured Ralph's deviated septum.

"Follow me," Ralph croaked. Daylight was doing horrible things to his eyes, and he wanted to escape.

The roadie ambled back to the tailgate and pulled out a steel-reinforced tour locker with KNOX BOX stenciled on the side in white spray paint. "If I'm gonna follow you, ace, somebody by-damn better be watchdogging this truck. Unless you wanna pay for what might walk off by itself."

Ralph put his expression of executive pique on hold. He yelled into the depths of the theater, and Aabel, a sandy-haired gofer wearing an AC/DC tour shirt, burst dutifully forth to await orders, so eager to do something that he was almost jogging in place. Ralph thought of a hunting dog waiting for the order to fetch. "Tell Jimbo and Ferrett we're offloading and to keep an eye on the truck."

Aabel fetched.

Keep an eye on it. That was rich, thought Ralph. The road-burnout cowboy only had one eye to spare.

Once the bucket brigade of rock and roll ordnance commenced, Ralph phased back to the more important tasks of terrorizing the bartenders and hired help. And the cowboy . . . well, the cowboy could just go jerk off into his eyehole. He watched the man sling the footlocker up with a practiced air of robotic boredom. Then he pushed past Ralph without comment and strode down the corridor. Amid the junk dangling from the cowboy's belt was the usual biker's wallet, linked by chain to a mountaineer's snap ring. There was a big lock-back knife in a scuffed leather sheath, a thousandweight of jangling keys, and a teardrop-shaped sap with a handle of braided cowhide. Another rock 'n' roll soldier, Ralph thought with distaste. Another dude who got off on being a mean motherfucker. The lead shot in that sap could powder your brains and send them flying out your nose—*wap*!

The thought of nose powder made him wince.

When the roadie came back, Ralph said, "Hey—when does the great man and his band show up?"

The cowboy swiveled slowly, considering Ralph as though contemplating a cockroach on a doughnut. "Jackson always shows up one hour before the sound check. One hour. Always. The sound check is always two hours prior to the first show. Always. You, therefore, have a while to wait, ace."

Jackson. Now Ralph was starting to fray. Jesus, this guy is on first-name terms with the son of a bitch. And it means nothing to him. Ralph's anger, of course, was veiled envy. He knew it. And it made him angrier.

He spun with a sigh and left the whole scene to his inferiors. In half an hour that fair-looking lady reporter from *L.A. Weekly* would be awaiting an audience in his cramped office upstairs, and already Ralph was putting her through *Penthouse* pet poses in his brain. He wanted to appear firmly in control when he met her. He snorted some more coke off the edge of his hand. It tickled the backs of his eyeballs.

Later, when the police were grilling him, all Ralph would remember about the cowboy roadie were the southern-fried accent and the eyepatch.

"Are you Jackson Knox?"

Knox straightened and evaluated the man asking the question. He said nothing because, as the Rockhound's headliner, he felt it should be obvious to the unwashed masses just who the hell he was. This better not be an autograph hound, not *before* the show could be talked about. . . .

The man had a few years on Knox. The beige-tan color of his hair reminded the guitarist of an attack-trained German shepherd he had once owned. He'd dumped it. Too much trouble to baby-sit a dog.

"You've been looking for Gunther?"

That lit Knox up. He'd been cursing Gunther Lubin's lineage for half an hour, wondering just where his number-one roadie had gotten to. He assumed Gunther was in the kip with some twelve-year-old; the roadie was known to prefer women small enough to revolve on the end of his cock.

Knox's gaze fell on the Rockhound sticker on the man's bush jacket. He sniffed and looked around the stage where the instruments had been set up.

"I'm Mason Kellogg," the man said, extending a hand. "I'm staff here."

Knox shrugged. On tour, all staff in all the clubs looked exactly alike. This guy was more behind than most. The bush jacket, the styled mop of hair.

"Gunther had some problems with the truck. Cops cited him or something. He phoned five minutes ago to say he's on his way in. That's all I know, but he said to tell you."

Knox inspected the drum kit setup. It needed to be two feet farther back, to give him more gesturing room while he was wailing on his guitar. Dumb, for him to get accustomed to having clones do all the setups for him. He must not get spoiled. He must remember his roots, and the dog days spent slogging through shithouse clubs before Whip Hand had made a good impression on a scout from Atlantic. On the other hand, plugging male jacks into female sockets didn't require a member of MENSA. Maybe his jumpiness was flop sweat, preconcert nerves. This was his comeback—his first California gig in two and a half years; what he hoped would be his triumphant comeback to the West Coast. More scouts would be in the audience tonight. Ralph "Sandjock" Trope had guaranteed it. Knox wanted to make a headline or two while he was in San Francisco.

"Thanks," he mumbled. The staff dude in the bush jacket loped off into the maze of cable coils and spotlight racks that litter the offstage perimeter. You never could get to know them all. The faceless ones who did all the scut work so he could sleep late in the mornings, and abuse room service, and sign autographs, and make headlines.

Knox raked his stool toward the lip of the stage. Right in front of him, tilted upward, was his monitor speaker. Its purpose was to give him true tones through the din of performance. The monitor obliterated the ambient band noise and the bounceback from the rear theater wall. The other amps and speakers, plus two columns of speakers forming the P.A. system, were directed toward the audience. During his shows, his anchors had always been Gunther and the monitor. The monitor did not lie to him. Gunther lurked backstage, poised to spring forth in case Knox popped a string or needed a quick drink.

The foot switches for pedal effects were strapped to the stage by swatches of gaffer's tape. There was an archaic, accelerator-style foot pedal for the fuzztone and wah-wah. It was even foot-shaped, like the gas pedal in a surfer's Woody. It was Knox's sentimental nod to earlier days, when the fuzz and wah-wah were the nastiest effects talkin'. The pedal had seen a lot of miles on the road. Next to it were the high-tech boxes for the flanger and the digital sampler. There was a microsynthesizer patched in as well, its twenty slide pots preset to Knox's accustomed positions. In the background, the telltales on the amps winked green.

Knox laughed to himself and spread his fingers out before him, palm flat. No tremors; not yet. Cool down just a hair. Get ice. Get control.

Because of Gunther's absence they were running half an hour behind on the sound check. Gregor, the bassist, was sprawled in a ringside seat, his feet up on the scuffed club table, pulling slowly on a beer. Comet, the drummer, was MIA, probably sniffing for nookie. Knox could see his rhythm man, Fudge, holding forth at the bar, watching the stage in the back-bar mirror. Knox picked up the gray coil of wire and knotted it around his shoulder strap. It was live and buzzed when his thumb touched the contact. They weren't up to the status level of radio mikes and instruments. Knox liked feeling physically connected to his equipment. The knot on the strap was to keep the cord from yanking itself out if the wire was pulled during play. He plugged the silver jack into his agate-black Gibson and strummed a few wandering chords, warming up.

At the sound of his guitar everyone came to attention. The gofers stopped what they were doing to look up. Faces appeared behind the glass of the crow's-nest, the sound booth of the Rockhound. Women were magically present.

He got a few friendly catcalls when he picked out "Don't Sit Under the Apple Tree." His E string was sour, and he tuned it carefully. He'd do the same regimen for his two identical backup Gibsons in just a second. People were now paying attention. It was better than any drug.

Knox decided to rattle the rafters, just to wake everyone up and cut through the dense atmosphere of the Rockhound. He twisted the volume knobs on the Gibson to full and gave the strings a hard broadside. Give the people already waiting in line outside something to look forward to, he thought. The rich, evil croon of his axe filled up the chamber and drowned out everything else.

He slid through a nasty, fret-melting solo, then teased the guitar into a simple but impressive A-E-C riff. After one repetition he kicked in the wah-wah on the pedal board and began to twist the progression into a new shape.

Then his faithful monitor exploded.

With a flashbulb pop of searing blue fire, the front of the monitor speaker disintegrated, blowing out steaming metal shrapnel that put three dozen large holes in Knox's body even before it tumbled backward off the stool and hit the stage floor in death. Superamplified feedback screeched up and up, pegging everyone's ears. The breakers blew and chopped off the sound. Knox was spread-eagled on the stage, wide eyes gaping at the empty space where the monitor had been. His mouth was locked open, speechless. Pieces of his beloved Gibson were sticking out of him. The last thing he saw was his picking hand, quivering spasmodically, spattered with his own blood. Then his eyes fogged and he was dead.

The prep man and other band members had hit the deck in panic. Now some of them conquered fright and jumped to smother the chunks of flaming wreckage that littered the stage. Aabel hurdled one of the P.A. columns, which was lying on its side. He had a fire extinguisher. Foul yellow fog blotted out the flames.

Ralph "Sandjock" Trope and the woman reporter from the *L.A. Weekly* ran out onto Ralph's private office balcony, the vantage point that the Rockhound employees called the Spyhole. Ralph immediately broke for the stairs. The reporter fast-drew a Leica from her sling bag and began speed-snapping pictures on 400 ASA film as a crowd formed around Jackson Knox's ravaged corpse. From the Spyhole, it looked as though someone had pushed the guitarist through a tree shredder. He was framed in a widening pool of blood. The people below milled around, stepping gingerly to avoid soiling their shoes.

The photo proof sheets would later reveal Ralph "Sandjock" Trope, trapped in individual frames like the main character of a nickel "flicker," dashing to the center of the gawkers, slapping his hand to his head in theatricalized shock, then turning away to toss up some very genuine vomit into the bowl of the upended bass drum. The drum kit was in an alphabet-block scatter all over the stage thanks to the force of the concussion, which had also blown out the back-bar mirror and the soundproof glass of the crow's-nest. The light wrangler got away with superficial lacerations; he had been able to drop his smoldering joint and shield his face as the glass of the booth imploded.

The reporter continued snapping pictures with total dispassion. She did not care for Jackson Knox's music. Ugly pictures could provide years of photo royalties. The dumb luck of being in the right place at Jackson Knox's particular wrong time was the sort of chance upon which entire careers could be founded. She was able to ignore the carnage below and fantasize picture credits in *Rolling Stone*.

She also knew that Ralph Trope's final response to this unscheduled surprise would be anger. Anger at having to cancel four sold-out shows, at having to refund ticket money to disgruntled rock 'n' rollers. That particular task could be assigned to a lackey, but Ralph himself would have to primp for the TV news crews and try to squeeze out a quotable sentiment for the record. Quickly, with admirable skill and sure hands, the reporter dumped a film roll and screwed on her zoom lens. Ralph Trope had his hand over his mouth and was facing Knox's bloody body. That was the tableau shot she wanted. "Call me Sandjock," he'd insisted, all the while feeling her up with his eyes. Now she'd have to ask him nicely for a portrait shot—something that could be boxed, mug shot style, next to an exclusive depicting Ralph onstage, a sort of before-and-after effect. She had no doubt she could sweet-talk him into one more pose. Right now, she had to keep shooting until the guys with the body bags showed up.

The early birds loitering outside had been scared by the boom. When police and ambulance units responded, the tight little rock 'n' roll army did their best to impede those who would disrupt their squatter's domain on the sidewalk. It was a great opportunity to harass uniforms.

At last, the component remains of Jackson Knox were carted out. The crowd oohed and aahed. The vinyl body bag was mercifully opaque. It drooped in ways a human body could not normally bend.

Gunther Lubin was discovered in a garbage dumpster owned by Rico's, a pasta parlor three doors down from the Rockhound. Despite the bulging, purplish-yellow egg growing behind his left ear, he was arrested and charged with murder one. His semi had been located five blocks away, devoid of evidence, its wing mirrors broken off by a sloppy exit from the alley. Several shining gashes decorated both sides of the truck. The only prints inside were Gunther's.

In the following weeks it would become a measure of rock status in San Francisco to claim membership in the brotherhood of the waiting line outside the Rockhound on That Evening. The club experienced a brief spurt of attendance caused by the desire of various ghouls to touch the place where one of their minor guitar gods had been sacrificed. Ralph "Sandjock" Trope found it wise not to clean up *all* evidence of the explosion.

Less than three hours after Knox's death, Ralph watched himself on the news. Squinting under the bar of lights held high by a camera assistant, he expounded at length to fill up the holes of commentary left by the paramedics, who would not make statements about the condition of the corpse; the police, who would not make statements about anything; and the bomb squad boys, who would only say that a "high-velocity fragmentation device" was their best guess. Ralph, wearing an expression of woe that might have been peeled off a dime-store monster mask, grandly compared Jackson Knox's death to the assassination of John Lennon.

Naturally, Ralph was quoted in all the write-ups.

It was a two-hour drive back to Point Pitt. Lucas did not notice the time.

He was amazed at how easily his combat senses had slipped back. His body hummed on high burn. No mistakes had been made.

Sapping the dude with the marine corps buzz cut had been child's play. Lucas had checked the guy's wallet to get a useable name, ditched the unconscious body, and pulled a perfect fakeout with the effete club manager. The eyepatch, cowboy hat, bush jacket, and all other props were knotted into a neat bundle on the seat beside him. In the center of the bundle was the sap. And the backstage pass, folded carelessly into quarters.

He had looked right into the eyes of the enemy.

Are you Jackson Knox? You've been looking for Gunther?

The enemy had even identified himself. Egomaniac. If he had known that Mason Kellogg's handshake had been his final chance to beg for his own life, he might have been more polite, less the rockstar. Courtesy was an almost nonexistent idiom in the rock scene. Perhaps if Whip Hand had ever stopped to consider the safety of their fans, Kristen would be alive now.

But then, so would Jackson Knox.

Knox might have begged harder, too, if he had known just what degree of damage could be done by a directional antipersonnel mine. They were designed to be unforgiving. The only touch-and-go part of the whole operation had been slipping the mine into the monitor cabinet and wiring it to the pedal board. The device was a crescent of steel with the detonation works on the back. Stamped into the metal was the most basic instruction of all: FRONT TOWARD ENEMY. The alligator-clip connections had been quickly made. Things had to be done quickly and quietly in the jungle. There had been time for a fast costume change (no one had noticed that "Mason Kellogg" was wearing "Gunther Lubin"'s pants) and a final, tasty gloat.

Mission accomplished.

There was a phone carrel outside the Licorice Pizza store at the intersection closest to the Rockhound. Lucas pretended to converse with a dial tone for fifteen minutes. He hung up when he heard the muffled boom half a block away. And when the vehicles with the flashbars converged on the Rockhound, he bought a can of Pepsi from a machine and took his leave. Specifics he could get from the news. There was no rush, now.

Back at the cabin, all was tranquil and ordered. It was late, but Lucas decided to grill a steak after cleaning up the hand-built brick barbecue outside the rear door. He added a delicious ash-baked potato and six bottles of Dos Equis. Again, his almost ravening thirst surprised him. When he had checked in at Olive Grove, he had certainly had nothing approaching this sort of passion for the brew. It seemed the perfect complement to his food. It seemed just the right amount. Everything was extremely balanced.

He burned the bundle of clothing after dousing it with gasoline. The burning gas smelled like napalm. Then he tossed in the cardboard jackets of Jackson Knox's two solo albums. The shrink-wrap hissed and shriveled. The vinyl discs smoked and sagged down into a topographical mimic of the pile of coals. The record labels blackened and ignited. The polychloride plastic bubbled hotly, releasing evil tendrils of carbonized waste floating into the air like fibrous black snowflakes from hell. Maybe the crackpot fundamentalists could use that. When you burned the cursed records, black demons fled into the air, momentarily visible, like a spirit relinquishing possession of a Haitian. Like a soul or animus departing a human corpus at death. That ought to be good for at least two newspaper articles full of ignorant outrage. And free publicity for folks like Ralph Trope. As an employee of Kroeger Concepts, Lucas never failed to consider the publicity angle of anything. Perhaps this knowledge might be used in some way back in L.A. The very idea almost prompted a tolerant little laugh. Lucas wanted no truck with religious nuts or their devils.

The records dissolved away to black puddles of plasma on the coals. One down.

7

THE KNIFE WAS A MONSTER.

Lucas jerked it from its heavy sheath. The noon sunlight sneaking in through the cabin windows made the blade glimmer. It was a matte-finish Randall combat blade, one of the type smithed up especially for the Green Berets. Everything about it was in aid of a single purpose—to help human beings quit this mortal coil. Catalogs called it a "survival knife." Survival, in combat, meant knowing how to kill people quickly and silently. The nine and a half inches of edge were honed discriminatingly enough to halve a piece of toilet paper floating in the air with one downward swipe. The blade was nearly four inches across at its widest point. Its backbone was serrated for gutting. At the butt of the haft, a screwcap sealed a tiny, waterproof compartment in the handle. The underside of the cap contained a tiny compass.

In unskilled hands, the weapon could do little more harm than, say, a large butcher knife. Lucas knew this. Back in 1965 the government had devoted two weeks to instructing him on how such a knife might be used skillfully. It had all come back to him. It was like swimming or bicycling—something your body never really forgot how to do.

Grab the enemy's head from behind. Seal off his mouth and snap his neck across the blade. You hardly move the knife at all. Let the blade do the work. Jam it between the ribs from behind. Twist and rip it out at an angle thirty degrees radical to the entry. Or plunge it into the V just below the solar plexus. Uncork your enemy and let his life dribble out. If they stab at you, shield yourself with your forearm. If the attacking blade penetrates your forearm, twist your arm so the bones trap the blade and you can take it away from your attacker.

He replaced the knife in its scabbard and left it on the spool table by the fireplace after tucking the little whetstone on its hide thong back into the secondary sheath. Hanging above the fireplace embers was a cowboy coffeepot besooted with lampblack. He used a rag to insulate the metal handle while he refilled his cup. Coffee steam was an excellent aid to contemplation and reflection.

That morning he had dumped all of his Jackson Knox ashes into the sea.

The trail leading up to the cabin door from the highway cutoff began as a dirt road, then narrowed to a rarely used path. After a hundred yards or so of careful footing, the path steepened into a virtual goat track. It had been a challenge for the Bronco to hump its way to the front door.

Out back were water and kerosene tanks. When the cabin foundation had been laid, Lucas had also sunk a well with a rudimentary pump and spout. Elbow grease worked the spout, and the water tanks were topped off a bucket at a time. They fed into the kitchen's tub sink and a wooden-partitioned outdoor shower. Power sufficient to Lucas' needs was provided by the butterfly-winged solar panels on the roof. For light there were kerosene lanterns, the fireplace, the sun. A pair of boxy battery lamps were racked by the rear door. Trying to find the outhouse in the dark without one had provided for some comic moments in the dark, which up here was totally unspoiled by light unless the moon was out.

A tiny collegiate refrigerator was wedged between the kitchenette shelves and the counter. It chugged softly to itself. Lucas found the background purr comforting; it provided just enough noise that he did not go buggy for want of solid, urban aural pollution.

After returning to the cabin from the beach, Lucas had opened up his Whip Hand room. That was what he'd unconsciously begun to call it.

The tiny locked cubicle had become a cramped control room. All of his audio and video equipment was wired together on a shallow workbench of four-by-fours and plywood that ran the width of the room. The Whip Hand discs and tapes were stacked to one side of the cassette player. Whistling tunelessly, Lucas detoured through the room to switch tapes from the Temptations to Jean-Pierre Rampal. Beneath the workbench was the exhumed footlocker, broken lid and all. Above it, thumbtacked to the split log wall, was the garish poster of Gabriel Stannard that Lucas had purchased at On the Brink. He had found a paring knife that had gone to rust in the kitchenette and used it to nail Stannard's liver to the wall. The blade looked like it belonged there. Next to the workbench he had managed to crowd in a card table to provide an additional work surface, which left a minuscule square of space for a creaky folding chair. Balanced across one corner of the card table was a fully assembled M-16 infantry rifle with a Nitefinder scope and flash suppressor.

The lead sap with the braided handle that he'd used on Gunther Lubin was the first thing Lucas had removed from the sealed plastic package inside the footlocker. The monster combat knife was second. Third had come the M-16, broken down into components, greased in cosmoline, coated with silicon, and wrapped in more plastic. It was absolutely cherry. Still unassembled was a special Russian sniper's rifle, a 7.62-millimeter Dragunov semiauto.

Jean-Pierre was blowing flute sonatas. Handel.

Then had come the flat boxes, packed against one side of the footlocker, each about the size of a brick, with designations like CAUTION and EXPLOSIVE and ANTI-PERSONNEL stamped all over them.

In a box under the card table was new ammunition and a squeaky-new leather shoulder holster with nylon web straps. Gun-cleaning tools; jeweler's textured cloths; solvents and lubes. Empty clips awaiting their loads. All innocuous items easily purchased without bothersome signatures and ID.

Lucas picked up the forty-five auto pistol and shoved in a full clip. The gun was a large-frame Llama ACP with a blue finish; the slugs were steel-jacketed hollow points. He snapped the action, and his eye sought the loaded chamber indicator out of habit. Then he popped out the clip, inserted one replacement round, reloaded, and thumbed the slide lever safety. The shoulder holster had snap pockets for two extra clips.

The guns had come into his hands without signatures as well.

Every man in every war meets good old boys heavily into ordnance. In Vietnam Lucas had met the sons of such men. A standout was Big John Lawson's second son, Billy, a hotshot ranger with an Olympian finalist physique and a cocky, lopsided grin. In 1978 Billy Lawson, beer in hand, had led Lucas down to a paneled basement room lined with some of the most awesome and frightening firepower conceived by the paranoid mind of humankind. And Billy Lawson had said, "Pick one"—such was his admiration for the man who had saved his father from being sawed in half by sixty-caliber fire a decade earlier.

Lucas had chosen the Dragunov, and Billy had smiled. It was a classic.

The rest of the hardware he had accumulated with time, like barnacle building. The flash suppressor and accouterments for the M-16 he had picked up from a gun dealer who was more than happy to sell the stuff under the counter for no other reason than Lucas's status as an adult Caucasian and a veteran. It was ridiculously easy to acquire a federal firearms license, and Lucas was eventually surrounded by men who were surrounded by guns. If they didn't have a specific item, they could tell him in seconds where one could be had . . . and at a discount, in exchange for the underground referral.

That was the how, Lucas thought as he snaked into the holster rig to size it up. *But what about the why*?

Why had he kept the weaponry all this time? In a way, collecting such instruments of harm was done with the same fascination people experienced when they thought of swerving into oncoming traffic. You knew you wouldn't. But. You knew you contemplated the way a knife in a kitchen drawer might be put to malevolent purpose, but you would never do such a thing unless you got yourself a damned good, defensible reason. Or were insane.

Lucas was not insane. He had had the procedure by which he had been cured carefully explained to him. His mind was not aberrant. They had even showed him pictures proving that his physical brain was perfectly normal.

And he had a reason. He understood that you kept such lethal tools close as an acknowledgment of control. There was life, there was death, and there was the tightrope between. Hefting the heavy pistol, Lucas felt a pang of revulsion, followed by a cleansing aftershock. The feeling of reaffirmed control. That was why people kept guns at hand—to constantly test themselves and to remind themselves that control kept them civilized.

Until the moment when violence was the only

option. *Pow*, as Burt had said. That was the big But that had consumed nations, redivided continents.

CAUTION. EXPLOSIVE. ANTIPERSONNEL.

He had stacked the remaining mines on the far end of the workbench, holding them in reserve. There might be some slip-up. It was conceivable that the mines would have to be seeded around the cabin as a fortification or as a booby trap to cover his absences.

Last night he had watched the late news on the convex-screened Sony Trinitron. The mountains made reception a hunt-and-peck session with the antenna, and he'd pulled in a multicolored chaos of static. But he did not need to see, only to hear Jackson Knox's name. The TV was mainly for use with the videotape deck, anyway.

Beside the TV, behind a stack of yellow boxes containing 5.56 cartridges for the M-16, was a framed photograph of Kristen. A professional portrait, done two months prior to Cory's suicide.

Kristen was looking frame left, head up, about to laugh. She had just turned sixteen; her honey-colored hair long and straight, and her very light brown eyes with predominant spokes of an almost lime-green color. She had Cory's eyes and snubbed nose. She had her father's jawline, but that wasn't too much of a handicap, though it squared off her face rather harshly. Lucas remembered thinking that soon every glandularly hyperactive male within range would start doing handstands. As it turned out, he never got the chance to fend them off. As Kristen posed, he had told her to say "cheesecake." The shutter had trapped her just before she'd made a face and said, "Say what?" She was wearing a dark blue blouse with several strands of liquid silver around her throat. The blouse had given up an extra button's worth of distance to highlight the silver.

Lucas, standing there in near reverie, strapped into his .45, thought it was an enchanting picture.

He opened the windows and swept out the cabin

again. He finished repairing the shower stall and the seat in the outhouse, nailing in fresh lumber. As a little reward for his industry, he lugged in two cases of Dos Equis from the Bronco. Let's see how long this passing obsession with the taste of mere beer lasts, he thought, amused. He chilled them and cracked one and studied his new collection of videos by the ex-members of Whip Hand.

'Gasm's feature film debut, *Throw Down Your Arms*, was intriguing. Lucas slotted in the cassette and slid the sound pots to zero-zero. Jean-Pierre Rampal played on while he watched the screen. When the flute sonata stopped, Lucas substituted Bob Seger.

For now he wanted to concentrate on the visual aspect.

First came a tiny corporate logo on a black screen. This was canceled out by a violent eruption of smoke and fire, as a frond-thatched hooch was obliterated by napalm. Cut sharp to an extreme close-up of the lead guitarist's hands abusing the strings on a mirror-finished guitar. Lucas recognized the instrument as the Ibanez imitation of the notorious Gibson Flying V. It had been customized, or "hotrodded," to pack in a bunch of DiMarzio humbuckers and "Mega-Drive" pickups, plus a cheap Kahler whammy bar with a locking nut. The strings had to be Ernie Ball Super Slinkies, just as the amps had to be Marshall stacks. It was all in the manual for heavy metalists.

The windmilling, finger-skinning attacks on the Ibanez were by a working class Aussie screecher named Pepper Hartz, alias "Mad Max," 'Gasm's front man. The rest of the band was just as bodacious; nasty-ass wolf boys on the prowl.

Hartz's manic playing was intercut with film of Latin American guerrillas executing captives via the one-bullet-per-one-head method. *Bang*. A snap of impact, and the spies or enemies or traitors dropped like cut puppets. *Bang*. Cut to Hartz, wanking away. The rest of the band gyrated on their stage marks; on fast video scan they would look like monkeys jumping around in an electroshock cage. *Bang*. Bob Seger sang "Turn the Page" over Lucas' headphones. A saxophone crooned. Then came a tight shot of 'Gasm's lunatic drummer, Jackal Reichmann, formerly of Whip Hand. He stood up from behind the octave drums on his monster kit and sprayed the concertgoers with mock death from a gangster-style, drum-fed machine gun. The brilliant flashes of discharge betrayed the loads as blanks. Planted squibs blew paper chaff all over the stage, to heighten the gunfire effect.

It would be interesting, Lucas thought, if someone was to fill Jackal's heater with a bit more oomph right before curtain time. He knew that blanks by themselves could do plenty of damage if there was a lapse in 'Gasm's quality control. He was willing to bet that the ticket buyers were ignorant of this risk.

He had not experienced the Kristen nightmare since leaving Olive Grove, not once. Sara, the good doctor, had been right, as always.

He clumped to the fireplace to lay kindling. The air chilled as the afternoon waned, and he locked windows and secured shades all around. When the fire was simmering he dropped to his sleeping pallet, a thick swatch of foam covered with a down sleeping bag. The slithery nylon hissed as he reclined, lacing his fingers behind his head. Fatigue settled in heavily, as though his body craved all the sleep it had squandered in the turbulence of nightmares. He no longer feared sleep, as he had just a few days previously.

Sleep had become unthreatening. And there was no rush. Brion Hardin, Whip Hand's ex-keyboardist, had proven absurdly easy to locate.

Alone in the mountains, close to the sea, Lucas lapsed into a totally untroubled slumber. Sara would have been pleased.

8

THE ROADRUNNER AND SPIDER-MAN held no giggles for Gabriel Stannard this morning.

Sertha Valich, a *Vogue* cover girl of good Russian aristocrat stock, peeked naked from the bathroom and was concerned. She was heavy-breasted for a model. Stannard enjoyed a good pair of firm pillows. Yet he had not been with her while they made love in the huge circular bed with the slippery silk sheets. His blue eyes had been flinty and distant. He had pounded into her for a very long time, and while she enjoyed this, she knew part of his control had come from distraction, not passion. Her perfect, ten-thousand-dollar teeth bit down softly on her perfect, million-dollar lip, and she was concerned.

Stannard was bunched up on one end of the bed, half-dressed. He wore a ruffled white shirt and socks. Cartoons unspooled on the monitor, ignored. He had discarded a vintage Marvel comic, abandoning Spidey in the clutches of Doc Octopus, to play with the pistol from the nightstand, a forty-four Magnum with an unbelievable eight-and-a-half-inch barrel. Sertha knew the gun only as the kind popularized by the mythic American law officer, Dirty Harry Callahan.

Click. Snap. Click. Snap. Stannard picked off the Roadrunner and Wile E. Coyote, dry firing. Six cartridges lay in a brass heap in the sheets. He thumbed back the wide spur of the hammer and fired at the screen, methodically, mechanically.

"Put that away," Sertha told him sternly. Stannard responded to mommy commands because he was spoiled, and he knew it.

His eyes went to hers, ignoring her fabulously nude body. She had hoped to coax him back into the real world with sex a bit friendlier than last night's session. She drank down six ounces of fresh orange juice from the breakfast tray and scooted over to him, her slim hand gently arresting the gargantuan revolver.

"Stop it," she said. He released the gun. She was unprepared for how heavy it was, even empty. Her hand was pushed down and mashed into the bedding.

He didn't respond. He was busy pouting.

She guided his hand to her bosom. Her moonstone-white skin set off dark brown nipples as large as Stannard's thumb. They became instantly erect. But Stannard's caress was still robotic, his eyes hazed. She paused to do two lines of coke off the breakfast tray. Stannard shook his head at her offer of the straw. Sertha swept her cascade of hair to one side and took his flaccid penis in her mouth. She heard him release an annoyed sigh, but his heart beat faster, and in another moment she was pumping her face up and down on his firm, slick shaft. He didn't make a sound when he came, and it took a long time.

Once Stannard's rocks had been gotten off, he became a bit more contrite. Sertha expected this; it was a strategic weakness. He kissed her and tasted his own ejaculate. Then he took a swallow of coffee and stabbed at the projection screen's remote control. The time appeared in the upper left-hand corner in square blue digits.

"Got to go," he said.

Sertha nodded. "All right, my love." She retreated to the bathroom to prepare.

Stannard stepped into a pair of leopard-patterned bikini undershorts, then into black leather pants and a pair of off-yellow cowboy boots. He mussed his hair in the mirror until it framed his face evenly, then donned a leather dress jacket. He tried on several pairs of mirrored racing shades from a drawerful until he found a good, dense pair that totally concealed his eyes from the public.

Thus attired, he was ready to attend Jackson Knox's funeral.

Responsibility for the Rockhound bombing had been claimed by a group calling itself the Mideast League Against American Fascism. The news showed two people wearing berets under heavy police guard, being escorted to judgment. Horus had watched the coverage with dour, unblinking eyes. The news drones always asked if terrorism would ever come to the United States. And every time it did, they asked again, as though purposefully ignoring the evidence before their eyes. As though *this* bombing or *that* bombing didn't really count.

When a commercial jetliner had crashed into the Potomac River, Horus had suggested that the whole thing was a grandiose attempt to assassinate the president. What better way, he opined, than to ram a jet right into the White House? And the conspirators had missed. When it came to political mop-up, it appeared Americans had lost their knack for killing.

Sertha emerged resplendent in black lace. Horus had Stannard's Cessna warmed up and waiting on the private strip.

They were back from San Francisco by dinnertime and toasted Knox's memory with Cristal champagne.

Sertha made sure that Stannard got plastered enough to be more romantic. That night the Magnum stayed in its drawer, unloaded.

Stannard and Sertha made love while *Overkill,* Whip Hand's first album, played full blast through the bedroom's tall Infinity monitors.

At first Lucas thought that the pounding was in his dreaming mind, that the voice commanding his attention was Kristen's, in a sneaky attempt to suck him back into the arena nightmare through a new mental breach point. He tried to roll over and ignore it. There was a flash image of Kristen's face, and for one second he felt a father's anger and wanted to smash the face down with a fist. Daughters should never try to trick their fathers so cruelly.

"Somebody be here. *Please.*" The voice was enfeebled by the heavy wooden door, a solid-core job that could body-block a car. The voice was weak, drained, dissipated.

The knocking weakened too, dwindling away to a halfhearted scuffing against the timber of the door, as though the visitor had conceded to the evidence that a loud knock on a small cabin, plus no response, equaled nobody home in the middle of nowhere. There came a watery sob that sounded like a cough.

It was the voice of a girl. A young woman. That helped shock Lucas to wakefulness. He rolled to his feet still fully clothed; he had not even gotten around to shucking his boots. He looked down at his hand. Even asleep, he had reacted automatically, and he paused a moment to congratulate himself. His hand had a positive grip on the .45, and the weight of the gun was instantly reassuring. When he had rolled, his hand had thumbed back the hammer on the first of eight waiting rounds and dropped the muzzle into the firing line on the door, dead center.

"Hello?" She had heard him moving around. She

might naturally shift to the window to check. Thank gods for the curtains.

"Just a minute!" he called, his cover blown. "Got to get my pants on!" In two big strides he was across the room, closing the door to the Whip Hand room and hooking the open padlock into the hasp. When he cracked the cabin door, his right hand waited behind his back with the cocked automatic. No telling what kind of scam a scavenger might try to pull. It really was the middle of nowhere.

It was dark outside. He had dozed into the A.M.

"Thought there was nobody here," said the voice as he opened the door.

Lucas missed a breath in surprise.

The young woman outside looked like the survivor of a train wreck. In the firelight spilling out the door, Lucas saw that her auburn hair, pulled back into a ragged cable braid, was streaked with dry blood from the left temple backward. An enormous shiner had closed up her left eye completely, and a dark, melanotic patch darkened her swollen cheek. It was dotted with blood. The skid marks of abrasion made crazy zigzags all over the left side of her face and neck, as though her head had been used to bark a pine tree. Her nose did not appear broken, but thick blood was clotted at the base of both nostrils. Her lower lip had sustained a hairline split, blood-crusted, and there was a track of cranberry-colored scabs where she had bitten down hard on one side. She was clinging to the door frame, dirt and wood pulp beneath her nails, and fairly collapsed into Lucas' arms.

"Jesus Christ!"

He caught her as she pitched forward. He supported her until she could drop into the nearest chair, then dashed to the Bronco for his first-aid kit. The damage he'd seen was nearly twelve hours old, maybe more. If she had a skull fracture, she might be dead in another thirty minutes.

"I saw your light," she said thickly. Her tongue tried

to moisten her lips and retreated at the sting.

"Wait," he said. "Don't talk. Don't say anything unless I ask you." He checked the dilation of her pupils, touching the blackened eye gingerly. Her eyes were very light green, with dark rings around the outer iris. "Can you inhale through your nose? Don't try too hard. Don't force it. Go easy."

Carefully she sniffed, watching him.

"I know it hurts. But it's not broken." He freed much of the clotted material using a cotton swab dipped in hydrogen peroxide. The abrasions on her neck and face were already scabbed over and did not look infected. She could focus her eyes rapidly. "I know this is stupid, but I want you to tell me how many fingers I'm holding up."

She might have smiled, if not for the pain of striating her lips. "Three," she whispered.

"Now?"

"None."

"And now?"

"Three again."

Lucas ran half a cup of tepid water, which she was able to take using a drinking straw from the medical kit. Lucas had included the straws himself. Whenever he was ill, he drank using straws. It was something he'd never paused to fathom. Perhaps it was more controlled or required less active participation of the mouth. Certainly the girl would be grateful for that.

"God, that's good," she said when the cup was dry.

"More?"

She swallowed again. "In a minute."

After examining her a few moments more, he was fairly confident he could risk giving her painkillers. She choked down a Percodan with more water. She had not swallowed any of her teeth, though some were loosened.

"You're going to get woozy. Don't try to do anything except fall asleep, okay?"

"I wish." Her voice was hoarse, pathetic.

Her arm moved weakly around his neck as he lifted and carried her to the pallet. He laid her down gently, like an Oriental making a careful composition of flowers. He unzipped the sleeping bag so it would better serve as a comforter and covered her.

"What's." Her consciousness was already flickering. It was best. "What's . . . your name?"

"Try to sleep." He hovered above her, a dark silhouette by firelight.

"What's your name? . . ." Her uninjured eye narrowed to a slit of white, and her respiration was coming in slow cycles, drawn orally. Her need for help had bested her automatic distrust of strangers, and now that she was convinced Lucas intended no foul play, her guard relaxed and the final barrier to sleep was removed. When the drugs kicked in she would numb pleasantly. Her body craved deep sleep as part of the healing process, which was abominably slow in the human animal, but at least marginally reliable.

Lucas knelt at the foot of the pallet to unlace her hiking boots. She was as still as a cadaver on an autopsy table, her legs dumb weights to be lifted and dropped. She had appeared on his stoop wearing a red plaid lumberjack shirt, flannel, over a violet sweat shirt, and faded denim jeans thinning at the ass and knees. The clothes had been stale for a while; she probably had not been out of them in two days or more. They radiated that peculiar aroma that combines great physical exertion with the crisp damper of fresh mountain air. The knees of the jeans had been muddied, dried, and muddied again. Burrs and foliage clung to the shirt and were confused into the weave of her hair, which was a ragged horsetail of flyaways and tangles. Lucas stripped away her socks and tossed them out the back door. Her feet were tapered but supple and grayed with dirt. She had been mucking around on foot for a long time, but her ankles and calves looked used to such exercise. She could be outfitted in substitute clothing without too much compromise. A few marks on her face still glistened with drainage, and he touched them up with medication. By now her chest was rising and falling in uninterrupted rhythm, and the bite of the antiseptic did not stir her. He spot-checked her pockets. No wallet, no money, no identification. The questions would have to wait.

She had never even noticed the pistol.

He had dropped it on the low table near the kitchen, forgetting it himself. Now he slipped the automatic into its black spiderweb of leather and nylon and stashed it in one of the kitchen drawers.

Above the sink, a single mirror tile was glued to the wall. He grimaced at himself in it. There was sleep crust in his eyes, and his own hair looked like a tumbleweed festival. A wretched, bilious taste lurked in the back of his throat. His fingertips and toes were as cold as moon rocks. He agitated the fire in the hearth and added lumber, then hung the coffeepot to warm whatever was left over. As the air in the cabin grew dense with the warmth, he dragged out a box from under the sink and rummaged. He found a dusty pair of overalls that had once belonged to Cory, now forsaken for future service as cleaning and polishing rags, but which had never gotten ripped up. Like his memory of her, they had simply lain for years, waiting for him to notice them again. There was also an old merchant marine sweater that was baggy but serviceable. He stepped out the back door to shake down the overalls. On the butt, right pocket, was an appliqué of a fat pair of lips and a red, lolling tongue—the icon of Jagger and the Stones. He added a pair of his own white tube socks to the folded pile of clothes and took a hot mug of coffee into the Whip Hand room.

The amplifier was still idling, indicators glowing in the semidark. He sat down and pushed the door to. He resumed his study of the 'Gasm videotape, *Throw Down Your Arms*. Several times he rose to check on his sleeping charge, but there was never so much as a change in her position. She breathed, and that was all.

Kristen's portrait was bluely illumined by the light emitting from the screen of the Sony. Lucas' instincts informed him that there was some similarity between his daughter and the girl unconscious in the next room. They did not look alike; this he knew even with the girl's face bashed in and bleeding. Their eyes were vaguely similar. They would have been contemporaries; Kristen would be twenty this year, and Lucas put the girl in the same age bracket. The tug in his gut told him there was something more obvious, more basic, that the two shared.

On the screen, Jackal Reichmann hoisted his gangster's chopper and sent sham bursts toward the audience. The bullet squibs detonated, shooting up mock ricochets.

He imagined Kristen looking up toward the arena stage in entreaty, mangled, bloody.

No, that wasn't it. Go slow. Let the subconscious do the work for you.

He thought of packing the girl into the Bronco and breaking speed limits to get her to the nearest emergency ward, but he decided to wait until morning to see if there was any damage that might require hospitalization. Taking her in for care would make him visible. He wanted to hear her story, find out how and why she had arrived at such a state. There was time, and he didn't want to share.

He might have been a bit more concerned, had he known that Sara Windsor, his friend and confidante, his doctor and budding lover, was already searching for him in Los Angeles.

9

"SOMEBODY NAMED SARA WINDSOR SAYS she's a doctor, and she knows Lucas Ellington, and needs to talk to you."

"Ask her to hold for a second, will you, Emma?"

Burt Kroeger pinched the bridge of his nose, hard. His patty-cake with Lucas at their luncheon had been difficult. He had hated assessing whether his old friend was bonkers or not, or cured, or had never been bonkers at all. Maybe just a little confused? Rather like the way Burt felt now—confused, wearied. He never dug up dead bodies once they were buried, and if Lucas' psychiatrist (or doctor or whatever the hell she was) was now calling for Burt specifically you could just bet it was to ask nosy questions and request impartial, objective opinions, and dredge up all the sludge Burt hoped he had sealed and delivered at lunch with Lucas.

Burt's desk was modern, glass-topped, open. On the wall facing him were rows of framed glossies and awards of merit—plaques and thank-yous. Tiny gold seals glittered. Kroeger Concepts had taken a Rubens Award in 1980 for a technical ad showing a stupendously ugly hound dog on a rural road, head in paws, face sagging into the most melancholy expression imaginable. Looming over him in the light of a country dusk was an empty mailbox—the barn-shaped type, with a little red flag. Nothing else for miles. The caption read: THERE MUST BE WORSE THINGS THAN MISSING THE LATEST ISSUE OF *RAW FOOTAGE* . . ." The dog was Evelyn's, the suggestion had been Lucas's, the game form of the ad had been Burt's.

Here was Burt shaking hands with Ned Tanen of Universal Pictures. Here was Burt with Steven Spielberg at a reception, a shot captured by Gustavo de la Luces. Here were Burt and Lucas arm in arm, frozen in a vaudeville pose, stopped in midkick, flourishing T squares in place of tap-dancing canes. The good old days. Before Lucas had taken his "vacation."

The pill bottle sat on the glass desktop, waiting for him, and Burt shot a pill down with water. Everyone wanted to remind him that Lucas had suffered a small mental setback. Burt wanted to forget and continue as before. The hold light on his desk phone blinked at him accusingly, rushing him. He already resented Sara Windsor. Lucas had said she was a friend, intimated that she might become even more—a stabilizing, healing replacement for Cory, a lover to fill the emotional hole left by Kristen. She probably knew volumes about Lucas. So why was she calling?

Why all this prodding, just when Burt's doubts had been comfortably filed away?

He sighed, then lifted the receiver. "Burt Kroeger here."

"Hello." Her timbre indicated she was used to being put on hold, not thrilled, yet aware of its necessity.

He could have made a grunt of assent or an encouraging noise, but he didn't. Let her set the tone, he thought.

"Once upon a time, Lucas told me that if I ever

needed anything, and he was incommunicado, Burton Kroeger could, quote, get it, do it, or fix it, unquote."

Burt chuckled despite his mood. "That's Lucas all right. What can I do for you?"

"Well . . . I won myself some unanticipated time off. I thought I might drive down to L.A. and spend some time with Lucas, you know, without the oppressive professional atmosphere up here. We'd planned to do the town, but set no schedule. I gather he filled you in?"

"In broad outline, yes."

"He told me that you are a happily married man, that your wife's name is Diana, and she wrangles real estate. Also does stroganoff worthy of the czars."

"I'm surprised he didn't set us up for a free dinner and invite you," said Burt, settling in. "I'd better be careful. You might already know enough to put *me* away."

She laughed politely. "He only said good things about you."

"And a smarmier tale you'll find nowhere. Except maybe in the pages of *Hustler,* which isn't one of our accounts right now. Which is a shame, because they bill high."

"Did Lucas mention his plan to get together with me once he'd gotten back to Los Angeles?"

There it was—the direct probing Burt had expected. He had to devise an answer that would not sound as if it were coming from a castle sentry on the safe side of the moat. What was it Lucas had told him? *We've arranged to get together later, after a few weeks. In a nonprofessional capacity.* He'd treated the trip to the cabin at Point Pitt as a matter of personal confidence, as if he didn't want Sara butting in, at least not yet. If she wasn't supposed to know where he was—and it sure sounded like she didn't—it was not Burt's place to spill any beans.

Play professional, he thought. Grab the reins and jump ahead of her next question.

"I think I know where you're going. Let me ease your mind on a couple of scores, Sara—if I can call you Sara?"

A sound of relief on the far end. "If you can be Burt to me."

"Great. Lucas isn't at home. He decided on the spur of the moment to get back to nature for a few weeks. Camping. Hiking. You know. Come back to deal with the city after dealing with the great outdoors. I'm sure he'll call you before he calls me."

A telling silence, then: "He didn't tell you where he was headed?"

"*North* was about as specific as he got."

"San Francisco?"

"No idea, Sara."

"That's not . . . good." She seemed to say this away from the mouthpiece.

"Anything the matter?"

"No. No, I'm sure he's just, as you say, getting away from it all for a while. But there's no specific address, no phone number for messages?"

"I'm it," said Burt. "Sara, forgive me if I presume on such a short acquaintance, but let me submit that the idea of being constantly watched at Olive Grove—not direct surveillance or anything like that, just that ever-present administrative air—probably inspired him to go breathe free for a few days before phasing back into the city grind. I know *I'd* go a little nuts—you should pardon the expression. But I'm positive he's okay. And I'm positive he's not running away from you, because I think you're important to him, and not just as his shrink. I caught strong vibes. Don't worry."

"You sound like a lay analyst yourself."

"Lucas always comes back, Sara. That's it. Simple, huh?"

"So he probably hasn't been keeping track of the news, or television, stuff like that."

There was a lot of hiss clogging the connection. Burt wanted the conversation over. "If you want to trade phone numbers, Sara, I'll give him yours if he calls me. You still coming to L.A.?"

"I do have some other things to take care of in the city. I'll be driving down, then driving back day after next." She reeled off several numbers, including her home phone in the bedroom community of Dos Piedras, near Olive Grove, and several extensions at the hospital. Burt saw no harm in giving her his home phone. He rather liked the idea of Diana lifting the receiver and being sent into a momentary panic at the fluid sound of Sara's voice.

"Since I thought of dinner, it's on as soon as Lucas resurfaces," he said. "Deal?"

"That doesn't sound too dangerous. I accept. I assume Lucas will."

She had not gotten what she wanted, Burt thought after they rang off. Wonder what she was looking for? Lucas himself had been very fuzzy about tacking down the exact location of his cabin, and Burt had a good sense of when not to pry. There was nothing but coastline up there. A cabin snuggled into the navel of some mountain "near" Point Pitt would be a challenge to sniff out. Hell, there were entire *towns* up there nobody knew existed.

He decided that mentioning Point Pitt, or the fact Lucas had taken a tape deck, would have no value. He'd idly wondered what Lucas would do with a tape deck, since he was supposedly camping out. But he'd know if he was supposed to.

He wondered what Sara had seen on the news. But he decided not to worry that one to death, either.

10

HER NAME WAS CASS, AND she had been beaten up and abandoned in the mountains by her boyfriend.

Ex-boyfriend, thought Lucas.

He'd talked her into a camping excursion, and once they were removed from civilization, he'd reverted to an anthropoid stage and punched the shit out of her. There had been a lot of screaming about sexual misconduct. She saw his massive fist flying toward her face, then sparks, and that was all until she heard his truck speeding away. All her stuff was in it; sling bag, money, ID, everything. The guy's name was Reese. He drove a Datsun long-bed with a fancy camper shell on the back and Montana plates. Lucas remembered passing the truck on his way north. Cass did not remember being passed by his Bronco, and that was just as well.

She had related all that while sipping hot coffee laced with a lot of sugar. Lucas had switched her from Percodans to stiff codeine pills. Now she was sponge bathing in the outside shower stall while he stood near the barbecue, hoping she didn't tumble and complicate the damage already done. She washed the woods off herself with slow, cautious movements. Her reach was restricted by pain.

Her rugged clothing had taken some of the abuse for her, but her chest was a disaster area. Reese had used her breasts for boxing practice, and the bruises were vast and ugly. Contusions outlined all her ribs on one side.

Her calves were firm and rounded from exercise; her thighs were almost muscularly expressive. The grace of her legs was interrupted by a ladder of welts. Once she fumbled and fell heavily into the side of the stall; Lucas was across the patio in a shot to catch her. She wiped a fat sponge along each arm, sluicing water down her body, rinsing away dirt and scabs and pain. She toweled off clumsily; she had trouble turning her head and was still using only her right eye for the most part. It obviously hurt like hell to move at all. Yet she had insisted on cleaning up.

"I can smell myself," she'd said. "Gag. You'll have to fumigate your sleeping bag." When Lucas had told her about flinging her socks out the back door, she'd almost laughed. "Yeah. Bet they were real killers. Maybe we should just stuff my clothes into the fireplace. They're beyond detergent by now."

With Lucas' help, over the tub sink, she'd managed to get the dry blood out of her hair.

Seeing her naked in the shadows of a sun creeping toward noon, Lucas felt a nagging stab of déjà vu. It wasn't just the idea of a surrogate daughter. It was the physical damage. Something about Cass' wounds keyed a nonspecific memory in him, a feeling of familiarity tied to Kristen.

But no positive connection. He would never think of wreaking such injuries on Kristen, not the Kristen he remembered.

Under normal circumstances, he realized, Cass would be very attractive. Not pretty. Pretty described twelve-year-olds in Easter dresses or costly trifles that were mostly frills and flowers. Cass would be attractive, with those eyes so direct and startlingly colored, with all that auburn hair untrussed, with her appealing shape and physique. She made no fuss about her nakedness; there were graver matters to be dealt with. He watched her fight her way determinedly into the merchant marine sweater.

When her head and one arm were trapped inside, he rescued her. "Here. Hold your right arm still."

"The sweater is winning," she said timidly.

He guided her into the garment. "Don't bend your other arm back so far."

"I *can't*, anyway." Her head poked through. "Jesus Christ, I never thought I'd wish for a bra, you know? But every time I move, my tits countermove, and it's like torture. Like what I imagine being gut shot feels like. Only higher up." She folded her arms, framing her breasts.

"Like being kicked in the balls."

She looked into his eyes to see if he was putting her on. "If you say so. My dear Reese never called them balls. It was always *nuts*, a kick in the *nuts*."

"I don't like that word."

"Aha—so you do have a delicacy threshold. The mark of the mature, older man." Once unclogged, her voice was low and resonant. He imagined her steering chat, kicking that voice over into sultry when she needed to. She spoke intelligently and did not trip over the English language the way her peers might.

"One of Reese's big hangups was getting kicked in the balls," she said. "He got that gleam in his eyes. I knew I was going to get stomped, and there was no place to run, so I let him have it. Boom—he folded up like a card table hit by a falling safe. Unfortunately, he also got back up. I kept thinking, *What do I do now*? He had the car keys in his pocket. He can run faster and jump higher. And he got up. And I stood there like a heroine in a bad horror movie, you know, screaming at the monster instead of running like hell? And the monster pounded the shit out of me, jumped in his rig, and sped away into the sunset. I suppose he thought I'd die from the exposure. More likely he just got crazed, and ran. Which is why I started blundering through the woods in the dead of night. He might have come back for more."

Lucas helped her into the bib coverall with the Rolling Stones patch on the butt. Before buttoning her up, he said, "Maybe we could use an Ace bandage to bind your chest as well as your ribs. I've seen it for breast operations—the idea is to immobilize the breasts so you don't open up sutures."

"Yowtch." She grimaced. "Is that for real?"

"Yeah. My wife had breast surgery once. Nothing serious. That's where I encountered it. Uh, my ex-wife."

"How ex is your ex-wife?"

"My *late* ex-wife." It hurt not at all to say it.

Cass paused. "You a widower?"

"No. She was an ex before she was—"

"What was her name?"

"Cory." He looked around, almost guiltily. "Yea or nay on the breast-binding technique? It'll be pretty warm inside all the clothes and bandages."

"I say let's try it. It can't feel worse than it does already. Hike up the sweater." She dropped the bib and held out her arms. She was full-breasted but not heavy, and her small nipples shrank at the shock of air. Up close, the bruises were much uglier. Blood had been forced through the skin.

Lucas slowly mummified her with an Ace bandage. "Why did Whats is name—Reese. Why did he go berserk?"

"Thought I mentioned it," she said. "We got into a tiff about who was sleeping with whom. Reese had formulated this unbelievable set of rules for me. It might have helped if I'd known what the hell they were. I guess, to Reese, worthy women knew his rules instinctively. Ouch!"

"Sorry."

"His ego required utter fidelity. At the same time, his ego was so huge that it made him fuck as many girls as he could pounce on. When I discovered how extensive Reese's pouncing had gotten, I brought it up. That was the first time he smacked me. Stupid me, I thought *I* had overreacted.

"I was doing temporary work for an accounting office, and I met this guy there, Jonathan. We'd had coffee a couple of times, nothing heavy. He told me about his separation, and I told him about Reese. Jonathan was frighteningly normal, almost boring. The type of guy you absolutely ignored in high school. But he turned out to be very considerate and caring."

Lucas furrowed his brow. She interpreted it as disapproval.

"Oh, no, it's not as if we met on the sidewalk and jumped into the nearest bed," she said. "It took a long time for anything physical to happen. And I never thought of anything physical happening, because Jonathan struck me as the type of guy who was a virgin on his wedding night, and I didn't need him for sex. Not at first."

"Reese found out about Jonathan?"

"I don't know. I don't see how. Maybe he was just guessing and read guilt in my eyes or something. Or sniffed it out, like they say a wolf can sniff out fear. I've heard some people can do that. Reese smoldered for a while. Nonspecific. Then, when we came out here, he brought it up."

"Convenient." He was nearly finished. The bandages were more attractive than the bruises.

"It scares the shit out of me to think he was planning to beat me to death the whole time we were driving up here. Just beat me, and leave me here to die. I never felt so removed from help. In the big bad city at least you can con your way into an ambulance, even if you're broke. Out here, the trees suck up the sound before you can even scream."

He buttoned her into the overalls. Back in the cabin, she swallowed two more codeine tablets with coffee.

"I was lying on the ground. I could feel my blood mixing with the dirt. And Reese said, 'You can stay up here and fuck the grizzly bears, puss.' And the goddamned thing is, when I finally was able to stand up, I was more scared of imaginary grizzly bears than I was of Reese. Although I'm sure a grizzly bear has better table manners. I just motivated myself the hell *away*, as fast as I could crawl. I'm not even sure there are grizzly bears around here, anyway."

Lucas shook his head slowly from side to side. "I don't understand how somebody like you could get tangled up with . . . with such a . . ."

She saw him groping for the word, avoiding it, perhaps, so she provided one. "Such an obvious psycho?" She pulled in a deep breath and released it in a sigh. "I really can't tell you. A girlfriend of mine, Tanya, used to go with a biker. A member of the Axemen, went by the handle T-Bone. A real righteous iron horseman. Had a lot of those pin-and-ink tattoos—a teardrop by his left eye for each prison stretch he'd served. T-Bone had four teardrops the last time I saw him. He'd killed at least two other guys in prison, in self-defense. The most humorless dude I'd ever seen in my life, and here he was going out with Tanya, who used to be Miss Super Yuppie, Miss Valley Girl. She was crazy about him; no explanation. How did I wind up with Reese? Maybe because I'd had a lot of guys who were all talk and nothing beyond. You know—if some junkie tried to knife us in a movie theater, my boyfriend would try to talk it over with the guy. Civilized behavior. And I'd be lying there with my trachea in my lap. Maybe Reese was my way of acknowledging the hazards of city living, my man of direct action. He'd take the junkie and turn him inside out while he was mouthing off, pumping up for the fight." She tried to turn her head to look out the window. At a stab of pain she gave up. "And look at all the benefits I reaped. I suppose you really *do* live and learn. Reese, I guess, was another in a long line of mostly failed experiments."

She fumbled the pill vial, and as it rolled to the edge of the table Lucas caught it. Her hands toyed with themselves in her lap. "I'm a tad woozy. All my friends use dope regularly, like jam on toast. I don't even touch the weed anymore. So any time I take a painkiller it knocks me on my ear. No fair, says I."

She was aware of Lucas's voice saying, "How old are you?" But she had not looked at him for a long time, and the voice seemed to come from a great distance. The effect was that of a gentle interrogation, on the fringes of sleep.

"Twenty-three. Twenty-three and a half."

"You look younger."

"People tell me I talk older. They always say that, like it compensates for something."

"Well, you're unusually articulate." Lucas leaned back, and the front legs of his chair disengaged from the floor, to hover. "You don't seem handicapped by the seven-word vocabulary most kids use these days."

"Oh, you mean fuck this, fuck that, fucking-A, in-fucking-incredible?"

He laughed lightly. "You remind me of my daughter."

You're my favorite asshole, dad.

"You have a daughter?" Now she looked at him with her good eye. The other one moved around inside the swollen eyelid, trying hard to see him. "You don't look that old. Old enough to have a daughter my age, I mean."

"Her name was Kristen. She would have been twenty this year. She's gone, too."

"Oh, god, I didn't—"

"Don't apologize. It's okay."

After a beat, she said, "I'd ask if you knew anybody among the living, but I'm afraid you'd have to include me out."

"Sam Goldwyn used to say that." He saw the non-recognition in her expression. "Never mind."

"Think I'll live, doctor?"

"I don't think we need to check you into an ICU. Reese didn't spend too much time bashing you, but he made the most of the hits he got."

"He's built," she said ruefully.

"If you're seeing and breathing okay today, I'd take a chance on your pulling through."

"I don't want to go back to the city," she said. "For what? Reese has trashed my stuff; I'm positive. And he's laying for me. No thanks. Cops can't protect you from someone like that. If he's blown town, there's still no rush—he's still trashed my stuff."

"The charges would be pretty serious," said Lucas.

"I have no burning desire to spend my life looking over my shoulder." Then, with an abrupt detachment that was chilling, she added, "If I ever see Reese again, I want to be whole, and functional. And ready."

"I could go with you," Lucas offered, strictly spur of the moment. "If he was around, and thought you weren't alone, then maybe—"

"That's sweet of you, but no good. It puts us in the position of fear, see? Besides, I'm in no hurry to leave here. Though that depends on how long you'll allow me to impose on your hospitality."

She was leading him. He could feel it. Like the feeling he'd gotten with Kristen sometimes. She was steering. He dismissed her gratitude. "No imposition, Cass. You were, and still are, in need of serious—"

She overrode him. "Come *on*, Luke, lighten up! That's my ploy. I'll be more flagrant: I want to hang out at your mountain retreat for a while. I know I'm not very formidable right now, but in a few days I'll be on the road to recovery, and—bingo!"

"Bingo?"

"You'll have a faithful Indian companion. Girl Friday. Whatever you want. I'll even launder my own irreclaimable socks. You've already told me I'm a terrific conversationalist, and I'm a person you know who's not dead. Think carefully before you turn down an offer like this."

It cut to the marrow; it seemed very correct. Lucas felt an undeniable sense of rightness while speaking to her. It was not just the vague echoes of Kristen. It was as though Cass was supposed to be part of what was happening. As logic, it was specious. As a healing thing, it seemed to hint at a vast good. She was very much like Kristen in the best ways: sharp and attentive and able to catch him off guard with wit. His mind raced ahead.

"You're welcome to stay as long as you want, Cass," he began, formulating a back story as he went. "But if you do . . . there's something I may need your help with."

"Anything." She said this with absolutely no hesitation. "I'm entitled to say 'anything' because I owe you my life."

He let it pass without protest. He did not feel like objecting. "Let me put it simply. There's a very remote possibility that my ex-wife will be looking to harass me. She may eventually sleuth up the location of this cabin. And when she does, she may come up here to cause a scene, possibly with her attorney in tow."

Her good eye widened. "Your *dead* ex-wife is going to show up here?"

"Oh—no." He backpedaled. Boy, had that lie sounded idiotic! "I've been divorced twice, once very recently, and it was a rough one. Nasty. It's one of the reasons I'm playing hermit up here. In the city, it's twelve phone calls a day, shrieking arguments, confrontations, endless angst. I don't need it."

"Who does? Looks like you're up here for healing, too. What you need is a diversion. No sweat."

"Nobody'll recognize my Bronco. It's new. Otherwise it'd be hidden in the brush."

"What's her name?"

"Sara. If she knew I was here, we'd be under siege right now."

"Sounds like a real harridan," Cass said, already on guard against the mention of any other women in Lucas's life. "Also sounds like you and I are kind of in the same boat."

On the remote chance that Sara could track him to this place, he could now utilize Cass to detour her, perhaps buy time if it was needed. Just in case Sara's smarts jeopardized his plans by figuring things out too much in advance. He had given Cass a motive for secrecy with which she could easily sympathize, considering the nature of the man who had assaulted her.

He worked on that angle, reinforcing it. "At one time, I loved Sara just as much as I'm sure you loved Reese." Don't slice the baloney too thick, he thought.

"Yeah, isn't true love just a casketfull of laughs? I think I can deal with your Sara if she shows up. Just promise me you'll take care of Reese if he ever shows up. Run him over with your Bronco or something." Lucas was certain she had a few good combat tricks in readiness and was probably a great actress when it came to the kind of fakeout he might need for Sara. "So. Anything else special? It's easy so far."

He brought her more coffee. "Something important. I have to go away from time to time. I'm usually gone about twenty-four hours; a day or two at most. But the trips are essential."

"Business?"

"You got it. I can't maintain my existence up here without the proper machinations. And I'd feel a lot more secure if someone was here to maintain the cabin while I'm gone. It's a pain to shut everything down and pack everything up, just for a few two-day absences."

"That one's easy, too. What's the room with the lock?"

"I have—what?"

"The room with the lock. Do I need to know what's in there, in order to run this place while you're gone?"

Lucas glanced toward the secured Whip Hand room. How far should he embellish this? "It's storage, mostly files. I have a stereo in there I can drag out. A gun, too. Thus the lock, for when I'm away. But if you're going to be here . . . well, I've got tapes of just about everything. From Motown to Mahler to Whip Hand. There's a radio."

She mulled this over. "What Mahler?"

"Fifth and Sixth symphonies."

"Sold." She sipped the hot coffee. Her eye considered the pill bottle again.

"Better not overdo it. Lie down for a while. You sure you're up to staying here?" He asked this more in worry about his immediate schedule than from honest apprehension about her injuries. There might be hidden complications, ones that could not be permitted to hamper his one-time-only timetable. But she solved that tiny twinge of conscience with her answer.

"Howzabout we don't worry so much, huh, Luke? I feel better already. All things considered, I mean. Let's look at this as another of my gambles, another in my long line of experiments. Just from staying here, I think I'll pull through. And if I don't . . . do me a favor and bury me in the forest. That's romantic. Funerals are a maximum pain in the ass."

He nodded. After suffering through Cory's funeral,

then Kristen's, he never wanted to countenance that ghoulish custom again in his lifetime. "Your wish is granted. And I have one more request, before you drop off to sleep in that chair."

Cass was fighting to hold her head up. "Sure. Like I said, anything."

"It's serious. The most crucial thing of all."

"Shoot. Before I pass out." She obviously longed to get horizontal.

"Don't call me 'Luke.' Makes me feel like Walter Brennan is hobbling after me. It's Lucas."

"Righto, Lucas. It's a deal. But let's not shake hands on it; I'd probably scream." She held up her wounded hand limply, like a dead sparrow. "I think I'm gonna need some help, to get from here to there."

He assisted her to the pallet. He had another sleeping bag in the Whip Hand room. He would haul it out later, set up another bunk on the opposite side of the hearth. "Okay?" he said when she was down.

She said, "Yep. Thanks, Luke." Then she was fast asleep.

11

THE INDEX CARD IN LUCAS'S shirt pocket bore a list of names.

KIRK MOORE
PHILIP T. LONGLEY
DAVID KLEIN
MARK FAWCETT
CALVIN WESTBROOK
MURRAY BANNER
BOB CALLAHAN

They were safe names, anonymous names, the sorts of names you saw on the badges of conventioneers and never remembered. Bland, forgettable, Americanized names, so unexotic that they slid easily off the ear and into oblivion.

All that was needed to pinpoint Brion Hardin, the keyboardist of Electroshock, was a concert schedule and an FM radio. Lucas admired all the convolutions of his little piece of espionage.

He had driven back to San Francisco and checked

into the Holiday Inn for two days, fronting cash and checking the Bronco into a pay lot across town. He stayed in the room just long enough to order lunch from room service and mess up the ordered neatness of the room itself. He tore the paper band from the toilet and the plastic from the drinking cups. Then, leaving his TV set on low and dialed to the pay-per-play movies, he hung the DO NOT DISTURB sign on the doorknob and caught a shuttle bus for the airport from another hotel.

That was Kirk Moore.

At San Francisco International, he loitered around the ticketing lines until he zeroed in on an elderly gentleman, one Nathan Downey. He explained that in order to fly at the standby rate, he could take no check-in luggage, and since Mr. Downey was only checking a single bag, could he render one small favor? Mr. Downey looked at the man who had introduced himself as Philip T. Longley and, while they were standing in line, delivered a brief speech on how the airlines were still gouging people despite the drop-off in business caused by terrorism. He would be happy to help Mr. Longley out. To Nathan Downey, this trifling subterfuge held all the thrill of cheating the phone company, and he relished the opportunity. Lucas promised to spring for at least one cocktail on the flight to Denver.

He had made sure to hit the counter up for standby rates in the middle of the week, so as not to get choked off by weekend commuters. Traffic was light, and his standby seat was ultimately secured. He and Nathan Downey toasted each other with overpriced airline liquor.

Standby flying was a worthwhile gamble. It probably would have been just as safe to check in as a normal passenger under an assumed name. Airlines never requested ID if you slapped cash on the counter. But that way he could not divorce himself from the bag that had to be checked—the bag containing the huge Randall knife in its combat sheath.

The temptation to employ ironic noms de guerre was amateurish. If any single thread of his trail attracted notice, then investigators would rapidly fix on joke names or names drawn, as Lucas had first considered, from the various record albums or performers themselves, such as "Bryan Harding" from Brion Hardin.

Despite the eastward loss of an hour, the Delta Airlines 727 arrived early enough to give him most of the day in Denver. Lucas slept through most of the flight.

He knew Denver was his next destination thanks to the latest issue of *Creem* magazine. *Creem* and others of its ilk were chock full of advertisements for current groups. If a group had a new album in the past two months or the coming two, inevitably there was a tour schedule included with the ad. Record companies were trying to make tours more "album supportive" these days. It had all become one grand, unending commercial—like the epic special-effects film that is nothing but a two-hour commercial for its own sequel. In turn, the videos made to boost album sales frequently included concert footage shot while on tour. Lucas thought of the snake swallowing its own tail. And in *Creem* he had unearthed an ad for Electroshock that included a tour roster. In the middle of the microscopic column of dates and venues, he had found the show slated for the Curriggan Exhibition Hall complex in downtown Denver.

The half-page ad showed two members of Electroshock engaged in a guitar duel onstage. Electroshock had begun existence as a hillbilly-rock band full of mountain men under the name Moonshine Express in 1977, just when punk was working up a full head of angry steam. Moonshine Express reorganized as the Badd Boyz and did an album's worth of what later came to be called "alternative country," more popularly known as "country punk" when the Vandals and the Beat Farmers came along later. Then bass player Roarin' John Masterson drove his Harley hog off a freeway overpass and met a Toys 'R' Us semi head on. Electroshock was born from the ashes a year later, with a decidedly heavier bent. Their promotional guys had crowed loudly about how an ex-member of the infamous Whip Hand had decided to link up. They were still an opening act, without their "breakthrough" song or album as yet, but they were respectable, reliable. Their following was strongest in the western deserts and the South.

Brion Hardin was just barely visible in the *Creem* ad, fortressed behind his keyboards next to a big Peavey box. Grizzly-bear size, with a full beard. Much clearer views were available on both previous Electroshock albums, *Force Me* and *The Crash of '86*. He was the biggest guy in the band.

Currigan Hall was a massive showroom suited to automobile exhibitions and Shriners' conventions; its concert arena was an adjunct that was more properly a part of the Denver Convention Complex. But the locals referred to the whole facility as "Currigan." So be it.

After thanking Nathan Downey for his help, Lucas grabbed a taxi from Stapleton Airport to the "Denver downtown" branch of the Holiday Inn on Glenarm and Fifteenth Street. He checked in as David Klein and gave a home address in Fort Worth, Texas. He paid cash for two days. His seventh-floor room overlooked Glenarm. A few floors higher and he could have seen the arena building from the hotel; it was only three and a half blocks away. His room in Denver was nearly identical with his room in San Francisco.

Electroshock was opening for Straight Razor, a speed metal riot that drew as many fans with spiked hair and marine corps buzzcuts as it did sullen teenagers in leather vests and studs. Both bands would most likely be holed up at the Denver Hilton, two blocks away from Lucas in the opposite direction. Or maybe the Executive Tower Inn. He was right in the middle of the hotel web.

He broke open the small suitcase containing the

Randall and pulled out a Panasonic radio/tape rig, tuning it to KOA-FM, a power pop station targeted at highschoolers and commuters. KBLO seemed too new wave for what Lucas needed. KPPL was a bit dirtier and more musically interesting than KOA's rigid commercial playlist format. Whenever songs were being broadcast, he tuned from KOA to KPPL and back. He was searching for commercials, not music, and he found plenty.

He had listened to both Electroshock albums enough times for the likely airplay tunes to be obvious to him. If a station dropped its needle on an Electroshock tune, it would be as a lead-in to an announcement of the concert. He shopped and waited for the taped and live ads to start repeating, to form a pattern. Simultaneously, he sifted through the local Yellow Pages and telephoned alternative papers as a fail-safe. Within twenty minutes he had the sort of information he was looking for.

Three members of Electroshock, not including Brion Hardin, were scheduled to do a half-hour live radio interview on KPPL that evening at 8:30 P.M. They would reprise the same gig on KOA-FM the next day, a few hours prior to concert time.

It was nearly four o'clock. Finding KPPL was easy. Lucas unpacked a silver-gray business suit and let it smooth out, knocked off his shoes, and ordered a strip steak from room service. Its price was breathtaking.

Downstairs, Fifteenth Street was littered with some of Denver's most colorful winos, panhandlers, and sundry dregs of humanity. Lucas finally found a liquor store that would sell him a case of Beck's dark, which he carted back to the Holiday Inn. Eight-thirty approached slowly.

As soon as the KPPL deejay cut to his in-the-booth interview, with the Electroshock contingent snorting and sniggering in the background, ready for anything, Lucas knotted his maroon silk tie and slipped into his suit. With the case of Beck's perched on one shoulder, he hailed a cab for KPPL.

He spotted them clogging the street corners and being hustled firmly out of the lobby. Groupies, fans, hangers-on. He passed the cabbie ten bucks over fare and told him to idle. Donning a pair of steel-rimmed glasses, he heaved the case of beer out of the taxi.

The crowd was not as hairy to dance through as he had predicted. They parted at the sight of the suit, the intimations of authority. Next problem was the brigade of security guards in the floor lobby of the building housing KPPL. But the one manning the heavy glass doors admitted him, reacting automatically, his eye contact suggesting that he accepted Lucas as an adult and unconnected to the general rabble.

The guard pushed the door shut, forcing the hydraulic closure to hiss at being rushed. The crowd jabber dropped in volume. The guard was young and did not quite fill out his gray uniform shirt, which was girded by a Sam Browne belt and festooned with patches, tags, and security passes in plastic. A matte-finish .357 Magnum hung heavy off his left hip. He was a day behind in shaving, and his complexion needed sunlight. He did not need more aggravation than he already had.

"Oh, now, what the hell kinda crap is *this*?" He indicated the Beck's box.

Lucas smiled. The brotherhood of the weary and put upon. "The rock stars in yonder booth have cried out for imported brew. *Regardez*. Any problem?"

"Problem," the guard snorted. His embossed name strip read TRENCH. He sighed and waved his walkie-talkie toward a check-in table. Lucas set the case down. More guards braced the elevator doors. Behind the table was an older man who seemed amused by all this craziness.

"Only problem I have," said Trench, "is that nobody bothered to tell me anything about this."

"I hear you," Lucas said while the guy behind the table peeked into the box. His eyebrows went up. "They never bother to do anything except give us orders. I don't even think the KPPL guys know. Marc Tobler phoned in the order."

"Who the hell is Marc Tobler?"

"Bass player for Electroshock. He's up there now, doing the interview. Look, you can check out the box. It's only beer. I'll be in and out in five minutes. You can even pat me down if you want. No weapons and no autograph books."

Trench snorted again, but this time it was like a laugh. Fucking rock stars thought they could walk all over anybody, go over anybody's head. . . .

"Hey," Lucas said. "Escort me if you want. I know you've got better things to do with your time. Me too. You want me to sign something?"

At last Trench was being consulted. He eased up. "Go ahead on," he said. "Fifth-floor suite. The booth is obvious. You can leave it with the girl at the desk. Houghton, let this gentleman go upstairs."

KPPL's receptionist was a gum-popping, eraser-chomping university dropout with a green streak in her Ish Kabibble haircut. She had pimples around her mouth and perpetually stiff nipples that punctuated the front of her jersey.

"Oh, jesus," she said when she saw the Beck's case. She rolled gray, vacuous eyes. "I dunno if you can take that into the booth, y'know what I'm saying? I mean, we got in trouble for the jocks smoking dope and drinking during the on-air stuff, y'know, like there's the FCC and stuff, and the jocks were sneaking in their friends who were high and they said 'shit' on the air and like we can't do that, and if my boss knew I let it pass without an okay I'd get reamed out, you know what I'm saying? If he says it's okay, then it's okay, but jesus, I wish to christ they'd check with us first, I mean, everything really got fucked up last month when Giant Human Sandwich was here, and the guys were cussing on the air and one guy farted into an open mike during a call-in, and I mean the shit really *flew*, right? And we're going out live right now, and I don't think I can, y'know, say yea or nay to—"

Lucas held up both hands, as though pressing down a huge manhole cover to choke off the torrent of babble. "Look, honey, it's no problem. I understand."

She finally shut up. Understanding was hard enough to come by.

"Just tell me where to deliver it. That way we keep the demon alcohol out of their hands while they're on the air, and they get it later, so nobody gets cheated . . . and my arm's about to give out from lugging this thing all over the building."

"Huh?" She actually looked at his arm. "Oh . . . right. Take it down to the Denver Hilton. Straight Razor and Electroshock have got most of the tenth floor, but don't tell nobody I told you." Then she grinned, a gamine, empty headed smile. "A case ain't gonna be enough. They put it away like—"

"Like a trout puts down eggs," said Lucas.

"What? Oh, yeah—like a fish."

When the burnished aluminum elevator doors parted to admit Lucas back to the lobby, case in hand, he immediately sought out Trench.

"Say, Trench. Do you have someplace to stash this?"

Trench turned his attention from the milling fans outside. Some fair-looking young heartbreakers were pressing up against the glass. "You mean hold it for the band?" Hostility lurked in his voice.

"No, I mean hold it for yourself and your buddies here."

Guard conversation in the foyer stopped, and all eyes fell to the Beck's case. It was the correct answer.

"To hell with those bozos in the band. All they have to do is snap their fingers, and alcohol condenses from the very air. You guys look like you could use some refreshment."

"Jesus . . . uh, thanks, I mean."

"No prob," said Lucas, tipping an imaginary topper. "You boys take it real slow, now. Enjoy."

Trench returned a mock salute as Lucas made his way back out to the waiting cab.

What a decent dude, he thought. *Should be more like him.*

Lucas had known the utter futility of phoning up hotels and asking outright for Electroshock's room numbers. Trying to penetrate the tenth floor of the Denver Hilton would require James Bond. Neither Straight Razor nor Electroshock would even exist, according to any registration desk in town. It was another groupie/fan deterrent mechanism. The exits, the elevators, all access to the tenth floor would be strictly monitored and regulated.

What was required was an audacious ploy. Outgrandstand the grandstanders. Shoes off, Lucas sat on his Holiday Inn bed and phoned the Denver Hilton. When the switchboard operator at the desk answered, he requested a random tenth-floor room number.

There was an official hesitation. "Who is calling, please?" There would be a screening list to consult.

Lucas made sure the man heard him sigh. "Mark Fawcett of Wolf and Rissmiller, okay? And I'm in a hurry, pal—we got a concert to put on, and I don't like having my time wasted."

"Oh. Oh. Just a moment, please." Lucas was put on hold. He knew that the operator would be scanning the list. There would be no Mark Fawcett. But there would be Wolf and Rissmiller—the firm that had booked the show. The deskman would assume, like Trench, like the KPPL receptionist, that no one had bothered to tell him. He would check the expressions of his fellow workers on the desk, making sure no one had noticed his little faux pas. Wolf and Rissmiller, of course. The firm was familiar to Lucas from his PR experience.

The voice came back online. "That was Room 1015, yes?"

"Thank you."

A line burred once, twice, with that blatting ring apparently reserved for business office systems and hotels. It sounded like a wet electronic fart.

The receiver was jerked off the other end on the third ring and dropped to the floor with a *clunk*. There was a loud, moist sniffle. "Starbase Six, come in?"

Lucas was out of the gate and running. "Yeah. Is Brion in there with you guys?"

"Brion? Shit, I don't think—" There was a brief gabbing, off phone. "Nah. I think he's still shacked up or crashed out or sleeping, still, in his room. You try 1021?" Another muffled consultation. Rapid, speed-injected talk cut through several other voices. Somebody giggled. "Yeah. 1021. Give him a buzz there."

Lucas cut the connection and punched in the Hilton desk again. A different clerk answered, and he asked if it would be any trouble to reserve a single room for one night. He gave his name as Cal Westbrook and explained that the TWA strike was forcing him to lay over in Denver till six A.M. The clerk explained that reservations were tight, but that Mr. Westbrook could be accommodated for one day only. He would have to check out the next day, though. The next day was the day of the concert, Lucas knew, and that was when the rooms would go at a premium.

Several hours later that evening, late enough to appear travel weary, Calvin Westbrook checked into his room on the seventh floor of the Hilton. He had little luggage. Just a sling bag.

It took twelve rings for Brion Hardin to answer his phone, in room 1021.

"Ahum. Yeah."

"Brion?" Pause. "We got major trouble with some of the equipment, specifically your computer. The guy who was backing the truck up to Currigan did it with the tailgate open. Guess what fell out."

"Aw, shiiiit." There was a rustling; Brion was either

in the rack, or dressing, or undressing. "Does Van know about this? Where the hell is Marc?"

"Can't say, Brion, they're MIA. It's not their stuff, anyway. You were the guy I needed to find. I just got the call myself."

"Who is this?"

"Murray Banner." Lucas played it fast, leaving no gaps for Hardin to jump in with questions. "I'm with Currigan, and I stopped by the hotel to see Bob Callahan, and I got the news. . . . Can we keep a low profile on this, please? I don't necessarily want anyone else to know. Not yet. You hear what I'm saying? I need you to go over to Currigan with me, pronto. Can you do it?"

"God, I don't . . ." The information raced through Hardin's head. "Yeah. Yeah, of course. Lemme get my pants on. Where do I find you, uh—"

"Murray."

"Yeah, whatever."

"Seventh floor, room 704. Bob Callahan is with me. You probably don't know Bob."

Misdirect him from the fact he probably doesn't know Murray Banner, either.

It all blew smoothly past Hardin. It was glossy and fast, without bumps to get stuck on. Lucas heard the keyboard man kibbutzing with his bedmate, whose name was Cheryl or Cheri.

"I'm on my way. Look, if I see Marc, should I tell him that—"

"No. Not yet. Let's not panic anybody. If the world needs to know, you and I will tell 'em. But *after* you've had a look."

Hardin appreciated the special attention. "Room 704. Five minutes."

"Gotcha. Bye."

The ensuing five minutes spilled more acid into Lucas' gut than a bad seven-course Italian dinner.

Hardin might encounter a familiar face in the hallway and stop to repeat the lie. He might drag along someone else from Electroshock. He might show up with Crystal or Cheryl or Cheri in tow. Lucas had gambled, to draw the man off the tenth floor. It was rather like the chances Cass had taken with her life. Close your eyes and jump. But the options were worse. There was no way to mountaineer down to Hardin's room from the exterior of the hotel. That was sheer fantasy. Bluffing past the guards on the elevators and exits was even stupider; he would be cutting off escape if anyone made a wrong noise. Why give a full floor of concert operatives a face to remember?

Room 704 was pristine, untouched. Ever since taking the elevator up, Lucas had been wearing surgical gloves. They had crinkled in his ear while he made the phone call to Hardin's room. And they crinkled now, as he wrung his hands together, wishing Brion Hardin would hurry the hell up so this could all be over with.

He turned on the television, for cover noise.

Four solid knocks on the door.

The sound snapped Lucas's head around, involuntarily. The blade of the Randall made a small ringing sound as he drew it from the heavy leather sheath. He threw the sheath, lightly underhanded, to the dark bathroom counter as he made for the door.

"Brion?"

The image, fisheye-distorted in the peephole lens of the door, was of a long face, framed entirely in woolly black hair. Hardin had grown a lavish beard since the photo session for *The Crash of '86*. Two blazing blue eyes helped unify the riot of hair into a face. They were nearly colorless in shade, bright and piercing as the highbeams of a truck. He was glancing impatiently up and down the empty hallway on the seventh floor. He was alone.

"Yeah. It's me." He shifted from foot to foot, worried about his equipment.

Lucas slid the Randall blade-down into the waistband of his pants, beneath the gray suit jacket. He prayed the jacket would not cramp his reach or tear. He had decided against wearing the glasses. They might fall off or go askew, or drop to the floor and get stomped on, leaving fragments, evidence of a hundred kinds. No.

He opened the door. "Come on in."

Hardin lumbered through. He was taller, wider than Lucas expected. A big man, a mountain man, former member of the Moonshine Express, topping six four. He smelled like beer.

"Brion, I want you to meet Bob Callahan." Lucas crushed down a jab of fear at seeing his intended victim's size.

Hardin stopped dead still in the center of the room, his eyes on the nonsense burbling from the TV. He was in the process of turning around, to ask whose joke this was, to wearily acknowledge more rock 'n' roll tour horseplay and bullshit, when Lucas shut the door and reduced the distance separating them to nothing.

"I don't see no Bob Ca—"

Lucas clamped his left hand over Hardin's mouth and shoved the Randall upward into his chest cavity from behind, driving hard from the renal area, perforating the right kidney, the pancreas, and puncturing a lung. He twisted the knife and ripped it out, stepping back for the follow-through.

Hardin's air *whoosh*ed out in a strangled cough as his body stiffened. He lurched forward, spinning the TV on its pedestal and slamming headlong into the window. He grabbed the drawn drapes to support him. The glass rattled thunderously when he hit. A ghastly retching noise escaped him, sounding like some grotesque Slavic jabber. His right hand pawed uselessly at the gushing crater gouted out of his back. Fresh blood slopped down to streak the legs of his pants. He spun and teetered back against the window, gasping, his eyes seeking Lucas, tipping over into shock trauma. The blue in them shone like comet coals as Brion Hardin recorded the image of his murderer.

He was still standing up.

His fists were tight around the curtains, and his eyes were still open, still seeing him.

"Come *on*, dammit!" Lucas lunged forward, sacrificing aim for thrust, and sank the blade into the middle of Hardin's wiry beard. He twisted, ripped, withdrew.

The blade had gone in to the haft. Lucas was ready to strike again if this did not prove fatal.

It did.

Hardin's tongue bulged out, rimmed with saliva bubbles. More blood coursed out. His eyes went wide with impact, then dimmed in death. His hand tried to reach up to his throat, to close the breach there, but never made it. He tumbled, top-heavy, like a tipped-over china cabinet, knees cracking on the carpeting, and fell on his face with a huge, muted thump. He was still. The carpet began to darken around his bearish, inert form.

Lucas stepped over him to check the window. The knife point had come out of the back of Hardin's neck and starred the glass. *Too much force.* He had nearly gotten sloppy with panic.

He leapt for the door to check the corridor via the peephole. No activity. Yet.

Spatters of Hardin's oral blood had shot across the room to decorate the front of Lucas' gray jacket. He hurried to the bathroom and filled the basin with cold water.

The body on the floor remained unmoving. Not even a residual twitch.

Blood scattered away from the blade to stain the pure whiteness of the sink. The stream from the faucet diluted it to nothingness. Down the drain and gone. He rinsed the gloves, leaving them on and drying his hands with a fresh Hilton towel. Behind him, the TV pressed onward with its uncaring, lunatic natter, filling the room with useless images, filling the brain with dazzling noise. He daubed at his jacket, not eliminating the stains, but at least neutralizing them to the cursory eye.

He looked out of the bathroom. Brion Hardin's body was still there, still unmoving, unbreathing, heart stopped like a busted railroad watch.

Lucas unfurled the wastebasket liner from his sling bag. He wrapped the Randall in it, sheath and all. He stashed the towel. There was nothing abnormal in the room.

Except for.

Lucas waited a few moments. Time to meditate his racing heartbeat down to normal speed, to stop sweating, to insure that Hardin was history. Boil everything else away to a sequence of mechanical events. Into the elevator. Strip off the gloves after you punch the button. Stuff them in the bag. Don't touch anything on the way out of the hotel. Cut through the parking lot. Take Court Place to Fourteenth Street and get back to the Holiday Inn. Lay low in the room. Behind the door of that room, you do not exist—like Calvin Westbrook doesn't exist, like Kirk Moore and Dave Klein and Phil Longley and Mark Fawcett and good old Bobby Callahan don't exist. They would all vanish, like 150,000 other people who vanished every year in the United States, leaving no earthly trace. A name on a computer reservation, a cash-paid bill, would be all that was left.

There was one more thing to do.

Lucas had thought of it while sitting around the Holiday Inn, waiting for the KPPL interview. He kept thinking back to his conversation with Garris, the guy in charge of On the Brink Records in San Francisco. Any diversionary tactic, however small, might buy breathing space later if it was needed.

So, on his way to the Hilton, he had stopped at a twenty-four-hour drugstore and bought a can of red spray paint from the hardware section.

He pulled the can out of the sling bag and shook it. The stirring ball inside clattered around. On the blank wall behind the TV set, next to Hardin's corpse, he sprayed a large cross, starting near the ceiling. Half of it extended to the mirror over the desk. He watched himself paint it, and his face was blocked out by a swath of wet red. He made his cross several strokes bold, about seven inches thick. Next to it, he added his message in equally large lettering.

KILL SATANIST ROCK.

The letters dripped glutinously toward the floor, to meet the bloodstain that was now approaching the wall. Paint mist stung his nostrils and obscured the fetid smell of fresh blood and exposed viscera. Let them think a religious whacko was loose in the Mile-High City.

More mechanicals: The cab back to Stapleton Airport. The jet back to San Francisco. A catnap at the Holiday Inn, as Kirk Moore. The maid would have cleaned up his premeditated mess, and he'd be back in time to despoil the bed again before leaving; proof he'd "occupied" the room. The Bronco, and the trip back to Point Pitt.

And Cass.

The woman who reminded him so much of Kristen, the daughter whose pointless death was now two-fifths avenged. The thought of turning his back on the slaughter and returning to the timeless reality of the cabin evoked a pleasant tingle in his guts and groin. Cass was so very much like Kristen. Maybe an improvement.

He smiled. He had stopped shaking. He dropped the can of spray paint into the sling bag and zipped up, checking the corridor again before opening the door. Before leaving he turned off the television. The cessation of the audiovisual barrage calmed him. He looped the DO NOT DISTURB card over the knob and closed up room 704 for good.

This phase of his plan had been successfully executed. Ditto Brion Hardin.

12

"ALL YOU OUTLAWS OUT THERE are eavesdroppin' on Robbin Banks here on KRZE—*cra-zy* rock and roll for the City of the Angels and all of suntanned southern Cal. As most of you already know, every Sunday in the A.M. we take our lives in our hands and open the lines for talkback. That's right—rock 'n' roll, social issues, riddles, suicide prevention, you set the goal and we does da roll. Whatever's in your head this morning. And if you're marooned in the middle of that clog on the Santa Monica Freeway . . . Rex just stuck his GQ profile in here to inform me that a tractor trailer has flipped and they don't expect to clear it for another fifteen minutes . . . well, hey, give old Robbin a buzz on your mobile phone, and the KRZE group consciousness will dump some grat-ti-fi-*ca*-tion on yo po' white head. . . . But first, we got Headbanger, with 'Outta My Face'—a request, natch, on KRZE . . ."

Robbin Banks snubbed her Benson & Hedges in the resident ashtray of the KRZE booth, a ceramic gargoyle with its head tilted back, its wide, toothy maw open to gobble butts. You parked your smoke between the Tolkienesque tusks. Reflex made her fire up a fresh cigarette as her eyes followed Rex's progress, watching him through the soundproof window. The cheeks on Rex's Sergio Valentes were worn thin, and Rex knew Robbin knew it. He had a splendid rump. Every male deejay at KRZE had tried to cut time with Robbin ever since her arrival, down from KUSF in the bay area, and Rex had been the first she'd succumbed to. He was a full meal that was difficult to resist. Oh, those calories, she thought. He'd begun his campaign by stuffing a single, long-stemmed white rose into the driver's side window molding of her Volks Rabbit, anonymously. Time did its dirty work. Ever since the night she'd slid her thumbs into his waistband and pushed his pants to the floor of her apartment in Venice, he'd sent her different signals. Alarums. His cool chilled. When Sandy Chin had joined KRZE's office staff, Rex's eyes had settled on her like sniper sights, and Robbin almost felt sorry for the new girl. She and Rex smiled dazzlingly in the hallways. There were still times when she wanted him so bad she ached. And he knew it. And she hated him for it. And life, how it did grind on.

Instead of Rex's buns, Robbin thought, I now have to deal with the Sunday morning loon parade. She hit the switch and repeated the station ID, and KRZE's phone numbers for Orange County, the Valley, and the 213 area code. Five of the eight lines on the board were blinking out of sync, like amber Christmas tree lights in a regimented row.

While all the TV stations were putting out dawn broadcasts featuring white-pompadoured, wide-eyed evangelists, KRZE opened its ears to its audience —highschoolers, blue-collar graveyard shifters, and the heavy metal faithful. A lot of whom didn't vote, couldn't read, and thought that Reagan's decision to "kick some radical ass" in Libya had been a fun idea. People who embraced Rambo chic. People stupefied by the spell of MTV. All the drones and the clones, thought Robbin, the great unwashed, the hope of America's future, play it loud.

She knew she was judging too harshly. A lot of the kids were good. They had verve and audaciousness. She had air time and the chance to open their eyes every now and again. It sufficed. She decided she was being sullen and pissed off this morning because there was Rex, right in front of her. Untouchable. Being male.

She punched in line two. Never do things in order, she thought.

"Hello there, line two, you're on."

"Uh. Yeah! Hullo there, Robbin."

She heard the guy's voice echoing back from his own overcranked stereo. The volume dropped. "What's your name and where are you calling from?"

"Uh, this is Donny. From Woodland Hills. We been partyin' since six o'clock last night, and we just wanna say that KRZE fuckin' *rocks*!"

"Yo, Donny." The FCC Demon of Swear Words jabbed his pitchfork into her neck. "Fuck" and "shit" could pass in song lyrics, but the jocks were admonished not to run a bad mouth too freely on air. KRZE couldn't afford an eight-second delay rig for the phone lines, so Robbin was stuck. Explaining federal regs to a heavy metal audience was an idiot's game. The call-in segment was not prime drive time, but it was an arena in which Robbin had proven her mettle. Female jocks got a lot more crank response, mostly from male listeners who were dying to talk to a woman, any woman. She'd fielded a month's worth of shows adeptly and so was sleeping in the bed she'd made—one that would later give her negotiating clout at KRZE. For now, there was Donny the party animal to deal with. So be it.

"What've you got for us this morning, Donny my

man?" She could make her voice so sweet it sometimes stunned them.

Donny was clearly overwhelmed by the mere concept of hearing his own voice coming out of his own radio, and he needed goosing. Robbin's rebound was automatic. She knew callers frequently had nothing to say.

"You got something to get off your chest, or a chunk 'o' news for us, or a question for all the other rockers tuned in? Any rap at all—it's all yours. All of southern Cal is waiting on you, so go for it."

That was the correct track. Encourage the idea of the radio family.

"Uh. Right." Donny marshaled his thoughts—such as they were. "Oh! Yeah, I gotta question. Y'know, like, how come there's these great groups, right? And they do like one album. Like Quiet Riot, y'know, like they did one album and it was like, rock *out*. N'then . . . shut up, Sasha, I'm like talking, okay? And then, they break up after makin' one album . . . like one album that's really great. So like, how come they gotta break up just when everything's, y'know, going real great?"

Robbin had answered this one before. "No way to predict how personality conflicts are gonna affect a band, Donny. Sometimes the sparks fly and the group can't hold together. Look at it this way: at least we got the one album, right? And the members move on to new groups. And other groups come along. And whatever music they're able to give us in the time they're with us is fine. Hey, thanks for calling KRZE."

She ignored the fact that Quiet Riot *had* cut more than one album, and cut the line before more time could be wasted. Rex had cruised out of the outer office. That helped her kick into gear. "Line five, you're rappin' with Robbin on the KRZE talkback."

Several girls, laughing.

"Hello-hello?" Robbin said musically, amused.

More giggling, more hysterical.

"Hm, well, *some*body's having themselves a fine old party out in the Basin somewhere," she said, chuckling. She cut direct to line eight and did her prefab spiel.

"Hi, Robbin, this is Ginger from Sherman Oaks."

Right away, this one sounded as though she was sitting with a cup of coffee instead of half a beer. "Hiya, Ginger. What've you got for us?"

"Well . . . this is *sort* of related to what that previous guy mentioned, about only getting so much music from a group?"

It wasn't a question, and I mentioned it, not that moron Donny. But let's be charitable.

"Groups breaking up is one thing," said Ginger. "But this thing where Jackson Knox got blown—er, killed, in San Francisco. And now, just a few days ago, this other guy gets killed in Denver . . ."

"Brion Hardin. He played keyboards for Electroshock."

"Yeah, and both guys used to be in the same band, right?"

"Whip Hand, way back when. Right."

"Well, is this a pattern of some kind? I mean, do the other guys who used to be in that band need protection or something now? I mean, why would anybody want to kill them? They're just musicians. They just make music."

While Ginger talked, Robbin sucked the last of the life from her smoke and stubbed it out in the gargoyle's mouth, then cleared her tubes with another jolt of KRZE's killer coffee. "What you're asking me, Ginger, seems to me, is this: Is someone trying to kill everybody who used to be in Whip Hand? I put that question to the KRZE group mind. But I'll tell you what I think. I think it's terrorism."

Dramatic pause.

"It's violence against heavy metal artists by certain people who, shall we say, have a different viewpoint on music and don't think people should be allowed to choose what they like." It was the sort of speechmaking that was permissible on Sunday morning, when the KRZE station manager thought no one was listening.

"You mean like those right-to-lifers that were bombing the abortion clinics?"

"You got it. They weren't even what you'd rightly call abortion clinics. They were health centers that made a lot of people healthier and better. Nobody ever forced anybody to walk through the doors of a health center at gunpoint. And the sort of person who would use *violence*, blow up a building because they don't like the ideology of the people who work there, that's twisted and sick. It's like blowing up somebody's house because you don't like what they watch on television. It's an animalistic response. Well, there are a lot of people out there who—"

"Mentally deranged," Ginger interjected.

"Well, that's your description, Ginger." In the back of Robbin's mind was the imperative that she could appear to take a stand as long as it wasn't one that threatened any of KRZE's sponsors. There was art and there was commerce, and commerce was what paid the rent on Robbin's duplex. The one where she and Rex had done the bump all night long. And might again someday. There *was* hope in the world.

"I certainly agree that people should not force their views on other people. All views on all issues should be aired in a forum. Information should be accessible, and people should make their own choices." That was a nice, high-sounding, thoroughly bland party line. Normally, Robbin hated cluttering up her brain with other points of view. She knew what worked for her.

"But what about the guys in Whip Hand?"

"I think the . . . the tragic happenstance that befell

both those men was terribly unfortunate. As far as anybody knows, Jackson Knox's death was some kind of accident. And there's no evidence that it was connected to Brion Hardin's murder. For all we know, he might have been killed by a robber or something, right?" Her tone indicated that she had her thumb on the pulse of the facts, was an all-knowing rock 'n' roll DJ. She was waxing authoritarian on something she knew little about because she knew no one would challenge her.

"People shouldn't kill the people who give us music," said Ginger.

"I think everybody listening to the sound of your voice right now would be in total agreement on that one. I hope that nobody out there is crazy enough to believe that killing musicians is ever going to stop the power of rock."

Whoa, back off, Robbin! That had sounded a bit too much like a challenge itself. The freaks out in bozo-land didn't need any new ideas. She was suddenly glad her radio handle was not her real name. Robbin Banks couldn't be looked up in any phone book.

"Well, I just think it's really sad. I cried when I heard. And I hope nobody else gets hurt, you know?"

That's right. And keep on believing the world won't try to harm you.

"I say if the solution is violent, it isn't a solution. We should all try to be more civilized toward each other, hm? I gotta move on, Ginger, but hey—thanks for sharing your thoughts with us."

She took a break to spin some vintage Ted Nugent —"Free for All"—then cut to the line three blinker.

"Fuck you, nigger dick!" bellowed a voice, followed by the hard clunk! of disconnect.

Robbin winced. "Whoops, wrong number. Let's check out line seven . . . and no more abuse, huh, gang?" She became instantly jumpy about what pleasures or terrors the next call held. "Yo, there, you're rappin' with Robbin on the KRZE talkback."

"Umyeah . . . hi, Robbin, this is Kyle from Garden Grove."

"Way south! Good to know KRZE penetrates all the way down to Disneyland land. What's doin', Kyle?"

He cleared his throat. "We work the night shift, okay, and me and some of the other guys at the Datsun plant were just wondering . . . like, if the death orientation of a lot of metal music, okay? And speed metal, and thrash, might have something to do with the fact that a coupla guys who actually *play* the stuff got wiped out, y'know what I mean?"

"I think the idea of metal music being 'death-oriented' is a misnomer, Kyle. Do you know what *I* mean?"

"You mean it's . . . like a mistake?"

"You got it. A lot of metal music deals with occult imagery, sure, and there's an aggression in metal music that implies violence, but the guys in the bands are not ravening monsters. I mean, Vince Neill loves his mom, okay? Blackie Lawless probably has a great pet dog. That's not what he chops up and tosses to the audience at his live shows. It's just slaughterhouse leavings, props. Like actors—just because Clint Eastwood blows away people in the movies doesn't mean he packs a Magnum in real life. Why, in real life he wants to make sure the citizens of Carmel can eat ice cream on the streets, man! The rats the Grimsoles toss into the crowd during their live shows aren't *rabid,* or anything. It's all show business. And like movie actors, the guys in heavy metal aren't very violent, or hung up on death. Some of them maintain a public persona that's pretty rowdy, but that's part of the image-making process. Unfortunately, some listeners can't tell the difference between fantasy and reality, man. And that's how people like poor Jackson Knox get killed. Heavy metal employs death imagery, but that doesn't automatically mean it promotes death or violence. A kid who listens to an Ozzy Osbourne track and jumps out a window had capital-P *problems* long before that record made it to his turntable. Some of the greatest poetry in history deals with death imagery. You gonna ban or label all poetry because of that?"

"No way," said Kyle.

Robbin was trotting out her responses and theories by rote today. She needed to focus a little more, but she was doing better than the callers so far, who were singularly uninspired.

Another puff. Another sip. The coffee had gone cold. Line one.

"Like, is it true that the lyrics to 'Sleaze Weasel' are about, um, oral sex?"

From line four to line eight, back to line two.

"Dude, you want the Grateful Dead, I think you're tuned to the wrong station, and I don't mean on your *radio*, can you dig it?" She cut to line six. A virgin Benson & Hedges kissed fire. Nigger Dick had been good for only one call. Wimp radio terrorists; no stamina. Kneejerks, one-shots. They'd make great line soldiers.

"I dunno *what* the hell they're talking about," claimed a blood named Kent calling from East Hollywood. "I played 'Kill Again' backwards on my stereo. And all I got was a headache and a fucked-up record."

Line seven: "Those bands, you know, they ask for it. By making so much money, and then braggin' about it, and gettin' their picture in *People* and stuff. Bound to get someone's dander up. So naturally someone's gonna pay the price."

Line three: "I think that last caller is deranged. But then, I think most of your callers are deranged."

Robbin Banks kept a straight radio face . . . but Tracie Nichols smiled.

"Public figures cannot accept responsibility for the lunatic behavior of aberrants or mental defectives," the caller went on. "There are a lot of kooks out there just ready to explode. Primed. No one can predict *what* will touch them off. Peter Kurten, the Dusseldorf Vampire, got sexually excited by listening to the Catholic High Mass. Then he went out and strangled women, stabbed them to death with scissors, killed them with a hammer. And maybe some other nut case apes what he sees in a movie, or acts out the lyrics to an extreme song. But the *artists* cannot be made culpable."

Inspiration struck Robbin. Now was the perfect time to cue up a Whip Hand tune for the next break. She selected "Drive It in Deep," from their second album, *Menace to Society*.

"Maybe if this guy, whoever, in Denver hadn't knifed Brion Hardin, he'd've raped some little girl instead, and the know-nothings and the brain-dead religious right would blame it on the *Movie of the Week*. My point is, that person would have exploded into violence eventually not because of movies or music, but because he—or *she*—was a disturbed personality. There are people out there with very limited horizons. They wear social blinders. They feel it is better to play it safe, to run scared, and blame the most convenient scapegoat. And that means censorship . . . and censorship is the attempted murder of our whole culture. Censure replicates itself until it engulfs everything. Slapping irons on a few artists who dare to be dangerous is in no way an acceptable solution. . . ."

Dare to be dangerous, I like that, Robbin thought. *And thank you, God, for this caller.* She set turntable #1 to spinning.

"Horus, turn that shit off, huh?"

Gabriel Stannard had once done a promo dub for KRZE-FM. They meant so much to the fans, those simple little station IDs, and they had a lot of recognition value. They cost zero—audio tape, no more—and took less than sixty seconds if done right, in one take. Stations were eager to have the voices of the top guns plugging them.

This is the man your mommy warned you about, Gabriel Stannard of Whip Hand. So what station could this be but KRZE-FM in Los Angeles, right? The supercharged 101.7 is gonna help you drive it in deep!

History now.

Now "Drive It in Deep" was coming back to taunt him, and he did not care to be razzed by some asshole DJ's idea of a ratings grabber.

Horus was doing fixed isometrics against parallel bars that were bolted to the poolside deck. He disengaged to flip off the radio remote. Sunday morning programming was usually all jabber, and he preferred something rhythmic to counterpoint his workout. His oiled ebony torso gleamed like dark, polished wood, intricately carved with sinew. He exercised wearing only a Grecian wrap. Stannard thought it looked like a potholder on a string, insufficient for covering his dong.

Stannard sat cross-legged on a tanning lounger near the deep end, with a tall Long Island iced tea and a couple of monster magazines to occupy his hands. He looked pale and ill and had snapped his order for the radio talkshow to be cut off. The tone of the calls had sunk a prong of fear into his gut. The song was the last straw.

Sertha Valich, who had accompanied Stannard to Jackson Knox's hurried funeral in San Francisco, emerged from the sauna hutch. She too gleamed, with perspiration from the steam. She wore a beach robe and had her magnificent hair wound up in a towel. Stannard watched her cross the terrace on slender, elegant feet.

"How's your head? Eyes still hurt?" Sometimes her accent came on strong. She stooped to clear a spot on the table so she could sit right next to him. Under one of the monster magazines was Stannard's .44 Magnum.

The blunt gray noses of the bullets were visible in the cylinder. "I wish you would put this . . . *thing* away. It frightens me. I dislike firearms, Gabriel."

"It's mine. I'll do with it what I want. You don't like it, cover it back up."

Sertha had stayed with him since Knox's death. She'd been there when the news about Brion Hardin came down. She'd been sitting in Stannard's office when Horus had delivered the news that Josh, the private detective, had lost track of Lucas Ellington, who had bought a brand new Bronco and vanished up the Pacific Coast Highway, leaving no tracks.

A knee poked from her robe, so he reached to stroke it. His blue eyes sought the blue water of the pool. Words came, but he could not force himself to speak. He was glad she had chosen to remain. Guns scared her, but he was pretty frightened himself. He dared not show it. That would be contrary to his established persona. He had put armed guards on the gates of the estate and was packing his Magnum to and from the bathroom, but he could not say he was afraid, any more than he could admit just how much he needed her to be around. Gabriel Stannard was not, *could* not, be pussy. Fickle fans were eager to judge him; should they even get a hint that Gabriel Stannard was not the macho wild man he purported to be, they would be just as eager to forsake him.

His mind raced around like a lab rat in a puzzle box. *Two accidents, sure. When Lucas Ellington braced me it was with a plastic gun, for christsake. Coincidence. Two unrelated tragedies. Right.*

He had begun to have nightmares about his own death. Shadow figures appeared at the foot of his Playboy bed to shove him off this mortal coil. See this knife? *Stannard exeunt.* Next act, please. Twice he had awakened with a yelp. Sertha's concern for him was not only genuine, but justified.

She kissed his cheek and spread a towel on a vacant lounge, dropping the robe and unfurling her hair. She was trying to work up a full body tan and would want him to rub her down with cocoa butter.

He held the first dollop between his palms to warm it. "Top or bottom first?"

She smiled and lay down on her stomach. "Save the front for later. Back rubs lead to front rubs, and you know what front rubs lead to." She finger-combed her damp hair so that it hung off the end of the lounge.

He was performing badly in bed, too, and he knew it. He wondered what she thought, and whether she was disappointed, and would endure. He worried, which was unlike him. Before, he had never worried about anything.

Right now, just putting his hands on her body to grease her up was giving him a nice, healthy hard-on. He thought of the way he fit into her, snug as a living glove, of the crisp abrasion of her pubic hair against his.

He massaged her methodically. Before he was done, he would touch every inch of her thoroughbred body.

But his eyes never left the loaded Magnum on the table. It sat there, likewise awaiting his pleasure.

13

EL GRANADA WAS A WIDE place in the coast highway, tacked onto a bedroom community. Lucas phoned Burt Kroeger, collect, from a phone carrel outside the local hardware store.

". . . and so I just told her that you'd headed north to camp out for a while. Meditate. Violate furry forest animals, that sorta thing. And that you'd be back soon, and that you'd get in touch with everybody when you did. No specifics, no maps. Okay?"

Burt had done well. Lucas had been apprehensive about Sara checking up on him.

"You positive you didn't mention Point Pitt? I mean, I like Sara a lot, but she might get overzealous, and I'm doing fine up here all by myself."

"You want a signed guarantee? Don't worry about it." For some reason, it occurred to Lucas that Burt had taken up his cigarette habit again. He could not hear him puffing, for the noise of the ocean, but the image of Burt sucking on a cigarette between sentences locked in and held. "But let me ask you something, old buddy. What the hell difference would it make if Sara *did* know?"

It was obvious that Burt now felt yoked with the responsibility of being the middleman. "I sometimes think that Sara is a bit too eager to deepen our relationship, Burt. She's a valuable person. But she's in a hurry. I don't want to screw things up by rushing. You know."

Burt replied that he did, in fact, copy and understand. The same sort of thing had happened during his courtship with his wife, Diana. Only in that mad race, it had been Burt doing the pushing. He was sensitized to the idea, and Lucas knew it.

"I'll get you off the hook, though, since you're such a swell guy."

Burt blew a politely brief raspberry into the phone.

"Give me the phone numbers Sara gave you. I'll call her myself, set her mind at ease, and that'll subtract you from the whole equation so you can go back to worrying about how much to screw Randell and Kochner out of on Gustavo's lawsuit."

Burt laughed and recited the phone numbers Sara had given him for referral. His response was concerned as ever, and helpful, and tinged with relief. He typically hated meddling, especially in other people's emotional entanglements. Tacit, well-intentioned interference was still interference, what he called Mary Worth-ing.

"And since you haven't brought it up, I'll do it for you," Lucas continued. "Sara put you on the spot, sort of. You did what a good friend should. Thanks."

"You don't have to be so nasty about it. As long as you don't cop out on the dinner commitment. Besides, Diana is dying to see you again, too. This is costing me money, so have yourself a time, son, and we'll see you . . . whenever."

"A week or two, yet. You can leak that to Sara if she bears her burden to your doorstep again." They both chuckled, not cruelly at Sara's expense, but merely as two friends sharing a confidence. Burt had accepted

Lucas's image of Sara and bore her no malice.

Far to the south, Burt hung up and allowed himself to feel at ease. It looked like Lucas was going to be okay. Everything was fixed, at last.

Across the narrow side street from the phone, the El Granada post office stood neatly closed. Next to the hardware store a small local eatery called the Village Green was still open for business. It was a short hop to the ocean, a city block or so away over a bit of vacant scrubland between the fire station and the highway. On top of a phone pole, right above Lucas, were the fire station's sirens in two collars of flared, multidirectional horns. It looked like an alien weapon from some weird science fiction saga.

Lucas decided to give Sara a miss. If he called, she would try to nail him down on the location of the cabin. If she was in Los Angeles, that meant she was already looking for him, and he would need all the time anonymity could buy.

Even if Sara knew what she was looking for, he could still outrace her. By the time she figured out the details, it would be finished. How many reliable starting points had he given her? How many times had he actually recounted the Whip Hand dream to her or the recurrent danger images in the Kristen nightmare? She had needed to see patterns in his dreams so badly, to justify her skill as an analyst. So he'd given her patterns to see.

The nightmares had been real, however.

Had she seen the news reports on Jackson Knox, on Brion Hardin? Would she associate them with a rock band that had not existed for years? Would the various news media make the association for her?

Would the police start using the same logic?

There were enough maybes falling out of the whole argument, left and right, that Lucas felt reasonably secure. His planning was so comprehensive that even if the killings were linked—which he did not mind and, in fact, desired in the long run—and even if he was exposed as having a prime-cut motive, there would still be an utter lack of concrete evidence to damn him. His vendetta had been blueprinted with the same conscientious eye he had used for so many successful promotional campaigns. It *was* a campaign. Battles were called campaigns. And time was his ally in this battle.

Time, in fact, was going to force him to miss some sleep, if he adhered to his schedule. Schedules were crucial to campaigns; timing was everything. Yesterday had been the Electroshock date in Denver; in about forty-eight hours he'd have to leave for the 'Gasm date, in Arizona. When the police tried to link homicides from state to state, they used the "connect the dots" method. By the time they had enough dots to connect, the line would lead nowhere. San Francisco to Denver to Tucson, Arizona. The shape of a big question mark.

He left the fire station and high-stepped through the muddy marsh grass, crossing Highway 1. North, to his right, was an imposing microwave dish perched on a spur of land run by the U.S. Air Force Missile Command. The electronic ear was tilted straight up, toward space. Nearer was a pull-over area for tourist RVs and campers. The beach led to a stone jetty that extended into the water as far as a good-sized pier, forming an enclosure known locally as Pillar Point Harbor. The jetty stone was a jackstraw piling of quarry waste in different colors, like a long bridge made of broken tombstones. Lucas jumped cautiously from rock to rock. The granite surfaces were slick with spume, and he tried not to squash the tiny crimson-and-black crabs that huddled in the million crevices.

When he reached the nose of the man-made breakwater, he threw the Randall combat knife into the sea, sheath and all, with a hard overhand swing. He was too far out for anyone to badger him about littering. Sea mist and the crash of waves pounding the jetty drenched him. From the sling bag he withdrew the spraypaint can and likewise gave it up to Neptune. Maybe the god could write an underwater graffito or confound some uppity octopus with a cloud of red ink. The surgical gloves had been burned back in Denver. He was about to weigh the sling bag with one of the smaller jetty stones and give it the heave-ho as well when he saw that the plastic trash can liners he'd used had kept the interior of the bag spotless. Innocent. Cass would see him return carrying the same two bags with which he had departed. Perfect.

The Randall was a monster, but it was no match for the Pacific Ocean. There was a little bloop and a weak geyser of saltwater, and that was the end of it. Case closed. Neptune (or Poseidon, as the Greeks had it—but then, there were no horses around, either) must have been cooping on the job. The ocean did not accuse Lucas of any wrongdoing.

He stared abstractedly at the water and the horizon for a few moments, the way most people do when evaluating themselves in relation to the sheer vastness of the sea. Then he turned back toward the parked Bronco.

He was anxious to see Cass again.

"You talk in your sleep. Did you know that?"

Caution jumped into Lucas' heart with a thud. "Oh? Nothing too provocative, I hope."

"Mostly incomprehensible." Lacking chores per se, Cass was moving kitchen stuff around in a ritualistic pattern, trying to find an arrangement that suited her idea of order. "Kristen's name. Something about teaching her a lesson."

Impossible. Teaching them *a lesson, yes.* But if he'd had the Whip Hand nightmare again, he did not remember.

"Oooh—if you could see the frown on your face right now," she teased. "Don't worry. I learned early never to try to read dreams."

Her facial swelling had dwindled, and her movements were regaining some of the natural grace Lucas had suspected, as the muscles unstiffened and healed. She was now seeing with both eyes, though the left one still had not completely opened. It gave her the attitude of someone with a perpetual half wink, like a comic delivering a sly punchline.

Say, have you heard the one about the doomed rock group? One bit a big blade, and then there were three. . . .

"I used to have a recurrent dream, when I was seventeen," she said. "I was being chased through a field of very tall grass, like reeds, head-high stuff. Maybe a wheat field. I never see what's chasing me, but I know it's big and ugly and hungry. And it's after me, specifically. The monster knows who I am, and it wants me. And I'm terrified that if I part the grass to either side, I'll be looking right into its face, all steaming and fanged and snorty, and a paw the size of a catcher's mitt will scoop me up, and that'll be the big finish. The end of me. The grass is both my protection and my greatest hindrance. If I was stranded on the fifty-yard line of a deserted football field, at least I'd know which *way* to run, see? Sometimes the monster is far away, sometimes it's closer, but always nearby. And I'll meet it inevitably, and that scares me, but I keep running. I'm determined to go down fighting."

Cass smiled slightly, gesturing with her wounded hand, getting into her own story.

"I come to a tree, a tall tree, a eucalyptus tree, maybe, something solid I can put between me and the monster. Maybe it can't climb trees. Or I can get high enough to survey the field and figure out where I am in relation to the monster. All I'd have to do is look for the swath it's cutting through the grass. As I reach out to grab the lower limb and swing up, that big fucking paw lands on my shoulder, puffing dust and fleas into my eyes . . . and I howl and wake up. End of dream."

Lucas had dumped down two Dos Equis without feeling a thing. Cass said the alcohol made her raw throat feel better. He returned to the table with two freshly uncapped bottles.

"So. My father, wheeler-dealer that he is, forks over money so I can go see a psychiatrist. Eight sessions. I rattled off my history, some of the exciting stuff, then I laid out the dream. Know what he told me?"

"That you were sick, sick, sick," he said. They clinked bottles.

"He told me I was afraid of losing my virginity. That the hungering, slobbering monster was phallic. The field of impenetrable grass was my fear of sex. And the tree was a biblical perversion of a celibacy facade, or something. I half expected him to pat me on the thigh, paternally."

It was what Lucas expected to hear. Cass' shrink had been another Freudian basket case.

"But the joke was on him, Lucas. This is what I meant about not trying to read dreams. I'd lost my cherry a year and a half before I'd ever had the dream, and gotten laid a couple of dozen times. Enough to think, even at seventeen, that there wasn't any mystique to sex, and certainly nothing that I was scared of. I'd lied to the shrink about being a virgin. I didn't want my father to know—don't ask me why, 'cos that'll waste a lot of time. So the shrink turned out to be full of it. End of story."

A conclusion reached as a result of faulty input. It had the fascination of a box puzzle. Lucas thought of Sara and her quest to figure him out. He had so enjoyed leading her where she wanted to go. The blackly depressed widower, the suicidal father of the victim daughter. He wondered whether Kristen had ever had sex before her death. He thought he knew the answer, but it kept being overshadowed by the weaker idea that a father should not consider such things.

"My recurrent dream was about Kristen, right before she died," he said. "Very stylized. Nothing useful there, either." His hands made an aimless effort to twist the air into something descriptive.

"How did she die? Kristen."

It was asked considerately but caused Lucas to worry his lips together a beat too long before he said, "An accident."

"Sorry." Cass looked at him directly. "Sometimes my big nose gets my big mouth in trouble." She regarded her empty bottle. "Want to switch off to coffee?"

He was pleasantly in half focus and willing to accede to nearly anything. He had not felt this good, this at peace, in a long time. Cass was really a remarkable young lady . . . no, a remarkable *woman*, with a tact and maturity that exceeded his low expectations of what twenty-three was supposed to look and sound like.

She fiddled gingerly with the coffeepot over at the sink. She still moved very carefully, as though afraid she might shatter. "And no, I did *not* spend my time engaged in domestic chores while you were gone. I've had a lifelong phobia about lapsing into housewifery. The Great American Dream. The white picket fence that imprisons you."

"White picket fence?"

"Yeah. All that stuff I'm supposed to want from life, but don't. The house in Malibu. An El Blando hubby who busts his balls to stay inside a six-figure adjusted income. A station wagon and matching Porsches. Two point five blond kids. An afghan hound that shits more than it eats, two spayed cats, and one exotic pet—a toucan or a tortoise or an aardvark. Hired minorities to swab the toilets and polish the jockey on the front walk." She shrugged and made a face. "You know the life,

Lucas: birth control pills, diet pills, sleeping pills, antacid pills . . . pills to counteract the draining effect of the other pills . . . vitamin pills to give you enough energy to swallow the sixty other pills you wind up taking every day. Yuck."

He thought of pills and of Cory. Pills could do good things, like expunge a harpy from your life. Like make a bad relationship into a good one. Cory had chided him about his performance in bed. After she was gone, he had done better. Maybe it was the pills.

"You get your first nervous breakdown at twenty-seven, first facelift at thirty. Then you move on to your first serious extramarital affair, having had a bunch of tacky minor ones already. Then a tumor at forty, a stroke at fifty . . . and a nice white picket fence around it all. You put it up so the serfs will steer clear of what's yours, and you paint it every third year, and it's always white and pristine and undespoiled. And when you die, it'll be sitting there, like some kind of perverted legacy to the world. *This is what I was, neat and attractive and forgettable*. And then you and the rest of your neat nuclear family get put in the ground, and somebody new comes along and puts up their own white picket fence after they've uprooted yours and recycled it, and that's the end. Dark, ugly nothing."

"That's sad," said Lucas as she brought him a fresh cup of coffee. She'd added cinnamon.

"That's why I'm giving it lots of room to avoid me. If anyone uses the word 'lifestyle,' it's a pretty good indication that they don't have one. Maybe they *bought* one. But they're trapped by the white picket fence."

"The WPF." He grinned. Despite the age-old cliché of the woman's touch, the coffee was really much better than his own brew.

"Life with good old Reese the psycho may not have lasted long," she mused, "but there was no white picket fence to worry about."

I'll be goddamned, he thought. Cass was talking about him and his old life. With Cory, his life had been aimed down the very path Cass was lampooning. And two people had died, and he had gotten a clean slate at a mental hospital in exchange for a year of his life, and things were much better now, thank you. Overseas, he remembered, there were no abstruse reasons *why*, no political fluff to cloud reality. You were there for one reason only—to stay alive. Yes, sir, I'm out there offing dinks for a damned good reason; the only reason. Staying whole.

"That's all done now," he said, as much in response to his own thoughts as Cass' abrupt stormcloud of depression. He was aware that he was examining what she said in an attempt to generate guilt over Cory. Guilt was his biggest enemy, Sara had told him. Guilt must not even enter into the equation.

The sun was falling. In another day he had to be packed and gone again.

"You're right," Cass said. "Another mood to slide into." She touched her fingertips to her face, appraising her shrinking bruises for the thousandth time. "Sometimes a traumatic experience forces you to become a better person. Sometimes you have to put up with an infinitude of assholes, and just when you're ready to give up, you stumble across somebody worthwhile, by purest luck."

"Maybe not," he said. "Maybe you're due for a good guy."

"Well, you're a pretty decent guy. Do you count?"

"Of course not," he said, getting up to refill his mug. "Wait till you know me well enough to really despise me."

She gave that an editorial *hmmm*, but intercepted him. "By the way, look—no more Ace bandage. Check this out, doctor." She unbuttoned her chambray workshirt and opened it up. Her breasts were unbound.

They obviously did not pain her as much as before. Yellowish smudges were all that remained of the bruises there, except for some dwindling dark patches where the impact had been the worst. She took his hand and made him touch them; a caress for each.

He gulped, more than a little surprised. "That's good," he said, feeling dumb.

She held his hand to her chest while she stood up and kissed him. Her lips pushed his apart; he felt the hard little rind of scab brush his mouth. The contact was galvanizing. There was the briefest, delicious touch of her tongue, making tentative introduction, then she withdrew.

"Thanks, Lucas."

His voice had dried up with amazing speed. "Uh . . . don't worry about it." His brain scampered madly, seeking some new subject. "Are you tired?"

"That's my good-night." She smiled her restricted smile. "I'm still too crippled for any heavy-duty action, if you know what I mean."

He was just far enough ahead of her, in years, to be embarrassed. "Oh, wait, I didn't mean—"

"*I* did. Lucas, you're blushing."

And that, of course, brought on the blush full blast. Cass could be very evil when the mood arose.

He sought a graceful escape and found none. "Oh . . . fucking hell," he mumbled.

"It's cute," she said. "Attractive, I mean. Men hate looking sensitive, I know. Get your coffee. It's not as if I'm a princess, and I'm repaying the White Knight for his chivalry by fucking him blind."

"That's nice to know." He drew the words out broadly, playing with her now.

"I just wanted to make sure you think about me occasionally. While I'm snoozing. Over there. In my bag."

"I do. And not wholly out of worry, not anymore.

I'm glad you're getting better. I'd like to steal credit for it. But . . . you *have* noticed that I'm old enough to be your—" He was thinking of Kristen again.

He was thinking of *fucking* Kristen.

"Oh, just barely," she cut in. "Besides, I don't recall bothering to ask if you were of age or not. Nor does that matter. You have to leave tomorrow; I just wanted to make sure you'd come back for some other reason than to make sure your cabin hadn't been stolen by a UFO."

"I've already got more here than I ever had," he said. He kept his distance from her, idling near the sink. "Wait. All right? Just wait a bit." His smile was genuine. Soon everything would be perfect. But not tonight.

"Sure." She limped over and held his face in her hands, touching, examining the planes, friendly. "Good night, Lucas."

" 'Night." Her eyes seemed to glisten at him. The cabin had grown uncomfortably warm.

She broke from him but kissed him again before she did, deeper, speaking volumes. and he enjoyed it.

White-faced haircut boys
They got their Jags and expensive toys
So-ror-i-ty pin
He gets her cornered and he sticks it in
White Trash!
Money to burn
White Trash!
You only yearn for
Cold cash!
Let yo' dollar bills fly
But rock and roll will never die!

While 'Gasm squirmed through the middle set of *Throw Down Your Arms*, Lucas put the finishing touches on the now assembled sniper's rifle, the lethal Dragunov.

Cass slept soundlessly nearby, unthreatening, uncurious. Now, if only Cory had been more like her . . .

. . . she wouldn't have taken the high dive into the pill bottle. And Cass wasn't like Kristen. Not really. Not yet.

With the barrel attached, the Dragunov was a few inches over a yard long and weighed a neat ten pounds fully loaded. The stock was an outline of wood, shaped like a wire stock but firmer on recoil.

Throw Down Your Arms spun out on the small Sony screen. Lucas listened through headphones at reduced volume. He watched Tim Fozzetto, the bassist, zip out of his outrageous checkerboard jumpsuit and expose his ass to a wildly cheering audience. *Boom!*—throw down your pants. Just quick enough to give the crowd a thrill, then all the onstage lights snap to dead black for Pepper "Mad Max" Hartz's big solo.

The solo spot was the part that interested Lucas.

A cobalt-blue spotlight picked out Hartz on his special stage dais as he writhed and belabored his Stratocaster. The Fender Strat was the guitar Jimi Hendrix had annoyed the world with.

Back in the good old days, Lucas thought, guitars had a hard time displacing the saxophone as the centerpiece solo instrument of rock 'n' roll. Solos were expected to have an inner consistency of structure that made them startling or notable. A natural outgrowth of this approach, due to the outspoken lack of talent in copycat bands and encouraged by the field hands of punk in the mid-1970s, was to use the guitar not to solo, but to provide the most grating and discordant noise of any individual instrument present—a kind of Big Stick theory for music. This begat the school of guitar abuse in which the strings were kicked, bitten, hammered with the fist, subjected to wine glasses and viola bows and chainsaws and anything else that could help produce a loud, obnoxious noise. Sometimes this was innovative. Most times it was tiresome.

Hartz pulled out the few stops he could manage. But he was a product of the bar-band rock gristmill that mistook energy for ability and desperation for outrageousness. All that was left to him was showbiz. Using a chromium phallus that dangled from his codpiece and tights, Hartz jacked his guitar off, bottleneck style.

The stage remained in blackness, except for Hartz's spotlight, for the duration of his solo. Using the digital stopwatch function on his Seiko, Lucas had timed the solo at three minutes and three seconds. Disorganized musical support was audible but ever-changing, as one band member or another sneaked offstage for a towel, a toot, or a quick gulp of something cold. Nothing was visible except Hartz, bathed now in scarlet light as the gels on his spot were rotated. He ladder-walked his fingers up and down the fretboard. It was an embarrassing cliché by now. Lucas was almost glad Hendrix had died in his prime and was thus spared this degrading of his style.

Rock and roll would never die, the lyrics reminded everybody. It would never grow up, either, apparently.

Embittered, Lucas thought of the bottom-line groups, the hackers, the clone bands who ripped off anything original and blanded it out. The creators of clichés, with their exhausted vocabulary of tired lyrics. You still heard the age-old lyrics today, but they no longer held any meaning; they were square pegs that fit into the square holes of building-block, formula rock: *We were made for each other. Love at first sight. Together forever. All I want is you.* Softened, obfuscatory versions of songs that now bore titles like "Slitlicker." Or, on the 'Gasm live disc, "Bend 'n' Spread 'Em" and "Cock Knock."

Gonna drive my skin bus
Gonna drive it on down
Right on down into Tuna town.

The Rolling Stones, god bless 'em, had cut a song called "Starfucker." And FM deejays to this day chickened out by referring to it as "Star Star." So did the album cover. It looked like something innocuous, but it was really a werewolf.

The sentiments expressed by this music, and the motives for writing it, were no different from those that had produced "Don't Sit Under the Apple Tree" a century earlier. When you thought it out, it was all a lie.

Lies kill people. Lies killed Kristen.

Kristen had swallowed all the hype and horseshit and gotten road-ganged into a concrete floor. The lies of love had nearly gotten Cass murdered. Lies had given Whip Hand a comatose following of apostles who were so unaware of the field's premier stylists that they actually believed the assault and battery committed on a guitar by a Jackson Knox or a Pepper "Mad Max" Hartz could stop the rotation of the Earth on its axis. In two decades, "Maybe Baby" had become "Wang Dang Sweet Poontang."

All the great bluesmen were laughing in their graves.

Boom—the stage flooded with light, and 'Gasm reappeared. The conjurers had returned for the magic show. Their stage moves were so pat they virtually carried a factory warranty. Lucas fitted the sniperscope onto the Dragunov, lifted the weapon, and socketed the rubber pad to his eye.

He was looking through a four-power scope with an integral rangefinder and a battery-powered rectile illuminator, enhanced with infrared. The whole cylindrical package was fourteen inches long. He loaded a magazine with ten rounds of 7.62-millimeter rimmed ammo and smacked it into the underside of the rifle. The Dragunov featured a flash suppressor and recoil compensator that helped to keep the barrel targeted. Muzzle velocity was 2,700 feet per second. It could kick a hole the size of a dinner plate through an oak door at eight hundred meters and made the M-16 look like a popgun by comparison. If he'd wanted truly outrageous firepower, he would have used one of those monstrous Remington riot guns—twelve-gauge pumppumps with twenty-inch barrels and folding metal stocks. The Dragunov favored skill and accuracy and was for deadly jabs in specific places, not industrial demolition.

"What're you burning?" Cass had asked him yesterday when she'd caught him disposing of the Brion Hardin Electroshock discs in the brick maw of the barbecue. He'd told her garbage, and she'd returned to the cabin, satisfied. Cass didn't pry. That was so good.

The rusty paring knife still jutted from the midsection of the Gabriel Stannard poster. Lucas leaned forward and levered it out. It reminded him of the way things had gone in the hotel room with Hardin—badly. Panic had come too close. He'd gotten scared, almost thought the son of a bitch would refuse to die. Not good. Expediting Stannard himself would have to be done differently, with no gutters for error. Lucas dumped the paring knife into one of the supply boxes, out of sight, and with it disposed of his thoughts of near misses and screwups. No lie.

Lucas killed the audio from the VCR and substituted another Doors tape. "Love Me Two Times" spun out while 'Gasm jumped and gyrated amid their smoke pots. He thought of the colorful smoke canisters he'd used during the war.

He recalled Burt Kroeger's loopy theorizing about the administration and the economy. Financial patterns had much to do with Lucas' personal war as well. It had been a mediocre year for the music business, preceded by a bonafide *bad* year marked by a buying slump. Consumers had hoarded their pennies. Bands were compelled to be more visible, less eccentric. They needed to tour more. Well-organized bands could blitz through three hundred concert dates in a year. This edict meant that Jackson Knox, Electroshock, and 'Gasm were all on the road and, conveniently, all in the West concurrent with Lucas's own liberation. Gabriel Stannard was not touring, but Lucas knew the singer maintained a palatial eyrie in Beverly Hills that was a twenty-minute drive from the Kroeger Concepts building. No rush there.

Stannard's ears would be pricked following the 'Gasm hit. His guard would be up. Maybe the best procedure would be to make him sweat for a year—two, perhaps—make him hire security guards out the wazoo, bleed him before finishing him off. Make him live in fear. It was already assured that it would be impossible to take out the 'Gasm boys in their hotel. The Hardin job had been a one-shot-only technique.

Security would be tight. Eyes would be open. The plan would have to be seamless. The war was hotting up.

Lucas touched the VCR remote and scanned backward to Pepper Hartz's solo spot. The band jerked in spastic fast motion; 78 rpm shock treatment. He played the sequence through several more times.

After locking up the Whip Hand room, he toted the Dragunov out for a bit of practical acid testing in the dark.

The main room of the cabin was still and quiet. In her sleeping bag, Cass rolled to one side. He heard her breathing in sleep cadence. A tiny trill of desire for her tickled his guts as he stepped out the rear door.

He was ready for Arizona, and his predawn target practice proved it.

14

"DOES THIS SHOT SUCK AS much as I suspect it does?" Logan McCabe growled as he bent to peer into the viewfinder of the big Panavision camera on its dolly. He cut loose a disgusted snort from beneath the visor of his baseball cap. "Yep. It do."

Gabriel Stannard slouched in the slingback chair embroidered with his name in golden glitter script. *Does rock 'n' roll suck as much as I suspect it does?* he thought to himself. They were even using metal music for beer commercials now.

David Lee Roth had Geronimo'd out of Van Halen. Eddie and the boys had gone reeling into mediocrity. Now Dangerous Dave was playing it safe, doing Sinatra, doing his ultimate party animal routine, lining up nubiles to ogle on one of Merv Griffin's sound stages. Dangerous Dave was playing it rich and safe, and he and Stannard didn't swap words much anymore. Time had defanged and neutered Ted Nugent. Sammy Hagar's plug had been pulled by the Springsteen brand of knee-jerk patriotism. Mötley Crüe had degenerated into a gang of prancing glitter faggots—chicks with dicks, as Il Duce, lead revoltoid of the Mentors, had observed on live radio.

Gabriel Stannard thought about the Mentors for a second.

The Mentors did puke-rock better than anyone else. Songs like "Clap Queen" and "Golden Shower," catchy little ditties concerning anal rape, venereal disease, pus, and other social issues guaranteed to make the elegantly circle-pinned ladies of the PMRC shit Tiffany cuff links. *On your face I leave a shit tower!* The Mentors' novelty was exceeded only by their gross-out factor; Dr. Demento would never spin their songs. But if it was inevitable that someone do tunes about herpes sores and killing queers, then Il Duce and his rat pack did them better than anyone else, with a gruff metal edge. The only company that would take them on was Brian Slagel's infamous Metal Blade Records, home of the napalm-attack speed metal act Slayer.

Gabriel Stannard sat watching, half-asleep, thinking bitterly about how bad boys invariably aged badly. His hair was acetylene-torch white and teased out. Lace gloves ran to midbicep. The fingers of the gloves had been sawn off. His top was designer-shredded, and his pants were Spandex. Boots, rags, hankies, all tied in the right places. He had done it a million times. It was comfy and secure. Rock 'n' roll was not comfy and secure. When bands grew comfy and secure, you got formulaic, torpor-inducing metal Muzak good for nothing beyond stringing commercials together on the AOR stations. What Stannard craved was a way to stay dangerous.

He thought he'd found it in a guitarist named Cannibal Rex, formerly of a group called Jonestown Massacre.

Jonestown had signed to Metal Blade in the wake of Bitch and Lizzy Borden cranking out a relentless brand of thrash guaranteed to make metalheads apoplectic with bliss. It was sticking your head inside a jet turbine to get off on the whine. The hardcore slant had reenergized the familiar patternings of heavy metal —the pro forma sexism, the punk biker look, the lyrics about hell and death and apocalypse. Two of Jonestown's songs, "Black Wedding Dress" and "Hell Wants *You!*" had even been played on KNAC, a so-called hard rock station that decried the metalzoid label. Stannard didn't care about labels as long as the contents were stimulating. He reevaluated his costume. Ten years ago, it might have been dangerous, different.

Jonestown Massacre fell apart a week and a half after Stannard's agents had gotten Cannibal Rex's signature on a contract. Cannibal—real name, Martin Killough Beecher—became the new lead man. The PR guys had stamped their hooves and moaned. Cannibal Rex was something they could not sell to the T-shirt-buying fourteen-year-olds in Stannard's constituency.

Cannibal Rex was bald. The scars on his pate suggested that he shaved his hair with a meat cleaver. He wore the urban punk uniform of Levi's, combat boots, and suspenders and affected a Special Forces green beret with a bullethole through the shield. He had lost the pinky and ring fingers of his picking hand in a gang fight and later had surgery performed to remove the useless hand bones. His right hand was in perfect proportion but only had three digits, rather like Mickey Mouse minus one. He wore one of the smaller finger bones as an earring. His eyes were very red, his pallor nearly blue. His complexion was that of an overdose victim on a morgue slab. He tended to spit on people when he talked. He rarely talked. Thick, murky wraparound shades hid his eyes from the world everywhere except onstage—he liked to glare at audiences, and those eyes were not something you would want paying attention to you for any length of time. His crimson glare was a laser, threatening to drill your heart and make you dead. He had recently begun wearing a combat knife, sheathed to the small of his back, while playing live gigs. He seldom spoke to the band in public, except for Stannard. When he spoke to Stannard, no saliva flew.

That was all the general public knew of Cannibal Rex.

"Rex, move on over here. One more time, right?" Logan McCabe pointed to Cannibal's masking-tape mark on the stage floor. They were shooting Stannard's new video on the old Chaplin stage in Hollywood, which was now an adjunct of A&M Records. The set suggested a bombed-out school classroom with a flaming sky visible through shattered windows. Cannibal dutifully moved to his mark, bone earring swinging. There was bullshit, and there was business. This was business.

What Gabriel Stannard knew about Cannibal Rex was another matter. He knew that Cannibal, as Marty Beecher, had killed two people in self-defense a long time back. Barehanded. He knew that Marty had been invited to enroll at Juilliard. Marty didn't want to study classical guitar, even as a prodigy. Somewhere between the two events, Cannibal Rex was born . . . and he could chop off two more fingers and still be a more versatile guitarist than most of the guys who made the cover of *Musician* magazine.

Logan McCabe had maneuvered into feature films by doing *Pimp Killer* and *Hollywood High Hooker Squad* for New World Pictures. Exploitation films for Roger Corman meant a furious production pace and a stranglehold-tight budget. If you were willing to shoot a movie in ten days, years of experience could be had on a shoestring. McCabe was willing and had gotten his chops. Stannard had previewed McCabe's movies on his VCR and requested the director because of the visceral way he handled action scenes. McCabe was not a director of videos, and Stannard had no interest in precision dancers, guest star cameos, or tinsel.

Neither did Cannibal Rex. Stannard recalled their first alcohol-stoked jam in Stannard's subterranean recording studio. Cannibal shotgunned a beer, blasted a line of good Peruvian snow up each nostril, and manhandled his Les Paul, sawing out a nasty improvised riff. He had repeated it a few more times before getting a vomitous expression on his face. His only comment: "This bites major hose." He bent his pick double and chucked it across the studio. But the riff existed, and like the one Keith Richards had picked out for "Satisfaction," it grew into a song. Stannard and Cannibal punched it back and forth, building and shaping the tune until it was a killer. The title was "Maneater," and it was sure to jump to number one . . . if they could ever get the damned video in the can. McCabe had tried thirteen takes of Cannibal wailing on his axe and was still dissatisfied. Time was wasting, the union's meter was running, and tempers were fraying on the set.

The oil smoke used to diffuse the stage lighting was giving Stannard a piledriver headache. All the starch was leaking out of his backbone, and he was sinking into his chair. Sertha appeared at his elbow bearing a glass of Sweetouchnee tea the consistency of Valvoline. It was cut with brown sugar and afloat with lime wedges; Stannard liked to think of the beverage as caffeinated rocket fuel. He crunched five Excedrin dry and drank half the glass.

"People, the *sun*. Has gone *down*. Out*side*. And here we stand." McCabe shook his head sadly, as if in sympathy at a passing busload of retards. "If this shot had any less juice, it'd be as dry as a nun's punky."

Sertha shot Stannard a questioning glance.

He smiled weakly. "Never mind. Another screwed-up American idiomatic expression, signifying boredom." The remark brought some tired chortles from the crew. Stannard knew they were all wearing thin; the gaffers and effects guys had even stopped ogling Sertha. He sipped his tea and snaked his free hand between her legs, to wrap around one thigh in a half hug. Ice clinked as he tilted the glass.

Her calm, contoured, almost Oriental eyes assessed him. "You're doing better today. There's blood in you, life in your eyes."

"That's from my daily Sertha injection." He polished off the tea, chugging it. "Wooooaahh, speed rush!" He made exploding noises, like a child playing with toy soldiers. "Horus says I've just shifted the focus of my anger. Horus is real big on shifting one's focus."

Cannibal Rex stood on his mark, shades on, expressionless, a mannequin awaiting the flick of the switch reading *detonate*.

"You've stopped worrying, is this what you mean?"

"Nope. Just that I'm worried more, right now, about the way we're pissing time on this one little piece of film."

McCabe's assistant director hollered for quiet on the set, and everyone ran through the motions for the ten-second take. One more time.

'Gasm had a concert date coming up in Tucson, Arizona. Stannard had taken very careful note of their tour schedule. Now he was dealing with his own timetable and observations, not those of the police or the TV news. Rather than sitting at home, gun at hand, wondering when doom was going to drop down on his head, he was beginning to formulate a plan. He was assuming responsibility for his own life, rather than waiting around for others to pick up the slack.

Horus' security force was stationed discreetly at the stage doors. They were joined into one mind by antennaed headsets. They wore bulky, zippered windbreakers and packed slim attaché cases that concealed all manner of brutal retaliatory capabilities. Sertha assumed these guards—three men and two women, not counting

Horus—were the source of Stannard's newfound ease. She was only partially correct.

Horus stood in the shadows like a dream idol from Stannard's subconscious, arms folded, face impassive, his golden earrings winking brightly. Sertha looked from him to Cannibal Rex and back, thinking of dark and light chess pieces of equal value.

Stannard knew his image was a lie. The macho posturing, the badder-than-thou stance, were mostly the product of his TV and comic-book fantasies. He had pumped up his body (artificially, so chided Horus), he'd become proficient in the use of weapons. His persona scared people enough to make him interesting and intimidated dealmakers enough to insure him a hefty income. But it was all on the order of the man who fanatically amasses a vast library without ever stopping to read the books. The collection implies knowledge, wisdom, worldliness. And if people thought you were knowledgeable, and worldly wise, you really didn't have to be because they deferred to you automatically. It reminded Stannard of the way clerks behaved in the face of presumed wealth.

The headache was making the hard comma of scar tissue bisecting his right eyebrow pulse. He wiped sweat from his face and felt the tough little bump there. His mark.

The stage was so hot that sweat generated all along his forearm, where it was in contact with Sertha's thigh. He released her. She was bearing up well in skintight white jeans and an oversized, sleeveless designer T-shirt with hand-painted balloons all over the front. Endless fashion shoots had inured her to the heat of klieg lights. Her face was perfect, like an antiperspirant ad.

Rock 'n' roll was Stannard's life. And rock 'n' roll insisted he do something besides dent his buns, waiting for an axe to drop and split his head. If his life were headed toward some kind of personal apocalypse, then rock 'n' roll and the persona that he had lived for so long demanded that he be the one to initiate the final onslaught.

There was an idea there. Part of his brain, the part that recognized hope, came to full attention.

Rolling over for an oncoming Fury like this Lucas Ellington guy was no answer. Depending on the real world to save his ass was no answer. Stannard had to take everything up he feared in two fists and choke it until somebody won.

He looked at Cannibal Rex, frozen in position, guitar jutting. What if he was to suddenly attack the camera filming the video footage? Just swing his guitar and smash dead on into that fucker? It'd cost a fortune. Everybody'd get supremely pissed. Violence—*wham!*

What if that violence could be interpolated into the video? The video could end as the guitar smashes the camera and blacks out the frame. Chop the music off; no fades, no lead-outs, just click and gone. Play it straight for half the running time, then the band goes berserk. Have cameras whirling around to catch the action as it happens. See the props and backdrops suddenly exposed, camera crews panicking, stagehands dropping their styrofoam coffee cups. *Bash*—a camera in the middle distance bites the dust. And the song grinds on, losing an instrument at a time as more band members fly into the fray, gleefully wiping out everything.

Stannard abruptly realized how the video should end. The camera—the final, surviving camera—pushes in on his face. Dark, manic, threatening. Cannibal Rex lurks to the rear. Stannard grabs Cannibal's guitar and mouths the final line of the song.

"C'mon, bad man—take me down if you can."

Then the camera gets knocked cold.

It was a modification of the song's final line, which spoke of bad girls, not bad men. But Stannard had the clout to get away with this one-time editorial change.

Hell, *Circus* magazine would devote a column to speculating on the secret hidden meaning. To the Bible humpers, "bad man" could only be the Big Red Guy, and that meant even more press.

A grin cracked across his bored expression. Yeah, this could stir up a lot of rock 'n' roll trouble. He loved it. The specter of Lucas Ellington had stolen his sleep, made him iffy in the sack, put him on the instant defensive. The solution was to call him out, on his own terms, and win. No cops. No headlines. To Stannard, the answer was to live his own myth at last and send out a message that only Lucas Ellington would understand instantly.

C'mon, bad man—take me down if you can.

The Sweetouchnee tea hit him like pure crank, kicking his metabolism into overdrive.

"Hey, Logan! Get your massively artistic ass over here! I've got an idea that'll save this dead meat!"

Logan McCabe squared off his baseball cap and ambled over. Standing in the wrecked schoolroom set, Cannibal Rex smiled as if he knew telepathically what was about to happen.

15

SARA WINDSOR DID NOT WANT to redden her eyes, so she rubbed them with the backs of her knuckles, gently, easily. Her day's workload had implanted weariness into her bones, but her brain was starkly awake, defying the fatigue. Her lower lip had developed a small chapped patch; her tongue refused to leave it be. She would worry it until it dissolved away and things were normal again.

Apt personality externalization, she thought. Her brain was chasing after Lucas Ellington. It did not want to take a break or defer work until tomorrow.

Her favorite chair was a broad, low-slung, hand-crafted recliner with wide, flat arms. When she had selected it at Furniture Barn, she'd known those wide arms would be perpetually piled with her take-home work. Everything, even the chair, related to her job. She was either terribly efficient . . . or the work had invaded every aspect of her life, even her love life, or her choice of furniture, or her favorite television programs.

Perched on the chair arms were two ungainly stacks of file folders, their machine-cut manila edges spiraled out of true by a random bump. Closer to the edge were several freebie notepads, the kind you pick up at xerography shops as a customer perk. They were covered with vagrant scribbles: *Laundry Thurs. or else!* Or else she'd have not a stitch of underwear pleasant to the nose. *Call Mom.* For the fourth time that month. The more she spoke to her parents, the less they talked about. She had begun to wish they did not speak at all, so that their relationship might turn around and improve. *PHONE BILL—by 27th.* Which bill the goddamned "diversified" phone companies, a system once the best in the world, were preparing to double, or triple, or tack on a surcharge, or some other surprise. *Sheffield: Marnie—Ghost & Mrs. Muir.* Work. Again.

Daniel Sheffield preferred hearing cassettes of Bernard Herrmann movie sound track music during analysis. It helped him concentrate. Lucas had been into music, too, but his method of focusing his thoughts when talking to Sara had been to stare at a candle flame until he achieved an almost meditative calm.

Enough stalling, she thought. Let's do it.

Several pens maintained precarious positions on the backward-slanted arms of the chair, listing against their pocket clips to keep from rolling off into oblivion. The purple one refused to write, she knew; it had given up two days ago. At the very brink of the left arm, just shy of the edge, she parked her steaming mug of black Laichee tea. The dripping metal tea ball was fished out and left to cool on a folded paper towel, its duty done. She balanced a yellow legal pad against the bare knee that poked from her bathrobe, flipped to a clean sheet, and began to write.

GUNTHER LUBIN—roadie for J. Knox—knocked cold ½ hour prior to Knox killing—found 1 hr. after.

The San Francisco police still suspected Gunther

Lubin of some culpability in Jackson Knox's murder, but they knew they had nothing concrete on him. Doctors had examined Lubin and decided that he had most likely been in dreamland at the moment Knox died. They'd probably kept a leash on Lubin and grilled the poor bastard mercilessly following the murder of Brion Hardin in Denver. If they had been able to add one plus one.

CRYSTAL DiPRIMO—(sp?)—Brion Hardin's groupie? Girlfriend? Daughter?—Asleep during Hardin murder and/or under from dope. No alibi. Time factor?

It had taken the staff of the Denver Hilton nearly twenty hours to trip over Brion Hardin's stiff, cold corpse in room 704. When they did, Crystal DiPrimo was still snoring in the keyboardist's room, sleeping off a load of Quaaludes and red wine. The police had awakened her, and she had not been polite. Even drugged, she might have been capable of knifing her paramour . . . if she could have overpowered a man nearly a foot taller and ninety pounds heavier; if she could have wielded a heavy blade like a trained marine; if Hardin had been already incapacitated. That last was mostly fantasy, since the only thing found polluting Hardin's metabolism was a couple of bottles of dark Heineken. The Hilton desk clerks recalled exactly zero about a man named Calvin Westbrook, the renter of the murder room. The rock and roll magazines and tabloids had not been charitable about the killings. All possible angles on intergroup hostilities had been enthusiastically milked. Lurid color shots of Jackson Knox's mangled body were run alongside newspaper photos of the Room 704 bloodbath, and it was immediately rumored that Hardin had threatened to quit Electroshock in midtour in order to form a new band with Knox, a band that would violate a number of contracts and rouse the ire of a lot of record company execs. It was further rumored that certain members of Electroshock did not appreciate certain other members sleeping with certain of the group's concubines and whores.

Speculation flooded in and engulfed the event. Media waves would evenly fill any gap the killer—or killers—had left behind.

One sobering trivium had floated to the surface in a *Nude Thymes* editorial. Clapper Boyette, resident cynic, writing in his popular *Slings and Arrows* column, had spelled it out.

> First Knox, then Hardin. Assess this. Knox was just beginning to blossom as a soloist—BFD—and Hardin's band was creeping up on the make-or-break third-album stage. No great loss either way, but a tragedy considering that more Whip Hand fallout still lives in a band called 'Gasm. It's a tragedy that 'Gasm wasn't wiped out instead, removing a metalhead buboe from the butt of rock and roll. Too bad. Oh, well. We can hope, can't we?

The hot tea stung Sara's raw lip. She licked it absently.

KNOX—land mine.

HARDIN—military knife.

She underscored *military*. The coroner in Denver had specified a "long, broad blade" and put forth an educated guess that the murder weapon had been a marine corps Bowie knife. That much had made the papers.

That afternoon, in a Dos Piedras hunting and fishing shop, Sara had found such a knife. Seeing it, she could not believe such things actually existed. The thing the shop's proprietor had dragged out of the display case looked like an enormous parody of a knife. She'd joked about it resembling a prop from a mad slasher movie. Doubtless anxious to assist this attractive lady and keep her in his store for a few moments more, the counterman had trotted out several catalogs and reference books from his stock room for her edification. In a glossy, oversized tome titled *Military Hardware of the US from WWII to Indochina,* Sara had gotten her first look at an antipersonnel mine.

LUCAS. Underlined three, now four times on the pad.

He was capable of utilizing such lethal-looking stuff, she was certain. That led naturally to that trusty cop show standard, *motive.*

The question marks were beginning to clog up the page. Superficially, Lucas' motive could be a member-specific vendetta against the former components of a now defunct band called Whip Hand. Cause: the death of Lucas' only daughter, Kristen, during a crowd riot at a Whip Hand concert.

Lucas had confronted the band's lead man, Gabriel Stannard, on the steps of the Beverly Hills courthouse with a purgative gesture that could be interpreted as an act of aggression, the promise of future retribution, or a threat. Low-wattage terrorism against someone protected by vast wealth.

But Lucas had been cured and was not capable of becoming a methodical hit man. Not now.

He had not been committed to the mental hospital. He'd come voluntarily. That man, Sara thought, could not be behind these hideous and calculated terminations.

Both Lucases had been cured. Hadn't he?

There was the Lucas whose wife, Cory, had left him, whose little girl had been stomped into the concrete at a Whip Hand show, a man full of remorse and suicidal tendencies. The urge to end his life had never radiated too strongly, but Sara had recognized the signs, the seeds, the little things that could resonate with deadly certainty and start a chain reaction in the mind. That sort of mental critical mass had sent much stronger men jumping off the top floors of skyscrapers. She had noted it, accounted for it, and treated it. She did her job.

Then there was the other Lucas.

The strength of the black tea was making her back teeth ache. She shifted the pad to her opposite knee, and her free foot tingled with pins and needles.

Cory Ellington had been found dead in a hotel room of a Seconal overdose. Lucas' complicity had never been suggested, but it had been intimated. Everybody knew that Vietnam vets were dangerous, homicidal, on hair triggers. It was a popular delusion on the order of catching herpes from toilet seats—untrue, yet holding the potency of mythology. Things did not have to be true to scare people. And wasn't the stunt with the plastic gun the sort of thing an unhinged vet would pull? The newspapers would certainly see it that way.

There was Lucas the grief-burdened widower and pain-wracked father. And there was Lucas the problem solver, the team component who interfaced so well with the group at Kroeger Concepts.

Nobody would care that Lucas' undistinguished military tour had in no way unbalanced him mentally. You never heard about the vets who had returned physically intact and totally blasé about their service, the guys to whom the military had been just a job, a duty to dispose. The image of the berserk Nam psychopath was ever so much more media fun. Likewise, these same nobodies would give not a sterling goddamn that Cory had ridden the suicide train, because the image of the wife killer was even more fun. Lucas was a victim of the Lizzie Borden syndrome. Lizzie had been acquitted, but that didn't change the rhyme about the axe and the forty whacks. Lucas was a victim of the same sort of prejudice. Please deposit Nobel Prizes for deductive logic on the pedestal by the door.

Sara listened to the breeze kicking up outside and

played devil's advocate. If Lucas was guilty, if he in fact had done it . . . well now, that really screwed up the TV viewing schedule for the evening, didn't it?

In both murders the weapons had been military in origin. Sara had no idea how difficult it might be to deprive someone of the burden of life, but if Lucas was constitutionally able to blow one man apart and gut a second like a dinner trout, it would surely have been within his ability to force-feed Cory five dozen reds and forge a suicide note or make her write one under duress. DIE AND ROT IN HELL YOU FUCKER THIS IS ALL YOUR FAULT. The note blamed Lucas; the logic was crystalline. If you accuse yourself before others can, then they hesitate to point the finger. What if the rough message of that note had been directed not by Cory at Lucas, but the other way around?

There was a second message to ponder: KILL SATANIST ROCK. All the photos of Room 704 had included that admonition, which dripped redly down the wall scant feet from where all two hundred-plus pounds of Brion Hardin had faded into rigor mortis.

Lucas was a stolid atheist; always had been. He enjoyed rock, and not just 1960s nostalgia, either. He'd introduced Sara to Peter Gabriel and Brian Eno and Tangerine Dream and a defunct group called U.K. and the resurgent Slade and even, god help her, a kicky little number called "Golden Shower of Hits" by the Circle Jerks. Scragging the demons of rock 'n' roll in the name of Jesus was totally out of character, a contradiction of all the facets of Lucas that she understood.

Think you understand, her mind nagged.

The legal pad was filled with accusations and dirty brainstorming. The thought of exonerating Lucas made Sara's heartbeat quicken in hope, but one word hung like a sty in her mind's eye to upset any neat deduction of innocence. The word sizzled in danger red and SOS yellow, and the word was *diversion*—from the medieval Latin *divergere,* to extend in different directions from a common point.

The art of diversion was a hallmark of military strategy, second nature to an experienced campaigner. Lucas qualified. *Didn't he?*

His suicidal tendencies had certainly seemed bonafide enough to fool a psychiatrist. What if they had been mapped out to do just that, on purpose, to divert her from other things?

What if the attraction she felt for Lucas Ellington had been programmed the same way, for the same purpose?

More question marks on the yellow legal page.

It dawned on Sara that Lucas could very well have planned his entire "recovery," leading everyone at Olive Grove along so they would unhesitatingly put the stamp of approval on his cured mind. *No, this man could not be capable of such a vendetta. We fixed him up. He was broke, but now he's all better.*

What if Lucas was out there settling his score, evening up, reachieving some balance? What could her role be? Perhaps he planned to recover all he'd lost, and that meant getting himself a replacement for Cory. And if he actually had murdered Cory . . .

Sara's eyes defocused suddenly in mild shock at the logic chain she'd just linked together. Bad as the idea of a surrogate Cory was, what if Lucas found himself a surrogate Kristen?

What if you strolled up to an epileptic and blinked a red light in his face until he tipped over?

Anger flared then, and she threw the legal pad across the room. The pages rattled, the wings of a chaotic yellow bird flailing in ungainly flight, and it crash-landed in a wad near the front door. She felt like crying. She felt like punching out the reading lamp, which hung over her shoulder like a peeking judge of her thoughts.

Why hadn't Lucas called her?

Two days. Two absolute meatgrinder days at Olive Grove, during which Lucas' slick disappearing act had nibbled, then gnawed, at her concentration. The Lucas she knew would have phoned. *Lucas always comes back,* Burt Kroeger had told her. The emotional weight she had assigned to Lucas' calling had become frightening.

Now that he was out, was this the noise of the boom dropping? Had the vanishing act been planned all along as well? Haven't you learned any *goddamn thing in thirty-eight years, Sara?*

"Aren't you glad you can heal people?" she said to no one. The dark tea mimicked the deep brown of her hair, the mahogany of her eyes. Her hair was in a short, stylish, executive crop. She had been raking her fingers through it, contemplatively, and it stuck out here and there. She looked at her reflection and saw her tongue busily belaboring the chapped scab on her lip. She felt like trashing the teacup for the satisfaction of hearing breaking glass. But that would be acting like a nut. It'd only lose her the cup, which had a big, grinning white cat on it and was one of her favorites.

Lucas had not called her. That had been the keynote of the evening, of the whole week. He'd gone incommunicado, and she felt jilted, left in the lurch like some highschool muffin clutching a corsage on prom night. To make herself feel better, she'd made Lucas into a superhuman assassin of rock musicians. In all likelihood, Lucas was tending a campfire someplace, as Burt had said. And the killings, which the papers were already calling "rock sanctions" in anticipation of a series of them, were probably the work of one or more religious fruitcakes, folks who wanted to kill satanist rock in the name of their god. The sort of fanatics who made the patients at Olive Grove look not just normal, but dull. Lucas' problem was over; she'd helped him solve it. It was *her* problem that she had to deal with.

It began to sprinkle rain outside. The Valley was thirsty.

Dos Piedras was an upper-income bedroom community tucked just off Interstate 5, due east of Santa Barbara. A fifteen-minute drive over pleasant country backroads led to Olive Grove, where the hospital was, and most of the local shopping. The terrain around Dos Piedras was hilly and rolling, still mostly open. A glut of condos was working its way up from the south, and a lot of property was subdivided into generous tracts for the well-to-do. Dos Piedras's main lure was that it was not shoved up against anything else, like an airport or a military base or a microchip plant. It stood at a fair remove from major highway arteries and most urban interferences, which enhanced a sensation of calm remoteness and thereby lent the area its identity. Olive Grove's fire department handled most crises; the sheriffs, law enforcement. There was a quaint little cemetery almost a century old next to a church that was more a tourist attraction than a sanctuary for worship. Small municipal airfields were all around in Santa Barbara, Lancaster, Mojave, and private planes could often be seen dotting the intensely blue sky or making steady, buzzing progress among the night stars.

Rough flying tonight, Sara thought, if the rain gets worse. It was pouring outside, battering her windowpanes and blurring the view.

Forty was creeping up on her like a mugger in an alley, and she hated the way she let it prod her. Lucas' attraction to her had been not only welcomed, but invited. So long as he was officially her patient, she never had to let him know that he was helping her, too. It was the safest relationship in the world—a secret, perhaps one-way infatuation. Now he'd bolted, evaporated with no forwarding address, and she was scared, and she reprimanded herself for her vulnerability.

It wasn't thirty-eight years. It was thirty-nine years,

two months from now. She thought of erosion, undermining her with slow inexorability. Hadn't her almost-forty years taught her anything?

Sara had been on the losing end of a made-in-paradise marriage to another doctor, Spencer Parrish. This ideal union had taken five full years to disintegrate. Spence had always been more interested in maximizing his investments than in emotional gobbledygook that might hamper his progress up the ladders of the world. He had planned a corporation, not a marriage, and Sara did not want to play vice president. Mismanagement had killed Spence's co-op when Sara was thirty-four. She had been painstaking and careful, not rushing into matrimony while too young. It hadn't saved her. She still had to learn the same tough lessons in the same impossible ways.

There was a card tacked near her desk at Olive Grove: *The difficult we do immediately; the impossible will be done by morning.* As she had discovered, the best way to learn how to do something was to do it wrong. The psychological weight of getting married had not rendered marriage immune to the rules by which she'd lived most of her life until that point. No fair, she'd thought. She broke, she healed, she learned.

She had rebounded from Spence into an on-and-off relationship with a writer named Stephen Grave, who masterminded several popular paperback series—what he called "violence books," with calling-card titles like *The Expediter* and *SSS: Special Sanction Squad.* The sole condition Steve imposed on their relationship was that Sara understand his deadlines, and that sometimes he would have to work to the exclusion of everything else . . . except perhaps for a therapeutic fucking session in bed after another twenty-five pages had been laid to rest. Steve pulled a pile of contracts. He tended to hole up in his rented cottage, working and working, rarely seeing daylight, sometimes at mirror odds with

Sara's waking hours. She told him that she understood and did not mind. They went to restaurants and to the movies in Olive Grove . . . and that was about it. She told him she didn't mind. She lied to herself. And Steve would nod patiently or murmur at intervals over the phone, until she realized that he was not really listening and was putting up with her in order to get back to his typewriter, where his attention was locked up. She finally understood that she did not wish to compete with Steve's endless writing. It was a bitch goddess that she could not beat. Ultimately she had fled. Another two years gone. To this day it was difficult to resist the urge to pick up the phone and talk to Steve; Steve was very good at talking and helping her get a handle on her fears. Even, she thought, if he really didn't give a damn about what frightened her.

When her rebound fizzled out she saw no one for six months, then overcompensated. It was a textbook pattern she hated herself for recognizing. She shared various beds with several monied, handsome nonentities from Santa Barbara's upper crust. The Mercedes and the overpriced eateries and exclusive clubs got boring when experienced in the company of men whose sole purpose was the pursuit of perfect meat, the cultivation of empty beauty. But it was a brief, comfortable time unmarred by thought. When she felt the need to plug her brain back in, she abandoned the fashion plates and retreated into her work at the hospital.

Then came the affair with a co-worker. A professional entwining of smart bodies, to be sure. Dr. Christopher Rosenberg dallied with Sara for four months, then hauled stakes for a juicier berth in Utah. With no regrets and no residue. He told her he was leaving exactly twenty-four hours before his departure.

Sara's life settled into the structure of routine. Work. Sleep. Groceries. Fashionable lunches with Angie and Barb and Charlene. Barb moved up from Los

Angeles with her husband, Vic. Sara smiled and was social, battling the urge to seduce Vic. She broke down and phoned Stephen Grave at last, because Steve didn't need preliminaries. Kept at phone's length, he proved to be a friend. When the itch got unbearable, she called in the guys with the Mercedeses. Rarely. More rarely as time clocked off. She had a quick and sordid fling with a friend of Barb's husband, a guy who had flown his own Piper Cub up for a weekend of think-tanking with Vic. The sex had been impersonal and hard, the way she imagined it must be for prostitutes. Another retreat.

Then Lucas Ellington had come to Olive Grove.

After a long time, she began to enjoy sending out signals and getting them back in measured, polite, cautious, and utterly unassuming new forms. Progress was achingly slow. That, oddly, had made her attraction to him more powerful. She had started feeling again. And now she was sitting alone in her house, depressed, pissed off, watching rain spiral down the leaded-glass panes of the west window.

Once she had made the error of trying to dredge up the names of everyone she'd lain with since losing her virginity to Harris Taylor, Jr., in the backseat of a Buick during a double bill of *Village of the Damned* and *The Time Machine*. She had gotten her legal pad, scribbled Harris Jr.'s name at the top, paused to think, then scribbled more names. She decided heavy petting did not count, penetration did, and crossed off two names. The list grew. Some were only first names. One was no more specific than *that guy at the Sinclair gas station*. She wrote for ten more minutes before she faltered and had to start thinking hard. Then she crumpled up the list and fed it to the fireplace. There had been too many names she had been sure of too many times she'd needed human contact and only gotten a fucking.

Her job was to help people with their problems, and she tried not to see herself as absurd. She permitted herself one irrational thought. If Lucas were standing before her now, she thought, maybe he could hold her, and everything would reassemble into some kind of sane order. That wasn't so unreasonable, so crazy, was it?

"Be empirical, stupid," she said to herself to block the oncoming burst of self-pitying tears. "Prove yourself wrong."

Almost fatalistically, she padded barefoot to the door, retrieved the yellow legal pad, and smoothed out the skewed pages. She rewrapped her bathrobe against the chill and tied it off. More exercise, less Italian food, she thought, finding the belt more snug than usual.

Lucas's untimely escape had to have a seam showing somewhere, a clue she could exploit in order to locate him and finish with her fruitless and destructive theorizing.

She could continue mooning about her house, eventually winding up in front of her bedroom mirror, opening her robe to spend a few narcissistic moments telling herself that her almost-thirty-nine-year-old body wasn't so damned bad after all. Or she could make a phone call and risk pissing everyone off with her somewhat extreme train of thought.

On the other hand, what if the stuff on the pad turned out to be nonfiction? Another big question mark.

Sara picked up the phone and called Burt Kroeger.

"Too bad you're not wearing a skimpy, revealing nightie."

Sara had no way of knowing that it was a typical Burt Kroeger line. It was the first thing he said when she let him in out of the storm, which had cranked up to a full-blast downpour by eleven o'clock. The thought that this compact, blustery man was looking at her body pleased her, but the comment was just nutty enough to make her cock her head for an explanation.

Burt shucked his water-speckled topcoat. "My wife,

Diana, joked about me rushing off to some illicit tryst in the middle of the night. She thanked me, soberly, for not lying to her. Then she started giggling. She finally had to go to the bathroom." His direct gray eyes shared the humor. "If there's a private detective tailing me in this typhoon, I was hoping I might at least get a peek at some cheesecake for my trouble."

He shambled inside, and Sara slammed the front door, which always swelled whenever the air got wet and refused to fit the jamb without a fight. "I guess that verifies your identity," she said, smiling at the joke.

"Oh. Yeah." There was a weary, hangdog expression on his face, but it was comic. "Allow me to introduce myself. Burton Kroeger, or 'Burt' as in 'just call me Burt, huh?' I'm glad to meet you at last, Sara. You're proof that Lucas hasn't totally lost his mind, you should pardon the obvious cheap joke."

They shook hands, and she took his coat. "Come on into the living room, Burt, so I can get a good look at you. Coffee, tea, something stronger?"

"Got any good bourbon? Could you put a slug of it in some coffee, not too hot, okay?" He stared gratefully at the gently crackling fire and rubbed his hands. His face was already reddening in the heat of the room.

"Sure thing."

Burt assayed Sara's living room. Near the doorways were framed art noveau prints from the commercial work of Alphonse Mucha. Over the fireplace was a large reproduction of "Girl's Portrait," from the Takamatsuzuka Old Tomb in Asuka-Mura, Japan, all sandy greens, oranges, and yellows. Varnished bookshelves supported rows of hardcovers. There were no textbooks in the living room, he noticed. The furnishings and drapes were comfortable and warm. A hanging lamp of stained glass threw interesting, watery colors around, and why the hell had he driven nearly two hours through a bitch whip of a thunderstorm to see Lucas' psychiatrist in the middle of the night, just on her say-so?

You're getting a little crazy yourself, in your old age, he thought.

But the answer was easy. Sara had said it was an emergency. A bit melodramatic, perhaps, but he had no reason to cite degree to her. She had told him there were things about Lucas she needed to know, and he had come prepared to answer questions. His own apprehension about Lucas' stay at Olive Grove was weighed down with unanswered questions, queries he'd dared not put to Lucas during their civil afternoon together, the back-slapping reacquaintance of old war buddies. Burt had come out into the night to put his misgivings about Lucas into a proper grave. Ever since Lucas' collect call from El Granada, something had begun to stink of decay. If he could barter what information he held in exchange for some straight illuminations from Sara, it would be worth the cold and the drive and Diana's loving gibes. He absorbed warmth from the fireplace and tried not to feel too silly.

"Here. This'll put hair on your hands." Sara handed over a steaming mug. "I hope Jack Daniel's is okay."

He smiled. "What a relief."

She motioned him to a chair across from hers, but he preferred to hang out by the fire. She sat in her work recliner, tucking her bare feet beneath her on the cushion. The light stubble on her calves rasped gently together. She had spent Burt's drive time trying to magic up some way to open up the not-too-pleasant topics she needed to deal with tonight. Her sense of the dramatic —or melodramatic—had not served her too well as she waited for him. She resisted the urge toward meteorological chat.

"Burt. How much do you know about Lucas's relationship to Cory, and to Kristen?"

He parked his chin in his hand, looking almost stern. He was really thinking about the question. He was not going to obfuscate, she thought, and he has his own reasons. Firelight shone through his thin but fluffy hair. Sara could see the outline of his cranium, as though through excelsior.

"After I met Cory, I saw her exactly twice, both times over a year before their divorce. Lucas was never fond of dinner foursomes, you know—two hubbys, two wifeys. Too much like a bad postcard of upwardly mobile Americana. He disliked that." Burt took a long sip and nodded to himself. "Cory made me . . . uncomfortable. Like I wanted to run from the room she was in. She was razor sharp, even caustic, and brutally polite to strangers, which I was, to her. She had a *very* superior attitude and enjoyed making people squirm. I think there was something in that intensity that attracted Lucas. We never talked about her, and I didn't like to ask how she was doing. She had one trait I know well: super-perfectionism. That's probably what drove her to kill herself. She could never live up to her own idealization of herself. Lucas did mention when she was pregnant with Kristen she refused to leave their house. She didn't want to be seen. She had Kristen at home, in fact. From what I understand, Cory never changed a single diaper. Baby care was something to be delegated. And you know what I'm thinking, just now? That maybe Cory *knew* she was on the way out, and had Kristen only so she could leave a piece of herself behind in the world."

Sara doodled on her legal pad while Burt talked.

"Don't ask me why their marriage lasted as long as it did, Sara, because I haven't a clue to that one. There've been wars much stupider that lasted much longer. I do know that Lucas was totally devoted to Kristen. As soon as Cory recovered from giving birth, she had an affair with a Porsche dealer from Westwood. Don't tell me—I know it sounds like a bad college joke. But that's when Cory probably entered her real drill-sergeant bitch phase." His hands worked in the air, futilely, as though wrestling with an invisible snake.

"What do you think about the idea that Lucas may

have helped Cory in some way to kill herself?" She had to tread cautiously here. She was accusing Lucas of complicity, opining murderous things about a man she was coming to love.

"That wind blew past me. I heard it and ignored it. Pardon my Sanskrit, but that's bullshit in a bowl, if you ask me." Burt, at least, was convinced of his friend's innocence on that score. "Besides, it's academic now. I think Cory was perfectly capable of setting up a rumor mechanism before offing herself. It's the sort of nasty, vindictive shit she was a pro at. I'm positive Lucas had nothing to do with her suicide. *Positive.*" Repeating the word made him sound unsure.

"Why, Burt?" She wanted to keep him on that topic without getting stuck in the quicksand of asking whether he was in a position to know the truth. "I'm not trying to antagonize you. But if you know something concrete, let's hear it." Sara the Analyst had shifted smoothly into gear. She felt a little ashamed; Burt seemed like a good man, and now she was demanding he prove it.

"That's all I know. Sorry. Lucas just . . . wouldn't."

Lucas had frequently mentioned Burt's fierce loyalty, and Sara wondered if that was what she was seeing now. As if it helped, he added, "Lucas just isn't a wasteful man, and suicide is wasteful."

"Okay. What did you know about Lucas when he joined your firm?" This was an easier question. He'd be happy to recite history for her instead of addressing the ugly problems of here and now. He would have to sift a lot of data in his head, and this would give her time to assess what she heard.

"Lucas showed me his portfolio. I hired him. It was a damned good portfolio. He'd been savvy enough to feel out Kroeger Concepts in advance, checking up on what our current projects were, so he could walk into the office with samples targeted directly toward our needs. Like the best people in PR, he knew his first sale was to sell himself. You might say we fell for his campaign."

Target and *campaign* were military words, fight-to-win terminology. Words that were part of one of Lucas's most successful personality facets.

"What about after Cory died?"

"I remember asking him about a million times who he was going out with," said Burt. "He finally chucked me on the arm and said, 'Don't worry, big brother, I'm getting laid regularly, if that's what's bothering you.' But I never saw the women he dated. He seemed happy. Cory was gone, and I thought that was a good thing, and I didn't want to push it. He *had* loved her, after all. . . ." Something dawned in his eyes. He looked around to nail Sara. "Now you're going to ask what effect Kristen's death had. Cory's death was a good thing; Kristen's was a bad thing, but he loved them both. How did he compensate—is that what you're going to ask? He found a substitute for Cory all right, but what about replacing Kristen?"

"Burt, that's one of the reasons I'm worried about Lucas running to earth somewhere up north. Finding psychological replacements isn't the greatest thing that could happen in Lucas' life right now. It'd be moving backward."

"Back toward Cory." His eyes told Sara a story about how nasty that might be.

She swallowed a blockage in her throat. This was getting rougher than she'd anticipated. "When Lucas first came to Olive Grove, we did a PETT scan of his brain."

"Is that anything like a CAT scan?"

She nodded. "It's shortform for—hold your breath—'Positron Emission Transaxial Tomography.' Know what a tomogram is?"

He gave back a sly smile. "Yeah. It's a roentgenogram." He paused a beat. A good punchline could give them both a small relief. "Sorry. A tomogram, as far as I know, is a little picture like an X-ray of a Hostess Twinkie that shows you the cream filling without the shadow distortions of the surrounding junkfood, yes?"

"A picture of the brain without the skull in the way."

"Gotcha." Burt's father had died of brain cancer. A lot of tomograms had been done. Whole stacks, before his corpse had been wheeled away on a gurney. They were rather expensive to do, and his father had not benefited.

"Lucas' PETT scan gave us a pattern that was markedly schizophrenic. It's a very distinctive pattern. The frontal lobes don't take up as much of the 2-deoxyglucose, the radioactive tracer, as they should."

"Schizophrenic? You telling me he had an alter ego, a Good Lucas and a Bad Lucas that killed Cory, or something?" Burt was gearing up to forcefully express disbelief, if that was in fact what she was proposing.

She cut him off before he could work up a mad. "No, no. Schizophrenia isn't the same thing as multiple personality. That's a popular delusion—"

He overrode her in return because he saw what she was doing. "You mean like the delusion that says if a car falls off a cliff, it'll explode instantaneously when it hits."

"Right. Another delusion fostered by television, I guess. Schizophrenia, the word, means *split mind*. The disorder is more a matter of a breakdown in the unity of the brain, as though one part takes over and begins to dominate all the other parts. A lot of scientists have spent a wad of government money arguing over what causes it. But the PETT scan gives us the kind of symptomatology we can treat. Treatment is still as hit or miss as it ever was. We put Lucas on perpenazine, and his tomograms gradually became normal."

"Meaning . . ." Burt paused to keep on track. "Meaning his brain absorbed the right amount of the tracer."

"It absorbed it at the rate a normal brain would. So we had a brain that was possibly schizophrenic, we treated the symptoms, and it became normal. After that, there were two aspects of Lucas' personality to deal with. The first was Lucas the unintentional widower and grieving father, the man who might have been upset enough to kill himself. The second was Lucas the problem solver, the man who engineers manipulative PR campaigns, and who plotted that brilliant stunt against Gabriel Stannard—Whip Hand's lead singer—on the steps of the Beverly Hills Courthouse." She picked up her legal pad. Under Burt's increasingly incredulous gaze, she laid out the sequence of events and the chain of theorizing involving the ex-members of Whip Hand, the "rock sanctions," and Lucas' possible vengeance motive.

She hated it as she read it off. It looked more convincing on the ruled yellow paper than it sounded coming out of her mouth. She rose to freshen Burt's drink and find the first of many filtered Salem 100s for a long night.

Burt shook his head a long time. "You just said he was normal. Cured."

"I know." She kept her eyes on her bare feet, on the polished stretches of hardwood floor separating the throw rugs, as she marshaled courage. "But bear with me for a second. I'm going to suggest something pretty wild, and I'm not sure it'll stand up to a lot of punching around just yet."

Burt folded his arms. Defensive body language was a bad sign. He watched his drink steam, unsipped.

"What could make Lucas kill someone?" she said. "There was no one to blame for Cory, but what about Kristen? What if he'd used a real gun on the courthouse steps? I'm sure he must have weighed the pros and cons of killing that rock singer. Instead, he pulled off something almost elegant. You know the guy sustained a head wound. He bled even though Lucas never touched him."

"He was marked. . . ."

"Something like that. But that brought me to another area, a touchy but relevant one. You see, Burt, I've always been interested in humankind's capacity to kill. What, exactly, forms it? You were in the military; so was Lucas. You know the ways in which circumstances can get screwed up, or become irrelevant. How killing is made necessary. The ways people justify it to themselves when the reasons aren't as clear-cut. Moral distinctions fly right out the porthole." She pulled a deep and deadly puff of her cigarette. "We're all latent killers. The question is, what makes a killer evil?"

Burt sped ahead. "I thought to myself once . . . that if Lucas had been involved in Cory's suicide, it didn't matter. Maybe she deserved it, for all the pain she whipped on him. I'm not contradicting myself; I'm really not. It didn't occur to me in any practical sense. More theoretically."

"That's part of my point: you thought of it." Puff. "At some point, we all think, *That person should die*. Not as a matter of corrupt morals, simply as an expedient. So let's say Lucas was innocent in the matter of Cory's death. But let's also say he had a mental problem. Let's say he was clay, waiting to be shaped by a catastrophe. Cory dies. Kristen dies. Catastrophes." With a weird detachment, Sara watched her body curl up in her chair, as though trying to contract, defensively, fearing an attack on her fragile guesswork. The cigarette was already sucked down to a glowing nub between her fingers. Acid churned in her stomach. The slight odor of the dead tea lees was making her stomach bubble. She butted out her smoke and lit another. "Did you know the chemical imbalances in the brains of schizophrenics have led some researchers to believe that schizophrenics are in the process of actually altering their physical structure? And all we know is that we can treat an aberrant PETT scan until the tomogram changes, becomes what we call 'normal.' When it does that, the schizophrenic tendencies conveniently recede."

"You said you'd cured him, Sara." Not that he needed to remind her.

Her voice became very soft. "Language is funny, Burt. It can mean contrary things. You know what I've begun to think? That technical expertise makes us arrogant. We treated a PETT scan instead of the patient, and put all our faith in a chemical, technical solution. The tomogram is what we cured. I'm not so sure about our friend Lucas."

"But you said the tomogram's configuration became normal. You treated symptoms and effected a change." He prompted her to continue. He was intrigued, if resentful. His gaze finally left the woman in "Girl's Portrait" and met Sara's.

This is it, she thought. The shit-or-git crunch point, the place where she laid down her professional reputation as a wager. "What if. What if by using chemicals to force Lucas' brain to become normal, we made it into a *new* configuration? Suppose the schizophrenic pattern wasn't an aberration. Suppose Lucas was abnormal all along, and *normal,* for him, is a guy who ruthlessly murders rock musicians. Because the consciousness of this new brain draws a vengeance motive from Lucas the grieving father, and the moral right to kill from Lucas the plan man."

Burt suddenly looked very tired, like a man waiting for a phone to ring, knowing bad news is on the way. Carefully, he said, "Lucas loved Kristen. Maybe he didn't love Cory so much; maybe he had brutal thoughts toward her. But I don't think his mind, his intellect, could countenance such an insane revenge fantasy based on Kristen's death alone. Because he *knew* her death was an accident. Regardless of all the smoke, it really was accidental. And he realized how much that upset him—" Burt cut himself off, as if he smelled impending doom. "And that's what brought him to you."

"I'm suggesting that to search for a single cause, a key event to blame, is fruitless. There is only a sequence of events—what came first hardly matters. Three things are important. Kristen died. That was fate, bad timing, a genuine tragedy. We treated Lucas . . . and perhaps made the mistake of believing that all solutions are chemical. And then there was a flaw in our raw material we didn't know about. Like the tainted ingredients that turn Jekyll into Hyde, and doom him because no other batch of chemicals is tainted in quite the same way. By treating Lucas, we force his new mind into being—the mind that looks so deceptively normal on the PETT scans. Three things—the gun, the bullet, the trigger finger." She made a mock pistol with her thumb and forefinger. *"Bang."* Saying it scared her.

"You're saying that we're all killers," said Burt sourly, "waiting for the right combination of chemicals and circumstances. The correct input to make us run amok."

"Not everybody—just Lucas. His brain was different in a special way none of us could understand."

"It wasn't circumstances or tragedies. It was *him.*" With a tang of justified sarcasm, he added, "Well, thank God he's normal now, if you're right."

"Oh, Burt, can't you tell how much this hurts me?" She damned her eyes a thousand times for tearing up. "This stings the hell out of me. I *care* about him. I'd never seen anyone as alone as he was when he came to Olive Grove. He needed someone who cared so badly—"

"Unless he was just playacting for you, stringing you along the whole time." His voice did not waver. "What if the whole gig at the hospital was a sham, to give himself an alibi? He's cured, there are papers to prove it, so no one could say *he's* the one out there killing." It was an insult to Burt to think he could not have known so much about his friend. Part of his rising anger was an attempt to wound Sara for giving him a convincing story that he wanted *not* to believe. "Suppose he was just leading you down the garden path? And to make sure you don't get in too deep and find out what he's really up to, he makes you fall in love with him. If you're a professional, how could you fall for a ploy like that? Part of Lucas' goddamn *job* is turning charm on and off like a light switch. *And you knew that.* Haven't you ever heard of countertransference, Sara? That's classified as dangerous malpractice—a doctor falling in love with a patient. And from the way Lucas talked about it, it's love. Believe it."

She was prepared for the accusation as well as she could be. "How professional are you, Burt, when it comes to love? To your marriage to Diana? People talk about not falling in love because they've gotten burned at it. They get fanatic about it. They vow never to fall in love again as though they had some kind of control over it! And the people who succeed in turning off their emotions turn to ashes inside. If you try to impose rules and logic on a process like that, you make yourself a little bit dead. How logical is anyone, for christsake, when it comes to getting married or having kids? I'm not a machine. I knew what I was doing, and I felt justified. Maybe I'm a little screwed up myself. Yeah, even doctors have problems—so sue me. But I'm not crazy. So just who the fuck do you want me to apologize to?" It was gushing out of her in a torrent now, all her own poisonous recriminations about her shattered past. Lucas had helped to heal some of that . . . and now Lucas was rotting away right before her shocked eyes, leaving her alone again. "A bunch of little disasters got together and made a great big disaster. We're *all* to blame, Burt. Even you. If you and Lucas were such tight asshole buddies, how come you never whiffed a thing?

You're to blame, and I'm to blame, and Kristen's to blame for dying, and Cory's to blame for being such a cunt. For all I know, it was her unending cruelty that was the initial catalyst. Lucas didn't fall, Burt—he was *pushed.* And even the poor fuckers in that has-been rock group are culpable. Assigning blame isn't going to solve the problem by a millimeter. That's rule number one in even the most elementary analysis. You have to fix what's broken and figure out who broke it later!" She trembled now with a kind of righteous anger. "All that matters now is finding out the truth. And if *any* of what I've told you is correct, then just maybe you and I can prevent a murder or two!"

She smacked the chair arm, and the Salem butt somersaulted from the ashtray and bounced, scattering orange sparks across the rug. Burt jumped to help Sara kill the smoldering particles chewing their way into the nap. It was comically mundane. The tension between them was vented in an instant.

"Okay. Okay." He was consciously controlling his tone. "I apologize. No vituperation." He seemed contrite, and she watched his large, muscular hands knead each other. "I always thought it was uncanny, the way Lucas in particular could turn it on and off. Seemed like a lot more control than was ever necessary."

"Don't worry about it. Uh—the carpet, either." Her own voice had become timid and apologetic.

"My mind—assuming *I'm* not crazy, too—cannot accept on any rational level how someone as radically changed as you suggest Lucas might be could appear so goddamned normal. And now you tell me it *is* normal. But if you're right, if even a degree of what you say is true, then we've got to find him. And quick. We may not think exactly alike, Sara, but I think we're after the same thing. I want him to be saved, and you want him to be helped."

"Close enough," she said. "If I'm wrong, then I'll be embarrassed as hell. That I can live with. I might be crippled professionally." She flashed on the thought that one more emotional handicap, in her current state, wouldn't increase her load an ounce. "However, if I'm right and we do nothing, the authorities will just scream 'coincidence!' until everyone in that band is dead meat. Worth the risk, I say. Put Lucas in your own place, Burt. Would you have you tilt at a friendship that way?"

"I'd insist he kick my butt, if that was what I needed." He drained his second mugful of spiked coffee. It had gone tepid. "Lucas has always been straight with me. I'd get mad if he didn't consider our friendship worth the risk of pissing me off."

"That's all I need to hear." Burt didn't need the history of her own emotional pecadillos right now.

"Good," said Burt. "Let's get going, then."

"Going?"

He smoothed his trousers. "Up to Point Pitt. That's what you wanted me for, right? To find Lucas' hiding place? Well, we can find out where his cabin is from the rangers. Let's find out *now*. I hate waiting for anything. I mean it. You and I can drive up there tonight. One sleeps while the other drives. Go on—put together an overnight bag. If you're really serious about this." His mind was locking into a chosen groove of action. Preparations he could handle automatically, and better than almost anything. It was mechanical, and less painful than further poking and prodding.

Sara felt a reactionary urge to protest, but that was overshadowed by a rush of relief. She had an ally. Her body impelled her toward the stairs while her mind raced through a catalog of the things she would need. She was smiling, though grimly.

Burt's voice stopped her on the threshold of the kitchen. "Sara?"

"Yes?"

"I hope we get up there and find him roasting marshmallows or something over a campfire. And I hope he laughs in our faces."

16

LUCAS LOOKED DOWN AND SAW at least a hundred Smokey Bear hats. He could not see where he was placing his feet, nor could he hear the sound of his careful steps on the flat black metal of the catwalk.

His feet were invisible because he was dressed in black down to the neoprene soles on his boots. He was deaf because even with earplugs, the sound flooding toward him from below was more than loud. It was internecine, fatal both to those putting it out and those receiving it.

'Gasm's concert opener was "Barbed Wire Babes," a tune from their forthcoming album, as yet untitled. The pulsating onslaught of the music vibrated the metal of the webwork of girders and support cables and access walks. This maintenance maze was designed to be invisible from below and hugged the black ceiling of the Arena at the Tucson Community Center. It was lit up only when the amphitheater floor was devoid of patrons, lit for lighting setups, or special effects, or the adjustments attendant to the conversion of the arena floor from concrete pit to a million-dollar plastic basketball court. Only technicians and some janitors ever ventured onto the precarious complex of singing wires and lurching catwalks. None were foolhardy enough to try it during a full-scale atomic-holocaust rockshow. When it was required—like the time Pink Floyd had insisted that artificial snow be dumped on the heads of the audience during an encore of "Echoes," the techs wore climbing harnesses and snap-ringed safety leads. It was easier than it looked, to be shaken off that catwalk while a rock and roll P.A. system was bombarding the arena with noise that threatened the structural integrity of the building.

Below Lucas, far below, the sold-out crowd was SRO—more than standing. Squashed together. A still life of a stampede. The bodies and faces formed an aggregate, like plankton in a rolling ocean, totally indistinct as people, a swaying, amorphous mass. There were at least a hundred Pima County sheriffs on duty; Lucas could pick out the tan circlets of their hats, and he suspected most of them were watching very carefully, hoping to spot a crazed assassin of rockstars. They milled around the central crush of bodies filling the open-floor, festival-seating area like languid antibodies around an enormous white blood cell. Some covered their ears against the music and grinned at each other.

How 'bout these stupid kids, huh?

Lucas looked ahead and down, to where the members of 'Gasm leapt and rampaged and posed on the curving stage, the body-building physiques and the spread-legged stances of Marvel Comics superheros made flesh and granted motion. Their output rattled not only the auditorium, but the city block on which the auditorium stood.

From his high vantage on the stage-right catwalk, Lucas could only perceive jumping shapes. He already knew who they were by position.

Hogging center stage, trussed up in bondage harnesses to flaunt his chest fur, was Pepper "Mad Max"

Hartz, in spandex tights, buccaneer boots, studs, and wristbands. His spring-loaded chromium dildo waited inside its special codpiece slot, an Alien ready to burst from its egg and do its bit. For this concert, Hartz's hair had been punked out into oily spikes with a blood-red streak. When he shrieked, the mike stand seemed to recoil.

Stage right, parallel with Lucas but at an extreme forty-five-degree angle to his position, was Rick Hicks —"rhythm guitar, temple blocks, and white noise," according to the sleeve of *Pain Threshold*. That was a lie, too. Hicks chorded the bass line in an altered, static key. He was not playing rhythm or contributing texture; he was adding volume. His job, along with that of the bassist and drummer, was the AC/DC bottom line—a tidal wave of four-four sound, period. Hicks' part was boring enough to give him plenty of latitude for onstage antics and elaborate flourishes intended to hide the fact that he knew maybe three keys in toto. He capered in and out of his spotlight, wearing black leather dunnage jazzed up with chains and a doggie collar.

Stationed far stage left was Texas McClanahan, tucked behind his bastille of keyboard equipment. Miles of wires webbed synthesizer to mellotron to electric piano. Texas had been a big fan of Rick Wakeman and resisted the technology that could combine most of his variations into a single keyboard. All Lucas could see of him was his wildly bopping head, which enthusiastically jogged up and down to the beat, though not the song itself.

After a sustain that held and held and held, like a chainsaw ripping through a log, the band leapfrogged directly into "Rock Rocket" from *Primal Scream*.

Between Texas and Hartz were the targets.

Tracking to the left of Texas, Lucas picked out bass player Tim Fozzetto. His area of movement extended from the keyboards, behind Hartz, past the drum set, and halfway to where Rick Hicks was jumping around.

Fozzetto was sheathed in an ebony jumpsuit with a weightlifter cut in the front. Bands of holographic foil twined around his thighs and wound down to the tops of his silver space boots. He teetered on at least six inches of platform heel; maybe Kiss had had a garage sale. He was stroking a long, mean-looking Fender fretless bass, pumping forth a growling low-frequency mimic of the riff Rick Hicks was diligently copying. Fozzetto's hair was a rag-cut rat's nest of bleached white, making him an easy pick-off.

Fozzetto strutted past the drum riser, planted in its traditional upstage center post. Behind a dental staircase of octave drums, Jackal Reichmann tortured his monster kit with the sadistic glee of a demented nine-year-old setting fire to an anthill. He was completely surrounded by drums. There was a double bass, three different floor toms, and a flat set of yellow Syn-drums wired in as well. It was like the vast control panel of an alien spaceship. Behind him on a trellis depended five bronze gongs in ascending sizes, plus a sheet of tin to bang on for good measure. Another rack, at a right angle to the first, held squeeze-bulb horns, cowbells, brass chimes, a xylodrum, other percussives. Hovering above, struts extended to the ridiculous popstar height espoused by good old Keith Moon, were the cymbals, at least a dozen golden UFOs. Reichmann loved them to death. He was clad in tight white leather bikini panties, white leather jackboots that reached to his knees, and an assortment of armbands from shoulders to wrists. He had given up the mohawk Lucas had seen on the back cover of *Pain Threshold* in favor of a weird loose crop that flowed around his head like seaweed underwater. To achieve the kind of hard beat 'Gasm needed to back up Hartz's guitar madman act, Reichmann could have done as well pounding on a trash-can lid.

The song ground to a finish, and Reichmann stood up, banging his sticks together one-two-three-four, inciting the crowd to put its hands together for the segue into

"Love Torpedo," 'Gasm's first FM hit. The first of three, as Chic Garris, manager of On the Brink, might have put it. Same beat, same pace. The audience went bananas. Lucas supposed that rock fans in Tucson would clap for any damned thing. Some self-proclaimed music critic would write the whole genocidal mess up for tomorrow morning's edition of the *Arizona Daily Star,* and if anything was more excruciating than the dreck reeled out by 'Gasm, it was the bilge that always sprouted by the column inch in the papers, courtesy of some talentless refugee of the University of Arizona's journalism department.

A working-class metal act, 'Gasm was not entitled to a gig inside the Community Center's "acoustically perfect" Music Hall. That was too prestige. 'Gasm's promoters wanted a venue that could be hosed down after the show, like the tiled interior of an Australian pub. 'Gasm was also, in the promoter's words, "too category," which meant they lacked the muscle to sell out a reserved-seating concert. Half the seats would be empty at showtime, and that was embarrassing. Better to lower the price than raise it and bank on ticket turnover instead of high-priced status. The result of this thinking milled below, jostling cattle awaiting not a slaughter, but perhaps a sacrifice.

It was a mock war. The band had to get the audience off. If they succeeded, the prize was acceptance. If they lost, if the fans refused to be impressed, then retaliation could assume a thousand ugly shapes.

"Love Torpedo" ended. Lucas mouthed Pepper Hartz's words soundlessly as he asked if the audience *felt all right.* In the roar that surged forth in response, they ran through the intro to a longish tune called "Agent Orange Blues." Fozzetto, as it turned out, could stroke a pretty fair blues foundation when liberated from 'Gasm's smash-your-head persona.

Penetrating the Arena was an operation that had required Lucas to leave his room at the Holiday Inn (formerly the Marriott and, before that, Braniff Place) in the predawn and spend part of the day camped out on the roof of the Tucson Community Center building itself. He'd had to duck an idly probing helicopter searchlight or two after the sun fell and showtime rolled near. Security at the arena's entrances was unreal. The sheriffs patted down all ticketholders, removing dope and liquor, a scut duty usually relegated to the ushers. But they were also searching for grenades, or switchblades, or Saturday Night Specials. A lot of people had raised hell, and the anti-authority mood was suitably ugly. Some raised hell because they didn't like giving up their weapons. Almost everyone had seen the news, and many were here in the hope of witnessing a tragedy. The band sensed this, and it had not provided for a spontaneous, warm rapport. At first the audience was howling because it had filled the arena, and it was hungry. Once the music started, they seemed to forget about the death factor, and it became more like a run-of-the-mill heavy metal show. The response 'Gasm had gotten to the intro to "Agent Orange Blues" demonstrated that.

Lucas had cut a hatchway in one of the rooftop industrial air-conditioning ducts, using a pair of duck-billed tin snips. He dropped in his nylon bundle, followed, and bent the metal shut behind him. The vents were three-by-three tunnels of aluminum. Lucas clambered about the system until his penlight and architectural sketches told him he was where he needed to be, and then he snipped himself another hole. He had spent the duration of the opening act, a band modestly dubbed the Nuclear War Babies, stretched out in the rush of cool air within the vent, eating a tuna-salad sandwich and sucking on a collapsible carton of grape juice. Then he eased through and landed silently on the catwalk. Being up top amplified the sense of distance to the concrete floor, which looked as if it were a hundred feet straight down. Actually, he was nearly level with the uppermost row of balcony seating, which was so far behind him it was not a consideration. His invisibility was guaranteed. His black clothing made him a ghost on the far side of the bright lights. He felt queerly like the Red Death sneaking into the Bal Masque.

Each 'Gasm album was a solid carload of five-minute-long cuts, which meant their live versions of the same songs ran seven to eight minutes. Rock bands aware of their own limitations tend to milk each tune for all the solo spots and fooling around they could squeeze in. As the obligatory blues tune "Agent Orange" droned on for nearly thirteen minutes, during which Hartz's true skill as a guitarist became wincingly evident. He posed, picking a single note forty-two times—playing not his guitar, but his audience, which grew more frenzied with each simple pluck. Jackal Reichmann, dusting his kit in a time signature way too lethargic to hold his attention, nearly dozed off while playing.

Lucas never took his eyes off the band except to spot-check the empty catwalk behind him. He unzippered the nylon satchel and drew out the Dragunov sniper's rifle. A small cardboard box sealed with gaffer's tape was affixed to the right side above the trigger guard. It would contain the expended shell casings as they were spit out by the Kalishnikov rotating-bolt breech, the efficient system that was the heart of the Soviet Union's number-one field weapon, the AK-47 automatic. The magazine and scope were already in place. The box had occurred to Lucas during his session of spin/sight/shoot in the forest. It would not do to have his brass raining down on the heads of the crowd as he gave them what they were really waiting for. This way was better. Less evidence.

The sound pounding out of the massive Marshall amps was beyond description. It made Lucas' face buzz, made him squint and grit his teeth. It was like being sandblasted. The bass line thudded inside his chest, compressing his lungs; the catwalk shook like a palsied dinosaur beneath him. He thought of the muscles needed to hold down a madly pistoning jackhammer. The physical challenge here was the same. Rock 'n' roll had come a long way from Chuck Berry . . . technologically speaking.

In his mind, he previewed the panic below.

He had allotted himself a generous fifteen seconds to take out both targets following his first shot. It would require another thirty seconds or so to backtrack to the hole in the ductwork and climb through. Once in the duct he would resheathe the Dragunov. The Arena bowl was seated in a man-made crater that put the bottom floor underground, but the roof of the building was still several stories up. The fire ladder Lucas had climbed up was not a viable escape route. It was not on the building's dark side. Lucas assumed there would be people watching it—later—so he had packed a light claw-hook-and-nylon grappling line. What was the joke the paratroops used in jump school? *It's not the fall that kills you, it's the sudden stop.* His physique was reliable enough to risk a fast downward rappel. Better to sprain his leg in a fall than get nailed on the fire ladder or gunned down while sprinting across one of the Community Center's football-field-sized parking lots. After that it was back to the hotel, and his room. The airplane sequence was virtually the same as it had been in Denver. This time, he had flown first class as Dexter Hayworth, a salesman of photographic supplies. His heavy suitcase was full of X-ray-sensitive film and plates. This precaution had been unneeded; American Airlines had checked the case through without nosing into its contents. Lucas had guessed correctly that there was no danger of anyone hijacking a flight from Oakland to Tucson International, anyway. That would take a *real* nut.

'Gasm let their end note ring, and ring, and ring, building audience applause like the airwash blast of an approaching jet fighter. The crowd had been caressed into a valley, and now it was time to peak them out. Hartz sprang into the air, legs pinwheeling. Lucas thought of Wile E. Coyote, making his getaway in a Roadrunner cartoon. Hartz landed on the boards on one knee, punching a raw chord out of his white Stratocaster. Reichmann woke up and began to bludgeon his hi-hat cymbal, thankful he could resume his endless four-four "Indian Giver" beat. This pounding, chording, and tribal prep gobbled up eight full bars before the band turned the song around a corner and bent it into "Doncha Want To."

Lucas seated the PSO sight against his eye and focused on Tim Fozzetto's bobbing white mane. As fast as he could, he tracked and targeted the four other band members in succession.

Flame pot explosions punctuated the refrain of the song, blowing columns of flash powder and orange fire twenty feet into the air on both sides of the drum riser. Then Hartz threw out both arms in a crucifixion pose, his Strat hanging free, still humming. A hidden pot positioned directly in front of Hartz's mike stand went off, obliterating him in a sheet of blinding white fire —*foom!* Lucas thought of Jackson Knox, eating chunks of his own guitar. When all eyes in the house recovered from the blitz, Hartz stood there victorious. The silver mike stand and the face of the Strat had both been painted with smoke paste before the show, and now they were blackened and steaming.

The audience berserked. Some were caught off guard. All approved, loudly, longly. Hartz was invincible.

Neat trick, thought Lucas. It was one that had not been on the videotape. Hartz must have gotten his eyebrows singed a time or two on this tour.

They wrapped up "Doncha Want To"—always a crowd pleaser—and bright red scoop lighting flooded the entire stage. Jackal Reichmann, laughing like a maniac, stood spread-legged atop his kit and hoisted his drum-fed machine gun. He held the trigger down and crisscrossed the front ranks of the audience, the ones crammed like lemmings against the orchestra pit barricade. The squibs, planted in triple rows along the footlight trench of the stage and salted around on the monitors and P.A. equipment, were detonated electronically. Reichmann's sham bullets blew glitter and paper shrapnel into the air. The front-huggers ducked and shrieked, and when the shooting stopped, Hartz was already filling the airspace with a freeform intro to "Loose Rivets" from *Primal Scream.* Reichmann kicked out and dropped back into place in the manner of an old-time cinema cowboy vaulting onto his trusty horse. The machine gun was still smoking as he began to pump and pound.

Lucas cradled the Dragunov against one thigh and waited, crouching, high above and in front of the band. From his vantage point he could see roadies snaking corrugated hoses for the smoke machines into place behind the P.A. system.

The crowd's initial hostility had been overwhelmed by 'Gasm's pyrotechnics. For at least two more songs, Hartz and company would have the audience palmed and wrapped.

The latent aggression Lucas had felt seething up toward him from the Arena floor earlier had had an additional source. At four in the afternoon, a lath-and-tagboard booth had been erected in the middle of the Community Center's broad stone patio. It was the sort of booth one sees at county fairs or during election weeks. Slathered across the top of the booth in stark red tempera letters was the admonition JESUS IS THE KING, *Not Elvis Presley.*

What Elvis had to do with 'Gasm, Lucas wasn't sure.

An advance guard of sweet, primly dressed, terribly earnest young women did their best to foist folded tracts onto the kids milling about the patio, killing time before the lines formed. At about six, when people began arriving in force, an enormous ghetto blaster appeared in the booth. It was the size of a large suitcase, all black and silver with twin speakers like begrilled insect eyes. A slickly groomed pastor was dropped curbside by a wheezing Chevy Nova. He made his way to the booth, tuned the huge radio to an empty AM band, and pulled a Mister Microphone from inside his coat. Though it was suffocatingly hot, he did not ever shed the coat.

The tirade that blatted forth from the radio had been energetic and incomprehensible, forming a surreal soundtrack for Lucas's waiting time. The pastor shoved forth the testimony that *a member of the rock metal group you are paying to see has admitted to consuming human flesh!* He did not waste time citing references. It was gospel. His young ladies and young men joggled their heads gravely at each apocalyptic pronunciamento. The pastor fireballed onward with that trapped but defiant look Sam Houston must have gotten when he saw his buddies dropping like mosquitoes at the Alamo. Lucas wondered whether this dude had ever wasted pulpit time on a consideration of the act of communion as symbolic cannibalism.

Just as the waiting concertgoers began shouting epithets and making threatening motions, the police dropped by to say howdy. A contingent of Tucson Metro officers hung close enough to the booth to discourage any spontaneous trashing of the wild-eyed pastor and his zomboid charges.

Ten minutes before the Arena doors sprang wide to admit the over seven thousand people waiting to see 'Gasm, a battered Ford pickup truck chugged and clunked into the loading zone near the booth. It had obviously come off the same lot for senile vehicles as the Chevy Nova and was loaded down with more of the pastor's minions. Each of these clear-eyed soldiers of the

Lord toted a cardboard box filled with books, posters, records, and other items any fool could recognize as sinful. The pastor continued babbling, his Mister Microphone in hand . . . but now a propane torch was in his other hand, and he waved it around for special emphasis. The icons of vice and corruption were dumped at his feet—'Gasm albums, EPs by the Nuclear War Babies, old Beatles discs, records by the Stones, the Who, Rude Boy, Patti Page, AC/DC, Merle Haggard and the Strangers, Jules and the Polar Bears, Jim Nabors, Leonard Bernstein, Street Pajama, even Alvin and the Chipmunks. Even an ancient copy of *Harmonica Harmonies,* amid a smattering of other records all picked up for 49¢ a shot at K-Mart to bulk out the haul. 'Gasm albums, after all, cost retail. Among the books spilling onto the heap were works by Robert Ludlum, John D. MacDonald, and Isaac Asimov. Newspaper accounts would later report that the pile also included copies of the *Destroyer* novels, several violence pulps by Stephen Grave, *The Guitar Fake Book, Monty Python's Life of Brian, Fahrenheit 451, Jane Fonda's Workout Book, Why Bad Things Happen to Good People,* and several dictionaries, including Bierce's . . . all of which had nothing whatsoever to do with the demon of heavy metal, but which helped make the potential pyre much more impressive, especially for the TV news cameras.

Rock 'n' roll wasn't the only thing that could distract the impressionable from America's old gods.

The police intervened. One officer fought to remain civil as he addressed people he thought of as Nazis in religious drag. He informed the crazy pastor—civilly—that burning records inside the city limits violated ordinances against combustibles emitting noxious fumes, and polyvinyl chloride certainly classified. The pastor stowed his torch in a huff. Both the cop and the pastor had to shout at each other over the catcalls provided by the line of concertgoers.

At the pastor's direction, the sinful pile was killed with ballbats and axes. By the time this was coordinated, the audience was inside the Arena. The cops directed the pastor's group to clean up their mess and watched, bored, while they complied. It was less than momentous.

The entire abortive moment had been set up on the local news by a Tucson minister the night before. Lucas had caught the guy's act on TV in his room at the Holiday Inn.

"I was in Haiti and Jamaica," intoned the stern elder, all brilliant white hair and glittering, point-making specs. "This rock music puts youngsters into the same uncontrolled frenzy of voodoo worship I witnessed in those places. Give them a beat, and Satan can slip into their souls with his message of doom. Youngsters set up these heavy metal rock and roll musicians as role models, like Ozzy Osbourne. Young people perish at Ozzy Osbourne shows; it's been proven. I have seen a record album by this group playing tomorrow night. There was no sticker or other warning on the record. The name of this group, which is in itself odious, and the names of their dark songs, all promote illicit sex, sadomasochism, pain, and death. A publicity gimmick is nothing less than an open doorway for Satan! People seem surprised that this singer was killed in San Francisco. He was blown up by the fires of Hell, and others have died violent deaths. Violence begets violence, and those singers sing with Satan now. We offer young people an alternative to damnation. Our interest is not to appear as fanatics destroying other people's property, but to save souls by any means! Jesus Christ is the king—not Elvis, not the Beatles, not this Bruce Springstein or any heavy metal group." He set his jaw for the camera, determined, as immovable as the Rock.

As it turned out, the record bashing pulled no coverage at all. Record store owners, FM deejays, and even reverends from other local churches were all given equal time. All condemned this particular minister's fascistic tactics to one degree or another. Lucas could not recall the man's name.

The gyrating performance below had blurred before his eyes. Had *he* started all that fuss with his simple, spray-painted diversion? Bunch of damned nuts. Yet here he was, squatting in the rafters, making ready to do 'God''s work.

Or somebody's.

He centered Jackal Reichmann in his crosshairs again. This deed was not on behalf of any god, any intangible spirit born of superstitious fear. This was for Kristen, born of his loins, whom he had loved . . . and whom the capering buck in the white leather panties had helped, in however tiny a measure, to erase from this world. His index finger teased the trigger. This time he would pull the trigger without blinking.

Quickly, he sighted Fozzetto again. He would hit the bassist first, since Reichmann was installed behind his drums and was not as mobile. In the scope, tinted red, he could see the smoke hoses leaking wisps of white fog, the dry-ice cloud cover that would flood the stage and transform it into a primordial tarn under cover of the darkness supplied by Pepper Hartz's big solo spot.

It was almost time. When the lights snapped out, Lucas would have three minutes not to screw everything up.

Hartz exhorted the crowd with the usual battle cries: *"You wanna ROCK 'N' ROLL SOME MORE? We're gonna PARTY HARDY tonight! Lemme hear ya say YEAH!"* He windmilled his arm and struck a hard, harsh note. *Whaannnng!!* He stroked the crowd and made them chant "YEAH!" with each salvo. Fists rose, made devil horns, and again Lucas thought of the Nazis. YEAH! Faster, faster, YEAH! American audiences were nothing if not syncopated—YEAH! The next song needed their participation, and Lucas knew it would be "Rip Me Off

(Blow Me Down)," one of the rowdier songs from *Throw Down Your Arms.* The stage moves for this one were recorded indelibly in his mind. This was the lead-in song to Hartz's big solo.

Yeah.

To Lucas' metabolism, his plugged-up ears and throbbing eyes, the music became a towering, unstoppable migraine headache. The shifting masses of air, pushed around by heavy amplification, redefined the reality in which he moved. The grubs below could never suspect the motivations of the being above, the man no one could see. Wasn't that the image that the nameless TV minister had painted of his god? A will-'o-the-wisp who guided everyone's destiny . . . comes and goes like Santa Claus . . . his handiwork plain for all to see, the presence itself unseen?

In the nightmare, he feels weight in his hands and looks down. I'm packed, he thinks. Thirty slugs should take the bastards down all right.

But the nightmare had not bothered him since his final days at Olive Grove. He'd killed it, too, and handily.

The audience surged against the barricade, yelling out the refrain lines to "Rip Me Off." The bouncers perked up and held steady, grinning grimly. They were a cadre of body builders who bulged mightily from their canary-yellow T-shirts, and they grimaced at each other to let the Tucson audience know they were not going to take any shit. You could put their guard-dog dedication in the bank.

Now Lucas tilted the Dragunov and used the dimred, incremented circle of night-sight to scan the audience itself. Now he could see them as individuals—aggregate neurons powered by the electrical jolts of music. Now he saw them as a tentload of Bible Beltists, swaying in unison, waving their arms in the air, born again as Hartz molded his song toward its thunderous and utterly predictable conclusion.

Perhaps lambasting the music as predictable was unfair. Predictability was part of the music's attraction. The very sloganism of heavy metal was its mainstay strength. Lucas was reminded of the social codes of the Hell's Angels, the permutated chivalry to which righteous bikers adhered. Their rules were absolute, and a lot of normal citizens couldn't handle a system in which there were no flexible ethics, no creative reinterpretation of peculiar and unwritten laws. Disputes were settled in terms of a one-to-one stand, whether it was between two hog jockeys contesting rights to the same old lady or two clubs claiming the same turf. The price for breaking the rules was ostracism . . . sometimes known as getting your skull kicked in and your corpse dumped in a wheat field. There was black and there was white. The basics were dictated by simplicity and expediency, and that was what 'Gasm's music held in common with the biker credo. The kids below Lucas had not showed up to be surprised. These were the people who watched MTV day in, day out. Instead, they had come to give trained reactions to stimuli they already knew by heart. They had come not because Pepper "Mad Max" Hartz's gimmicks were anything new, but because Hartz was nicknamed after a movie they had all seen, and they wanted to see him survive a fake pillar of fire one more time. They wanted to pretend to be shocked by Jackal Reichmann's blanks. They didn't give a damn about the music's originality, they gave a damn about how easy it was to duplicate. They all wanted to live the rockstar fantasy, and if Pepper Hartz stood up and proved to them that what he did with his hands was simple, they would all envy him and perpetuate his existence. 'Gasm took their money. In return, the audience expected to orgasm according to conditioning received via various media —manipulative selling campaigns like those Lucas had dreamed up to make a living.

(During his first visit to the local cathouse, the country

hick forks over five bucks and gets so excited when the lady of the evening takes his hand to lead him upstairs that he ejaculates in his pants. "Now what do I do?" he says, aghast. The painted lady, her mission prematurely accomplished, says, "Now you find yourself a ride home, lover. Y'all come again real soon.")

Here, below Lucas, as in that ancient joke, the conditions of an unspoken contract were being fulfilled. 'Gasm did not have to be innovative, not by a mote. So what?

So had that meant that Kristen had known exactly what she was getting into that black night? Was she as responsible for her death as Whip Hand?

Rolling fog, pink in the glow of the sniperscope, began to congest the stage as "Rip Me Off" wound up. The cobalt-blue spotlight perked on and singled out Hartz, who lashed into his solo with an earsplitting feedback whine that brought another breaker of wild applause.

Lucas was still scanning the audience, stunned, thinking, *Impossible!*

He shifted up hurriedly through the total darkness in the auditorium. Too hurriedly. It made him sloppy. He zeroed in on Fozzetto.

Where are you, you bastard . . . there. There, gotcha.

He was positive he'd seen Kristen in the crowd below. The nightmare and the reality had fused, blurring into each other. Long blond hair, Cory's nose and eyes, his own square, definite jawline, crystal beads, silk shirt, looking adoringly up at Hartz in his deep blue circlet of light. Goddamned little slut would spread her legs for anyone, anyone, and she had to be watched constantly. . . .

No, impossible. The girl was not Kristen. From this distance, under these conditions, Winston fucking Churchill would look like Kristen. There must be at least two thousand clear-skinned heartbreakers here tonight who looked vaguely like Kristen. Yet the sight—the imagined sight—had shaken him.

Five seconds gone.

Fozzetto was unstringing himself from his bass guitar, dipping from under the Fender's broad, tooled strap and poising it on a nickel-plated stand next to the drum riser. As soon as the stage lights changed to favor Hartz, Fozzetto was apparently bound for the wings. Maybe he had to take a quick leak. Lucas would have to tag him before he crossed behind Rick Hicks. He felt like swearing, but that would have bollixed his aim, and he would only have this one chance.

Lucas squeezed off, and the Dragunov bucked against the hollow of his shoulder. The flat crack of the expelled bullet was lost in the ear-pegging keen of Hartz's gorilla axe-handling. Fozzetto's hair flew apart on the far side of his head, and he stumbled into the drum riser as though shoved. One hand thumped the bass drum. Lucas put a second slug into him before he could collapse. No sound. The bass player's white mop of hair began to darken as soon as he hit the stage floor.

Nine seconds gone.

Jackal Reichmann's face was like the fifty-point hole of a bullseye. It would be fast and easy to plant a slug right into his mouth, which was now hanging open in a black oval that sat at ground zero in the tinted crosshairs. He was the only band member who had seen Fozzetto's head come apart, who had watched him crumple to the boards. Lucas gave him one extra second of life, to react. He might decide to stand up and provide a bigger target. Manufactured smoke billowed up behind him, and he was framed in the red light of the scope. During his bit with the gangster-style machine gun, red spotlights were used. This time the red light belonged to Lucas, and the shells were not blanks.

Eleven seconds. Lucas' finger pulled back on the steel tongue of the trigger.

Write a wet-dream love ditty about this, *ratfuck. Hope you enjoy hell.*

Before he could shoot, he saw something astonishing through the scope. A stuttering line of black dots punctured the double bass, then corrected trajectory and quilted upward into Reichmann. Five dark holes blossomed in a diagonal across his bare chest as he rose to take a look at his unmoving comrade on the stage below. His face scrunched up, and he did a backward tumble off the drum riser, dragging the long rack of brass gongs with him as his white-booted feet flashed in the air and he disappeared out of sight behind the platform. The gongs made a hell of a racket going down.

Rick Hicks had half-turned to see what in blazes was going on when a fan of hot slugs tore through both him and his guitar, impelling him into a clumsy pirouette.

Fourteen seconds gone.

Pepper Hartz's solo hitched and died. He had just turned his attention to Reichmann's fall when a fireline of bullets stitched toward him, blowing plastic and canvas splinters out of the prefab stage floor. There was zero time to react. He caught the burst in both legs and folded up, screaming. The blue spotlight was still on him, and in its light the fresh blood looked like chocolate syrup. Hartz's Strat thudded endwise on the floor and sent a thrumming bass tone careening through the Arena.

Lucas broke through the panic freeze of his total surprise and turned his head to fix on the bright flashes of light.

Somebody was standing on the stage-left catwalk, less than sixty feet across from him, cutting the band apart with an M-16 on rapid fire. Lucas remembered what he and every other soldier had called the rapid-fire setting in Vietnam.

Rock and roll.

17

THE URGE TO SPEND SOME time near the ocean struck Cass as she was picking her way down from the outhouse. Going to the bathroom in the woods was never less than an adventure, and however cleanly maintained, the outhouse nevertheless hosted a scary variety of curious life forms.

The clothes she had hand-washed in the kitchen basin hung, dry now, from tree limbs behind the cabin. She pulled them down and sniffed. Ahh.

There was ham and swiss cheese and tuna salad in the fridge, and she constructed a pair of thick sandwiches on seven-grain bread and folded them into a bindle made from one of Lucas' large kerchiefs, which she had also washed. She used the sandwiches to cushion two clinking bottles of cold Dos Equis beer and added a spiral notebook she had discovered in the kitchen drawer. Under the gun.

Finding the gun had sent a tiny lance of surprise spearing into her heart. It was some kind of huge pistol, wrapped up in a holster with a lot of nylon webbing. Her hands had absolutely refused to even touch it; she hated guns. She'd slid the notebook out from under it as though the pistol were radioactive. It had dropped back into place with a heavy thud—even the sound had been dark, weighty, ominous. She'd slammed the drawer shut and refused to look inside again.

Guy has a cabin in the mountains. Has a gun. Almost logical, for out here. Frontier security. Just because you don't like them doesn't mean lots of normal people don't have them. I certainly don't have to touch the icky thing. Case closed.

After she wiped off the surface of the notebook (what, me, compulsive?), she put the gun out of her mind. She did not feel much like reading, though Lucas had socked in plenty of paperbacks. Today she wanted to ruminate on the pad or just doodle by the sea, which held a degree of bohemian attraction for her. A pity Jack Kerouac was stuck with the squalors of suburbia and skid row for inspiration.

Thus provisioned, she checked the padlock on the door of the cabin's auxiliary room before leaving. She could not pinpoint the reason why she did this, other than her desire to be responsible on Lucas's behalf. It was secure. When she let it go it clunked against the plank door and shined at her. It was new, recently bought, as was the hasp on the door. The other hardware and cabin fixings were all worn or broken in with age.

It was none of her business.

If there was a single fact she had learned about men—whose weird body chemistry made them the closest thing to alien beings on earth—it was that men were addicted to the cultivation of their private little caches of secrets. The thing that had put the whole country in such a balls-up was the *machismo* hormone. That was why the backbone of politics was the mud-slinging smear campaign, why there were so bloody many nuclear bombs buried all over the map, why

Tanya's biker boyfriend T-Bone and Cass' own Reese had apocalypse written in their eyes. The *machismo* hormone. Lucas seemed immune, so far. At least he had not been demonstrably male in the Teutonic, patience-abrading fashion that kicks the female's automatic alarm system on like a fire klaxon. He seemed to live his life in balance, to know what he wanted. He seemed in control of his circumstances, and for that Cass envied him. At least he hadn't gotten himself puddled by a homicidal screwball like Reese.

She had taken stock of herself that morning and thought she was mending with fair speed. The left side of her face no longer stung abominably when she spoke or rolled onto it in sleep. Her crushed hand had freed up, and her grip was back to about three-quarter strength. Her shiner had deflated. The discoloration in the socket of her eye now resembled an inept makeup job. If she glanced at her face in the mirror tile above the sink fast enough, she looked normal. The progress pleased her. You'll be back on the cover of *Vogue* in no time, kiddo.

She used a flexible wire brush on a wide wooden paddle to brush her auburn hair straight back, then braided it into a single, thick, twisting rope that she secured with a rubber band at the bottom. It looked rather like the bell pulls used by the filthy rich to summon butlers and handmaidens in the mostly awful 1940s films that ran in the predawn on Channel Five or Thirteen, back in the city. It no longer hurt to comb her hair. She did not yelp with pain in the course of washing or drying it. Just a few days before, it had felt as though she was yanking blood vessels right out through her scalp.

She laced up her hiking boots and cuffed the slightly large coverall legs to fit. Then she hit the trail.

Near the cabin you could make out natural depressions in the ground that meant *walk here, others do.* But the footpath vanished almost immediately, giving way to a forty-degree slope of limestone bluff littered with rock chips a foot deep in some places, which led down to the timberline. She speculated that a huge chunk of limestone stratum had pushed its way to the surface and made a big scab where trees could not root. Only stubborn scrub plants poked up through infrequent cracks. It killed traction. Sometimes it allowed deceptively easy climbing. Right when you thought you'd gotten the swing of dancing downward, high-stepping, it would slip your foot and dump you on your ass. No wonder Lucas needed a tank like the Bronco to scrabble all the way to his stoop. From a postcard distance, it was picturesque. Up close, it was just a bitch of a hill.

She watched a squirrel watching her.

"Yeah, laugh all you want, buckaroo. I need the exercise, and nobody invited you to watch. Whoops!"

Cass slid feet first down five feet or so of the rock surface. Pathetic miniature avalanches of chalky rock trickled around her. Fifteen feet away, another squirrel joined the first on the branch of a crooked, dead tree. The soil could not nourish the tree here. But the squirrels could gather there to make bad squirrel jokes and watch the human burlesque.

"Fine. Wonderful." Her butt was sore, and her calf muscles were already twanging. She felt like throwing a rock until she remembered this wasn't her neighborhood.

Doggedly she continued downhill, bobbing and weaving and sliding only occasionally. She thought triumphantly, *At least I'm not falling around as comically as those two city slickers on their way up. . . .*

She petrified, a cat on freeze mode.

Two people had just emerged from the treeline far below her and were valiantly fighting their way up the inhospitable incline. They were about a hundred yards distant, mere specks. But it was obvious they were bound for her position as though homed in via radar.

She turned and bounded back toward the cabin. Going up was more of a challenge, but she did not fall, and her legs greedily welcomed the work. In the rare times she noticed her legs thrumming with strength, she would reflect that maybe the eight years of dance classes inflicted on her by her parents had been worth it. Her legs hit stride and propelled her upward with gazelle sureness.

She could lay for them inside the cabin.

Twenty minutes later the two visitors knocked on the cabin door. It was a city knock, no different from that of a group selling highschool band candy or proselytizing for the Seventh Day Adventists.

Cass opened the door fully prepared for a confrontation with Lucas' fabled ex-wife.

She met eyes with a tall woman whose conservative brown hair was windblown. Her tan boots were newly scuffed from the climb. She had removed her dark glasses to unveil direct, authoritarian eyes, also brown, which she narrowed in the sunlight.

"We're here to see Lucas," she said as though it explained everything. Then, less sure: "Lucas Ellington."

Ellington. Nice name. Cass had not known it. Yes, this had to be Sara, and the bulldog type with the fluffy gray hair, standing a respectful distance behind and to the left, that had to be her attorney, as Lucas had forewarned. Any residual fear drained away. She had this ex-spouse's number. No problem. She folded her arms and squared her body. She'd actually been rehearsing the routine in her head.

"Too late," she told them sweetly. "Lucas is long gone." If the legal bloodhound knew his business, it wouldn't be any use to try and convince them that this was not Lucas' cabin. "He expected you guys to show up a week ago." Just a hint of derision there. Perfect.

Bulldog stepped forward to flank Sara. "Do you suppose you could tell us where he is, Miss—?"

Cass' eyes did not leave Sara's, where a war was brewing. "Nope."

A slow breath escaped Sara, laden with the psychic smell of grinding teeth. "I don't believe her. Listen, whoever you might be . . . if Lucas is hiding, or if you're just covering for him . . . you might be in danger. He—"

"Sounds *horrible*." Cass smiled, dripping contempt.

"He is being sought statewide right now for possible connections in three murders," Sara overrode, despising the lie but infuriated by this girl's snide manner. *Splendid,* her professional imp poked her. *You've just changed from a potential equal in this argument to Old Bitch.* She had been put instantly on the defensive by a girl half her age. Almost half, since she was almost forty. Didn't she have *any* chops left? Her jaw muscles concretized. "I don't know how long you've known Lucas, honey, but I'm willing to bet it hasn't been more than two weeks, and you obviously don't have any idea of who or what you're involved with! If Lucas is here, he'll see me. I'm his doctor. . . ."

Now she was looking past Cass and into a depressingly vacant cabin. There was a locked door set into one wall. A hiding place?

"You listen to me now, *Mom,*" Cass shot back. "I really don't care if you're Doctor Jekyll and that's Mister Hyde behind you. Get some legal realities straight. I am the caretaker of this place. Lucas is gone; don't ask me where. That's none of my business and none of yours. You are trespassing. If you want the tour, bring a cop with a warrant. I know how that works, so don't jive me. I would tell you all I know is that Lucas packed up and left days ago, but you're not prepared to buy that. So we have nothing to talk about, do we? Goodbye."

She began to shut the door in Sara's face when Sara

interposed her boot, blocking it. Cass' green, dark-ringed eyes flared.

"You trying for forcible entry, *doctor*?"

Burt interceded. He approached with his hands open in entreaty, a gesture unchanged almost since caveman days, like the handshake, originally intended to prove the absence of hidden weapons. "Er—look, young lady. We're not here to cause trouble or make you angry. Seriously. I don't know what you've been told, now, but Lucas is a good friend of mine, and he might be in trouble I don't think he even knows about. Perhaps you care about that? I'm certainly not here to trap him, or compromise him. I'm here to exonerate him." His salesman voice clicked in; he made his eyes as warm as he could. More primal signals. That was how you sold products. "I just need to talk to him. I guarantee you that if he knew Sara—Ms. Windsor—and I were standing here right now, he would see us. So I believe you; I don't think he's here, either." *Christ,* he thought—what on earth had this girl been told?

Cass held the door fast, and Sara withdrew her foot. She looked from one to the other and settled on Burt. "You should have come to the door first. Your lady friend is less civilized. I'm not a hard-ass, but I've already told you: Lucas is gone. He did not say where. That is all I know." She shrugged.

"Fine," said Burt, still succoring. "Is he coming back?"

"In a month, maybe." That fib was harmless enough.

"Can I leave word for him here? That's all I really want—to get in touch as soon as I can."

"Sure. You can leave word, but like I say, he may not see it for four weeks or more. Four weeks equals a month."

Sara stopped smoldering. "Did Lucas do that to you? Black your eye?"

"No. I had an accident. I'm recuperating up here, and baby-sitting the cabin, and that's all." Then she pointedly turned back to Burt. "I think your lady friend wants to ask if I'm Lucas' significant other. No. Lucas is a touch too old for me." Unspoken was *He's more in* your *range, Mom.* Cass watched her barb sink and seat.

"Any idea of what's in the locked room?" said Burt, pushing his luck.

"Not the foggiest."

He craned his neck but could not see the video gear Lucas had borrowed from Kroeger Concepts. "Then that's all I can ask without force," he said, conceding defeat and hating it, for it offended his problem-solving mind. "Let's go, Sara."

She spun on him. "You mean we just walk off, Burt, just like that, after the drive, after . . . everything? Just pull out because she wants to play some stupid game?" Her eyes were wet with fury.

"Hanging around here gains us nothing. Lucas would have poked his head up by now."

"Lucas!" Sara shouted at the cabin, at the woods. It was immediately apparent how futile it was. "Lucas, goddamnit!"

"You've got quite a backbone, young lady," Burt said to Cass. "I sure as hell hope you don't come to regret it. Because if you're spinning me 'round, you will."

He took Sara's hand to avert her, and they crunched away down the footpath. She looked back. He did not.

"You're welcome," Cass said, knowing they could not hear. Then, in a whisper, she added, *"I win."*

She watched from the door until the pair could no longer be seen. Lucas would be very pleased. Maybe he would tell her what their tale of three murders was really about. Probably this Sara woman, playing soap opera, trying to scare her. She might have tried saying they were from Internal Revenue; that scares the shit out of most people. For all the results they walked away with, she might have said she was a Russian counterspy or a Roman demigoddess fallen on hard times.

Cass reveled in her handling of the situation . . . but now her stomach lurched sourly, and her knees wanted to unhinge. Her hands trembled. Battle fatigue. The thought of the fat sandwiches packed into the bindle became less than appetizing. It was just adrenaline backwash. She recognized the nausea. She replaced it with anger. She would *not* let this spoil her plans for the beach.

Murder. Sara had used the magic word, and it hung around to hamper her.

They might come back. If they did, things might escalate. They might bring up the Rangers to roust her. Would her backbone give out at a crucial point, making her faint or puke while they ransacked Lucas' place looking for god knew what? She sat down heavily on one of the kitchen chairs, drawing slow, deep oral breaths. Gradually things swam back into normal focus, and the iron returned to her blood. If the interlopers were to hang back a day, then try again, Lucas would have returned and the matter would be out of her hands. She would help him any way she could.

Just who was Lucas, though, out in the real world? Did it matter, as far as her relationship with him was concerned? She wiped her brow; found it sweaty. Nervousness, leaking out through her pores.

Then she heard footsteps outside, or thought she did. She stopped in midbreath. A shadow disturbed the light in the front window. She pushed out of the chair. Maybe the pair had thought of some new angle to throw in her face.

When she pulled open the door, she was pissed off.

Then she found herself staring up, up into Reese's

crooked smile. Lucas' long-handled axe, from the chopping stump outside, depended loosely from Reese's right hand.

"Hi, puss," he said.

"Just who the hell are we?" Burt said.

They had traded the fantasmagoric milieu of the woods for the push-button urban familiarity of bucket seats and tinted windshields, and now they were headed north. "Be realistic, Sara. We can't demand anybody do anything. Even if we had any kind of authority, we'd still need guys with badges to deal with that girl. Is that what you want? I thought the idea was to *avoid* guys with guns."

Their descent down the mountain had made Sara's coat a hot purgatory to wear, and she had stowed it in the backseat. She nursed a keen whomper of a headache, and the Excedrin tin in her bag was cunningly empty.

"Overreaction from acute frustration and paranoid delusions." She sighed. "Hysteria and headaches are textbook responses. Goddamnit, Burt, where is he? Off making my reasoned Sherlockian deductions come true? Boy, that would change all our lives really fast. And if not—where is he? He's not in the cabin, and that means he lied to you on the phone the other day. That snotty little bitch might have been telling the truth. For all you and I know, Lucas hadn't even been to the damned cabin in the first place!" She constricted her face in pain. "Christ, I'm making my headache even worse. The sun is scouring out my eyeballs." Her sunglasses were not much of a buffer.

"What if Lucas had just stepped out to get groceries or something?" Burt's eyes stayed on the highway. He was back in the realm of questions and answers, relentlessly sorting data and seeking possibilities.

"Big joke on us." She spoke softly, to deny the thin claws of pain a tighter hold on her belfry. "Ha. Ha." The girl had been so spunky, so self-assured. Sara detested being shot down by someone who had been a squalling baby while she was busting hump to survive her sophomore year at university. "But she saw Lucas, Burt—he might have been up there as recently as a week ago. Why should she bother to construct an elaborate lie when the truth works even better?"

"Just what I was thinking."

The Rolling Stones rolled through "Ventilator Blues" on the sound system of Burt's Eldorado. He'd twiddled up and down the FM dial until he found a station he could stand. Heavy metal was not to his taste; Mick and the boys, just barely. He thought about killing the music in deference to Sara's headache but never got around to it. For the next four miles it was the only sound in the car.

"So we're back to square one. Where is he?"

"We're not leaving for real, are we, Burt?"

His mental gears had been grinding. "I thought that if you were amenable, we could enter the dreaded metroplex and shack up in one of its finer motor lodges. Tomorrow, we'll check again. Just in case Lucas went to the 7-11. He's got to be driving something. It'll be parked somewhere if he is. We can quietly spy. He's probably using a Jeep, or something similar, if he drives right up to the cabin's front door."

"If we were just looking for his *car*, we could have avoided that hysterical scene up there."

Burt thought it best to ignore her embarrassment. It had gone badly, yes. But that was the past, and they were planning for tomorrow. "We didn't know that until we went and checked, now did we? Now we know better than to go knocking."

"Unless something is parked there."

"Now you're catching on." Burt was not one of those half-wit drivers who stare at their passengers while carrying on a conversation. His attention was on the driving. When he did sneak a glance to check her condition, he said, "Look in the glovebox. There might be something ancient and painkilling stuffed away in there." It was about time for him to choke down one of his awful blood pressure pills as well.

"There's another problem." She rummaged and held up a rock-hard pack of chewing gum. "I can't do overnighters and mountaineering indefinitely."

"Not the outdoors type? You weren't bad on that hill, you know."

"That's not what I mean. I'm shirking my duties at the hospital. I've already cashed in most of my sick time for the fiscal year. What if Lucas takes four weeks to come back, like that girl said?"

"I'll stay. I can get away with it. I'm president of my own company. You can drive this car back to L.A. After all, Lucas might show up at Olive Grove, or at Kroeger Concepts, if he really isn't up here. I'll rent myself a Jeep and tool back to the cabin—maybe to charm the harpy therein into balming me with all the hot poop there is to know." He paused, pleased with his own turn of phrase. "Sounds good, anyway."

"I wonder what Lucas told her. You notice that she seemed to be fully briefed? Ready for us?"

"Yeah. I thought about that, too, and it might be another reason Lucas might show up sooner than she says. But he didn't rent her along with his camping gear. Who is she, where did she come from?"

"If Lucas was out there avenging Kristen, killing the guys in Whip Hand, and he somehow acquired a substitute daughter, a surrogate Kristen . . . would he stop his vendetta?" She was speaking with her eyes shut.

"What about that combination-brain stuff? What if he's—I don't know, programmed. And can't stop." Burt was thinking of the death junkies he'd known in the service, the guys who thrived on night patrol, the machines who collected VC ears and balls and didn't *want* to go home.

"I was just thinking that if he got a surrogate Kristen, it would nullify the motive for the vendetta, wouldn't it?" *It also might mean that a surrogate Cory would be next, and his brain would rebel at that thought. Cory was death for him.*

On the radio a few seconds of burp-gun deejay patter bled over into the opening of Wall of Voodoo's "Mexican Radio." For a moment Burt wished he was back at Kroeger Concepts, chiding Gustavo de la Luces good-naturedly about the silly tune and busting his brain on stratagems that were, in Gustavo's words, "do-able, get-able, and cashworthy." Lucas had once joked, long, long ago, that those three words sounded like a Beverly Hills law firm.

"Something else," Sara said. "What if that girl has slept with him, Burt? She might be the Cory substitute, not Kristen. Those bruises we saw might be Lucas' fault." Her voice trailed away. "I . . . I just don't know . . ."

"Yet," he said, hoping to deter her from further self-excoriation. "But if he's all the way back to Cory, and that girl's not dead, maybe it means he didn't help kill Cory after all. Remember, he was seeing other women after she died."

"Yes. Yes." Maybe *she* was a bigger victim than Lucas. Maybe it was all innocent and hubbed on a third explanation no one had thought of because there wasn't enough information. Yet. "Oh, God, Burt—where the hell *is* he?"

"Best we can do for now is—"

"Wait, shh!" Her hand flew to the radio knob.

The deejay was reporting that there were no new developments in the 'Gasm concert tragedy in Tucson, Arizona. Three members of the band were dead. Two were in critical condition. Their assailant, a middle-aged man who had opened up on the band with an automatic weapon during their Community Center show, was in the custody of the Pima County Sheriff's Department. His name was being withheld, but he was described as a "religious fanatic."

Sara blanched. Burt suddenly wanted a drink, very badly.

As far as the deejay was concerned, the attacker was "one of those ass-backwards backward-maskers. They condemn us, gentle listeners, yet they kill and we don't. Let's just hope that lynching hasn't gone out of style in woolly old Tucson, you hear what I'm sayin'? Here's 'Toledo Breakdown.'"

The song was one of 'Gasm's few slow numbers, like "Agent Orange Blues." The inevitable ballad, as Chic Garris would have put it. Song style #3.

The Eldorado slowed to a stop on the shoulder. Burt was staring at Sara. "Now what?"

Her trusty words had failed her, and she felt useless and dumb. The jock had referred to the assassinations as the "latest Whip Hand murders."

18

THE AXE SWUNG DOWN IN a sharp silver arc toward Cass' head as she slammed the cabin door.

She had reacted to the sight of Reese instantaneously, trying to engage the heavy sliding bolt on the door. In a single, horrible moment of elongated time, she saw Reese's thick wrist *flick*. The cording defining his arms jumped into hard relief, and the axe pivoted upward with frightening speed. She knew how heavy it was; she'd levered it from the chopping stump the day before, and its mass caused the blade to thump to the ground, wrenching her still-mending left hand.

She threw all her weight into the door. No good. The blade thudded in and blocked. Its crescent, dirty and pitted, was inches from her nose.

A savage kick snapped the door inward, freeing the axe and sending Cass sprawling on her ass to the cabin floor. She looked up at Reese, framed in the light filling the doorway, as his foot drifted back down to its starting position.

"Jackpot time." His lips barely moved when they

formed words. His voice was a nightmarish memory, whisper-soft, sandpaper-hoarse, a deep and purring register that issued from somewhere black and demoniac inside of him. The axe, which had moved in a blur, now hung idly in his grip, at ease. He gave the cabin interior a bored once-over with eyes the color of anodized aluminum. "Nice place."

Cass hoisted onto her elbows but did not try to stand, not yet. Reese's pupils were pinpricks. His habit was to pop Dexamyls like black M&Ms until the steady beat of the speed pounded like rock 'n' roll in his bloodstream and made his chest and arm muscles twitch and tic at random. Reese preferred crank to sugar in his coffee.

He wore steel-toed mountain climbing boots, tight, roughed-up jeans, and his favorite denim vest. No shirt. His solid pectorals bulged to fill the gap between the vest's thonged button slits like sculpted rose-colored marble. The vest's bone fasteners dangled with nothing to do. A wild, lightning-bolt scar interrupted the hard muscle of his abdomen. It was a keepsake of some long-ago buck knife fight, and Reese's recently begun tan made it obvious, a white zigzag etched into his flesh. *What his brain waves must look like,* Cass thought. Bound to the hollow of his throat by a strip of leather was a lozenge of ivory, cold and alabaster. It held an opaque disc of jade in a pewter setting. It was the only thing close to personal jewelry she had ever seen Reese wear.

His tongue slid behind his teeth like a snake in a chuckhole. "Miss me?" The viper's gaze, unblinking, sought and engulfed her. "Sugar daddy ain't home. I know. I watched for a whole day, just to make sure. Your other pals drove away, too." He was talking about Sara and her companion, Mr. Hyde. Reese's mouth pulled back slightly at the right corner—his version of a casual smile. "The mountains just ain't for them, puss."

His right leg arched up and back with a practiced

aikido motion, and the door crashed shut; Cass heard loose junk sifting down out of the frame from the impact. He took three measured strides forward and straddled her at the waistline, gazing down at her, the axe off to her right, hanging like the pendulum of a lethargic grandfather clock.

Her mouth tried to moisten, to form words. "How . . . how did you know I was here?"

Interest glinted in the metallic eyes; they ceased their random scanning of the cabin to nail her. "I'm a timber wolf, puss. I followed your smell." The eyes flickered to the kitchen, then back. "Any food here?"

The normalcy of the request allowed Cass to flush away some of her terror in favor of anger. "Why don't you just get the hell out of here, Reese? Leave. Just leavc me alone." She did not unclench her teeth; they might start chattering.

Again the peculiar glint came and went in his eyes, as though he was receiving orgasms in his brain via electroshock. "Or what? You'll kick me in the nuts again? Hey, make your move. I'm even spread out for you. Give it another shot." His tongue tested the cutting edge of his incisors.

She didn't want to try. She needed to maximize whatever time she had left, not to touch off his fuse. She visualized him crouching in the forest cold in the middle of the night like some genetically mutant Indian guide, bare-chested and not feeling the temperature. *Kick me*, sure.

"That's good." The hooded gaze started to mesmerize her. "We don't want to fight. We want to make love, don't we?"

She remembered the time he'd swerved the Datsun long-bed across two lanes to splatter a darting rabbit all over the grille and front bumper. Blood and viscera shaded the headlights and steamed on the pebbled glass. All Reese had said was *got him*. He had just said *make love* in the same tone, rippling stalactites of ice into her spine.

"Forget it, Reese, no way."

"Sorry I got pissed at you. You shouldn't've kicked me." He planted the thick tread of one boot against her shoulder and pressed until her back met the planking again. Then he leaned on it until her face tightened in pain. "Bad girl." He gripped her jaw and squeezed, mashing her mouth until it parodied that of a goldfish. He examined her head like a melon. "You healed up nice." He bent closer; something popped wetly in her shoulder. His unblinking eyes filled her universe. "Remember Jonathan?"

"Oh, no . . ." Her world was coming to an end.

"Poor guy. I *feel* for him, puss. Because you had to spread your legs for him, he's gotta spend the next four months in intensive care." He *tsk*ed, released her face, and stepped back. "Terrible thing. Poor dude."

She lost it. "Motherfucker! What did you do!" She was halfway up, the door at hand. She tried frantically to calculate the success potential of running.

A pained look stabbed his features. "Don't be so crude, puss. Watch your language. Jonathan had himself an accident. Little accident. Can't move his head, has to piss through a tube for a while . . . that's all."

Cass' imagination spun grisly stories as she got to her feet. Her hands brushed off her backside to keep from shaking.

Reese has spotted Lucas' tapedeck, on the kitchen table. "Nice," he said. That meant the deck would leave with him. "Are we going to eat something, or what?"

Buy time! Do something! "Right," she said dully. To move toward the sink she had to pass Reese.

He caught her quick glance toward the door. "Don't run." His voice was quite calm. "Don't even think of running. You can't outrun a hungry wolf." The cocked twitch-smile came and went.

Mechanically she untied her bindle and pulled out the paper-towel-wrapped sandwiches. She pulled open the first kitchen drawer and took stock of the knives there. No good. He'd dare me to try, and I'd need the fire department and a gynecologist to get the knife out of me. Behind her, Reese leaned on the axe and propped one boot on a chair.

"What's inside the secret room with the padlock?"

"I don't know." She moved to the fridge and considered Lucas' stock of Dos Equis. Maybe if she could get enough alcohol into him . . .

And then? Take the axe away, or bash him with something solid, or run? Run where, with him chasing her? Distract him enough to sneak out a knife? Sure. She swallowed hard; it felt like trying to swallow a votive candle. *You can always kick him in the crotch again*—hadn't that worked out great?

"Sugar daddy's big secret, hm? Hey—pass one of those beers over."

He twisted the cap off. She didn't know if they were twist-tops or not. She pulled open another drawer. Plastic bags, a knife sharpener, batteries in store packages, a flashlight, a card of thumbtacks. Useless.

"Let's take a gander. Maybe more tapedecks and stuff. You got the key?"

"No."

He drew off half the brown bottle in a gulp. His dark hair was strewn lankly across his forehead, making his eyes glow chromium. "You sure the key ain't in your pocket? Or on a string around your neck?" He stroked his ivory pendant. "Or stuffed into your underpants? Sure I shouldn't check you out, puss?" He licked his lips. Wolfishly.

Her minimal control was eroding fast. Reese was revving himself up to pummel the shit out of her, this time for keeps. That was why he was so calm. He was going to catch her face in his hand with big, molar-loosening slaps, then punch her in the stomach until the fight leaked out of her. Then shove himself into her, fuck her till she bled, as he was fond of saying. He would rape her until he'd come three times. For Reese, it was three orgasms or it wasn't sex.

And then, if she wasn't dead, he'd kill her.

"I don't have the goddamned keys, Reese!" she shrieked. Fear was what he wanted to see. She was certain that if she looked down, she would see the erection prodding forth inside his pants. If she saw that, he'd win the fear he craved. She kept her eyes locked on his.

A humming sound stopped halfway out of his throat. It was almost a laugh. "No prob," he said dismissively.

Cass recalled telling Lucas about Reese. Somewhere along the road, she'd told herself that life would never be dull with Reese around.

The hasp on the door dented into a crooked V with Reese's first roundhouse swing of the axe. With the second, the door splintered loose. Flat-headed screws chocked with wood pulp hung like pulled teeth. Reese gave the door his boot, and the whole cabin shook as the top hinge ripped free. The door skewed inward on the bottom hinge and rasped across the floor. The padlock hit the floor with a clank, tangled up in the bent hasp. Reese peered inside but did not step over the barrier. "Looks like good stuff," he said. "Nice." He set the empty beer bottle gently on the floor—Reese did not believe in littering—and motioned for a fresh one.

Cass' sandwiches sat on the counter, hardening and looking ridiculous. Her pupils were stopped down with shock. Mechanically, she pulled another Dos Equis from the fridge. Then she remembered the gun in the kitchen's third and last drawer.

She nearly dropped the bottle to shatter on the floor. Instead, she moved very methodically, fighting for control. She used a church key to open the beer. They were not twist-caps. This was going to be touchy.

I certainly don't have to touch *the icky thing. . . .*

At the sound of Reese's footsteps crossing the cabin, she turned and held the beer out to him. He touched the mouth of the bottle to his forehead, saluting her. Toasting her imminent death, perhaps. Time to find a new girl. Then he turned back to Lucas' cache.

The drawer was missing a knob, and she had to jiggle it open. Confused into the candle stubs and wads of tinfoil was—it. The crossgrained butt of the .45 jutted from a contraption that looked like some kind of leather knee or shoulder brace, with tiny sawtoothed buckles and loops of nylon webbing. A shoulder holster, that's what it must be.

Touching the butt of the gun made her want to wet her pants.

In one more second, Reese's attention would be back on her, wondering what the hell she was doing by the sink. In that eyeblink of time, too many questions froze her. *Is it loaded? What do I have to do before I shoot it? Can I get it out of the holster? Does Reese see it? Do I* want *to get it out of the holster?*

She pushed the drawer halfway shut. Dumb, careful Cass; since when did she have to make sure of something before she went ahead and did it?

She just might get that forest burial she'd mentioned to Lucas—today.

Reese tilted the axe against the door jamb, gulped some more cold Dos Equis, and started to swing one leg over to enter the tiny auxiliary room. That might have been the moment, but he was still facing her. Brilliant —one blown free turn. What if he found another gun in there?

"Don't go 'way, puss." He ducked his head inside.

Cass' hand dropped back to the drawer. The thought of Reese's cock being the last thing she'd see before she died gave her a rush of strength. One strap was wound around the pistol, binding it to the holster. Swiftly her hands untangled it and slid the automatic free. It took days to get all of the barrel out. God—it must weigh twenty pounds.

She put her back between Reese's vantage and the gun she now held above the counter, struggling to remember what little she knew about such a thing. This sort of gun was clip-fed. The clip held the bullets. She'd seen movies with supercops adroit at fast clip changes. The clip dropped from the butt of the pistol as the supercop whacked in a new one. She tilted the butt and saw the bottom stoppered up with metal—the end of the magazine. Ergo, this gun must be loaded. If it *isn't* loaded, then why does it weigh so goddamn much? . . .

The change in the resonance of Reese's voice told her that he had stuck his head back out through the door. Careful, now.

"All kinds of nice stuff. Too bad the Datsun won't make the climb. Might have to use you as a pack mule, puss." She heard a stack of plastic cassette boxes rattle as they fell to the wooden floor. Lucas' tapes. "Check this out," commanded the low, graveyard voice.

Suddenly her mind insisted that this was hopeless and futile. In the movies, they fired these things with both hands, grimacing while they did it. One of her hands was still crippled.

"Hey." She still had not turned, and now the reptilian eyes were sought on her, drilling into her back through the merchant marine sweater, seeing her secret prize with some alien form of X-ray vision.

She took casual chances with her life; she'd told Lucas so. Now she had to live up to the brag.

"Just a minute." She tried to sound irritated, thinking phony normalcy would buy her another half second.

She turned. Reese was standing, one foot in, one out of the doorway, holding Lucas' portable Sony Trinitron television. Wires trailed from it back into the room. Reese wrenched them free with an irritated expression; more stuff clattered as it was swept off the table inside.

Cass finished her turn by raising the pistol and pulling the trigger in a single smooth motion. Her left hand braced her wrist, as she had seen in the movies.

Reese's eyes locked on the gun. Instead of widening in surprise, they narrowed as his whole body tensed. Recognition was instantaneous, and his reaction time was blindingly quick, juiced by the speed in his system. His lips curled back over his teeth, and his body had already jerked to shield itself within the tiny room when he realized that nothing had happened.

The trigger was frozen solid; it had not budged. Cass' eyes were squeezed shut, but the expected booming report and the slam of recoil had never come. Her finger jerked on the trigger again. Nothing.

In that second Reese, still holding the TV set, decided to take her down. Four sure steps accelerated him across the room, and he swung the TV wide to extend his reach. To him it weighed nothing.

As Reese took his first step, Cass' brain screamed that there was a thing called a *safety*, that it immobilized the trigger, that it was a little thumb lever on the left side of the butt. She turned the big Llama ACP sideways to shove up the safety with her good hand, and when she glanced up she saw the TV set swooping down in Reese's hand like some damned ICBM targeted right between her nice green eyes.

The pistol seemed to go off by itself.

It kicked, almost snapping her wrist bones, and yanked itself violently to the right, jerking her arm out straight. The steel-jacketed hollow point mushroomed as it plowed into the blank glass eye of the Sony. The TV exploded like a magician's jack-in-the-box with an eardrum-compressing pop, peppering them both with whizzing slivers of glass from the disintegrating vacuum tube. Reese collided heavily with the counter where Cass had been standing before the recoil had jerked her out of his path. His free forearm shielded his eyes. Flying pieces of the TV set made an incredible hailstorm din all over the cabin in the aftermath of the gun's loud and obliterating voice.

An animal roar jumped out of Reese as he pushed himself upright against the counter, amazed that he was still alive. His right ear was a ruined casserole of tissue that sparkled with fresh blood. His eyes, fixed and gleaming, caught Cass, and his face split into a hungry grin that showed all his teeth. His forehead was lacerated; blood began to bead there instantly. The sticky mass that was once his ear welled red, and blood coursed down to drip off his chin like candle wax.

And he *smiled* at her, saying, "Okay, you cunt."

And he reached for her.

Cass forgot the agony in her arm and fired again, from a distance of less than four feet. There was no time for aim or thought; her fingers simply snapped shut around the gun.

The noise and flame and impact stunned her again. Tears ran from her eyes and wove cold webs on her face. Reese was yanked backward. He hit the table, collapsing two of its legs. His right arm flailed out and slapped the floor as he slid diagonally down. His left arm, the arm with which he had just tried to grab her, had been blown off at the elbow. It was lying in the sink, fingers still trying to close.

She heard him breathing as he lay there on his back, his blood starting to pool around him on the floorboards. His second Dos Equis had rolled off the table and was upside down in his lap, gushing yellow foam, mixing with the blood, making the liquid orange. Blood jetted from his left elbow joint in gruesome arterial gushes.

The trick with the gun, it seemed, was to keep it

from launching toward the ceiling when you shot it.

Reese was trying to get up, making guttural noises of effort. With one arm gone and needles of glass sticking out of his forehead, he fought to lift himself, watching her as she stepped closer. There was no fear in his eyes. If there was any expression, it was that of a robot who dumbly tries to complete a programmed task as more and more of its parts fall off. His breath husked in and out, becoming labored.

The gun trembled in Cass' raw and throbbing hands. He was halfway up, sitting now, reaching for her. She became aware that she was murmuring under her breath in a nonstop litany.

"Stop it . . . *stop* . . . stop it . . ."

It looked as though Reese had been bashed in the side of the head with a meat-tenderizing hammer. His ear was pulp. Cass thought she could see a white bit of skull exposed to the air. He chocked a boot under himself and leaned forward.

". . . stop breathing . . . stop . . ."

He looked at his left arm, which ended at the elbow. No reaction. He looked at her. She saw in his eyes what he wanted for her. His right hand stretched toward her, a bloody claw.

". . . stop . . . bleed to death . . . stop . . . *die, god-damn you, Reese!*"

One more shot reverberated through the forest, quieting the chatter of the birds. Then stillness.

Except for the gentle sobbing.

19

GULLS TRIED TO TILT INTO the buffeting wind, and gusts hurled them around like so many scraps of dirty white paper. As the day had darkened, it had turned surly and hostile. A gale-force storm had blown in with the dusk, soaking everything in mist, stinging the eyes and ears with the chill. The sea churned, shifting itself massively and pounding the beachfront with vast, frothing breakers. Here and there a lone vehicle—a municipal safety rig, or highway patrol blazer, or some hapless, behind-schedule traveler—inched its way south against the hurricane of motive force, motor grinding with strain, door and window seals leaking.

He was a free man.

The realization replayed for the millionth time in less than twenty-four hours. Free. And, as Burt Kroeger undoubtedly would have added, exonerated. Free. And forced at last to admire the fortuity of absolute coincidence, free to concede the existence of luck, as a rational man would have to under such circumstances.

Pain still ossified his hands. Steering the Bronco

against the whipping wind trying to shove it off the road was a necessary torture. His leg fought the accelerator the way his hands fought the wheel. It shot pain through the roof of his head in regular tick-tock jolts. His kneecap had been crowbarred off and nailed back into position with a rusty cement spike. The backbeat of pain made his complexion look drained and cheesy in the green glow of the dashboard telltales. His stare was fixed, his jaw clamped, as he made slow but inexorable meatgrinder progress toward home base at a careful forty miles per hour.

The storm had puffed up a while back, scouring the tarmac with its violence. The Bronco's wipers strobed erratically in the splattering pellets of rain, which rendered the roadway nearly invisible.

By comparison, the desert night had been too warm, arid and stifling, making him sweat profusely, making his pores weep from exhaustion and depletion and the fear he hated to see in himself. Dehydrating him spiritually as well as physically. Never had the security of his cabin seemed so out of reach as it had the evening of the 'Gasm concert, when the foremost thought in his brain had been—

I've finally lost my mind, I've slipped all the way down the trough into gibbering madness.

Sometimes time defies its own rules and elongates. For one achingly clear second, the Kristen nightmare had not only come back, it had become real and true. As the tale spun out, he watched it like some vagrant astral spirit dispassionately monitoring the hell suffered by its recently vacated physical shell. In that cruel moment, he had looked up—and seen *himself* strafing 'Gasm to shreds with a machine gun. And that sight had scared the marrow right out of his bones.

But it had not been himself. Of course. That would be . . . well, crazy.

It had been someone else, another man with another mission. An insane mission. Lucas remembered thinking, *Why, that nut is trying to scrag the whole bloody band!*

Pepper "Mad Max" Hartz's smoking white Fender Strat hits the stage and bounces, the screech of its feedback blanking out the popping report of automatic weapons fire. Band members Reichmann, Hartz, and Hicks get chopped down one two three. His own finger is still stalled on Dragunov's trigger after picking off Fozzetto. He sees gouts of yellow-white fire spitting from the muzzle of another weapon on the catwalk level, even with himself. In the flashbulb light of the discharges, he registers a single image of the attacker, legs splayed atop a girder, sweeping his weapon back and forth. Then his own feet move him from the scene, pronto. 'Gasm never gets to perform "Cock Knock."

Had he actually seen Kristen in the crowd? No—that had to be dismissed as a hallucination.

He runs, fast yet cautiously, and through the catwalk grids he sees, in a blur, dozens of faces turning from the stage to the ceiling of the Arena. Almost at once comes the cattle panic of bodies compelled to flee and meeting the resistance of fellow bodies in the lethal illogic of the mob. He only has a second to think of this before he is tearing away the mesh screen of the duct through which he invaded the amphitheater. Then a brief, furious period of crabbing awkwardly along on hands and knees, needing more speed and feeling the panic he had felt in Denver when Brion Hardin had almost refused to die. The fear tries to wrap him up in its arms and squeeze. The riot noise behind him cycles down as he gains distance. Blindly, he shoves away the curling flap of metal that served as his breach point. He gashes his palm and hits the graveled tar of the roof. The Dragunov skids ahead of him like a broomstick as he rolls. It doesn't discharge from impact, as he fears. He is gasping now, terror sliding in and out of his lungs and rawing them with the hot, dry air of the Arizona desert.

A deep, murky puddle exploded upward on the left as Lucas plowed the Bronco through it. It was not much of a distraction from the pain of his wounds and the infuriatingly slow countdown of green posted mileage signs. There were still twenty miles to traverse. He was alone on the road.

Yesterday, the problem had been too much traffic.

Below the fire escape ladder are maybe ten cops, milling around, just beginning to ask what has occurred inside the Arena. In ten more seconds they'll catch the drift. He yanks his grapple and climbing line from the nylon slipcase and runs full-tilt for the opposite end of the roof. Less light there. If a police whirlybird has been called in, its spotlight can still nail him like a butterfly on a board. Like Pepper "Mad Max" Hartz. He hears push-bar exit doors crash open below. A stream of shouting and running people is unleashed. Most will remain inside to bungle the cops, to gape, to be part of the Event. He thumbs the release, and the tri-clawed grapple snaps open. He slips it through a square rain vent and unfurls the thin nylon line over the side. It hangs straight between two pools of diffused lighting from decorative standards at ground level. He sleeves the Dragunov in its black pouch and digs for his gloves. They aren't there.

At first he had thought, *Oh, yes, the gloves weren't in the dream, that's why.* Perhaps his alter ego on the opposite catwalk had borrowed them. Then he realized those notions were crazy, too.

No time for panic. He zippers the pouch shut and loops the strap over his shoulder. He kicks his leg over the lip of the roof, into the void, and begins to rappel down the coarse brick surface of the wall without looking. And without gloves, on the thin nylon cord. People are beginning to fill up the parking lots in the distance as he hangs heavy on the line. He is a vague shadow against a dark wall. The stiff toes of his boots brace agreeably against the abundance of toeholds on the wall. He feels a tiny spark of relief that this might not be impossible after all. Not that he really has any choice. He who hesitates is busted.

The damned gloves were probably still up there on the catwalk. They'd dropped out of the pouch while he was fiddling with the rifle in the gloom. It made him feel sloppy and stupid; here was his first accidental clue for the sleuths. The gloves were leather, traction-palmed and calf-lined. They'd carry finger oil but no prints. It wasn't good enough. Two successes had made him careless, and it had taken no time at all for him to—

Slip.

His foot misses a perch, and he yaws heavily to the left after only five downward steps. The line yanks taut and skins his palm like a wire cheese cutter, laying wide the incision made by the ducting just a moment before. A bark of pain dies in his throat, and he clamps both fists shut on the line. Three feet greases through and comes up dark red before his plunge is aborted. He hangs dumbly, legs splayed to keep him from twirling, since the line is not belayed from below. With slices of flesh and pattering droplets of blood he buys several more crucial feet, then his friction checks out for the night. Agony flares in both hands, and he releases the line, lurching vertiginously out from the wall, into space. Picking up speed. The ground gets bigger. About the same amount of time as a dive from the high board. Air rushes past his ears as he plummets. He tries to tuck and roll as his boots thud into the turf. He hears the fresh carrot crunch of his right knee dislocating on impact. This time he screams into the crook of his arm. Nobody notices him. He scrambles into the darkness, back against the wall, terror oiling him from top to bottom. This is no time for wimping. The adrenaline is making him ill; his breath speeds in and out. He grits his teeth and kicks out to reset the kneecap. This time the sound is the crack of dry kindling. The pain is utterly fantastic; it makes him forget his bleeding hands for a second, and, weirdly, he hears the jingling of the two spent cartridge casings inside the box taped to the Dragunov.

He had tossed his knee out several times in his life. Each time it was about ten days before he could stop walking funny. Now his leg was bitching that gas pedal duty was just too goddamned much to ask. The cure for the hurt had been an even worse hurt. His knee was black and swollen. Before the storm, he had tried to glean some information from the radio news. He had seen the face of his alter ego last night, on Tucson's *News on Nine*, thinking perhaps he should sue KGUN-TV for defamation of character.

The only person he encounters while limping back to the hotel is a wino, loitering on the tiled patio of a mercantile adjunct to the Holiday Inn called La Placita Village. It is a short walk from here to the Community Center, something Lucas had factored into his plan. The wino looks exactly like the ones he had ignored in Denver. He sits with his feet in the pool of a novelty fountain that only operates during business hours. He has pissed in the pool, and his coat front is caked with vomit. He stinks of sour alcohol and hydrochloric acid. He laughs at Lucas and mumbles something in Spanish.

He recalled thinking that he probably looked worse than the wino, and even though his vision was spotting and he could barely stand, his universe fuzzing apart, then reestablishing in near-total blackout, he could not let any of the hotel employees see—and remember—his state.

The wino laughs as he gimps onward. Come back and shoot the motherfucker later, he thinks. Later. He peeks through the patio entrance to the hotel, then edges through the glass door with his rifle bow-slung, shapeless in its sleeve. He whangs into the door and draws a few fazed titters from the lounge. There is a stairwell door that permits him to bypass the lobby and any more questioning glances. He feels like Sisyphus, clopping up seven flights of stairs one by one, acrid bile crawling up his throat at the same pace. In the room he stays on his feet long enough to gobble painkillers—the same ones he'd given to Cass —and wrap his hands in damp hotel-issue towels. He wakes up facedown on the bed five hours later, rolling over and staring into the recap of the ten o'clock news. The towels have grown pink with juice.

The Bronco's cab windows seemed to melt under the onslaught of the high-velocity rainfall. Beyond them, the ocean seethed and swirled, inviting fast death, anxious to wash over its borders and come to a boiling point. Ten more miles . . . then Cass could nurse him, for a change.

His original plan had been to shovel out a final resting place for the Dragunov on the roadside somewhere between San Francisco and Point Pitt. The storm and the uselessness of his hands had erased that idea. It was too agitated out there to stop at El Granada and heave it off the jetty. Disposal of the evidence would have to wait. It seemed an acceptable risk, more sane than his previous slips. Even if they noticed the difference in caliber between the slugs that holed Fozzetto and those that took down the rest of the band, the guys hunting for the mystery gun would be a time-zone distant. Perhaps they weren't bothering to search or to mess with lab workups, since they thought they had the killer in custody. His alter ego. Perhaps they wouldn't see the gloves or consider their importance.

But there was still the nylon line, dangling from the north end of the arena, stiff with Lucas' blood. He'd had to ditch at least five blood-saturated towels (they weren't dry and were too many to burn discreetly). People had taken notice of his injured hands. Even innocent notice was too much attention. The Holiday Inn staff would remember that "John Case" had slipped away without officially checking out, the day after the tragedy. Maybe the predators clogging the hotel's lounge would recall the man walking headfirst into the closed glass door. Maybe they had seen blood.

A double baker's dozen slips, on this job.

The color on the room TV is cockeyed. The hawk-faced man on the screen has a chartreuse face and dayglo orange tufts of ear hair. His American Gothic go-to-meetin' suit is obviously black, but it swims with poisonous rainbow patterns, like the moire of an oil slick. With the suit he wears combat boots. An aging urban middle-class country punk? He flashes the video news crews a peace sign from within a ring of six Pima County sheriffs who aren't laughing. The cuffs, linked to a steel waistband, restrict the man's reach as he is escorted away. The voice-over labels him a "right-wing fundamentalist." His story, told by robotic, blown-dry news mannequins (one for each local station) is "a simple one."

Eldon Quantrill, of Clifton, Arizona, enthusiastically noted for the record that he was a close personal friend of both the ghetto-blaster pastor who'd engineered the abortive book burning on the patio of the Tucson Community Center and of the voodoo-obsessed Falwell clone Lucas had seen on the same TV screen the previous night. Each of these worthies disowned Eldon with hot blushes of embarrassment when a TV camera was shoved into their faces for comment. This upset Eldon's kilter not a particle. Such rejection, he said, was another facet of his lifelong penance.

What penance? he was immediately asked. Lucas thought old Eldon was a lot more canny than he let on. He played the news media like a fiddle from the first.

God, it seemed, had instructed Eldon. God had told Eldon what needed to be done. God had told him to do it using his trusty M-16 and home-loaded mercury-tipped ammunition—poison bullets left Satan that much less leeway. Eldon did as he was told. Any devout man would have, but Eldon was eager to atone for his past. He obeyed God because it was God who had marked him with a large, ungainly facial mole that sprouted thick white bristles as punishment for having carnal knowledge of his farm mother at age fourteen. "Knowing her," as Eldon put it. Now, at age fifty-two, he was still trying to make up for that sinful goof . . . or rather, those eight sinful goofs over a one-month hell of gracelessness. Since that grand yet troublesome time, in the final year of the Second World War—(Eldon's father had bitten the big one at Anzio Beach, thus his mother's distress) —Eldon had tried to keep himself pure and await a Sign. The Sign had finally come via God's instrument on earth, television, in the divine form of the *Old Time Gospel Hour,* which Eldon watched religiously. It had been Father Dunbrille's words less than twenty-four hours prior to the 'Gasm date that snapped everything into focus, and Eldon did not hesitate to exercise his Second Amendment rights and mow down that godless zoo of pagan troglodytes who suckled the Devil's bilious teat, unquote and exclamation point! His path was clear.

Police, attorneys, and professional interrogators would unearth reams of such trivia during Eldon's intense and protracted debriefing. The investigation would ultimately consume a six-figure sum in man hours and squandered taxpayer dollars, all because one of the cops had asked Eldon if he had any knowledge of the similar incidents in Denver and San Francisco.

"Why, certainly, shorty," Eldon said with a grandfather's jaunty grin. "His will be done. You just tote that microphone back over here, and I'll tell you all about God's plan to eliminate that Gabriel Stannard guy, next."

Eldon Quantrill remained a darling of the media for about two weeks before the truth became known, the ratings dropped, and audiences moved on to seek other diversions.

And Lucas was a free man.

Stannard was the Whip Hand member in whom Lucas had the most interest. His plan had been to let the singer wilt on the vine, mulling over the deaths of his former comrades for a long, destructive time. Let paranoia erode his life. Let him fear imminent death for years; poke him, prod him regularly, keep Eldon Quantrill's devout fear of a god singing high in his veins. Eldon's holy inspiration had come along at just the right moment to make Lucas consider altering his plan. Call it luck, he thought. Call it divine intervention.

It had been common sense, not a magnificent constitution, that had denied Lucas the services of Tucson doctors. His blood, on the nylon rope, would be discovered eventually. It had been luck that had let him choke down enough room service protein to permit his damaged body to catch his outbound flight on time, with bandaged mitts and a noticeable limp and another suitably opaque alias. All luck.

His muscles burned mordantly, particularly the hamstrings behind his knees and the bundles on the inside thighs connected to the groin—pectineus, adductor longus, gracilis. The tension of maintaining uncomfortable, stressful positions on the roof, in the air vents, and on the catwalks for hours had caused sweat to flood out of him. He had lost seven pounds last night, and today he hurt. He hoped the pain also meant that he was on the mend.

Despite the slithering lime chips and rainstorm mudslides, the Bronco valiantly billygoated its way up the slope to the cabin. The idea of stumping up the hill in the storm and the dark held no attraction. When his lights finally splashed across the face of the cabin, he tooted the horn twice and dismounted carefully. Icy sleet stung his face. But he was not in pain anymore.

She almost started shooting out the front window without thinking at all, like an Al Capp cartoon hillbilly filling a trespassing "revenoor" full of rock salt. If Lucas' former wifey and her bulldog-faced lawyer wanted to harass her in the dead of night, let them swallow some lead hospitality. She had major problems to solve before she could be sociable, or even snide.

Thank Christ or Allah or whoever was in charge for this good storm, she thought. Rain could rinse away so much.

She had fled. She had run as fast as she could downhill, toward the coast road, because her body needed to flee. It had been straining to run ever since Reese had come axe first through the cabin door like the ghost of Jack the Ripper. *Hi, puss.* That awful whisper of his had been the charnel sound of graves and gallows. It could make snakes shudder.

Run!

At the bottom of the hill, back in the real world, her brain had decided to check back in. She found Reese's Datsun, hidden in a stand of brush and camouflaged to be undetectable from the road. She smashed the driver's side window to silver-faceted dust with a stone. There was no way in hell she was going back to the cabin to dig through Reese's pockets for keys. The monster might open his eyes and seize her wrist with his teeth.

Her saddlebag purse was still in the back, most of its contents mingled into the sleeping bags and camping gear. Reese had sacked it, taken fifty in cash, and ignored the rest. Her favorite hairbrush was MIA. Damn—of all things, he would have to lose that. . . .

What astonished her the most was not dropping the gun after she and it had sung their duet. Horrified heroines *always* dropped the gun, especially after it fired. She had clutched it as she ran, a heavy metal throttle to steer her mad flight. Its solidity, its presence would make returning to the cabin a lot easier.

She found Reese still capsized in a wide pool of tacky blood, his position unchanged. Maybe he did not require a stake through the heart. She stood and looked at the corpse for a long time, as day shaded into twilight.

It was hours before she actually crossed the room, to touch it.

She had been certain that Reese would be gone. That she would return to find a pool of blood and no body. *It's Friday the thirteenth, and Jason Voorhees never dies, not really*. And now that she saw the body, she was equally certain that it would roll over, grinning and hungry, capture her in a rape both physical and spiritual, and drain away her life force like some weird paranormal leech.

Reese remained very dead as she dragged him out the back door by one leg. The dark swath of semicoagulated blood left in his wake reminded her of the wide water trails left by street-cleaning machines. The body seemed to gain two hundred pounds in death—another of Reese's little jokes. *Just try to move me, puss*.

She stripped the tarps from Lucas' lumber stack and shrouded the body, partially to obscure the fact that this lump was a dead body, but mostly to kill her fear that those inhuman metal eyes were going to snap open while her back was turned. She weighted down the corners of the tarp with firewood, fighting to quell the voices in her head.

You have to bury them before they can rise from the dead.

She backed away, sneaking glance after glance at the unmoving lump.

In a perverted burlesque of dull routine, she restored the interior of the cabin to normal. Try this: Just ignore the fact that the mess you're scraping up is shell casings, an exploded TV, and moist body parts. Ignore the fact that you're doing it with a roscoe stuffed in your coveralls, and your heart is stopping at every tiny noise. Ignore the fact that when you mop, you're mopping up blood and tissue. To mop, she had to use the sink, and to use the sink meant lifting Reese's arm out of it, hoping madly that the fingers did not close on any part of her while she did it.

She worked methodically, with an utter lack of expression.

Thank hell I got the body out before it started to . . . uh, stink. What if animals smell it and wander down to snack? What if Lucas' wife—ex-wife—and the lawyer saw Reese? Why haven't they come back? Maybe I could put Reese into the Datsun; drive the Datsun into the sea?

I wish you were here, Lucas. Luke.

When she checked Reese again, he was still dead. Her insides finally began to uncoil.

She thought of Reese's grizzly bears, making themselves known at last, closing a circle. Then the cleansing storm had rolled in and cleared up that qualm. She was inside, where it was warm and safe and there were food and weapons, and Reese . . . Reese was *outside*.

While neatening up, she made a conscious effort not to nose into what Reese had called *sugar daddy's big secret*—the room with the invitingly skewed door. Certainly Lucas' big secret was not the Trinitron. That caused laughter to jump from her, a bit too shrilly: *My big secret is that I'm a vidiot, Cass. Forgive me. I have to watch* Green Acres *reruns. I have no choice*. The portable Sony had been the first thing Reese had spotted. He'd pulled it out to show her, then tried to kill her with it.

The tapedeck had been supplied by Lucas from that room, too. He'd been perfectly nonchalant about it. Maybe he was a fence for stolen electronic gear?

The tapedeck/radio was most welcome. It supplied blissful noise while she did her dirty work in the cabin. It would also hide the sound of Reese crawling in through the back door, wobbling, homicidal, like the limbless killer in *Freaks*, squirming toward his victim in the dark with a knife clenched in his teeth, an undulating human snake, another monster that came while it was raining. . . .

Stop it!

Pulling in radio stations was difficult in these hills. She endured the static just to hear snatches of live, human voices elsewhere in the world as she picked up bits of TV and wiped blood off the counter and invented self-conscious busywork to keep her eyes from seeking the secret room again.

She finally ran out of domestic chores.

The first thing Reese had noticed was the Sony TV set. Cass lifted one of the Coleman kerosene lanterns inside, and the first thing she noticed (eyes widening with a horrific alternate scenario to the carnage of that afternoon) was the M-16. It lay on the floor, its black stock poking from beneath the workbench. It must have been leaning against the table, must have slipped and fallen while Reese was axing the door. The sight of it froze her. Her eyes saw Reese brandishing the rifle like a scepter of doom, filling her with perhaps twice the bullets needed to kill her. Saw Reese raping her spasming corpse, then venturing into the forest to blast trees and slaughter anything that rustled in the leaves. And laughing, all the while laughing, as his chromium eyes sought new things to kill.

If Reese had not seen her holding the pistol, he would have turned back and seen the M-16 . . . and Cass would never have had to worry about cleaning up.

She put down the lantern and clicked on a Tensor light on the workbench. It was an M-16, yes. It had some kind of huge, bulbous scope on top. It seemed almost weightless; it felt made of plastic, toylike. She put the obscene thing down on the table. Here was a poster of some rockstar. A big hole was gouged in his paper belly. Here was a stack of albums and tapes, but no turntable. Lucas had mentioned an affection for rock 'n' roll, as a kind of anti-cliché for his generation. Here were nondescript boxes and memo pads and the mess caused when Reese had yanked the TV out of the nucleus of its webwork of wires. Facedown on the card table was a gold 5x7 picture frame, its stiff cardboard foot sticking up like the stabilizer on a jet plane. It was the sort of frame anyone could pick up at Thrifty Drug for family snaps, prom-night shots.

Cass tilted the photograph into the minuscule circle of work light. It was a young girl, a teenager with straight blond hair and a bitter little smile, a smile somehow too cynical for such a youthful, unblemished face. The brownish-green eyes seemed very old. A curving diagonal fracture in the glass divided the girl's head from her silken blouse; the picture had struck the corner of a cassette case while falling. Thanks again, Reese.

She eased into the chair; it was reminiscent of settling into the cramped cockpit of a jet, with the equipment and gear all around. The closeness of walls in the smaller room was comforting. She stood Kristen's picture in the light and contemplated it for a long time.

The axe was still cocked against the doorframe where Reese had left it. The kitchen table could probably be repaired, but attempting that was beyond her right now. On the counter, the tapedeck radio lost the Stockton radio station Cass had nailed. Its feeble beep fuzzed out to pure static, courtesy of the storm. Getting San Francisco was impossible this far south, under these conditions, but a broadcast from San Jose or Santa Cruz might seep through the mountains. She would have to try AM next.

The ritual of preparing coffee was also soothing to her. When the pot was on she fiddled with the radio some more and caught an all-nighter news hook-up in midsentence concerning something called "the 'Gasm concert tragedy" in Tucson, Arizona.

Just as a chain of facts linked up for her, with the dizzying suddenness of a freeway smashup, she looked up to see the afterburn of headlights flashing across the cabin's front window.

20

"—HIS WILL BE DONE! YOU just tote that microphone back over here, and I'll tell you all about God's plan to eliminate that Gabriel Stannard guy, next!"

"No more," Sertha said sternly, and reached across Stannard to touch the remote control. The video image of Eldon Quantrill blinked out on the large video-beam screen. It was a considerably better image than that pulled in on Lucas Ellington's hotel TV; here, Quantrill was all the right colors. Stannard had videotaped the news coverage of his arrest and all subsequent updates. He had one of the mansion's maids sitting in a room in the west wing, right now, watching television, poised to record anything new. If he monitored the news himself, he'd miss the Porky and Daffy hour at four o'clock.

Stannard's eyes remained on the blank gray screen. "I've got all the puzzle pieces," he said. "I just don't want to miss anything obvious, lover. I've gotta be ready when my time comes."

"I don't understand." Trying to appear helpless to elicit his sympathy—and get a sensible explanation —would not work; she knew him that well. His behavior had become scary. At least when he had acted like a victimized child she felt a maternal protectiveness. That haunted look was gone now. The color was high in his face, but the price had been the bright, almost glazed aspect she now saw in his ice-blue eyes. It was a little like the expression she'd seen in Eldon Quantrill's eyes as Stannard replayed the videotape over and over—that look of righteous certainty. Like the certainty of a Salem inquisitor that you must be a witch, for example.

Her eyes ached, and her neck was sore. Why was she so tired all the time? It had become a draining ordeal for all of them, but she could not escape the impression that Stannard was psychically vampirizing them all to feed his newfound purpose and keep the light in his eyes burning brilliantly.

She finished her cigarette with a sigh of smoke. "I'm going to take a hot bath. I'm sore all over."

There was nothing on the screen. Stannard watched it anyway, barely glancing back at her. "Have Horus give you a rubdown with his infamous collection of oils."

At the threshold of the master bathroom she paused. "I'd rather it'd be you putting your hands all over me. . . ."

He grunted. "Maybe later."

She closed the door, relieved at the definite sound of the latch clicking shut. This, too, was new—she generally bathed with the door open, so Stannard could wander in and out as he pleased, which pleased her even more. She twisted the hot taps in the tiled Roman tub full on and let steam mist the mirrors so she wouldn't have to consider the ravaged state of her body.

Nude, she was angular and graceful, with an unmistakable thoroughbred hauteur. Her long, contoured legs had helped make her internationally famous. Her dark eyes, her flood of dark hair, made warm promises to the world at large. Now her hipbones seemed to jut out; her belly seemed sunken instead of flat. Her breasts hung, looking out of proportion to the anorexic state of her body. Her hair had lost luster, her eyes humanity. Her fine, slim feet looked bony and old, roped with blue veins.

She lowered herself into the simmering suds and felt her skin drink up the bath oil. Time for repairs to commence.

Sertha closed her eyes. Long black lashes—her own, not cosmetic fakes—drifted down to blot out the world. First, she thought, the drink. It was a mess of juices and protein powder and blenderized calf's liver and other disgusting gook her doctor had invented for her. Then a lot of steam and some time on the Uva-Sun table; some passive electronic exercise followed by a light workout in Stannard's impressive weight room. Laps in the pool. Then she could insinuate herself with the kitchen staff, to construct her own special salads.

Horus seemed to have twice the number of muscle cables in his arms as a normal human being. She thought of the delicate interplay of those tendons and ligatures, all working in concert to squeeze the fatigue out of her body. It was pleasant, not frightening, as her halting consideration of Stannard's recent personality shift had been. She did not desire to have sex with Horus, though Stannard understood he had no right to protest if she ever did. To be sure, it would be an adventure, but she had long ago opted to spare herself the hassle. When dear Gabriel did not get his way, or disliked another person's decision, he was capable of acting like the most monumentally spoiled brat in the cosmos.

Perhaps it was because he *was* a child, she thought —an overly pampered one, used to getting his way. He hated arguing fidelity with her, because it was a rule for grownups. The concept of faithfulness to one woman was, for him, a chore above and beyond the call of his profession. Part of the baggage of his chosen public persona was the parade of women—most of them girls, really—convinced that their lives would gain new meaning, and their hanger-on careers in the lightning-strike field of rock 'n' roll cemented, if only they spread their legs for Gabriel Stannard and partook of the power he represented. He handled this pressure ably—that is, he paid it next to no attention. Most couplings with his fans were restricted to sordid one-nighters in hotels while on tour. He told Sertha of needing such women only as steam valves for the pressure of the road, as a sexual analgesic. Horus was always there to hand last night's bimbette cab fare and usher her out of the Presence Magical.

But the first time Sertha had accompanied him on the concert circuit, she had seen the cheated look in his eyes a hundred times. She resented being the villainess who had locked this jaunty child out of his candy store. Later, he had admitted to her that too much candy was never good for a kid, and she smiled. He smiled back. For a moment it was all genuine. He was capable of a mature attitude, but generally only for brief bursts. He was one of those men who always wanted whatever someone in authority told him he could not have. Sooner or later he would begin to resent the lack of new flesh, and Sertha would catch the flak.

She knew the extent to which it was all part of his job. Calculated. Even the Beatles admitted to forming a band, at first, to "meet birds."

When Sertha had been introduced, she had barely known he was a musician, although his wardrobe had tipped it instantly. He was fascinated by the concept that someone could *not* know who he was on sight. Naturally, she was not from this country. She was not blinded by his light. And he came after her with the ardor of a stable boy setting sights on a princess.

Sertha wondered if the great passions of history had ever sat down to round-table the terms of their "relationship." He was not only childlike as well as childish, but like a narcotic—a golden, delicious drug, so pleasant to take and oh so difficult to resist. His charm could knock down her defenses like two double shots of vodka and sneak up on her in exactly the same way. Whenever she mustered and rehearsed the complaints that needed airing between them, he used his uncanny power to wipe them from her brain with a mystic pass, a perfect smile, a flash of heat from those ice-blue eyes, and the fine music his body could make against hers.

And she had let him get away with it, times beyond measure. That was how good he was. But when she had looked in the bathroom mirror—actually *looked*, without lying to herself—she was forced to acknowledge that her vitality was somehow being leached away . . . and the most obvious suspect loomed large, with his ability to send blood rushing to her groin and fog to mist her brain, blotting out her little dissatisfactions. He was tapping her battery to keep the embers of his hate banked. He was stealing her heat and replacing it with none of his own. It was not the empathic transfer of energy she resented, it was the lack of compensation. Up until the events the press had labeled the Whip Hand Murders, Sertha had always gotten something back from her best lover.

She could hear his voice in the next room as she simmered in the king-bed-sized tub. His words were unclear, but his tone told her he was busy sandwiching new layers onto his budding scheme of vengeance. She thought of what all that energy could do if it was channeled in her direction, applied toward keeping and pleasing her.

She regretted recognizing the progression so easily. She had seen it before. Sex had become unimportant to Gabriel because he had discovered a new karmic vitamin. But the thing fueling him now was tainted, poisonous, ultimately fatal. That was the part he had not yet tasted. Basking in the healing heat of the tub, Sertha asked herself how much of the responsibility for saving him was hers.

She stepped out of the tub and belted herself into a lush black terry robe, to hold in the warmth pulsing from her. Her damp hair hung untoweled. When she cracked the door, steam wisped out around her. Stannard was still talking.

When she thought she might redirect his concentration so that he could become as hung up on her as she was on him, it gave her strength. "Love," she said. "I was nose-deep in the tub when I suddenly thought of two places. The Bahamas. And Europe. Suddenly I began plotting, and a lot of possibilities jumped up. The Paine villa is empty right now; they're friends of mine, and we could move right in . . ."

Sertha became aware that she was addressing an empty room. The big bed was cold, and the videotape deck was running. The tape chilled her down immediately.

It was *Hollywood Weekend Wrap-Up*, playing again.

The perverted parlance of America's so-called news programs had always confused her. No news report needed more than five minutes to impart its information, yet on television there was no such thing as a five-minute timeslot. In Southern California the malady of news overload was acute. The four o'clock hour bled into the five o'clock hour, which segued into the six o'clock hour, which was updated at eleven and repeated at one-thirty in the morning. Almost none of it was essential information. It was cluttered with sports scores, the cult of local personality, and time-wasting "human interest" features about people you would cross the street to avoid in real life. And that was the key—none of this represented life as Sertha knew it.

The entertainment industry programs stole their

format from the news shows but banked on sensationalism to an even more extreme degree. They were the *National Enquirer*s of the airwaves—bright, glossy, fast forward, and empty of caloric value. They were hosted by blown-dry, vapid nonentities, all acting hopefuls who craved advancement via the art of the million-buck smile. One of the worst of these minicircuses of disinformation and thinly veiled advertising come-ons was *Hollywood Weekend Wrap-Up*.

Buzz words were lifeblood to such programs, and the Whip Hand Murders buzzed loudly indeed.

The phone had rung until even Stannard's attorneys had advised him that some sort of statement, some minimal public exposure, might be a good idea. Don't make the public think you're hiding, they told him. That perked up the hunter-killer in him, and a *Hollywood Weekend Wrap-Up* van was soon dispatched to the Stannard estate, bearing an anchorperson with a fierce smile, fabulous legs, and the dead hiss of deep space between her ears. Her name was Mardi Grassley, and the first question she asked Gabriel Stannard was, "Do you feel that rock music has caused the deaths of your fellow former band members?"

Stannard's uncoached response was deleted by unanimous decision in the editing booth.

Take two.

"That's a simplistic charge." His annoyed sigh spiked VU meters in the van. The background noise could be sweetened later. Everything could.

"It avoids the issue," he said. "It's like making you responsible for the guy who watches *Hollywood Weekend Wrap-Up* just to see your legs so he can whack off. And believe me, your producers make sure viewers can see *lots* of your legs, Mardi, during those phony reaction shots you guys pretape to stick into the interviews later."

A fascinating social insight, but too complex for

Mardi's viewership. And you couldn't say "whacking off" in prime time.

The musical segment of the program was called *Rock Wrap*. Stannard had seen himself on it numerous times in the past. It had previewed the new video of "Maneater." Perhaps someone at the studio had done some elementary addition after seeing it, and that was why Mardi Grassley's crew was all over his front lawn now. Stannard found himself constitutionally incapable of hiding from their cameras.

He had seen Mardi Grassley's legs before and could see them now. They were wondrous fine. A strategic advantage. It was easy to imagine her in a leather teddy, assuming positions you'd never hear discussed on *Donahue*.

The most ironic aspect of the entire interview was that Mardi Grassley wanted to ride Stannard's boybone in the worst way. Maybe it was real lust, maybe just the latent physical promise she used to get a hook into interviewees, but either way Stannard felt the air grow dense with palpable sex vibes. Even this TV clone wanted him.

They let the tape grind, so he rattled on for a while about rock music and social responsibility. Blaming rock for sending misfits into berserk sprees, he said, was a criticism that people *outside the entertainment industry* had been leveling for years. He compared it to the buck passing that went on in education. Kids were stupid. Parents blamed schools. Schools blamed parents. So much finger pointing went on that the kids never got any help . . . but they sure as hell thought they knew who was responsible for fucking them up. Round and round. It all avoided the issue. Placing blame was no solution. And if there was a single person responsible for the Whip Hand Murders, what kind of upbringing did he have that permitted music to trigger him into homicide? Was the fact that Jessica Savitch was once held hostage by a crazed fan of her news show *her* fault—or her producer's, for the way in which she was presented?

Stannard put forth these points with effortless eloquence. He was doing what he was good at—controlling audiences.

None of it was used, and Grassley and company finally settled for splicing in a lot of reaction shots of Stannard. She theorized, he nodded. Closeups of Stannard meant a guaranteed viewership for *Rock Wrap*. It was not necessary for him to actually say anything.

What he told them became passionate, inflamed, potent, and utterly unusable. What they invented to fill the gaps was vapid, promotional, and by rote, like weather dialogue enhanced by steroids. Mind Chee-tos, thought Stannard. They looked like food, but when you crunched them you got nothing but orange scum on your teeth.

Mardi Grassley had played him. In person, she had been dripping for him; on tape, she had spun and bitten, with a challenge uncomfortably like the one Stannard had tossed down at the close of the "Maneater" video. Now Stannard had to shit or git . . . because everybody was looking at him now, and as usual, the watchers hungered.

Sertha saw it replay as she came out of the bathroom, realizing Stannard had lit off, taking his .44 Magnum with him. Steam uncoiled from her bare skin in the cooler air.

If Mardi Grassley's expression had been any more portentous, her face would have ruptured. She wound up in her most unctuous Rona Barrett mode. "So, the question remains: Is Gabriel Stannard, the macho bad boy of heavy metal, for real? Can he just stand idly by while his old comrades drop like targets in a shooting gallery, or is there enough fiber beneath the tough, strutting, and oh-so-safe stage persona to compel him into direct action? We expect no less from Gabriel

Stannard than for him to burst forth with six-guns blazing. This reporter isn't so sure anymore. Tell us, Gabriel: *Are* there any bullets left in your gun?

"This is Mardi Grassley, for *Rock Wrap*."

Her piranha smile dissolved into a freeze frame of Stannard's face above the caption WHIP HAND KILLER'S NEXT VICTIM?

Fade out. Commercial. Next segment. *Hollywood Weekend Wrap-Up* was incisive, penetrating, pushing the limits of hard-line investigative journalism.

"This cannot be healthy," Sertha said to the empty room.

The videotape ran varicolored static.

Sertha was not used to being unseen, unnoticed, or worse, ignored. The concern surprised her with its mundanity: Why could things not continue as they had before? This phase of her life had been amputated midway. Her mind naturally recoiled from the thought, the way the eyes recoil from a sudden bright light.

She might have to leave this place. Already she felt the tug; now she had to choose whether to acknowledge it.

She could not be more uninvolved. Stannard had locked her out.

She wondered how many of her things were here and how long they might take to pack, were she ever to think seriously of leaving.

"You guys look like a coupla dicks wearing shirts," Stannard smirked as he strode into the poolhouse.

Both men in the room, chocolate and vanilla, speared him with acid glances. To retort would be to rise to unwanted bait.

Cannibal Rex's serpent eyes flickered up to spray Stannard with caustic blood, then declined. *You're spared*, they said, *this time*. He finished working his gums with the lees of coke dusting his pinky finger—the pinky on his left hand, the hand on which he could still count to five. His bone earring jittered to and fro as he polished off the dope. His punctured Special Forces beret was discarded atop the long folding table next to all the hardware. Even though it was nearly night, he slid his radiation-proof wraparound shades back on. The only light inside the poolhouse, a dim forty-watter in a billiard shade, hung right over the table and the goodies arranged on it by Horus.

There was one other light source in the room. From the corner the "Maneater" video spun out on one of Stannard's army of 24-inch color TVs. Over and over again, Stannard and Cannibal Rex laid waste to the schoolroom set on the Chaplin stage. Each play of the video faded out on Stannard's face, filling the maw of the camera, repeating, *C'mon, bad man—take me down if you can.* The image on screen was replicated in the lenses of Cannibal Rex's shades; two hot points of cool fire in the dark.

Horus was draped loosely in his workout silks, a cacao-colored man in funeral black. He did look rather like an enormous black phallus wearing a shirt. All he would give Stannard by way of retort was, "You just wish you had a cock this perfect. But then, I know that you were circumcised as a tadpole, so it's difficult for me to believe you know anything about real dicks."

Cannibal snorted. Whether it was from the blow in his snoot or the gibe, no one could tell. His eyes were masked.

Stannard cracked a huge smile the moment he saw the gear on the table. Eagerly, he said, "What we got?"

Horus worked his way from one end of the table to the other, lifting and demonstrating.

"Okay. Exhibit A. We got your American 180—also called the Buck Rogers gun. Laser-sighted .22 caliber; empties a 177-round clip in five seconds. Lightweight. Recoilless. Police departments and government agencies use 'em. It's got a hit rate fifty percent higher than any other rifle ever tested. The laser concentrates the bullets onto the target. It's a battery-powered helium-neon job." He activated it, and a dot of red light the size of a pencil eraser skittered across Cannibal Rex's forehead. "At fifty feet the sighting dot is no bigger than a quarter; at six hundred feet it's three inches wide. The slugs can penetrate wood, concrete, car doors. Depending on how fast you reload, this thing can fire over 2000 rounds per minute."

Stannard nodded, a well-fed look in his eyes. Cannibal Rex belched and reached over to crack a fresh bottle of Jack Daniel's.

"This is a standard Auto Mag," said Horus as he picked up a large pistol. "I've had it blued to cut the reflection of the matte finish. Kicks just like Dirty Harry's revolver, except this is an auto pistol. They couldn't manufacture these until recently; the fire rate of an automatic caused parts of the gun to melt."

Stannard held a clip to the light. It was loaded with eight big 240-grain lead slugs. "Man, firing six of these mothers numbs my hand and nearly breaks my wrist. I think I'd rather stick to my revolver."

Horus shrugged. "The handgrip is too fat for you. The reload rate's too slow, even using speed loaders —great fun for the target range; not such fun when the target is you. Even urban police departments are beginning to admit that the revolver is a dinosaur. The bad guys watch *Miami Vice* and tote submachine guns. FBI stats say the average shootout consists of twenty-three rounds fired from seven feet in poor light. The six shots and awkward reload of your Magnum under firefight conditions aren't optimum. You told me you wanted the maximum advantage."

"Yeah, right." He dropped the clip back onto the stack. "What about the shotgun?"

Horus tapped it. "Italian SPAS autoloading riot

gun." It was an awesome weapon, with a fat slide, rectangular vents, a pistol grip, and a fixed stock. "Twelve-gauge rounds'll blow down a cinder block wall. Push this button and it converts to a pump—lets you clear a jam that would stop a normal auto shotgun cold." When Stannard hefted it by the pistol grip, Horus laid in with his qualifiers: "Another pain in the ass to reload. The reputation of a shotgun as an alley sweeper ain't all it's cracked up to be, either."

He moved on. "These are flash-pops, also known as stun grenades. Used well, they can immobilize an enemy you may not be able to see, with a *very* loud bang and a burst of bright light. Used badly . . . well, you get what those idiot sheriffs got at the Van Cleef and Arpel's shootout got, which was dead and scorched hostages."

"Move over, Arnold Schwarzenegger," said Stannard.

Cannibal Rex cracked into a parody of the body-sculpting star: "Ahh, ahh, ahh, be garful you don't blow abb!"

"More than this and we'll have too much crap to carry," said Horus. "And I, for one, think the idea of all this firepower is pussy."

"I like 'em," croaked Cannibal. "Pretty guns."

"Strictly backup, failsafe material," Stannard noted. "If it was my choice, I'd do the son of a bitch with my crossbow. But we gotta be ready in case we find him arsenaled in somewhere—that's the bottom line. And if you hate guns so much, how come you know so many statistics?"

Horus turned his mouth down. It should have been obvious that he preferred any endeavor to be executed well. If Stannard did not want expertise, he could have sent some amateur to do the job.

On the TV screen, Cannibal charged a large white Panavision camera and began to batter it with his Les Paul. Both camera and guitar began to splinter apart, hurling fragments. The sound on the TV was turned all the way down.

"The cops are too stupid to see they grabbed the wrong guy in Arizona," Stannard said. "But they'll catch on. In the meantime, Lucas Ellington is saving me for last. It'll all be old news by the time the cops do anything effective."

The nasty challenge of Mardi Grassley hovered about him, taunting and echoing.

"You don't know for a fact he's after you," Horus said.

"I don't need a bouquet and a card to tell me." He patted his left pectoral. "I know it in here. And if you can't understand that after spending all your spare time sunk to the upper lip in that Eastern mystical bullshit, then I can't explain it to you."

Cannibal Rex touched the three fingers of his picking hand to his sternum, nearly duplicating Stannard's motion. "When someone wants your blood," he said in that odd voice of his, "you know it. There ain't nothing else except to play it out." The cocaine had dried him out, and his voice sounded remarkably like a gas bubble in a tar pit.

"Whatever you say, bwana. We live but to serve. But I say again I think this is all hot fart wind." Horus folded his massive arms.

"If it is, then we've got nothing to worry about. That's what I mean by fail-safe. Josh is checking out the guy's shrink, the one from Olive Grove. I bet he'll check in with her sooner or later. Personally, I hope it's sooner—before the cops whiff the fact that their killer is still at large. That way it'll get done before they can muss things up—and I don't want a bunch of amateurs in my way."

"Amateurs, wow," snickered Cannibal Rex. He grabbed his beret from the table and mopped his shaven, scarred head with it.

"Seriously. The LAPD is one thing—those dudes are *professional* cops, rated the best metro police force in the country. But the hypos and sheriffs . . . shit, man, those morons got their jobs by 'calling the number on your screen.' They got their training by spending two years beating up prisoners in the county lockup. They're walking around out there with more hardware than anybody. They're the worst fucking gang in the whole city. And I don't want them in my way."

Horus released a huge breath. He had not determined whether there was karma to be balanced here or not. "I've spoken my words. You call it. We'll do it."

Cannibal Rex hoisted up the American 180 by the long, padded SIONICS silencer screwed onto the snubbed barrel. A stretch clip protruded from the grip. He worked the bolt and perched the gun against one forearm. "Yesss. Anyplace around here we can acid test this honey?"

"Basement." Horus nodded. "It's soundproofed."

"He's gotta see the video," Stannard said, noticing the TV set. "Once he sees the video, he'll know I'm after him. If he was planning to leave me alive, make me sweat, then maybe this'll force his hand. He'll have to try to take me out before I can do the same to him. Showdown time." He held the auto Mag end up into the light, popped the clip, and thumbed up one of the cartridges. He turned it between his fingers like a jewel.

"Target practice," said Cannibal Rex, up for it now. "Firepower! Crush, kill destroy!" He laughed, and Stannard joined him.

"You gentlemen start without me," Horus said. "Right now I've got to go put my hands all over your girlfriend."

Stannard's eyes did not waver from the gun. "Do whatever she needs," he said, as though Sertha was the furthest thing from his concern.

21

CASS UNBOLTED THE DOOR IN a clumsy rush, yanked Lucas into the cabin, and threw her arms tightly around him.

When he had called her name from outside, her fear had washed away and she had literally leapt for the door. Lucas caught many impressions in a finger-snap of time.

The echoes of her ordeal had made her newly healed face haggard, and he saw animal trepidation haunting her eyes as she pulled him in out of the rain. His Llama ACP pistol was in her right hand as she answered the door. The door to the Whip Hand room was battered to junk, the table was collapsed, there was blood dried on the floor. Lucas knew the dark stain was blood—no excuses. The air in the cabin hung thick with recent violence, and he felt the phobic dread that radiated from her as she clung to him, her face buried in the hollow of his neck. He tried numbly to still her shaking without using his crippled hands.

They stood that way for a while, the storm raging outside, as he spoke her name repeatedly and said other soothing, meaningless things in a succoring voice. The muttered nonsense helped distill some of the anxiety and pain; it solidified the bad feelings so they could be spat out and eliminated. It was a two-way exchange, though Cass was oblivious to this at first. By the time they settled down, Lucas himself was close to tears. They parted, looked into each other's eyes calmly, and Cass' mouth unhinged when she got her first good, rational look at what was left of him.

"Jesus *Christ*!" She saw his mummified hands, watched him list stiff-leggedly to the nearest unbroken chair.

"You first. I've got to—ahgh!—sit down." His leg gave up, and he landed heavily in the seat. He cleared his throat of the thick coating that impeded his voice. "God. You know, on top of everything else, I think my foot's asleep."

The coffee was on, and fresh, and they both needed it. Lucas was rapidly running out of pain pills. They dragged their chairs closer to the hearth, where it had taken Cass an hour to get a good fire going. Orange light illuminated them in flickering, shifting patterns as she wrapped one of his injured hands up in both of hers, carefully not squeezing.

"This day has been a million years long." She cleared her eyes with the sleeve of the merchant marine sweater, looking like a first-timer on the high-diving board. Then she took the plunge. "Reese came back after me. He found me. He's out back, now, behind the cabin. He's dead; I shot him with your pistol. He was going to kill me. I killed him. He broke into the locked room, looking for stuff to steal, and I found your gun in the kitchen drawer, and it jammed and I tried to shoot him and he ran at me with—"

"Calm, calm," Lucas said. "He's not here now. I am. Calm."

A nervous laugh rose and broke surface. "Almost became a runaway, didn't I? Damn it." She swallowed dryly. "I shot your television set. Pretty slapstick, huh? I blew away a TV set. Reese was going to bash my brains out with it." The enormity of her luck made her shake her head in dull awe. "I shot the TV, and then I shot Reese. How am I doing so far?"

"Just work your way through what happened. Nobody's going to land on your head tonight. Reese is . . . that is, his *body* is out back?"

"I covered it up. I was gonna bury it. I found his Datsun down at the bottom of the hill, hidden in the bushes."

"Anybody else around? Does anyone know he came up here, do you think?"

"Reese wouldn't tell anyone. He's a lone wolf. He went back to the city and beat up Jonathan pretty bad. Everything but my cash was still in the truck. Everything except my favorite hairbrush, which the son of a bitch probably threw away."

Lucas looked speculatively to the kitchen window. The storm hammered on. "No one is going to come snooping in this weather."

He lifted the .45 from the kitchen counter, slid out the clip, and thumbed up five slugs. Another shell jumped from the chamber when he snapped the action. His eyebrows went up. "Three shots? It should only take one bullet from this gun to put anybody away."

"Not Reese. And I missed the first time. I've never fired a gun in my life." She shut her eyes, segueing back. "I shot the TV. Then Reese. Twice."

"He must have been pretty close, if you shot him twice and never fired a gun before."

"Point-blank, as they say in the cop movies. Another second and he'd've noticed that nasty-looking M-16 you've got stashed in there."

Lucas' eyes darted to the Whip Hand room, then back. "But he didn't. Look . . . I'll do something about the body when the rain eases up. Maybe Reese and his truck can disappear into the good old *Mar Pacifica*. That sort of thing isn't unheard of, not in storms like this." He had no way of knowing that this was exactly the option Cass had considered, but her reaction to the suggestion was acquiescence, almost resignation, and not the queasy discomfort he expected to see. He had, after all, just proposed ditching the corpse of a murder victim.

Cass sat grinding her teeth, eyes focused on the floor. "I would not enjoy dealing with a whole platoon of nosy cops," she said at last. "Or laying out everything that happened, in detail, over and over. Or blowing more of my life than I already have on Reese. All it would gain me is more grief. No, not for him." She wrung her hands. "As far as I'm concerned, Reese went into the forest and never came out. Besides, I get the feeling that the police are the last people you want poking around up here."

"Why?" Lucas was aware that he was playing games, that he should just be straight with her. But what harm could paying out a little more rope do now? Let's see what she says.

"The stuff in that room over there. The stuff I've heard on the radio about the members of an old rock band called Whip Hand. A room full of weapons and a poster of the lead singer with his gut torn out. Two plus two. I hate to be chill, Lucas, and I hate to rope you in regarding Reese . . . but what I saw in that room looks awfully incriminating to me."

He sat, evaluating her. His unblinking assessment was too much like Reese's flat lizard gaze.

"Lucas, listen to me: I don't *care* one way or the other! It all has something to do with Kristen; it's what you wouldn't talk about before." She moved closer, trying to touch his injured hands gently. "I'd be willing to bet that what you're doing—what you *seem* to be doing—is no more murder than what I did today. Sometimes things don't fall neatly and cleanly into the boundaries of the law! Can't you understand that I saw the stuff in that room, and that none of it matters to me? What I care about is the fact that you saved my ass, and that you're a good man, and if you're involved in this Whip Hand stuff, then you must have a damned good reason—a reason at least as good as mine. Nothing else matters." She waited a beat, through more of his stoic silence. "Would you like some more coffee?"

The moment was poised between them, like some dark predator deciding whether to kill or let live. Finally his eyes came up to concentrate on the crackling fire.

"I love dealing with intelligent people, I really do. I think I've just had ten seconds of the most significant eye contact I've ever experienced . . . and yes, I could use some more coffee, Cass."

She rinsed out their mugs. There was dry blood staining the ring of the drain. It looked like a coffee stain. She did not want to flash back on what she'd fished out of the sink earlier. "Another thing," she said. "Your ex-wife? I think I met her and her lawyer right before Reese showed up."

"You said nobody else was up here." The hint of accusation in his voice was level and reasoned, but damning just the same.

"No—I said nobody else saw Reese. He showed up after they left. He'd been camping out in the trees, watching the cabin, biding time. He made sure nobody was around when he made his move. A half hour earlier, who knows? A half hour later, I might be dead." Yet unspoken was a flat verification of murder on Lucas' part: *I did it, Cass.* Part of her was frantic to know. Part of her needed to know how she fit into, or disrupted, Lucas' plans. One possible answer was ugly and total. Lucas' words had suddenly taken on a defensive tinge. What he said seemed to hold deadly dual meanings and unvoiced threats. She had started babbling to fill the hole left by his scary silence, while Sara's odd protest echoed in her mind: *I don't know how long you've known Lucas, honey, but I'm willing to bet it hasn't been more than two weeks, and you obviously don't have any idea of who or what you're involved with!*

Who was Lucas? *What* was Lucas?

A realization jolted her as she mechanically did her bit with the coffee. It was one of those unsettling puzzle pieces that had been sitting all along, only it had taken her till now to think of it. Sara had been angry and reactionary. Maybe the reason was because she thought Lucas was up here fucking a girl half his age. But why should that make his *ex*-wife so steamed?

And she hadn't said she was his ex-wife, but his *doctor*. And that meant Lucas hadn't been entirely straight with her.

"You don't look so disheveled now," Lucas said, intruding on her accelerating thoughts. "Despite Reese."

"I'm a fast healer." She was going to start mumbling and circumventing if she didn't dive in and hope for the best. Detouring Sara had committed her. She had lied for Lucas before she had any real idea of what he might be doing out in the real world, beyond the mountains.

Cass dove.

"Sara said you were being sought in connection with three murders. Her words. I think *she* was seeking you. I think if there was a real dragnet out for you, neither of us would be here right now. There'd be cops dropping out of the trees. She looked to me a lot like a lady who has put a whole bunch of facts into a stack —enough stuff to come after you. But she doesn't want to nail you. She just wants to find you." She found the Bronco's first-aid kit, still in the kitchen, and brought it over. In a curious, role-reversed replay of their first meeting, she began to unwrap the stiff dressings on his hands. "So who is Sara, Lucas? Really. Maybe it's an unfair question. But I don't want to keep up with the evasions and meaningful silences."

He decided to play proper croquet. "It's over, Cass. It ended yesterday. And no matter what Sara does, there's no real evidence. All the evasions have been mine—you've been perfectly honest with me. I'm not used to that. But since I found you—or vice-versa—things have changed. The whole . . . what I was doing . . . doesn't seem as important now." His palms felt the air. "Careful . . ."

"Holy *shit*." Cass' mouth pulled back.

"Skinned them on a climbing rope. Damned stupid."

"In Arizona." There it was—a direct accusation in one color, sizzling crimson.

"Right."

She refused to let it rock her. She busied herself with cleaning and rebandaging the ravaged hands of the man who had just admitted to killing off the members of Whip Hand. But then, hadn't she just killed someone herself, less than ten hours ago? "I think Sara and that guy will probably come back. They didn't have that give-up look in their eyes. I told them you'd cleared out for a month, but I don't think they bought it enough to keep them from checking one more time, maybe tomorrow. Hold your hand like this. Better."

He winced as medication stung him, sterilizing, cleansing away what his hands had done. "They had to have driven up from L.A. It must be Burt who's with her, which means he's gotten curious by now. They're probably in a hotel somewhere between here and the city. Maybe one of those mom-and-pop beachfront stopovers you can get for twenty-six bucks a night. They'll be back all right."

She unfurled a roll of sterile gauze. "So what do we do? Both of us, I mean?"

"Nothing will happen till the storm goes away, and no one is coming up that hill in the storm unless they have a tank. We've got to get rid of Reese's body *and* the stuff in that room. Maybe Reese can serve a purpose after all. Everything—including evidence—could be dumped with him. Once that's done, we could wait for Sara and Burt and just face them off. Or you and I could just move on, and I can deal with them in my own time." The new bandages were brilliantly white in the firelight. He pushed himself up and stumped over to the back door. With the baton flashlight from the kitchen, he scanned until he located the soggy mass of tarpaulin.

"That's Reese," Cass said from behind him, grateful that the lump was still there, had not crawled off into the night to stalk her another day. "The firewood's wet, but I brought a stack inside before it started pouring. Don't know why I thought of that, considering the mental state I was in."

"The mind does weird things to keep itself on track during stress," he said. Behind them the fire had calmed down to glowing embers, pulsing good heat.

She moved past him to close the back door and slide her arms around him. "I'm just glad you finally showed up," she told him, and this time he knew she meant it.

Cass was a woman who would not lie to him.

She had been broken and now was healed before him, like the void left by Kristen had been healed by his masterful plan. He was still a bit stunned by the knowledge that his careful vendetta was over. Gabriel Stannard would be crushed by paranoia, without being touched by a single glove. Lucas' own skill as an assassin had been (in the parlance of Kroeger Concepts) "trending steadily downward." It was time to finish it.

Cass took his face in her hands to aim, and kissed him. His arms crooked under hers and pulled her closer, drawing her up onto her toe tips as their kiss waxed into a healing charge of energy. Her fingers dallied in his hair. As she stretched up to meet him, she squeezed his uninjured leg, oh so gently, between her own.

Their talking was done for the evening.

22

THAT NIGHT THE COASTLINE FLOODED from Santa Cruz to Santa Monica, where most of the pier submerged at an estimated cost of two million dollars. The PCH buckled, and expensive Malibu homes glissaded muddily down to meet the riptide. Movie stars bitched on the late news, helicopter flybys were bollixed by the downpour, and the Red Cross came out to sandbag. Phone communications went completely to hell.

At the very moment Lucas and Cass were slowly and carefully undressing each other in the warm yellow radiance of the fireplace, Sara slammed the hotel room phone into its rack. Its red bubble pager light winked once on impact, as if in pain.

"Damn it—I had them, I was on hold, then I lost them. Or they lost me. It must be a sign that I'm not supposed to do this." She plopped into a weary lotus position on the left-hand bed, her jeans stretching taut as she crossed her legs in order to knead her bare feet.

Three feet away, Burt Kroeger rubbed his face until it was ruddy, then rose from his recliner fortress of pillows to pour more coffee from the room service tray. His gray cloud of hair was frazzled enough for Sara to perceive that his hairline had retreated, but the arrangement of his hair was artfully designed to conceal this.

"If you don't get through soon, I'm going to start spiking this coffee. And we'll both start drinking it. And by morning neither one of us will be capable of interfering anymore." He looked back at her. "That's a joke. Sara—don't second-guess yourself. You're not turning Lucas in, you're merely seeking assistance in Los Angeles to try and locate him—if he's down there at all. You're a professional; they'll take an educated guess from you seriously. And if they will, why won't you?"

"It's still a betrayal," she said. "I hate that feeling." She seemed small and lost, there at the edge of the large and hardly rumpled bed.

Burt lit up another filterless Marlboro from the hard pack he'd pulled out of a vending machine that morning, and coughed on his first puff. "Filthy habit. I started up again almost as soon as Lucas came home from Olive Grove." He paused to smoke a bit. "If you and I were going to sit and do nothing, we would be much more rested now, and our credit cards less abused. So let's not play this game of woulda-coulda-shoulda. We're in it. It's too late to go back and pretend we're not involved."

"I know, I know. . . ." She squeezed his hand. Daddy image. Father figure. "It's just that—"

"You care about the guy." It was obvious to Burt, perhaps just as obvious to the world at large. "Me, too. That's why we're out here in alien territory while the whole state drowns, acting like jerks—because we both love the son of a bitch. End of story."

"Maybe they *will* turn up Lucas in L.A. . . . hitchhiking, or wasting time at the movies, or . . . something." It sounded lame. It *was* lame.

"We've called in the marines just in case. Look at it

that way. We have a better chance of finding him this way even if he has to endure a nasty little search and seizure. At least then we'll know. Calling the cops was a good idea, Sara. I sure as hell don't know where else to look for him."

She bunched pillows into the small of her back, and her spine popped when she eased back. "I'm beginning to think that at Olive Grove we treated him exactly the opposite of the way we should have treated him."

Burt crushed out his smoke. "How's that?"

"Suicidal depression usually involves a load of guilt. The therapist must help the patient alleviate the guilt and eliminate the impetus for the urge toward suicide. But if you're dealing with a psychotic personality, sometimes you have to do the reverse—instill guilt, because he doesn't have any built in. They don't care about things the way you or I might. They don't worry about good or bad in the sense we were brought up to understand."

"Lucas a psychotic? That's news to me."

"My age is showing, sorry. We supposedly stopped calling them psychotics in the 1950s. The APA's buzzword became 'sociopathic.' By 1970 that had expanded conveniently to include 'antisocial.' The psychopathy I'm talking about is the textbook form, not the splatter movie form. I was thinking, what if you reinterpret Lucas from this slant? A lot of items suddenly link up."

Burt sneezed. "Stuffy in here." She saw his eyes automatically seek his vial of blood pressure medication on the desk. "I don't know anything about psychopaths except the Hollywood brand."

"There's a certain kind of psychopath whose behavior turns toward pure problem solving. His urges are translated into instantaneous action. He wants to *do* something, anything to correct whatever wrong he sees in his situation. It's the same kind of frustration that makes teenagers break windows."

"Or saints make what the history books call *bold steps?*"

"Anything but inertia. Oh, the classic psychopath has many qualities we groundlings often envy. They are very driven individuals. Obsessed, almost. They can be utterly pragmatic, or charming to get what they need, or aggressive and unrestrained. A fellow named Cleckley noted this more than forty years ago; he wrote a seminal book on the subject called *The Mask of Sanity*. He acknowledged the existence of what he called 'the successful psychopath.' A restless, gallant, daring type who generally gets what he wants, is bored spitless by most of life, and who finds most pleasures transient and most disappointments recurring."

"You're describing most of the uptight three-piece-suiters on Broker's Row," said Burt.

"No doubt." She sought her Salem 100s, slid out a slim ciggie, and occupied her hands with it. It was comforting to sit and speak pseudoacademically, as though she were still a student, arguing theory in some campus cafeteria. "Some doctors speculate that this sort of 'psychopathy' is the survival mechanism we've evolved for coping with the 21st century. There are studies revealing that the children who had well-rounded upbringings and responsive, loving parents grow up to be dominated by the psychopaths—the kids who were rejected, or treated with cruelty or indifference. So the question arises: Do we mistreat our children on purpose, so they'll grow up to be survivors, or do we raise meek 'good citizens' who will ultimately be pushed around by the psychopaths?"

"Sounds like something essentially very seductive," he said, turning on to the idea. "You're talking about dressing your *mind* for success—programming for a competitive society. Part of me likes the idea already. Part of me is frightened by it—the lure of altering yourself to win. Put a price tag on it, and a lot of people would line up to pay cash money." Even now, the promotional aspect of Burt's consciousness was at work: *How can this be sold? Who would want it?*

Only every person who wasn't as successful as he or she *thought* they should be.

"It *is* seductive. This kind of psychopath has the gift of being able to maneuver people, but at the cost of his own innocence. He can hug someone mechanically because the hug is what is required to gain some objective . . . but he has no concept of what other people feel when they embrace. To him there is no such thing as the emotional rights of another person. No idea of 'good' or 'bad.' When he's caught in what you or I would consider a sin, he's repentant only because he's pissed off at being caught, because for him there is no such thing as guilt. If you accuse him, he'll act the outraged innocent—*I didn't do it! It wasn't my fault!* Or he'll vigorously protest that he's been framed. But as soon as you let him go, or forgive him, that repentance evaporates. His goal has been achieved; he was never really at fault. He'll steal from his friends, and say he loves those he uses. The only thing he'll ever feel is a sense of accomplishment. For such a person, the only beauty is domination, the wielding of power, attracting attention. To be outwardly seamless, never stumbling, never unsure of himself, never admitting it if he is, never looking awkward or stupid. The only grace is in speed, in performance. The psychopath is 'on' all the time, or tries to be, and has nothing but contempt for those who cannot match his level of performance, or who lack the proper skill or defenses. Harrington called them 'Zen sadists.'"

Sara seemed wearied, as though her explanation had brought things she did not wish to see floating to the surface.

"Suppose the Whip Hand plan was in Lucas' mind

from the very first?" said Burt. "I mean, assuming he's guilty."

"Then I was misdirected by an expert." She thumped her skull against the padded headboard. "If, if, if! Not knowing is . . ." She petered out in frustration.

"Driving you nuts, I know." He ruffled his own hair again. "I think it's hot shower time. Bang on the door if you reach anybody on the phone."

She smiled wanly at his shambling exit. The door thunked shut, and the sound of hot water gushing made her think of warmth, and how that warmth could pound the weariness right out of your bones.

Calling the cops had ultimately been her decision; Burt had deferred to her all along. He, too, took her professional credentials seriously. But it was also a way of abrogating responsibility for what happened. In turn, the burden of guilt would fall to Sara, since her treatment of Lucas had been so wrong. She wasn't sure she was ready to acquiesce, to accept that horrible feeling without protest.

The police would ask why she hadn't proffered her theories earlier. She would say she'd only just put the chain together herself. They might ask how possible it was for Lucas to seek out his doctor. She wasn't so sure of the answer to that one. There had been no messages for her at Olive Grove and no taped news on her answering machine at home. Lucas knew where she lived, had her address and number and vital stats. The police would check her records as a matter of course. They would discover that Sara held a carry permit for a .38-caliber Colt Diamondback revolver. It had been a gift from her father, who'd taught her to shoot. She had fired it maybe twice since 1976, and it was hidden at the bottom of her overnight bag. Burt had not seen it.

The police might want to slap a watchdog on her. She wondered if Gabriel Stannard had given them a call yet. He was now the last surviving member of Whip Hand—unless you counted Jackal Reichmann, currently a resident of the intensive care ward at Tucson Medical Center. Reichmann was currently in deep coma, inside an oxygen tent, his heart, lung, and bowel functions monitored by racks of beeping machines, with twenty tubes carrying fluids in and out. His bed was next to that of Pepper "Mad Max" Hartz, the only other survivor of the massacre at the Arena.

Do you really want to ignore that, Sara?

Burt showered, and she was left alone with her mirror image, the brainless snow on the hotel TV, and her own noisy, intrusive thoughts.

On more than one occasion she'd emphasized to Lucas that guilt was his enemy, to ignore it, to push guilt from his mind, to evict this unwanted tenant that was trying to make him kill himself. If that wasn't programming for psychopathy, what was?

One thing she had not mentioned to Burt stood out saliently now. The books all took pains to note the male psychopath's "strange ability" to inspire fervent devotion in women . . . even women who had been lied to, or ripped off, cheated on, or fucked over. Of course, the reverse applied equally to female psychopaths, but that condition wasn't what was making Sara nervous. Her hands wanted to jitter because there was a distinct possibility that she was trying to find reasoned, academic, professional excuses for Lucas . . . because she loved him. Lying alone on a rented bed, she knew he had somehow won, and she wondered if he felt anything for her beyond the satisfaction of successfully manipulating her.

While still in school she had memorized a quotation from Casper Sotheby, and she recited it almost subaurally to herself: "'Compassion does not exist for him, nor love, except as a means to an end. He makes the sounds of love by rote, having collected them for their functional use. He is the one who says, "I love you," without having any practical comprehension of what it is to love. And the tragedy is that he will get what his handicap tells him he wants, without ever understanding the tools and capacities he holds in his hands. It is akin to the analogy of a blind person never missing the color red.' "

She let the tears come, and they did not shame her.

And when the room phone finally rang, its red light sputtering insistently, she picked it up.

23

CASS WAS CURLED UP NEXT to the fireplace, very still, while Lucas paced around the cabin to vent pent-up energy.

His first thoughts had been of Cory, and how fine his life would be if she had been more like Cass, more human. Everything would have turned out all right instead of the way it had. Mindful of his wrecked knee, his gauzed hands, Cass had pulled him into the warm nest of pads and sleeping bags on the cabin floor. In the firelight it had been so easy to overlay Kristen's face on hers; Kristen had once had the same sorts of bruises that Cass had now.

She feels heat at her temples, a surging at her groin. Her eyes are captured. The green spikes of color in them flare and become prominent, as they do whenever she is excited or happy. . . .

Cass' eyes were light green with dark rings bordering the iris. It was easy to make the substitution, and the expression on her face had been identical to Kristen's in the nightmare as she returned the cobra-seduction gaze of Gabriel Stannard. He thought of power surging back and forth, from the Arena floor to vibrate the catwalks, from the amps to the stage and back again, from eye to eye, setting up echoes that bounced back, growing stronger, reverberating, swelling in potency until nothing could stop them. The same force that fed amperage through thrumming cables to Whip Hand's storm-trooper P.A. system was alive in Stannard's hooded gaze. It was enough power to twist time, to change reality, to jump-arc from the past to the present, to now.

Cass' legs rise and enclose him; he feels her hands on his buttocks, and she is pulling him into her faster and faster, her voice becoming breathless, a whisper, her eyes tilting shut as her own control deteriorates and she begins to gasp. He looks at her face and sees—

Kristen, bruised, beneath him, teeth bared, fucking energetically. He thought of Cory, controlling him, directing him, telling him what to do through orgasm after orgasm. She is never completely fulfilled, never satisfied. Climax, for her, is like accrued interest in a savings account. The only reason for having it is to pyramid it into more.

—Cass, who reminds him of Kristen, who inevitably takes him back to Cory. Cass is thrusting hard with her pelvis now, working at it, distilling away her massive reserve of pain, helping him to help her. He feels as if he is outside himself, standing across the room observing two strangers engaged in this farcical positioning. His detachment gives him an unsuspected sexual endurance. Locally he feels friction and little else, but Cass comes a second time, tiny, gemlike grunts escaping her. She relaxes, opening her eyes again, clumsily bucking and rolling him over so she may pounce and straddle him, hips moving slowly, rotating liquidly, her rich auburn hair untrussed and falling like wing curtains to obscure her face.

He recalled that the position had been much easier

on his ravaged hands. She was a considerate person even in bed, Cass was. He wondered if she had a motive. So he asked her, "What are you thinking?"

"I'm th— Ahh!" Her body tightened up, rising, then came down, slow, slow, slow, relaxing. "I'm thinking that I'm about to fall right off the edge of my third climax and want this to be a tranqu . . . nhnmm . . . tranquil one."

More silence and velvet motion; the muscular flower enclosing him.

Then: "Mmm, I guess I was right about you, Lucas my dear."

What had she meant by saying that?

She suspects something.

In his mind's eye he saw Kristen, fifteen, glowing, the bruises fading now. Kristen lifts the fat vial of oblong red capsules into the light and smiles speculatively. He feels a surge of love for his little girl. She wants to make him happy. She perceives his pain and wants to help.

The one power he thought beyond his reach was the power to reach into the nightmare concert and grab Kristen back. Yet now the nightmare events had congregated to compose a reality. He'd seen Kristen in the milling crowd at 'Gasm's fatal Arena gig. He'd perforated the motherfuckers who had caused her death. And now he had her back—in a manner of speaking, of course. She was here, beneath him, helping him, as before.

He had loved her enough to kill for her. He knew she hadn't been dead, not *really* dead. . . .

"It was a lie," he murmured. "The way the music was a lie."

Either she does not hear him or disregards his talk as the nonsensical jabber of coitus. Her tempo speeds up and turns feverish. There is a delicious itch burrowing into the head of his penis. The soles of his feet start to tingle. His stomach teeters on the brink of a rollercoaster drop.

He had seen her startlingly colored eyes in that moment. He had looked deep into them, into her mind, into her soul.

Her eyes are glittering.

"I love you," he whispered, just barely disturbing the air with his breath.

She jerks, making a breathy whooo *sound, and tightens all around him, her tempo hitching. He feels his cock and balls spasm and all the pictures in his brain flow together like warm oil paint, running.*

Kristen had not been as good in bed.

She flowed to his side and hugged him with her arms and legs. Wetness brushed his thigh. She wrapped him up tightly because he had been shaking all over, in shock.

"Oh, baby . . . no, no, it's okay . . ."

By the time he stopped shaking she was drowsing, slipping into that never-never land that beckons you after really good sex, the soft, warm cloud that lets you come down slow. When he freed himself from her, her hands would not let him go. He stood before the dying fire, the air movement making his damp crotch and legs chill. The fire needed stirring up and refueling.

She had rolled onto her stomach then, her round butt poking up saucily, flowing into her legs, which tapered into the magnificent calves he had admired. She had crooked herself onto her elbows and swept the hair from her eyes.

Her eyes are glittering. It's encore time.

"Lucas?"

She had been saying his name when he crushed her skull with the stubby split of firewood. He'd hit her twice, and she had not moved or drawn breath since then. She was curled up next to the fireplace, very still, where she had died.

Kristen was dead. Cass was dead. So now they really were the same.

They'd gone off to join Cory. He stood before the renewed fire, into which he had tossed the chunk of split birch. Cass' blood sizzled as it evaporated. Heat sheeted the front of his body. He knew about that nightmare glitter in Kristen's eyes. He had learned to recognize it. Even though he had not been at the Whip Hand concert, he knew the glitter. It was the same queer golden light he'd seen in her eyes as she watched him hold the knifepoint to Cory's temple and feed her the red pills, one at a time, with a swallow of water every tenth pill.

Sixty-eight, sixty-nine, seventy . . .

Kristen had gotten that glitter from her mother. She would have matured into the same kind of creature. If Cass was anything like Kristen, the same chain of events would be set in motion once again, and it would lead to his destruction. Lucas understood why he had a naked female corpse in front of his cabin fireplace.

Reality was slipping in and out of his grasp. The dream and the here and now; the past and the present; the old Kristen who was the new Cory; the new Kristen who was the old Kristen, it would hit critical mass and blow his circuits soon if he didn't get help.

Sara had helped him the first time.

He had to find her. Pretend he was being chased by a demon. Sara had made everything stabilize for him; Sara could explain what was taking place inside of him. Without Sara, he never would have gotten his little girl back. For that he was grateful . . . and now he did not want to be afraid.

He dressed hurriedly, yanking on his pants, groping around in the darkness for his boots. His frightened mind could find comfort in order, in the dissolution of problems, and now his mind considered the problems at hand.

The body of Cass' monster boyfriend, Reese, was still outside in the rain. Bodies had to be dealt with. All the Whip Hand *incriminata* needed to go up in smoke or into the sea, and soon. The remaining ordnance waited to be piled into the Bronco. He turned his back on the corpse in the living room and concentrated on cleaning up. His fingers were steady as they broke the boxes of 5.56 ammo and loaded the clips for the M-16. He mixed in fifty Teflon-tipped rounds. Developed for police use, then officially rejected as too dangerous, Teflon loads could punch through a stack of four Kevlar vests as easily as ripping through a cotton shirt, and the SWAT squads of Los Angeles disliked such abrupt vulnerability. The range and penetration the Teflon coating gave the comparatively small-caliber bullets were awesome. Lucas tucked the loaded clips into their canvas pouches on a garrison belt. Good to be armed, just in case. . . .

The shearing wind made the rain outside needle-like, and it stung his face. Cass' body was shrouded by his sleeping bag, and he was stopped by the sight of it on his way out to load the Bronco.

He thought he had helped her, too, in return. Now she would never have to worry about the White Picket Fence screwing up her life.

24

THE RANGER'S NAME WAS LUBBOCK, Trace W.

He barely scraped five-five in his Smokey Bear cap and shitkicker heels. Thanks to his mom's mom, he was one-quarter Paiute Indian, but that blood did nothing to push along his suntan. It was still too chilly to go shirtless along the Diablo and Santa Lucia ranges, so Lubbock had resorted to a sunlamp to get his coveted ruddy-outdoorsman's cast, with mediocre results. Now he looked like any other displaced Staten Island Jew with a sunburn. This abraded both his purely western sensibilities and his ranger persona.

Trace Lubbock wore tailored, starched, dun-colored uniform blouses with a tight fit and knife-sharp collar blades. He squinted on purpose to make his face craggy and weathered. To assure tenderfeet that he was indeed a seasoned mountain badass, he spoke in a low, dry growl through clenched teeth. If it worked for Clint Eastwood, it'd work for Ranger Lubbock. Usually, though, grinding his jaws gave him muscle-spasm headaches. The pain settled in between his shoulderblades and defoliated his cool in a mohawk-straight furrow up and over the crown of his head, with a silver dollar of pain dead bang between his eyes.

The seed of another such headache was sprouting right now, and he resisted the urge to knock it down with a slug of coffee. Norma had warned him off caffeine. Everything Norma warned him off had been regurgitations of the TV commercials that divided up her daily soap opera intake. He felt manfully entitled to his four morning cups of joe even when headaches were the price. From what he'd experienced, caffeine withdrawal was worse. When he was late getting to the ranger station below Los Gatos, he lacked time to brew at home and had to drink the turbid crud shat by the station's wheezing Mr. Coffee. It hadn't been cleaned since its purchase in 1970, and the stuff it produced reminded Lubbock of the silt that had caked his feet when he had made the mistake of wading into the Salton Sea, farther south. That one-time goof had come before Norma and before rangerhood. He had reached a detente between the coffee, the headaches, and the four pint bottles of Pepsi-Cola he put down every day (number one came at lunchtime). Hell—tomorrow would bring the first paycheck to reflect his recent salary hike, and Norma's VCR would be paid off, and didn't that translate as progress in the long run? Life wasn't so bad. Just dull.

Lubbock was also a harmlessly superstitious man. He knew that if he took the trouble to get more coffee, make sure it was the right temperature, measure in his cream and sugar powders with assayer pickiness, by the time that precisely prepared mugful was ready to drink . . . that fella from Los Angeles was going to stroll through the door and make him strand that coffee on the radio desk, to grow cold. Besides, he did not wish to give the impression that all he did at the station was dump coffee down his chute. The only call that had been logged this morning had come in from this Kroeger fella.

Trace Lubbock, Super-Ranger, sat without his coffee, looking tough and professional. Waiting.

The radio in front of him spat ranger drivel and fuzzy crosstalk. The bad weather and overcast conditions were juggling the airwaves. When he clumped to the station's freezing bathroom to relieve himself, he dared the phone to try ringing. Norma had told him that the caffeine in all his coffee and Pepsis was a *diuretic*. Whatever a *diuretic* was. It sounded like just another cute name for the Inca Squat Dance—*ain't that the shits?* Lubbock firmly believed that a man pissed out what a man poured in; you drank a pint, and a pint of a different color emerged, and that was all. Norma was so foggy sometimes.

Superstitions always had some basis in fact, he thought, and sure enough, as soon as he was laid bare with his cannon in his hand, he heard the front door rattle as it was slammed shut. He took his time buttoning up, having learned at age thirteen not to try pissing through a zipper because *you can shake, wiggle, squirm, and dance—but the last three drops always hit your pants!* He checked the mirror and made sure his Ranger Face was on before saying how to the L.A. fella. Kroeger—same name as the supermarket to which Trace once hauled wagonloads of deposit bottles during his boyhood in Roswell, New Mexico. Kroeger and his weird phone call about a matter of life and death and all that TV stuff. This was going to be weird.

Kroeger had needed Trace to pinpoint the location of a cabin owned by Lucas Ellington. When Trace considered the map reference, he whistled through his teeth. The location was prime—a couple of acres that cost more than five of the ticky-tacky double wide he kept Norma in. The mobile home was cheap, and Trace was still feeling each payment hard. Norma had selected a trailer corral where every other double-wide tin firetrap enclosed a story like their own. Christ—you could always hear your neighbors humping in the next trailer. It wasn't like a home at all. Checking out the sort of retreat Lucas Ellington's money had bought reminded Trace that not everybody relaxed by watching the tube inside an anonymous foil box. One day, he'd win his own modest Xanadu like the buddy of the fella Kroeger had.

Rich folks, Trace thought. Not like me. But Kroeger had done his matter-of-life-and-death dance. Seemed like drastic stuff always befell people who had a lot of money. If he ever got rich, he would never make a rich person's mistakes.

The fella waiting for him in the outer office looked well-to-do, too. But he also looked dog-tired, and the first thing he said was, "You wouldn't happen to have any coffee running loose around here, would you?"

Trace liked this city guy better already.

It was so easy to abstract into the rain. Burt rubbed his face and deeply inhaled cold, damp air. The Jeep Ranger roared through the storm, water mist sluicing to either side, wipers squeegeeing miniature waves cleanly to the left. The chuck-knobbed tires cut glistening lines across the rainswept pavement, lines that held their pattern for one fragile second before dissolving into the flat, wet sheen of the road.

Abstracted, Burt thought that the foundation of this whole mission was mistrust of a friend. Once again he had become the manipulator of events. Sara's workload demanded her return to Olive Grove, and he had dispatched her back to Dos Piedras in his car after mouthing a lot of promises. He had talked her into tipping off the Los Angeles police. Her call imposed a deadline on their activities—Lucas had to turn up soon, or it would all be in the hands of the authorities. Burt had pledged himself to take one more shot at the cabin, taking a

Ranger along, thinking perhaps the presence of a uniform might help to loosen the tongue of the girl who was fortressed in up there.

All bases covered? It was the best he could do. A gnawing sense of his own impotence demanded that Burt do something. And here he was.

He still felt that if he could see Lucas, meet his eyes, the whole potpourri of events would assume a sensible configuration. If not, and if Sara was right about Lucas . . . the ugly alternatives scraped away at Burt's composure like a planer defeating a sticky door one peel of wood at a time.

The Jeep's CB chattered sporadically, its tiny bank of red LEDs freezing whenever they caught a stream of good, pungent nonsense: *Big Fat Firestone, you've snared the Hub snatchin' two flatcases smokin' it signwise hip deep and fast asleep; lay it down for me if ya dupe, rebound!*

"Goddamn truckers," muttered Lubbock.

"Sounds like a Russian code or something," Burt said.

Lubbock sighed. "The Hub is setting up a deal. He's in a citizen car, pacing a truck, on the lookout for highway patrol speed traps so the truck can cut ninety miles-plus without a bust. It's still cheaper for the truckers to pay off pace cars than to bribe the hypos."

Burt nodded. The stuff coming out of Lubbock's mouth wasn't much clearer. A sign flashed past on the right: POINT PITT: 10 mi/6.2 km. Two miles past that was a scenic lookout.

Burt was trying to figure out how he was going to suggest to Lubbock that they just might be dealing with a killer today. Lubbock shoved a cassette into a dark slot on the dashboard, and the cab filled up with an old J. J. Cale song, "They Call Me the Breeze." The Ranger's hands tapped the wheel in time, and the speedometer oozed past seventy-five. The coiled cord for the CB mike swung between them from the top of the cab. Competition with the music kept Burt quiet for a few more miles until Lubbock just spat it right out: "Why is it we need to visit this fella, Mr. Kroeger?"

They passed the place where Burt remembered parking the day before.

Burt hoped his nonchalance quotient was up. "Mostly to make sure he's okay, if he's still up here at all." He said "atall," unconsciously lapsing into Lubbock's good-ole-boy speech pattern. "I scatter-assed up this anthill once, after I got lost twice before that. Figured I needed some local help. A guide; one with a four-wheel drive to get me up the hill in the rain, and get my friend out if he's hurt."

"I can do basic rescue," Lubbock said as he twisted the stereo's volume knob down a notch. "Used to work as a paramedic for an ambulance service." That brief gig had come during a hellish eighteen months Lubbock and Norma had spent in a jerkwater piece of nowhere called Bisbee, Arizona—another misstep in the long haul from Roswell, New Mexico, to Los Gatos and the trailer court.

"Well, we might have to restrain him," Burt said. "Or pull him out of the cabin bodily. You see . . . er, he was recently released from a . . ." *Mental hospital,* his brain screamed at him. There was no nice way to pussyfoot around it. Acid boiled sourly in his stomach. "Uh, institution."

"Oh—this guy Ellington is a Mental?" Lubbock's tongue was digging furiously inside his right cheek, trying to dislodge some ancient morsel of breakfast. "I've handled Mentals before. No sweat. Hadda restrain this fella we hauled out of a bar brawl once. Kept hitting us while we were trying to hold his guts and brains in. He didn't feel *no* pain; he was lubed to the crow's nest. Thought we was trying to boost his wallet, which had nine hundred and eighty bucks in cash falling out of it.

We finally put him down with an injection. Technically we can't give 'em a needle, that was a job for a doctor. But we did—*I* did. We were trying to keep him alive, and he wanted to kill us on behalf of his billfold, so we compromised and spiked him to settle him down. I don't drink, myself, not after seeing that." Lubbock's lush caffeine habit did not count as drug use. Burt noted with perverse amusement that the Ranger omitted mentioning the fate of the fella's wallet. "Yeah, I've done Mentals. Single guy, you 'n' me, shouldn't be no problem. No sweat, like I said. Why you checking up on this guy? 'Cos he's a Mental?"

Lubbock's cruelty was astonishing, but Burt could not allow himself the luxury of protest. It would be dangerous to argue the point before they knew whether Lucas was in the cabin or not. "His doctor is worried."

Lubbock let it ride. He was more interested in conversation than in motives and investigative logic. He'd checked Lucas' cabin for signs of vandalism many times over the years and never noticed anything provocative. Teeth clenched, he bucked the Jeep up the rain-washed hillside and over the slippery obstacle course of limestone shards.

Burt grabbed the chicken bar bolted over the glovebox, and a few stomach-lurching moments later they were looking at the front door of Lucas' cabin. Lubbock killed the Jeep's motor, and the sound of the downpour became unnaturally loud. Droplets speckled the windshield and obscured their view. No lights were on inside.

Lubbock pawed around behind his seat and located a holstered .357 revolver stopped up with six Light Special police loads. He strapped it on beneath his rain slicker. The look of alarm on Burt's face was almost comical, and Lubbock overrode the protest he saw coming out of his passenger's mouth. "Mr. Kroeger, you say this guy's a Mental, then I'm walking up to that front door with my goodbuddy here. Don't worry. I ain't never had to draw this thing seriously."

"My friend gets nervous around guns," Burt blurted out. "Better not flash that firepower." He had a nightmare preview of Lucas and Lubbock swapping lead; of Pretty Boy Floyd getting a high-caliber calling card from the Feds. What if Lucas got his head ventilated by this cowboy?

"He won't even see it." Lubbock patted the slicker. It was fairly clear he could not be argued out of packing his gun. His sunburn was even starker against the danger-yellow of the rain slicker.

Burt didn't like the light in Lubbock's eyes.

He thought of the murderous calm that would enshroud the dog soldiers in his unit whenever they got tapped to flush Vietcong snipers out of the trees on night patrol. At first the newcomers gobbled up battle duty, but after about a week of nightfighting with no sleep they became glutted with death, and their eyes would gleam in the same wet, fixated way that Lubbock's were right now. Burt's stint in Southeast Asia was the history of two decades past, but memories of it were keyed too damned easily. The steel slivers he felt in his stomach were battle jitters. He and Lubbock were poised to jump into the unknown and *find stuff out* . . . for good, bad, or worse.

"Let's do it," Lubbock said, and dismounted.

Burt began to sense that the young Ranger might be a more dangerous piece of machinery than Lucas at any depth of madness. Lubbock was dangerous because he was bored. He thought he craved action. *Let's do it*—that was what Gary Gilmore had quipped on his way to the frying chair. Burt climbed down from the cab of the Jeep, and his city topcoat speckled with dark raindrops.

As they approached the front door, he felt absurdly like a gunfighter stepping his way to the final showdown.

Nothing happened.

Burt wet his lips. "Lucas?"

Rain pattered the forest, hissing on the trees and rocks. He felt totally removed from civilization. Maybe Lubbock's hogleg was a good idea after all. Emboldened by the lack of response from inside, he called again, louder, thumping a fist against the door.

The door creaked open three inches.

There was a huge eye-level gouge in the blank wooden face of the door. The axe was missing from the chopping stump out front; Burt had noticed it there yesterday. But only a boob would leave a good axe out in the rain. Right?

"Hey, Lucas. You home?" He spread his fingers against the door planks and pushed gently. Peripherally, he saw Lubbock's hand travel beneath the slicker to unlimber the pistol. His head was tilted forward, and a tiny stream of water spouted down from his Saran-Wrapped hatbrim.

They could both see inside now. The axe was leaning against the counter near the kitchen sink. The fireplace was black and cold.

"Lucas! Yo! It's Burt!" Disappointment began to slow his heartbeat.

Lubbock pushed past in a swish of plastic, stiff-arming the pistol out into the open. "Come on."

Burt scanned around. Nice and dry inside. No wet footprints on the floor. Bits of broken glass strewn near the fireless hearth. Sleeping bag bundled up in one corner—unused? No cups or plates racked in the dish drainer. A table with only two legs leaned face-into one wall.

"Outhouse out back," announced Lubbock. After a fast glance out the kitchen window, he shifted his aim to cover the door to their right. It stood open just a crack. Serious gouges tattooed the wood, as though a monster cat had tried to claw its way in. The hinges had been ripped out and reset. The frame was splintered in axe-sized bites.

Halfway to the door Lubbock stopped and wrinkled his nose. "Smell it?"

All Burt had noticed about the dead air inside the cabin was that it was wonderfully dry. Now he caught an underlying scent, like rotten stew.

Lubbock's brain shifted into overdrive. Part of his pseudo-paramedic job had been collecting the bodies of elderly people who had died alone in their homes. Sometimes they sat for days, weeks, before they were discovered and reported. When bodies settled, they leaked. He and his hundred-hour course mates picked them up from bathtubs whose water had long evaporated or peeled them from their stained deathbeds. A surprising number of deaths occurred while the victims were sitting on the toilet. Bones crackled inside papery skin envelopes stiff with rigor mortis and plum-purple with dependent lividity. Their homes always smelled the way Lucas Ellington's cabin smelled now—clogged with the reek of slow decay.

Burt had been one of the first of Bravo Team to discover the Viet Cong body pit. He had nearly done a somersault into it in the dark. It was at least three bodies deep. Most of the bodies retained scraps of American olive drab, and none had kept all their parts. The rush of smell was rich and heady. Think of fresh shit, think of acetone, think of steaming, greenish-black maggot oatmeal plugging up your throat. Burt had turned away and blown his Type-B combat meal. He spent an hour cleaning vomit out of the Stoner rifle he had been carrying. You could catch hell for a dirty weapon. He had not been one of the unfortunates assigned to clear the pit or reassemble the corpses of his comrades, like grisly jigsaw puzzles. He hadn't been able to keep food down for two days afterward. The pressed mystery meat inside the combat meal tins reminded him of ripe hanks of human flesh; its smell was too much like the miasma of rot that hung like a malign thundercloud over the mass grave. The smell in the cabin now was a soft echo of that long-past stench. Burt's intestines shivered.

With a hard swallow, he thought that now was no time for cowardice and barfing. Here were two grown men dicking around in an obviously unoccupied cabin, skittish of a closed door and a funky smell.

He crossed the room and pushed open the door.

Lubbock yelled, "Wait!" and Burt heard the .357's hammer click back twice, into full cock.

Burt forgot the sickly vibrations of his body. All of his perception centered in his eyes, and the fleeting image they were able to absorb in the quarter second used up by the swing of the door. Even in that brief piece of elapsed time, he recorded too much, visually over-loading, thinking that in front of him was the most shocking thing he would ever see in his life. He was too correct.

His last sight was of the tripwire on the door twanging taut as he pushed it all the way open. Then the booby-trapped mines waiting at chest level blew him and Lubbock clear across the cabin.

25

SARA'S ATTITUDE WAS PRAYERLIKE. SHE bent her head and watched soapy rinse water spiral down the bathtub drain as the massage spray pounded the kinks out of her thickly knotted neck and shoulder muscles. Funny, she thought, to step from the hostile shower outside, freezing and uncontrolled, to the one inside, which was rejuvenating and hot as a sauna. A force she could control with the twist of a spigot. That was the essence of civilization—control over nature.

Her drive down from the bay area had been monstrous, like touring the ocean floor at a crawl. She stopped often because of the null visibility. Once the rain ceased, she hit fog so dense it reflected her headlights hard enough to sting her eyes. It was tough to shake the idea that Burt's undeniable utility became more lost to her with each mile, a lantern flame of sanity bullied by an ever-stronger wind.

At Olive Grove she had checked in early and clocked out late. During all those hours, Burt had not called, as he'd promised. Not a peep from Lucas, either—not that she expected a windfall like that. By midafternoon her concentration was destroyed every time the phone sounded off. By six o'clock she felt ready for the gibber and slobber ward. Anticipation could turn even a doctor who recognized the patterns into a basket case. She thought of the anecdote told of Cleckley, author of *The Mask of Sanity*. One day while in court, he looked up to see the psychopath in the docket dutifully reading his book. Knowing the rules didn't mean you were immune to them. Defining a psychopath did not cure one.

She hated the idea that Burt had let her down or forgotten her as soon as she was out of range. *You go on home; we men can fuck this up all by ourselves, thanks.* At dusk she had moped home to nurse an entirely self-indulgent drunk of defeat.

There had been one call. From the police. It had not brightened her day.

Gabriel Stannard, rock singer and sole intact surviving member of Whip Hand, had neatly vanished from his Beverly Hills manse and could not be accounted for. Now everyone who had been alerted was engaged in damning mathematics: Stannard was gone. Lucas was gone. The rest of the Whip Hand members were dead, except for poor Jackal Reichmann, ex-drummer of the ex-'Gasm, who was busy becoming a veggie. Two and two usually equaled four . . . and four, in this case, was not the devoutly dedicated Eldon Quantrill, who was still in custody in Tucson.

While at work, calls to Sara's home phone were automatically forwarded to her office; another line was added to her monthly GTE phone bill. Her home phone had remained inactive. *Dead* was such an ugly word.

She had even thumbed the little adjustment wheel on the bottom of the phone to make the bell ring as loudly as possible. So, naturally, it did not ring . . . until she was in the shower. She jerked her head from beneath the spray and heard the end of the brassy ring, then listened until it rang again to verify that the sound had not been her imagination in fifth gear. Then she was through the plastic curtain, planting soapy footprints on the blue plush of the bathroom rug, ignoring towels as she came out of the door in a burst of trapped steam. It took her one more ring to traverse the hallway, naked and dripping, and snatch the receiver from its cradle.

"Hello?" Her breath quickened.

"Hello. Is this, uh—787-8821?"

She did not recognize the voice. "Yes?"

"Congratulations. You have just been selected as a potential winner for over two thousand dollars in services, food, discounts at local retail outlets, even expense-paid trips to Las Vegas and Hawaii. Sound good?"

Soap sneaked into her eyes, hot and stinging. A sudden plunging feeling overcame her stomach, and her vision began to spot. Her constitution did not agree with this sort of prolonged suspense.

The phone solicitor took Sara's befuddled pause as a license to forge ahead but had obviously lost his place on his spiel sheet. "Then you can . . . no, wait. Are you over eighteen years of age?"

"No." Disgust finally surfaced. "But I fuck like a guinea pig anyway, my father tells me."

"Beg pardon?" The minimum-wager was not sure he had just heard what he had just heard.

"Listen, ace. This is a crisis number, not a residence. You've just called the Emergency Heroin Addict Suicide Prevention Hotline. My board is lit up, and somebody out there is probably dying right now because you're tying up the line." The water all over her had gone cold, and she was freezing.

"Oh. Huh. Geez, *really*?"

Sara had worked the phone-soliciting scam in college, suffering three and a half psychologically degrading days in the name of extra income. It had made her feel like a burglar, a rapist, invading people's privacy and trying to sell them stuff they did not want. She'd finally quit without earning a single pie-in-the-sky commission and virtually had to drag the sleazy ringmaster of that telephonic circus to small-claims court to get her base wages. Now she could hear the other callers in the booths beyond her boy and knew they were all hungry and desperate enough to spend eight hours with phones in their ears, breaking and entering. It was shit work, strictly steerage class. She suddenly felt sorry for the guy and added, "I know the phone number lists are all random things, computer-generated. Sorry. Hope you find a real job soon."

The other voice stayed silent for a moment, then: "Yeah, lady, so do I. If you've done this, you already know it sucks the canary."

"No harm done. Bye now."

She almost hated hanging up on the poor slob; he would certainly hate disconnecting from a sympathetic voice since now he'd have to dial another total stranger . . . unless he did what Sara had done when the phone game became too much for her, and she discovered how she could pretend to be doing her spiel with one end of the receiver cord disconnected.

The minute or two she'd wasted on the line, however, was ample time for Burt or Lucas or the police to get fed up with a busy signal and hang up for another five minutes before trying again. Or ten. Or half an hour.

Her breasts and back had been dried by the air. Outside the bathroom it was definitely chilly, and she wanted to get back into the shower, embrace the steam, pull it deep into her lungs, and let it cleanse her. She belayed a moment to stare at the phone, daring it to ring again. That magic would not work until she was back in the shower. Fate was a sadistic bastard.

It was dark outside. Burt had mentioned taking the ranger up to Lucas' cabin. Surely something had happened by now.

She shuddered despite the renewed gush of steaming water. Yeah, maybe something had happened all right. Maybe they had dragged Lucas out of that tiny locked room at the cabin, kicking and frothing. Maybe Lucas had opened them both up with gunfire at the first sign of approach. Maybe everybody was too dead to pick up the phone. Or maybe Lucas had taken his adolescent wonder girl and shagged ass to Vancouver hours before Burt knocked on the door. The options all seemed as ugly as that word. *Dead.*

There was no telling what the new improved Lucas was capable of.

On the other hand, maybe Burt was on his way to a phone at this very moment. The nearest-available pay phones were a good drive from the cabin, not counting the hike up and down the mountain or the progress-retarding factor of the storm that was still slamming down full bore, drowning everything. Maybe he was punching in her number right now.

Each thought of the young girl at the cabin hollowed her stomach, achingly.

Sara was not a believer in precognition, but as soon as Lucas took leave of Los Angeles, she swore she had felt a string break between her soup can and his. Had she foreseen the derailment of her budding relationship with Lucas so soon, and was the girl at the cabin culpable? The wily little bitch was young, young enough to be a surrogate daughter *and* a substitute wife . . . Kristen and Cory, all back in a single package. Sara knew that while that conclusion held a thousand intriguing possibilities, she did not yet have the right to draw it.

She had to talk to Lucas. That was the wall she kept bashing into. She wished Lucas were here. He could explain the mysteries and the dropped-out puzzle pieces that were now making her head hurt as well as her stomach. Even if his answers were crazy, they'd at least give her more information so she could play analyst and invent the real answers, yes?

And there was angry jealousy, too, a hot rivet of it sizzling in the wall of her stomach. The girl was competition; preferred company for Lucas. Sara could not rationalize her way around that one. And had she blinded herself to the extent Burt had suggested because she wanted Lucas—wanted him enough to ignore obvious danger signals? A pang of guilt settled in next to the hot rivet.

Soap-clouded warm water rose over the tops of her feet. She bent to clear the drain mesh of loose hair and felt the hot water flow begin to pale. It was time to trade the warmth of the shower for that of the fireplace and her favorite chair, the one with the broad, work-area arms.

There were other kinds of warmth, too. She toweled off slowly, catching her breasts in a humid double handful of terrycloth, her slim hand sneaking between her legs to investigate the droplets suspended in the fine down there. No gray hairs, she thought, feeling amused and a little scandalous.

She reached back into the shower to crank both taps to full stop. The hot water spigot sometimes leaked. The faucet shut-off that diverted water to the showerhead clinked down with a loud echo, and the phone rang again. She turbaned her hair in a turquoise-colored towel and left the bathroom door open to defog the mirrors.

She actually had one arm extended to the phone on its antiqued corner table before she registered the dark figure leaning on the kitchen doorway.

A yelp of surprise forced its way out of her, and her body tried to backpedal, her feet still wet and treacherously slippery. She was totally naked except for the towel on her head. Reflex thoughts of rape defense scurried through her overloaded brain as the man at the end of the hallway stepped into the light.

"Hi, Sara," said Lucas.

He was clad in black from top to bottom. There was a neutral grin on his face. And crooked into one arm was the largest automatic rifle Sara had ever seen.

26

AT FIRST, TRACE LUBBOCK THOUGHT that his own faithful .357 pistol had gone off prematurely in his face. He did not recall pulling the trigger. Second thought: *No round in the world makes a muzzle flash like that!*

That PR fella from Los Angeles, Kroeger, had rushed a closed door and wrested control of a potentially hazardous situation from Lubbock. Lubbock had thought *he* was the authority here. But that Kroeger fella had jumped the gun and relieved Trace of all responsibility for what had happened next. Lubbock had learned to think this way while working ambulance duty. The country was gorged with scam artists who loved to pin lawsuits on public service guys like paramedics. Or Rangers. It all boiled down to the placement of responsibility, and Trace judged himself blameless.

His eyes had filled with so much white light that his pupils had snapped shut before his eyelids. The blast erased reality. His ears were slapped into deafness by coarse hands. He was lifted, turned, and spat out; he'd caught a glimpse of the cabin ceiling whirling past underneath him.

Underneath him?

His senses had popped all their fuses, shutting him down. This was death, he had thought, the Big D. So long, Norma, babe, wish you'd come off your period a week sooner. . . .

As Lubbock floated up toward the light, toward consciousness, the images that were compressed into a corner of his brain began to push apart. They were too packed, too fast in coming, to permit individual review. Now they broke away and resolved into separate impressions.

. . . stupid civilian—don't charge a closed door!

. . . bodies—oh, god—like the old folks we used to collect—a man and a woman?

. . . a co-op suicide, that's what it looks like—he killed her, then killed himself, but why are they—

. . . blood oh jesus blood their heads are all red and dry their eyes are still open—

. . . is this guy the Mental?

. . . the wire on the door's gonna snag hey don't—!

. . . Holy FUCK!

. . . that fella whatsisname Kroeger flying toward me—

. . . he's hit he's hit MY EYES!

Without opening his eyes, Lubbock saw the bodies again. They had been sitting on the workbench in the tiny room, feet dangling, leaning together like a pair of winos, the girl's head on the man's shoulder in a sort of postcard lover's pose. The caked brick color of long-dried blood had transformed their faces into shining masks punctuated by the unseeing, dulled jewels of their dead eyes. Their garments—or lack of garments—went unnoticed. They seemed drenched, entirely dyed in that horrible brick red, which had dried to a metallic crust. Lubbock had been surprised that there had not been more flies, nibbling at this feast with their microscopic proboscises. Maybe the rain had kept them away.

Now the pain faded up, as though on some volume control knob. Goodbye J. J. Cale, hello five-inch woodbiter corkscrew-twisting agony into each kidney.

Lubbock uttered his first strangled cry of pain. Air whistled past his broken front teeth. His next convulsion was motionless and silent, an internalized shot of pain. He did not know that he had bashed himself in the mouth with his faithful .357, the ramp sight shattering his two front teeth and his left canine at the gumline. His mouth had filled with blood, but since he was facedown on the floor, he had not strangled on it while unconscious.

Look, Ma, no hands. . . .

One of the corpses had been missing an arm. A strange disc was fastened to its throat, winking through the dry blood like an evil-eye fetish. A vision that transcended death; the All-Seeing Eye that Lubbock's Paiute grandmother had told him about. Lubbock's mind classified the other corpse as a woman because he saw her breasts; everything else was hideously androgynous. Her hair was very long and completely shellacked with blood. Most of her right brow was reversed inside-out, and a huge ditch in her head had pulled one side of her face up into a ghastly bogus leer. The man wore a vest and jeans. The woman was completely naked . . . naked, bludgeoned, and dead. As dead as you could get.

Then he remembered Kroeger flailing toward him, end over end, and the hot birdshot of pain clipping his ankles, and the din of shattering glass, and long splintered chunks of the door Kroeger had just opened flying at them like a jagged fusillade of arrows. Kroeger's airborne body had formed a black silhouette surrounded by a corona of blast-furnace white. A rush of broiler heat had puckered Lubbock's skin, followed by moving air, like the slipstream of a freight train going full throttle. He had been picked up and laundry-bagged on his head against the far side of the cabin. More pain began to pound at his skull in new and torturous ways.

Trace Lubbock stood exactly five-five, with two inches added by his cowboy boots. He couldn't know that if he had gotten his lifelong wish and been taller, by even two more inches, the top of his head, eyebrows included, would be splattered all over the cabin's front yard.

Before he risked opening his eyes, he indulged in the frivolity of wishing he was still kicking back at the Los Gatos station, swilling down cruddy coffee from Ajax Ballard's shitty Mr. Coffee machine. Ajax was probably weighing down a counter stool at Paulette Barnum's diner out on Route 152. He wasn't due into the Los Gatos station until . . . late. Trace had warned Ajax about Paulette. She was out to snare herself a Ranger with those fabulous plastic tits of hers. Trace had dented the mattress a few times with her; it was comforting to know she was willing whenever Norma got cranky. Paulette Barnum's sexual needs were basic and uncomplicated. Trace figured that was why Ajax Ballard was so hot for her—maybe he wasn't any bull in the sack. Old Ajax, with his marine corps haircut and his beer belly . . . he was doubtless swapping lewd remarks with Paulette and wolfing down his never-changing order of two double cheeseburgers and cottage fries . . . and he was probably nowhere near the radio in his Jeep . . . the Los Gatos station had put in an order for those portable FM units that holstered to your belt, but those would not be a reality until after next February, so for now it was the old game of catch and listen. . . .

The radio!

He had to get to the CB in the Jeep. Call. Anybody. Send out a mayday before the pain got so bad he could not move . . . if he could still move at all.

Trace Lubbock opened his eyes. His panic and alarm held just below the frothy boiling point. Only one of his eyes still worked.

A swimming image of the cabin came into cloudy focus. His yellow rain slicker was sprinkled with gelid slops of blood—whose blood, he could not estimate. Burt Kroeger was on top of him, an unmoving mess, one hand extended toward Trace's face in a petrified claw, the other twisted beneath his body. He was sprawled face up over Lubbock's legs. Face up, that was a laugh. Burt Kroeger's face was gone.

Trace tried to scream, but nothing came out. His vocal works were locked. Rust choked off his gullet, and his tongue sat like a dead blowfish in his mouth, swollen and dry and spiky. He saw his right hand shaking uncontrollably, knuckles knocking on the floorboards. His right leg throbbed with hot cactus prickles of pain, nerve endings shrieking. His left leg was completely numb and dead.

Crippled! Oh, jesus god, crippled, no! Better off dead.

The rain outside sheeted down with Olympian vengeance, scrubbing Trace's rawed eardrums with demon glee. It was a miracle he could hear anything; the concussion had punched out every window in the cabin. He did not yet realize he was hearing the rain with only one ear. The left one, on the same side as his dead eye, was sealed up with a gooey bloodscab and was as useless as a dustball.

He grabbed with his right arm and pulled. Kroeger's leg rolled to the floor, the heel of his shoe thunking. The foot toed in and was still again. Kroeger's other shoe was twelve feet away.

When Trace tried to sit up, the chopping blades of agony in his back cut him down to floor level.

Try that one again.

It took him half an hour.

He reached, this time with both hands, tendons bitching, hooked his fingernails into the grain of the wood on the floor, and *pulled.* He shifted two or three inches. The lower half of his body was dead freight. But he moved two or three inches. It was only a hundred inches more to the cabin door, maybe two thousand inches more to the Jeep. Piece of cake, if he didn't die in the next five minutes or pass out from the floodtide of pain eroding his consciousness.

Pull, sonofabitch, pull! Pretend you're grabbing a bedpost and fucking the tits off Norma or Paulette. PULL!

He bought five more inches, then ten, sliding like a snake with a broken back. Kroeger's other leg spilled off. *Thud.* Softer sound—no shoe.

He reached, and pulled, and reached. The reach was restricted each time by the vise-grip of pain in his arms, the stakes penetrating his skull, the horrifying numbness below. At least he could not feel his scrotum sanding against the floor as he dragged himself along, a primal amphibian crawling out of a prehistoric sea for the first time, its undercarriage useless on land.

Breathing quickly became torture. Something was ruptured. Expanding his chest hurt. The air touched off his broken teeth in the way candy foil shocks a filling.

His hand filled with little round white pebbles that ground to powder when he pressed down. They were all over the floor. Pills, miniature pills. His hand closed around half of a smashed, nicotine-colored vial, and Trace read BURTON KR on the ripped label. He'd seen Burt pop one of the high blood pressure pills while in the Jeep. Medicine was a wonderful thing; it was supposed to keep you from dying. Right.

Six, maybe seven more repetitions of the Paraplegic Two-Step would win him the door prize. He reached out. His fingernails were peeling back and bleeding. Something in his chest broke apart and voided hot fluid.

Trace's good eye rolled up and his forehead hit the floor when he blacked out.

It took a long time for him to come back up.

It would be wasteful for Norma to get insurance money. She'd just buy a bigger TV set and spend the rest of her life in front of it, growing fatter and paler. It was his responsibility to pull them both out, to start over. He wondered if the dying were always so repentant. *I'll fix everything this time around, just give me that second chance. . . .*

The pain switched from memory to reality, no less potent. Tears were streaming from his eyes. His eye. But he was awake and alive, and still facing his objective. Outside was the dark, the rain. The storm had not paled at all.

It took centuries to make his slug's progress. As a reward for curling his fingers around the rough texture of the cabin door, his body kicked in its final shot of epinephrine.

Trace dragged himself out into the rain.

It was totally dark, the all-enveloping, suffocating deep forest dark that only nocturnal hunters could penetrate with their lemur eyes. The moon was just a sliver, and thunderheads blanked out the starscape. The unseen rain sang down like ball bearings on sheet tin, it pattered on Lubbock's uniform cuff to darken it as he tried to grab his first handful of distance. Clammy moss and mud clogged up his fingers.

Outside, it was quite cold.

The darkness helped him blot out the horrors available to the eye inside the cabin, the cavern of death he was slowly leaving behind. Reach. And. Pull. Now he was squirming in the mud, a dung beetle, lolling and caking himself with swampy cesspool grime. It was better than looking at all the blood in the blurred depth perception of his surviving eye. Dogs rolled in bank mud when they were wounded, didn't they? Better mud than blood. Crawl, you jarheads! Grovel, worm, locomote with your fucking upper lip, but get closer to that dim curve of Jeep canopy.

Lubbock prayed the Jeep was no illusion.

The storm wanted to press him to the ground, tempting him to stop, relax, and leak his life away into the mud. In the morning, all signs of abnormality would be rinsed clean. He could sink into the earth, return to the loam to nourish the trees. The ecosystem of the forest was slow but inexorable. Relax; become one with nature. If he gave up; if his body gave up for him.

He cursed himself for being lax on the calisthenics, for giving up jogging—too Marin County for his taste, for not giving up Norma's starchy meals and the fried goodies hashed up by Paulette Barnum. Mud insinuated itself into his pants, filling his holes, making him more ponderous. It topped off his Tony Lama cowboy boots with thick sluice the temperature of morgue-slab marble.

Perhaps the mud might set and solidify, like hot-top on a roadway, a poultice to seal his wounds. He was using this fantasy to occupy another five seconds of pain when his fingers brushed the bas-relief pebbling of the Jeep's left front tire.

There was no relief, no surprise. This job was still far from coffee break time. The thought of a shot of good, dark, steaming coffee nearly made him swoon. He fastened on to the hub rim and pulled . . . grabbed the chassis and pulled . . . grabbed the running board and pulled . . . and rose . . . and reached, and missed, and fell on his ass in the mud.

The second try took longer. He thought he could feel ligaments snapping like rubber bands as he tried to extend his reach. Two fingers hooked on to the icy silver of the driver's side door handle.

The CB rig was inside, mere feet away now. Inside, there was a padded seat, and dryness, and the miracle of a heater. From his wounded splay in the mucus slime of mud, the interior of the Jeep looked like Valhalla.

Let's DO *IT—*

First pins and needles, then scalpels and icepicks invaded his arm from elbow to fingertips. His traitorous limb rattled on the door handle, and Lubbock felt himself plunging again. He ate a double mouthful of mud spiced with the sharp taste of his own fresh blood.

Lubbock screamed.

With a backbone-rending shriek, high and uncharacteristically feminine, he swung at the door handle with his other hand and smashed it down. He strained but could not see if his blind strike, his last chance, had mattered. It was so damned dark, and getting darker. . . .

Hanging drunkenly, he nearly lost it when the door glanced off his temple. He groped out with his nearly useless right hand and felt the vinyl seat cover, which yielded to his weak grip.

The CB unit was mounted above the wide bar of the wraparound rearview mirror. It was far enough away from his reach to be a cruel joke. Its pinhole LEDs blinked importantly, ignoring his emergency. Why hadn't he mounted it on the dashboard? Why did he have to be so fucking *cool* all the time? The blinking row of red lights was almost hypnotically seductive.

Red means stop. Stop. Give it a rest. Go to sleep.

His eyes began to hinge heavily shut. At last. The LEDs blurred into a thin red line, glowering at him.

Redline. DANGER*—*

He pulled his good leg beneath him and shoved hard. Something else burst apart, and the agony that flamed upward through him made him sure his guts were trailed behind him in gray, slick runners. A new scream died in his throat. His good leg was no longer that.

He went facedown into the driver's seat. He fancied

he could smell his own ancient butt sweat.

Now roll. Roll one more time and grab the mike cable.

His dead legs tried to pull him back toward the ground, a viscera-covered infant sliding forth from a metal womb. He got the edge of the seat in his mouth and bit down hard with his broken teeth. The pain was beyond description.

But he did not slide out of the Jeep.

Unable to look toward the CB, not daring to release the seat, he pawed overhead. There was sudden sharp pain in his fingers.

The black microphone was knocked from its cradle and fell with the coiled cable accordioning out behind it. It struck Lubbock behind the left ear. His consciousness tried swimming for the deep end of the pool one more time.

His remaining front teeth had bitten through the vinyl, and the foam beneath was dark with his blood. He could not hold, so he let go. Gravity hauled him back out the open door of the Jeep. The mike hung, touching the rubber mat by the accelerator, and Trace's hand slapped at it as he fell out. He caught it and took it with him.

The coiled cable payed out to full length and twanged tight enough to jerk the plug out of the CB unit. Trace was sure that would happen as he collapsed back into the slime. But when his body went down, his arm was suspended by the still-connected cable.

If he sneezed, the cable might pop out.

He managed to slide around until he was sitting with his back to the Jeep. He could feel the running board digging into his back just below the shoulderblades. And the mike was still in his hand, a marvel to behold. His broken face tried to smile, but there was no victory, not yet. No Pepsi break until he finished his job.

Close the mike in your hand. Don't let it go. If it's connected, it'll spring out of reach. If not, it'll go into the mud, the dark. Depress the button. Make your face talk. Call in the ATVs, the evacuation crew, the choppers. Talk. Talk now. Do it as though your life—

The cabin had been so nice; it had never been any trouble. Why had all this happened now? There were two dead people in there, one of them a girl with no clothes on. This was not normal. He and Kroeger had walked in and boom—now there were three dead people in there. Three going on four. And nobody knew about it.

Medic! Medic! Corpsman!

Corpse-man, he thought.

Lubbock tried to raise the mike to his face. He tried to depress the talk button. Alone in the dark, dying by the second, he tried.

27

JOSHUA KNOPF WAS AN EXPERT at sitting on his duff and waiting, patiently. He often mentioned this singular talent to people as a means of procuring employment.

Joshua sat, waiting, while the rain eased up and showed some mercy to his Honda Accord. He snapped off his book light to conserve its batteries; the flexible penlamp was clipped to a paperback copy of James Crumley's *Dancing Bear*. Cheeseburger detritus littered the passenger seat, and a huge silver thermos of coffee warmed his thigh. The coffee was thick with Kahlúa, and Joshua was relaxed, glowing warmly. The sound of the rain was soothing. None of this was sufficient to lull him into a doze, however—sleeping was not part of his job. Waiting was.

North Claremont Street in Dos Piedras was badly in need of a bit of slurry sealing. The pavement was ruptured and ancient. The property, however, was upscale. North Claremont allowed access to eight homes on the soft eastern slope of a hill; on the west side of the street the hill flattened into open scrub field. The street was a dead end terminating in a yellow-and-black-striped barricade dotted with orange reflectors. Part of the hillside had been gouged away to accommodate the street. If some drunk lost control and rammed the dead end, Joshua thought, he'd be nosing his car into a berm of dirt ten feet high. It had long since become overgrown with brush as it settled into the local ecology. The field and the open hillside were seeded with paths; past the dead end one trail led down into the little cemetery behind Grace Methodist Church on Weaver Avenue.

Maybe, Joshua reflected, if the drunk hit the berm hard enough, they could just tote him right over the hill and into the graveyard's next vacancy.

KNOPF FOR HIRE, read the business card clipped to the visor above Joshua's head. He had a whole glove compartment full of business cards pinpointing expertise in a dozen occupations, from contributing editor to *Soldier of Fortune* magazine to insurance adjuster to IRS representative to the clergy. None were bonafide. All had served at one time or another to get Joshua Knopf the things he needed in the course of his work. Below his name—it annoyed him that clients rarely got the pun—in maroon ink on the gray card was the line PRIVATE INVESTIGATIONS, with his phone number.

The P.I. license had come by mail order seven years earlier. Joshua was retired military (navy, seventeen years starting in 1960). He had also tried, as a tax dodge, a card-carrying ministry in the Universal Life Church. Before opting for the correspondence course, he had decided that a calling as a letter carrier for the post office, a night watchman, a shoe salesman, and night manager of a convenience market was not for him. Thus KNOPF FOR HIRE.

At first he had been astonished at how dull it was. But as he moved away from domestic surveillances and automobile repossessions, he developed a modest measure of pride in his closed-case load. He did all right.

Then people began recommending him to other people. Joshua Knopf was your man for a taste of discreet fact finding. Joshua Knopf got the job done.

One of Joshua's night-watchman stints had been for the huge Holiday Inn that overlooked the sea on the coast road to Santa Barbara. One memorable weekend, the tenth floor had been invaded by a band called Whip Hand, and Joshua had been the man tapped and tipped for twenty varieties of midnight errands. Gabriel Stannard, leader of the band, had remembered Josh Knopf and ever since 1981 had kept the detective on a yearly stipend, so his services would remain on call. Stannard was always businesslike—he always discussed his needs with Joshua in person, not through intermediaries like some of these rock and roll guys—and always paid well. The money took the pressure off. Joshua was always happy to work for Gabriel Stannard.

And Stannard had apparently been able to use the file dug up by Joshua on Sara Windsor, psychiatrist at Olive Grove Hospital and resident of 7764 North Claremont Street.

The neighboring dwellings were dark, shut down for the night. The residents here were professional people with things to do in the evenings, or well-to-do older folks who rose with the dawn and were abed by nine o'clock. No one had taken note of Joshua Knopf, private investigator, sitting in his car in the rain, doing what he did best.

Detective fiction tickled the hell out of him. TV programs ditto. Fat chance he should ever wind up rubbing elbows with Cybill Shepherd or waving around firepower like one of Robert Parker's hapless characters. No—detective work was mostly sitting. And waiting. Occasionally one was mistaken for a burglar or peeping tom.

Another pleasant thing about working for Gabriel Stannard was that the singer never imposed complex instructions. So many clients who resorted to the use of private investigators felt the urge to gussy up their assignments, pump them full of wind and mystery and speed, to make their cases seem more significant, more like the cases they experienced in fiction. Stannard's instructions regarding Sara Windsor had been specific and succinct.

Joshua sat in his car and watched Sara Windsor's house. He'd been logging reports ever since Sara had returned home. When Stannard had advised him he would no longer be available at the Beverly Hills number, Joshua had been given an emergency number that he had not yet used.

Every hour or so, Joshua unhorsed himself from the Honda and trekked up the slight incline to Sara Windsor's house to play voyeur. Missus Windsor was quite a good-looking woman. For the most part she had spent the evening puttering around the house in a robe. The first time Joshua had spotted her wearing the robe, he had experienced a sudden lack of maneuvering room inside his jockey shorts. She logged a lot of time in a comfy chair by the fireplace, making notes. This was a woman who brought her work home with her. She seemed a bit antsy whenever she got near the phone. She was waiting for a call. Joshua did not feel the need—yet—to attach his lineman's handset and tap in. He had it in a case on the backseat if he changed his mind or something drastic went down.

In the glove compartment of the Accord was a nine-millimeter Smith & Wesson automatic. The clip was in. Joshua carried a permit for the gun. In his entire career as a private investigator, he had drawn the gun once and fired it never. So much for romantic notions of Bogartry.

The blue neon digits of the dash clock told him he'd have to do a spot check before he could help himself to more Kahlúa. At dawn he'd call in Mickey Rounds, his partner. Mickey would park in the brush on the hillside, between the cemetery and Claremont Street, and use binoculars until Joshua told him to stop.

He shrugged up his collar and ducked out into the rain, which had receded to a light, miserable drizzle. This leg of Claremont had a single streetlight planted in front of 7041, and most of the houses were dark. The street glistened. The only sound was the ambient hiss of moving air—like a stereo turned way up with nothing playing.

Joshua's chosen vantage was a crack in the curtains near the kitchen on the north side of the house. It was dark enough for him to pick his way through the shadows there with no fear of being spotted by chance from the neighboring house. His rubber boots squished in the saturated grass; the incline from the street to the front porch—about forty feet—made footing iffy, and he would skid if he wasn't careful.

It had been forty-five minutes since his last check, and the same lights were blazing in the house as before. Joshua assumed his half crouch at the window. There were steam beads on the obverse of the cold glass. Maybe she was bathing.

The thought of catching a fast cut of Sara Windsor in the buff inspired him to tarry. His basic requirement was to note, each time, that she was alive and moving around and nothing overt had transpired.

The curtains stirred. Air had moved inside. Joshua's automatic thought was of a door opening and closing, shoving interior air around.

Through the window, he heard the phone in the hallway ring. He could almost see the little phone table from his position. When Sara talked on the phone, she usually leaned against the opposite wall of the hallway —where he could see her just fine—or dragged the unit on its twenty-five-foot cord to another part of the house. Once, twice, three rings.

A shadow blocked out the light from the kitchen. It was a man, a big man, clad in black. He had an M-16 with a large nightscope cradled against one arm. He wore black leather gloves.

Sara stepped out into the hallway, totally naked but for the towel on her head. Joshua saw her from behind. He thought her ass was a touch on the large side, but nice and soft. She had good, long legs.

He sighed. He was not being paid to intercede.

As soon as the pair began to exchange words, Joshua humped down the hill to his car. If the guy had come to kill her, he would have wasted her in the hallway and left. They were going to spend some time talking—like the characters in mediocre private-eye fiction always did, explaining the plot to each other.

The emergency call number was clipped to the visor next to Joshua's spare business cards. Stannard's very curt instructions had not included anything about gunplay, or violence, or maverick risk. Joshua did his job. He would not fire his gun tonight, either. He would do what he was being paid to do. He was good at his profession.

Sertha Valich watched Stannard mutter monosyllables into the phone, his body english gradually torquing up. He punched the extension for Horus' quarters, said, "Tell Cannibal we're a go," and hung up.

The horrifying thing to her, in retrospect, was that during the whole sequence he did not look at her, not once.

From the moment he had answered the call on the first ring—"*Yeah*?"—her mind began recording every feeling. Time would allow the moment to resonate, so she could interpret all of it later.

Stannard's mad little gig was on, and she was not a part of it. By design or oversight, he was excluding her. In an American movie, at least, this would be the scene in which she would reel off expositional dialogue, explaining for the dullards in the audience all the deadly reasons why Stannard should not embark. *You can't go!*

Instead, she thought of the term *tactical fuck*. She had learned it from Stannard. For him, it meant strategic gain via sexual favor.

The single memory that stood out—not burning with pain, just there, like a clog in a pipe—was of a rotund and depthless man named Greg Seligman. He had been overweight by fifty pounds, not so much fat as puffy. His shirt buttons put up with a lot of stress. His clothing always appeared fully packed and two sizes shy of comfort. Any exertion, such as rising from his desk chair, caused him to exude sour sweat. To Sertha the droplets always looked yellowish. He insisted on wearing dark plaid shirts that showcased a plague of saltgrain dandruff wildly out of control even though his hair was fluffy and looked as if he washed it once a day. She remembered how the heels of his Bass Weejuns were worn down on the insides because he walked with a slight pigeon-toed cant.

She also remembered the time Greg Seligman had instructed her to sit on his green desk blotter and raise and spread her legs *this way*, pointing her toes. She recalled the clamminess of his grip on her hipbones as his undernourished peenie sniffed its way in. His bulk hampered penetration despite her buffet position. He bumped against her pelvis and squirted without making a noise, and the next day Sertha became a client of the Bache Agency. A week after that, she was posing for men's cologne advertisements, and her snowball started rolling apace.

Greg Seligman had made a big mistake. Thinking the reverse, he had given her power over him. Her air was superior the next time they crossed paths, and he had flushed crimson to the roots of his flaky hair in front of twenty people.

There was no pain attendant to the memory, no psychological rent, no sense of rough trespass unavenged. As a localized memory it was as silly and insubstantial as Greg Seligman himself—an absurd, plump, tiny-minded man who once had something Sertha needed and whose sweat still stank of desperation. Sometimes even the most highborn must swab out their own toilets. At least when you are done the thing is clean again.

This aligned with Stannard's definition of a tactical fuck.

The extra access permitted by the conditioned suppleness of Sertha's leg muscles gave her pleasure beyond human speech when Stannard went to work on her. When she thought of making love with him, she always smiled. Now, watching him realizing that the time of madness and firearms was at hand, she saw the power she had given him over her.

One part of her could appreciate the corner he was in. It was a career crisis—the kind sometimes solvable through tactical fucks. He was facing a showdown with his own public image. The rest of his professional life might depend on how he dealt with Lucas Ellington and how visibly brave he was when he did it. He really had no choice, if he wanted his fans and the media to keep treating him just so. The *Rock Wrap* incident was a pale hint of the nightmare to come if he did nothing and let "the authorities" take their meandering procedural courses. Running down Lucas Ellington like a cheetah was Stannard's own form of tactical fuck.

But Sertha had not been consulted, let alone asked.

So instead of playing the movie scene, with its hyperadrenalated hysteria and bad speeches, she waited until he cradled the receiver and had to look up at her.

The look in his eyes was defiant, committed. He expected her to protest.

What her eyes saw was different, and as ominous as

a lump in the breast. She saw in his eyes the possibility that she might be used up completely to fuel his mad need for retaliation. He had been burning protein at an astonishing rate and dropping body weight to match. He seemed to exhaust whomever he spoke with. He was taking it anywhere he could get it . . . and he had not spared her. She extrapolated the sore and scarified condition of her body into the husk it would become if she tried to oppose him now.

She backed off, lowering her eyes, hating herself for rolling into a surrender position so quickly. She had known physical power games for too long to permit herself anything but an instinctive survival response.

He took that for an answer and stalked out of the bedroom. Wordlessly.

Sertha felt weaker than ever. Her knees did not want to bend in the correct directions. A nasty, icepick headache made itself at home behind her left eye.

She stared dully at the telephone. The light board was dead now, inactive.

Enough time had passed that she would have to unearth her book and page up the number she knew she had to call.

28

NO POLICE AWAITED THEM AT the Oildale airfield, but what eventually happened was not pretty.

Stannard jumped from the Cessna before Horus wheeled it around to full stop. His blood sang with electricity as his white-gold hair flew in the backwash from the twin props. "No cops!" he shouted into the wind. "We caught 'em circle-jerkin!"

Cannibal Rex refused to budge from the aircraft until it was stilled down to the engine vibrations. He climbed out with a large zippered nylon duffel slung over one shoulder. The finger-bone earring jogged spastically as he wrestled with the bag's weight. When both boots were solid on runway tarmac, he scanned the night and the tiny airstrip from within his murky wraparound shades. So what.

Before them were two dilapidated hangars of rusty corrugated steel. Fastened to the side of one like a moray on a whale was a battered, single-wide mobile home—a sixteen-footer whose traveling days were long past. Inside it Stannard found a middle-aged fellow tucked into a greasy jumpsuit, feet propped on an old army-issue desk, attention funneled into a dogeared copy of *Penthouse* that was two years shy of current.

Above the man's head was a mimeographed sign that read WE DON'T GIVE A DAMN *HOW* IT'S DONE IN LOS ANGELES.

Stannard knew he should play it broad, firm, and definite. "Hi there." He nailed the man with the intense, ice-blue gaze he kept powered up for the shutterbugs from *Rolling Stone* and thrust his open hand unavoidably forth. Hicks always thought you could take handshakes to the bank.

George Kellander's wife, Margie-Marie, had always told him that he tried to do too many things at once. Right now George needed to get his big engineer boots down from the desk, finish dislodging a stray piece of ham from between his two front teeth, put Stacey Butterick (August's *Penthouse* Pet, a couple of birthdays removed) on hold, and deal with the stranger who'd barged into his little office. George was zipped inside of what Margie-Marie called his "overhaul overall." An oval name tag sewn to the breast declared him to be Georgie O.—O for Oswald, his middle name—in embroidered red script.

He draped the *Penthouse* over the desk edge to hold his place. August indeed. He had no idea why those crazy-as-a-shitfly New York publishers dated magazines so far in advance. Some computer bullshit, most likely. His visitor looked like one of those windblown Hollywood faggots. Crazy as shitflies, everybody in Hollywood and New York. They didn't know squat about how the real world functioned. Probably because most of them were hustlers and queers and dope addicts, all hot for each other. You'd never see a sweet piece like Stacey Butterick walking the streets of Hollywood, no sir. The *Penthouse* copy said she was a small-town girl from

Lebanon, Indiana, and why would they lie about something like that?

Nevertheless, the stranger's hand was out, and George took it. The force of Stannard's grip reassured him a bit. George tried to be polite and surreptitiously wiped his hand on his overhaul overall. You never knew which one of these guys might be carrying AIDS around.

The visitor's white-blond hair was wound into a bunch of tight little curls, the way the coons over in Ruckerville favored their hair. His clothes were pure faggot—jeans too close at the crotch, yellow cowboy boots, some kind of fruitcake black deerskin shirt that laced up the front. He was wearing an earring. That was a sure sign. But George had forgotten which ear meant AC and which DC. The earring was a tiny double-bladed axe in pewter. It hung upside down. George couldn't even guess what that might mean.

But the guy obviously had muscles on his muscles. George knew that gayboys were into bodybuilding, and this guy was just *too* handsome. For somebody like this to come blowing in on the ass end of a storm might mean serious trouble, and a guy would have to be a little crazy to fly around in weather like this. Just what the hell did he want?

Stannard cut loose a bright burst of smile and teeth. "Georgie, I got me a slight emergency here, and I think you might be able to help me out. I'm needing a car. I gotta get someplace in a hurry with no hasslements."

That was Horus' entrance cue. The room seemed to shrink when it filled up with the big black man, and George's eyes hastily digested a flood of new input.

Stannard then brought into play the only *other* thing hicks swore by—hard cash on the deck. He drew out his wad and began thumbing up Franklin notes. "Now, you wouldn't know where I maybe could *rent* transportation like that for, say, an hour or so?"

George nervously considered the huge bald bodyguard with the ear studs, then the newly born fortune in Stannard's hand. It helped him keep his gaze off Stannard's bulging package—as George's old navy buddies designated it during jump practice from the high board. He didn't want this bend-over boy to get the idea he was interested or something else perverted.

George forgot all about L.A. queers and perversion when Stannard slapped a thousand bucks down on the desk next to Stacey Butterick's moment of glory.

George only looked at the money once. He felt safer since this was a game he knew how to play. "Well now," he said, stroking his chin, pretending to think. "Well now. I just might be able to give you boys a hand at that. An emergency, you say?"

"I gotta get my pal here to the doctor real fast."

George glanced at Horus. He drew his clasp knife out and unhinged it to pick at his teeth, purely as an innocent gesture clarifying that there should be no funny business. "What's the matter with him?"

"He's got a throat problem. Altitude makes him lose his voice. It's happened once before. Might be serious."

Horus pointed to his neck, grimaced, and shrugged.

"Well now. The only car I have here is my son's car. It's my only car on account of my truck is laid up with valve problems and won't be ready till Thursday. Now, I don't know if I could let you drive my boy's car, even if I was inclined to . . . uh, *rent* you it. It's his property, after all."

Stannard peeled away another five hundred bucks as though the dirtier bills in the stack offended him. "Like I said, we're kind of in a hurry." Another smile. *Wham!*

George's eyes were catching the light from the money more often. He narrowed them and tried for shrewdness. "You boys wouldn't be robbers, or wanted by the police, or something like that, now, would you?"

"I've never been arrested in my life," said Stannard, giving George his press profile one more time. "Not even for jaywalking. And if we were bad guys . . . why, hell, we would have just coldcocked you and *taken* your son's car, instead of leaving your son an extra chunk for his kindness. And yours." He slid the wayward stack of bills closer to George, who suddenly needed to clear his throat.

"Don't look like it could do any harm, at that." He was wrapped up in dreams of untaxable income that Margie-Marie would never have to know about, if he could get his boy Clyde on the phone quick enough. He could slide some cash to Clyde, and they could both prosper. The evening was beginning to look less rotten, despite the dog weather.

On the other hand, if he said no, there might be guns and trouble and ugliness. George smacked his lips to clear away the taste of stale ham. "Er—could I have another one of them?" He indicated the stack of hundreds. "You know, for beer money?"

"Sure thing, Georgie." Stannard's smile did not waver. "Keys first."

George produced Clyde's keyring from a coverall pocket and tossed it. Stannard caught it one-handed and dropped an additional hundred-dollar bill onto the stack. "You're a real prince, Georgie."

Then blondie and his nigger buddy were out the door.

George resumed his chair with a twinge of excitement tickling his belly. Definitely Los Angeles, he thought. Probably one of those billionaire hippie kooks. Maybe bank robbers, with a hot haul. Either way, from this moment on the money before him did not exist. He folded the stack double and stuffed it into the same pocket from which he'd fished the keys. He knew Clyde's personal stuff was gone from the glovebox—that was SOP when loaning your car to your old man.

George picked Stacey Butterick up to tell her the good news.

Cannibal Rex had been sharp enough to stay out of George Kellander's sight. He might have queered the deal.

Horus found Cannibal occupying himself with the American 180, removed from the black duffel bag. He had fitted in a stretch clip and waved the weapon around. In the time it had taken to procure the car, he had obviously paid a visit to his cocaine vial as well.

Clyde's wheels were parked—almost hidden—by the backside of the trailer. Stannard discovered he had rented a refurbished 1971 Dodge Charger with Hooker Headers, a paint job that was mostly gray primer, and road-grabbing mags. He jumped in and fired the engine.

It was *good*.

The ass of the Charger was radically jacked, and the powerhouse grumbled liquidly as Stannard twisted the padded-doughnut steering wheel and made it emerge, like a big cat slinking forth from a cave.

Cannibal Rex grinned at Horus, brandishing the 180. "Budda budda budda budda," he said. "Kapow. Kapeewingg!"

"Seems like everybody in the sticks has a set of wheels like this stashed somewheres," Stannard said as his private assault force boarded. Horus took the blue vinyl bucket next to him while Cannibal Rex piled into the cramped backseat with all their hardware. "Nothing else to do in the sticks except watch TV, make babies, and work on your engine."

Stannard's limbs seemed to merge with the pedals and gearshift and foam doughnut. His stark blue eyes considered every piloting contingency; as the car warmed to him he seemed to mutate into a hybrid of driver and machine. Behind the cold epinephrine sweats and the mental shields that had settled in to opaque the hard blue of his eyes, what he was thinking was not an open topic. He drove. The car responded to his firm hand. Outwardly, he looked like he was digging it mightily.

He sprayed Kellander's trailer with peel-out mud. In seconds open roadway was unreeling in front of them, faster and faster.

They were five minutes from the first police roadblock.

The rotor of the L.A.P.D. helicopter whipped up a tornado of wet leaves and litter at the north end of Vista View Park. Some spectators had already gathered, people whose dinners and favorite TV shows had been disrupted by the hellacious eggbeater racket. Sullen teenagers loitered, shrugging at the pow-wow of waiting cop cars. There was a sheriff's cruiser, a highway patrol Land Rover, and an unmarked car, dead gray, circled in readiness.

The chain of events Sara had set in motion with her phone call to the authorities from the storm-beleaguered motel room on the Pacific Coast Highway was ending here, tonight. The police had taken the information supplied by her, formed logical outlines in their inevitable Joe Friday way, and chased them like a rat in a cheese maze. The most obvious conclusion had been drawn, and the chopper had been dispatched to land in Vista View Park, which was the most practical place to set down according to local law enforcement concensus.

The sniper pinched the bridge of his nose hard, pushing down to duct pressure from his sinuses. He had popped pseudoephedrine hydrochloride to handle the altitude and quick descent, but for him there was always a residual twinge in his head, like a warning sign. He shut his eyes and turned the moment into a bit of fast-food meditation, a shot of stilled-pool mental calm on the run. Then he wired his stainless-steel-rimmed shooter's glasses around his ears and snugged his ballcap down tight as the chopper settled heavily on its runners.

The pilot dealt him a good-luck punch to the bicep; the sniper returned a cocked smile and a mirthless little salute. A topcoated form disengaged from the nearest car and humped up to slide back the door. The sniper and his long, waterproof rifle case were gone, doubletime.

The unmarked car had blackwalled tires, a red bubble light on the rear deck, and a whip antenna that thrashed about in both the man-made wind of the chopper blades and the more formidable wind of the storm, which was marshaling for a renewed siege. The sniper ducked inside, and before his door was shut the whole convoy lurched into motion, gouging ruts out of the wet turf, flashbars igniting and bathing the park and nearby homes in red-and-blue light.

Marty Danvers hung his headset on the throttle and grimaced up at the turbulent night sky. The lull in the rainstorm had provided an almost perfect window to permit his full-tilt jump from Los Angeles to Olive Grove, and now that his pet helo was grounded he acknowledged that he'd have to hang out awhile. He dropped his rain hood over his head and got out to chock down the props with roped weights. Then he unfolded the couch behind the two front seats, looped a single-phone headset around one ear to monitor the police band, and found his place in the latest Trevanian paperback. Waiting was dandy. He was getting hazard pay for flying up here in the storm.

Little by little the gawkers dispersed, returning to their meals, to the cool fire of their video windows on the world. That was what you did in a place like Olive Grove. You commuted, you ate, you reproduced, you watched a lot of television. You got cable. You achieved a tranquility that was rarely disrupted by noisy urban intrusions like helicopters. The next day, at work, you talked about the weather, what TV shows you watched . . . and the damned helicopter that came in the night and woke up your babies. You swapped theories about what a helicopter might be doing in Olive Grove, over coffee at a place that invariably served "home cooking." Surely this was nirvana, for anyone who had survived World War Two and the turbulent 1960s.

Nothing ever happened around a place like Olive Grove or Dos Piedras. When something did, it became the stuff of gossip, and legends, for decades to follow.

29

"HE'S COMING," LUCAS SAID AS the rain started again. "He's coming here."

In his eyes, Sara could make out her own darkling outline, defined by the bathroom light behind her. Her hand, stalled halfway to the phone, still hung, reaching, from the end of her arm. The phone had stopped ringing.

His eyes moved up, then down, cataloging her body with mild curiosity but no discernible interest; not at all the way most men looked at her. He was seeing her naked for the first time. "You'd better find a towel or you'll be sneezing your way into next December."

It is more than bravery not to broadcast raw fear when one is buff-ass naked, dripping, with a towel lopping sight from one eye, with a phone blowing reveille every five seconds, with a heavily armed killer sharing your hallway. It has to be on the level of autonomic reflex, like breathing. One holds or one folds. One cannot train for it. For a moment she feared a shot of urine would be startled out of her, to course down her leg and pool on the hardwood floor. That would have broken her. Instead she locked fast, heedless of her nudity, careful to appear nondefensive, *Dr. Windsor*, not just Sara.

Her hand withdrew. "Lucas, that was probably Burt Kroeger on the phone just now—"

He closed his eyes and nodded as though he knew this. His hands seemed thick with padding beneath the black leather gloves. He wore a bulky ski sweater, also totally black, and black fatigue pants with combat pockets on the thighs. The butt of the Llama automatic poked from its brown leather nest in his left armpit. The black woven canvas garrison belt around his waist was filled with clips for the M-16. Was it even legal to strut hardware like this? She had voted for the handgun control initiative in the 1982 election, when California was supposed to set the trend for the entire nation. Instead, Proposition 15 had been humiliatingly trounced, and the gun lobbies had been victorious. Citizens shrugged. She thought of her own gun, the Colt Diamondback revolver, still at the bottom of her overnight bag. In the bedroom. Miles away.

She had to wrest more control. "Lucas, I want my robe."

"Later," he said, with no pause to think. "I want every psychological advantage I can get right now. Nudity is a great deterrent to rash action. Go sit by the fire, Sara. Get warm." He motioned with the M-16. The enormous Nitefinder scope looked like a space shuttle sitting atop a 747.

Sara's dinner roiled in her stomach. She pulled the towel from her hair and tucked it around her torso, defying Lucas to do anything retaliatory about it. He did not protest. Thank god for large towels. She swept her damp hair back to keep it out of her face. Warm air from the fireplace tingled her skin and tried to make goose-flesh; it didn't need much help.

"I browsed a little while you were in the shower," he said, following her into the front room, his gaze constantly jumping to the windows and back. From the sofa he picked up a cloth volume Sara recognized as *Psycho-Therapeutics,* by Robert Collier Young. It was tented open to a particular passage, which Lucas read aloud for her.

"'. . . psychotherapy, like meteorology and economics, is an art rather than a science,'" Lucas recited. "'There are psychiatrists and psychologists who have had some success with a certain type of patient under certain circumstances, but there are an awful lot of imposters, quacks, failures, and just plain incompetents running around in that field, and they exert far too much influence. They have become the modern priestcraft. They have supplanted the religious infallibility of previous centuries. One hundred and fifty years ago, phrenologists enjoyed as much status as today's psychiatrists; yet today, phrenology is dead. I don't know how much longer psychotherapy is going to last.'"

He snapped the volume shut and put it down. His right arm and hand were ever occupied with the ugly M-16.

She thought, *Will I be alive when the sun comes up?*

"Dear Sara. You came up to my cabin. Why?"

"No," she said, fighting to bypass his terrifyingly stoic manner. "You're going to answer some questions for me, Lucas—about that girl at your cabin, for one thing."

He seemed to defer. "She killed somebody. Remember Kristen, Sara? Kristen killed somebody, too."

"Is the girl at the cabin dead, Lucas?" She kept using his name, searching for any breach point. She wanted to rise from the chair and dared not.

"Kristen is dead," he clarified. "She was alive for a while, and then she was dead again. It's not my fault."

She remembered her minilecture to Burt. *If you accuse him, he'll come on as the outraged innocent or vigorously protest that he's been framed.* You and your big mouth, Sara. But there was really no reason to be scared of Lucas, for *her* to be scared of Lucas, unless she became part of the hideous pattern he seemed locked into repeating. Cory and Kristen, Kristen and Cory, a new daughter and a new . . .

"Tell me what happened, Lucas. *Who* is coming here? Cory? Kristen? Burt? Who?"

He had been watching her with an odd expression, waiting for her to challenge him with some accusational shuttlecock he could swat down. The attack he expected did not come. Sara wanted to help. He could confide in her. That was what had brought him to this place.

"When I left, Sara, it was all clear. No problems. Everything had worked out crystalline, as Gustavo de la Luces would say. Just crystalline. He's a guy I used to work with."

"Burt mentioned him to me."

"Yeah." The muzzle of the gun was not pointed at her. His voice had tuned down to a quiet, hoarse whisper. "You know about Whip Hand, right? You wouldn't have gone all the way up to Point Pitt with Burt if you hadn't figured that part out. And Burt wouldn't go unless he had a goddamned good reason. He's that kind of guy, a problem solver, very direct. I liked him."

Psychopath? *You're describing most of the businessmen on Broker's Row.* Burt had said that.

"I wasn't as good at it as I thought. Revenge, I mean. I did the first one okay; pretty seamless. The second one was sloppy; I got frightened. The third one was nearly a complete wash. I thought I was up to it. It was for Kristen, you know. But I guess I wasn't."

A knot of scrap pine began sizzling in the fireplace.

"You're a problem solver too, Lucas," she said. Her heart was banging about inside her ribs like an enraged ape trying to fight its way out of a cage.

"Then that crazy religious nut chanced along, and I

said to myself, perfect. Perfect. I could stop with clean hands. Except for . . ."

"The girl at the cabin." She was gambling, and she knew it. "You were avenging Kristen, and all of a sudden you got Kristen back. And that meant you'd get your old life back. And that might lead all the way back to Cory, and Cory wasn't good for you, so—"

"You're not so smart, Sara," he snapped. "You think you know every goddamned thing. Well, you don't." The M-16 swung back up, and Sara felt as though she had attracted the unwanted attention of a cobra. "You don't at all. You just don't understand. Kristen was . . ." He stopped, sighed, then refocused on her with something like anger. "You made me forget things at that hospital. You took away elements that I needed to remember. You convinced me, with your psychiatric horseshit, that my little girl Kristen was perfect and I was mourning her loss so bad I wanted to kill myself. You took Kristen out of my head and laundered her and stuck her back in."

He had seemed so broken, so consumed with guilt. Sara had wanted to help him up out of the black well of depression. The man's wife had overdosed on pills and left him a note reading DIE AND ROT IN HELL YOU FUCKER THIS IS ALL YOUR FAULT. Then his teenage daughter had gotten killed at the Whip Hand show. This was all true, a matter of record. And Lucas *had* pulled that stunt on the courthouse steps with the plastic gun, as if in deadly presagement of what was to follow a year later. Gabriel Stannard had been scarred, marked by his future murderer. Lucas had been driven by love for his daughter.

Hadn't he?

Cory had committed suicide. *Remember,* Burt had said, *he was seeing other women after she died.*

What other women? Where were they now?

Pow! The pine knot exploded in the fireplace, scattering embers.

"Kristen had to be watched constantly. Or she'd

tell. Eventually, she'd tell. She was not the little angel you reinvented her as, Sara. You messed with my head. You changed my reality. And look what has happened."

"Lucas." She tried to stay calm, level, reasoned. "Lucas, what did Cory's suicide note really mean?"

He thought about this, like a man who sees the inevitable barreling toward him and realizes he'll have to tell because time is leaking away. No force could stop it.

"I wrote the note," he said.

Lucas had written DIE AND ROT IN HELL YOU FUCKER THIS IS ALL YOUR FAULT in a flawless mimic of Cory's hand. *She* was blamed. What was all her fault?

"We don't have a whole lot of time, you and I, Sara," he said after checking the windows again. "He's coming here. There'll be cops and noise and madness."

"Lucas—listen to me. What did you have to do with Cory's death?" The idea that Lucas had killed his wife rose like a ghost seeking trouble. "I'll take care of you. Nothing'll happen to you if you just—"

"I didn't kill Cory," he overrode, working up anger. "Killing Cory was Kristen's idea."

He knew about the nightmare glitter in Kristen's eyes. It was the same queer golden light he'd seen in her eyes as she watched him hold the knifepoint to Cory's temple and feed her the red pills, one at a time. . . .

"Kristen never really came back, not really, not back up from the grave," he said. "I *would* be crazy if I believed that. The girl's name was Cass. She was everything Kristen could not be. More, really." Then, almost as a whimsical afterthought, he added, "She was much better in bed than Kristen. She wanted to take care of me. She didn't care if I killed people. . . ."

Sara's stomach became an elevator car that dropped into freefall for twenty floors, then got hung up in its own cables and bounced to a gut-imploding halt. Mere feet from the fire, she began shivering. She thought of Lucas' mind, literally evolving to a malignant third level while the technicians at Olive Grove watched, secure in the knowledge that they were curing him. And the truth had backed up so far in his brain that the pressure was seeking any vent. It was pouring out of him now and reminded her of her pathetic assessment of her own love life. Once it had been Lucas who was going to help save her. Now she watched the fragile jackstraw structure of her planned future begin to drop parts and buckle.

"It was rage, at first, I was so angry with Cory. Then I was angry at Kristen. I . . ."

Sara's imagination sketched in a picture in nightmare chiaroscuro, of Lucas attacking his thirteen-year-old daughter following their murder of his wife, then—

"I was going to stop, but I *wanted* to . . . and I thought she would stop me, and instead she wanted it, she *liked* it, she begged me for it . . ."

—then becoming trapped by Kristen, who had clearly been the product of her parents' union, the sum of both their minds and personalities, a combination of potentials for disaster and tragedy patiently waiting for the right catalyst—

"And I got Kristen back, just like in the dream; in the dream I was able to change things if I put my mind to it, and I changed what happened at that concert and got Kristen back again. I did it in the dream a million times, then I did it in real life. And it worked. But I . . ."

—to cause an explosion.

"Sara, I didn't know what to do next. It got all foggy. So here I am. Help me."

He sagged into the plush chair across from her, the M-16 across his knees now, perhaps her biggest victory so far in this exchange. Sara had to remind herself how to inhale.

"Maybe we program flaws into our lives," he said. "Maybe it's just another pattern, another cycle moving through predetermined motions with nothing to stop it. Once it starts, it has to play itself out. And now he's coming here. Don't ask me how I know. I know."

"Lucas, if you're talking about Burt, that was probably him on the phone a moment ago. He was going to get a Ranger to take him up to your cabin to check on you again the day after we both went up. I thought the girl there might be lying."

"Then Burt is probably dead now." Lucas said this with a lack of inflection that was chilling. It was just another cog turning in the clockwork pattern.

She couldn't let it faze or stop her. "Then the police, Lucas. I spoke with them in San Francisco. They've probably guessed you'd come here."

"They don't matter. The firepower's mostly for them."

"Then who—" Sara caught herself. "You mean Gabriel Stannard? But how would he know to come here?" She had not thought of this before, and now, inexplicably, it scared her. "*Why* come here, especially if he knows you're after him?"

"He has to. He's a self-made badass. He has to prove himself, walk through the fire now, or his fans will vanish. He has to take me on and win. He wants to kill me for the same reason I wanted to waste the rest of Whip Hand . . . and with that kind of motive, I'm sure he knows just as much as, if not more than, the police do. And that's another reason for coming here, Sara. In case I don't survive, I'll need you to tell everyone what happened. You're the only person I can really trust, you know."

"He's coming *here*?" Disbelieving, Sara was out of her chair without thinking. This madness had to be cut short, and now.

"*Sit down!*" he roared in her face, springing up, the M-16 ready to rip her in half with its deadly Teflon loads. In an instant his face had turned vulpine, wolfish. Before

Sara now was an unstable and heavily armed man who had not twitched an eyelid at rape, at incest, at murder, at the thought of the death of his best friend.

Sara sat back down as though yanked, the blood draining away from her complexion, her knees watery and quaking. She was going to die, and she was trapped in her favorite chair with no clothes on.

Lucas simmered for a couple of beats, nearly panting, reining his control. "Just sit. We sit and we wait for this cycle to finish itself. And don't worry, Sara. You're doing your job in the best way. You're helping me to eliminate those nightmares for good."

As he spoke they heard the first sirens, distantly.

30

THE CHARGER ENCOUNTERED THE HIGHWAY patrol roadblock just as the rain turned nasty again. Two growlers were nosed into a V formation with about three feet between their grilles. Two men in yellow rain slickers reluctantly got out to do their duty, as they had for every car on this road for the past hour. Datafax copies of Gabriel Stannard, Horus, and Lucas Ellington were clipped to the visor in each car.

Stannard geared down, cutting speed to fifty. "Poor fuckers," he mumbled. The battle light had settled into his eyes. "Get the Auto Mag."

Cannibal Rex dug through the black duffel and brought up the blued automatic .44.

"When I do my trick, cripple those." His manner indicated the police cars; his eyes could just as easily have been saying "Kill them." Cannibal grinned and worked the action to chamber the first slug.

The officers in their frisbee-brimmed, Glad-bagged hats had split to approach the Charger from both sides as Stannard slowed. Their reaction time when he shifted into first and stamped down was good. The car's fat radials ate wet pavement, and the cops backtracked several paces. Stannard stood on the brake and cranked the doughnut steering wheel sharply.

The Charger was a pre-oil-shortage extravagance, a gas gobbler big on size and performance. The trunk must have been weighted with cinder blocks, because the mags barely squeaked whenever Stannard laid on the petrol. Old Clyde Kellander had hot-rodded his car well.

The car spun sideways. The cops were uncertain. It could be a loss of control on the wet road.

The tail of the Charger swung like a hammer and demolished the right front fender of one cruiser, folding the metal and jamming it through the tire, which burst with a gunshot noise and flattened. The cops dived for the embankments on either side of the road. Next they would be clawing for their service revolvers.

Cannibal Rex leaned out the window on Horus' side and put a huge Magnum slug into the engine block of the second cruiser, right through the hood. Only the monster Magnum was capable of penetrating all that heavy metal.

The cops ducked for cover, squirming around in the slimy mud of the embankment as Stannard put the car in motion. The Charger charged, slewing around the leftmost cruiser and tearing twin traction ruts out of the shoulder. Bilge spewed skyward and came down in a brown rain. Stannard saw one of the patrolmen's eyes go as big as tea saucers when he concluded that the Charger was trying to flatten him. He dove facedown into the pool from which he had just risen.

Another spin of the doughnut, hard over, and the Charger fishtailed back onto the road with a dragster screech of tires and instantly generated distance, farting thousands of highway stripes. Before the hypos could run for their radios, it was slot-car size in the dim, rainy distance on the road to Dos Piedras.

Quiet approval settled over Horus' face. He enjoyed violence that solved problems without loss of life. His right hand was firm on the door handle, to maintain equilibrium through all the thrashing around. "You do know where we are going," he said, "don't you?"

"I think I bought my grandmother a house up here," said Stannard, his forward view unconcerned with obstacles. The Charger's needle crawled back toward the century mark. "There's a street, Claremont, that runs parallel to Center Avenue on the other side of a hill. Claremont is backed into the hillside. The house we want is about two-thirds of the way up Claremont." Joshua Knopf's directions had been very specific. "He's holed up in there. By the time those cops back there call us in, we'll be there. The rain'll slow 'em down. There's a goat path that dumps into Claremont from the far side. I think we can get away with using that. Hope it's not flooded."

Four blocks shy of the right turn that would put them on Center Avenue, a county sheriff's vehicle ass-slid into the rearview mirror, lights and siren popping on in an all-out, berserk maniac code three, making tracks behind the Charger like a puma running a rabbit to ground.

"Shit." Stannard was actually amazed their luck had carried them this far. His hands tensed on the doughnut wheel, and the Charger charged again, a bull seeing red.

Miles behind, in the trailer office of the Oildale airstrip, George O. Kellander finally got around to phoning his son Clyde. With the conspiratorial glee of a twelve-year-old, he told Clyde that his news was man-to-man stuff and not for the ears of his mom, who would not understand anyway.

"You remember that gashog Charger with no muffler?"

Clyde's teenaged sigh said, *Why shouldn't I remember my own fucking car?* But he was still living at home, at least until next summer, and in the Kellander household the fathers still used three-inch belts. "You place the ad, finally?"

"Better." George had Stannard's hundred-dollar bills lined up, two bills high, eight bills across, sixteen hundred bucks' worth of good news right next to the fingerprinty centerspread of Stacey Butterick. "We don't need no ad. I just sold it to some hippie queer from Los An-gee-lees for a thousand bucks. Split it with you, fifty-fifty."

Clyde whistled through his teeth. His mother was in the front room dozing through a movie on CBS and probably could not overhear, but he whispered anyway. "You want me to come pick you up? You ain't got no wheels there." He wished he'd had the opportunity to strip some of the frills from the Charger's powerhouse before his dad had sold it. But five hundred bucks was more than twice what he expected his cut to be, and delays often made for no-sales.

"Come on in about ten o'clock. I got paperwork."

Clyde knew that this meant his dad was most likely going to spend the next hour warming a toilet seat. "I'll bring the Camaro," he said.

"Good." George hung up.

George Kellander had not lied to Stannard about his truck being in the shop. What he had neglected to mention in his quaint rural way was that he and Clyde owned five other functional automobiles between them, including a refurbished 1968 Mustang with a police chaser engine and a classic 1967 Camaro with Naugahyde buckets and fuzzy dice.

Clyde wondered whether he'd left half a lid of stale marijuana in the Charger and decided it did not matter. He was already spending his five hundred bucks in his mind, wondering how in hell his father had *really* wrangled a grand for the Charger.

They burned intersections and red lights like a seven-year-old gobbling potato chips, and when Stannard's cold blue eyes checked the mirror again, he had to look hard to make sure he was not seeing a double image. A second sheriff's car had sprung into view, bobbing in and out behind the first one. They'd been whistled up by the highway patrol. Stannard was willing to bet cash that the call-in had neglected to mention how he had turned two chase cars into scrap steel back on Route 5. Two more junkers wouldn't change the course of history. He put his foot down. The acceleration mashed Horus and Cannibal Rex into their seats.

The cop cars hung on about a block back and would have gained had they not slowed and swerved twice for other cars and once for a pedestrian in the rain. Stannard didn't bother.

The turnoff on DeLacy had to be sacrificed. Stannard kept his contingency plan foremost in his mind as he burned up Fifth Street and hung a gliding, smoking skid turn past the One Stop convenience mart on northbound Weaver Avenue. The One Stop clerk, a college student named Abel Langtry, gawked at the car chase as it hurricaned past in the rain. His only customer, a ten-year-old named Dennis Chambers who had tarried late to fill the store's Slime Wars videogame with quarters, took the opportunity to pocket three Milky Ways free and clear.

It could be said that religion was the buffer between Olive Grove, where the stores were, and Dos Piedras, where the residences were. Weaver Avenue featured five houses of worship. Their differences were cosmetic. The last church on Weaver Avenue was the imposing Grace

Methodist, which was backed into a scenic, rolling hilltop. Grace Methodist Church was Gabriel Stannard's contingency plan. He'd seen it once and known immediately what might be done with its layout.

The church was at the end of the street. From there, one turned right onto Center Avenue to get over the hill and onto Claremont, or left, which led to a winding, tree-lined drive of five minutes that emptied back onto Highway 5. When Stannard caught Weaver Avenue, the chase cars would assume he was headed back for the highway. Other units were already enroute to Claremont. If he was foolish enough to hang a right, he'd find cops waiting to scoop him up.

The pilot of the lead chaser was alone and busy calling in his hot pursuit when he was forced to drop his mike and match the speed turn Stannard had made onto Weaver Avenue from Fifth. The two sheriffs in the second car, as well as One Stop clerk Abel Langtry and ace shoplifter Dennis Chambers, all watched as the lead car angled into the rain-slicked, double-wide street, slid wide, and started spinning. It plowed into a row of three cars parked slantwise in front of the post office and mangled all of them. Fiberglas and chrome shrapnel sprayed into the street. The first car was goosed up onto the sidewalk. The police crash bumper banged a mailbox loose from its bolting; it fell onto its wide-mouthed face with a loud ashcan noise and lay there like a dead robot, bent feet sticking out. The car settled creakingly onto its left rims as the driver tried vainly to focus his vision on the passenger door and crawl out of it. A pair of late-night postal customers, checking their boxes, peeked timidly out to see how their cars had been customized.

Several blocks away, the convoy of police vehicles from Vista View Park piled through the intersection of Fifth and DeLacy, bearing down on Center Avenue and, beyond it, Claremont Street. Everybody's target.

Watching the deputy ahead of him botch it caused the pilot of the second chase car to think hard about his repertoire of aggressive driving techniques. He nearly clipped the ass of the wrecked cruiser as Weaver Avenue tried to spin his car, too. It almost ended ugly, right there. *Nearly* and *almost,* he thought as he began to hydroplane, only counted in mortar attacks. He corrected deftly, then put his pedal down on the straightaway just as Stannard had. Churches blurred past.

Stannard saw in the mirror that he had dropped a cop. Only a single chaser was sniffing his tailpipes. Then Weaver Avenue suddenly ran out for everybody.

The Charger scorched up the inclined parking verge of Grace Methodist and hit the front walk at one hundred miles an hour. When the pavement quit, the wheels left the ground and the car spent a scary half second in flight over a row of concrete planters. Stannard cut loose a throat-rawing war whoop as Clyde Kellander's pet Charger went airborne, and everybody aboard clamped on for dear life. A planter clipped by one of the rear wheels exploded. The highballing half ton of Detroit steel crashed down and chewed turf, destroying a decomposed fence and spitting white pickets rearward. Sod and mud fanned out in the car's wake as traction was wrenchingly reestablished. The headlights played over the oncoming row of graveyard markers, throwing jittering shadows.

Two sets of sheriff's eyes bugged as the stone wall of Grace Methodist grew in their windshield to monster size. Darkness descended inside the car, leaving only the eyes, dull white with fear. The end was right on top of them.

The driver of the number-two car chickened and mashed the brake down hard enough to spring a tendon in his ankle. No fucking way *he* was Steve McQueen. He had a goddamned family and a wife and Sears payments to live for.

Smoke blurted from the wheel wells, and the cruiser slid to a halt, its nose kissing the stone steps leading to the cemetery gate with a hollow bump. Both cops inside could hear the Charger's engine racheting, growing distant. They listened to the hiss of their own radio and the clicking noise of their flashbar lights. *Tinka-tinka-tinka-tink.* The woop-woop siren had malfunctioned, cutting itself off about the time they rounded the corner. In the mirrors they could see their fellow officer's car belching up steam clouds into the moist air, leaking its vital fluids all over the pavement. Crashed autos only blew up in the movies.

The two sheriffs looked at each other. Simultaneously, both said, "Son of a *bitch*."

"This damned street's as empty as a collection plate," said K. C. Dew to his deputy, Chris Carpenter.

Carpenter curbed their cruiser at 7764 North Claremont. The vacant slot they filled had been provided by the departure of Joshua Knopf, private investigator.

K. C. disliked city cops trespassing on his preserve and resented the suggestion that he and Carpenter were to do nothing more here than await the arrival of some bigshot from the L.A.P.D.'s collection of SWAT lunatics who wanted to land his goddamned helicopter right in Vista View Park. His men had been ordered out on roadblock duty. Everybody complied. It wasn't the shitwork that K. C. bristled at so much. It was the suggestion that psycho killers were some kind of urban specialty.

Out here in the sticks, he knew, there were crazies, too. But they were quiet crazies—the senile, the juvenile. Rarely did you pull a one-hundred-proof whacko. Out here, they didn't dress like the village idiot or drop clues like they had holes in both pockets. Out here, a quiet madness waited, and to K. C. that threat was more frightening than the more concrete disposal problem presented by a loon in a tower with a rifle.

He remembered Mrs. Kalish. Her husband, Jack, had gone to Southeast Asia and come back in a KIA bag. She had hung herself in 1972, leaving an incoherent note about the coming UFO invasion. The Vietcong were aliens. She had been thirty years old.

He remembered Buddy Simonsen. That one still hurt. After a decade and a half of tipping hats and picking up checks for coffee and danish and pie, Buddy simply forgot who and where he was and hadn't remembered since.

A silent street, a quiet house like this one, could be signs of serious trouble. They might have to deal with a dead body today. K. C. was convinced there was something wrong with a community like Olive Grove/Dos Piedras, so friendly and countrified, where the dead could go unnoticed for so long. Chris Carpenter had been a deputy for nine months, the same amount of time it took to make a baby. Like a baby, Chris had done a lot of hard growing in nine months. He'd dealt with his first dead body his second day on the force. He'd blanched but not puked. He'd dealt with it. It had been an easy one, thank god. Mrs. Keeley had been found in her bathroom, dead for ten days until a neighbor noticed the smell. She had been ninety-one, also a widow, who still took evening constitutionals and cooked her own food. Her homemade preserves were locally famous. Old people often died in the bathroom, K. C. knew.

K. C. and Joel Carpenter—Chris' old man—had gone to high school together. They still took fishing trips twice a year. K. C. fought regularly not to be overprotective, over-proud, of Chris.

"So what are we supposed to do?" Chris said. Rain hissed down all around them and speckled the windshield.

K. C. rubbed his florid face. "I guess we stroll up to the front door and knock in the name of the law." His casualness did not appear forced. He kept his thoughts to himself. He had spent a good slice of his sheriff's career amortizing the horrendous discoveries he often made at times like this; the starved, forgotten dead people he'd tripped over, the domestic scenes out of *Peyton Place* by way of de Sade's *Justine*. His duty was keeping the peace.

He opened the door and hefted one massy leg out. The wing lights popped on, red and white, and the door buzzed with a cheap smoke-alarm sound.

Chris turned up his coat collar and grabbed his plastic-bagged hat. Claremont's single streetlamp tossed down a long thin shadow from his football-toned frame. As the rain ebbed and then descended with renewed vigor, they could hear frogs chittering in the distance. The street was oiled and gleaming. Their Wellington boots made soft sounds on the pavement.

"Car's in the driveway," Chris said. "Datsun. It's hers." They took no notice of Burt Kroeger's Eldorado, parked curbside two cars up.

"Anybody asks, you and I are investigating an anonymous call regarding a suspicious disturbance." K. C. knew he was circumventing the desires of the police in Los Angeles by poking around. But he'd damn himself for sitting and waiting.

Both men were three paces from the car when a single gunshot ripped through the fabric of the rainy night, to silence the frogs. The cruiser's right mouse-ear blinker disintegrated in a spray of red plastic chunks, and the bullet *zing*ed off the roof.

K. C. hit the deck with amazing speed. "Chris!"

Carpenter dived headfirst over the hood of the car and rolled. Hearts racing, they huddled up behind the far side of the front fender, sneaking glances at the house through the cruiser's windows. Chris jacked open the door to grab the radio.

There was an absolute lack of practical cover. Past a

recently laid strip of sidewalk, lawns sloped up to houses. It was wide open, punctuated only by standing lamps at the sidewalk level and flagstone or concrete walks winding up to each residence. Decorative foliage was mostly tucked against the houses.

It was no popgun that had taken out their blinker. K. C. wondered if the shooter had a good scope, or excellent aim, or both. It had definitely been a warning shot.

"Everybody's enroute," Chris said, hugging the street with the riot gun he'd retrieved. "Can't contact half our units. They don't respond. B-two, B-five, B-eight."

"Jesus." Sykes and Fowler, Preston alone, Dalton and Schlacter. They were all on roadblock duty or patrol. What the hell was happening?

Chris sat gauging range. Impossible to hit anything with a pistol at this distance. The shotgun in his grip seemed a bit futile. Scattershot would get a lot of attention but accomplish little. When he dropped to one knee beside K. C. and met his eyes, both men heard sirens gradually pushing back the stillness of the night.

"Don't do nothing," K. C. said. "No shooting, not yet. It ain't our job to get killed for these guys. Not yet."

31

REASON AND SANITY HAD TO prevail. It was Sara's duty to manipulate the tools of mind and logic to win. But her phobic side told her that Lucas might pivot on a whim, a misspoken phrase, or even a neutral silence, and cut her to pieces, using the inequities only he could perceive as justification. He had been honed away to nerve endings, awaiting stimuli. His response would be ruthless and final. Lucas was a problem solver.

Problem: People jaywalk. Solution: Kill people for jaywalking. Next case.

He was at the front windows again, M-16 slung across one forearm, the .45 hanging butt-down and ready. All the ammo hanging off him clinked comically when he moved. Sara did not laugh.

She was dry now. The thought of what Lucas' mean weaponry could do to her chipped away her courage. She had seen what kind of damage mushrooming slugs and hydrostatic pressure could do to a human body in several emergency wards. Spence, her first husband, had kept a hunting rifle in the bedroom closet. She had never seen him fire it. It had been an expensive gun . . . but she had never seen him fire it. If she got a chance to grab any of Lucas' guns, she was sure she could operate them, although the M-16, a new sight to her, looked a bit intimidating. That weapon, and the reasons for its presence in her living room—*her* living room, with the fireplace and the books and her comfortable furniture and the reproduction of "Girl's Portrait"—was not as easy to deal with as a mechanical intimidation. It was awesome; it was like the end.

He did not need the guns for her. She could be killed with any of the hundreds of blunt instruments and cutting edges scattered innocently around her own house. Bare hands could dispatch her . . . although from observing Lucas, it was now clear to her that he had seriously hurt his hands. It was a tiny advantage, not reassuring. It would be imbecilic to try to bash or stab Lucas while he had the guns, and Sara was not confident that she would exploit an opportunity if one presented itself. She wanted reason and sanity to prevail. She wanted everybody to live happily ever after.

She had become lost in a maze. Each time she turned, she smacked into a wall or dead end.

"Lucas." She spoke softly, head down. "Gabriel Stannard will never be able to evade the police long enough to come here. They've probably corraled him into protective custody by now. Even if he wanted some kind of crazy . . . showdown . . . with you, the police would never permit it."

He looked back at her with something like pity for the stupid. His gaze held the party line: *He's coming.*

"Sara. Dear. I think you're very wrong." The timbre of his voice had changed. Moments ago he had been faltering, scared, confused. He had needed her help. As soon as he had moved to the window and begun the rigid business of surveillance, his fear had dropped away like a chrysalis. The way he avoided line-of-sight contact with the windows, the stiff efficiency with which he moved, saddened her deep inside. Lucas—her Lucas—was receding.

"I think Stannard's fuzzy little rock-and-roll brain will make it imperative for him to seize any opportunity to kill me," he went on. Even the tiny hesitancies had evaporated from his voice. "He knows how mucked up the law enforcement and judicial systems are because he's a victim of them, just like me. Eye-for-eye justice is something his limited intellect can encompass without causing a headache. His persona *demands* he pick up the gauntlet. He really has no choice. I've turned his manufactured image against him, forcing him to live up to it. His wild-man reputation will compel him to face me, even while the timid good citizen inside him will persist that the safest course is to hole up behind a lot of guards and whistle in the police. To preserve the myth of what he is, he has to come. The cult of personality says so. Rules of promotion and publicity say so. I'm an expert in that field. For him to cringe now is bad advertising." He turned from the window to offer up another of his odd, scary smiles. "I may be crazy, but I'm not *stupid*."

She tried anger. It was all she had left. "I want my goddamned robe, Lucas, and I want it now. No more of this screwing around. If *you* think you're crazy, then shoot me. But I think—"

Her heart shoved its way past her voice when Lucas released the bolt on the M-16 with a metallic snap that rang in the high corners of the room, cutting her off like a splice in a movie. Her body tensed, anticipating a bullet. The shot would seem very loud.

Then she heard what Lucas was hearing. The hiss of tires on damp blacktop. Two car doors closing. Lucas was back at the front window, parting the curtains with the muzzle of the M-16. They heard sirens, shrieking tires growing closer. The sirens were no longer dismissible, faraway noises.

"Looks like showtime," he said.

Bracketing the front door was an arrangement of oblong, delicate windows that latched at the top, bottom, and middle and swung inward when unhooked. Sara had filled the little frames with thick stained glass. Lucas opened the middle one on the right-hand side of the door, flicked a microswitch on the side of the Nitefinder scope, and sighted. There was no light in the foyer. He was invisible.

She had expected more noise.

She thought of bolting for the kitchen. He could easily see her in the periphery of his vision, but now his concentration was focused outside. The kitchen door could not be locked or barricaded. The bathroom was a trap with a minuscule window. She could flee out the back door, but how far would she get, panicked, her bare white ass an easy target in the dark? She could flee upstairs, but how long until Lucas got fed up and started shooting through the ceiling?

Her thoughts of escape steamed away into pipe-dream mist at the sound of the gunshot. All gone. It sounded like a bark, a loud cough, a plug blown out of a hole by explosive decompression. It stiffened her body and slammed her eyelids shut. The sound was irresistible in the way it forced her to flinch. She wondered if what she had just heard was someone getting their skull ventilated. Time and physics suddenly failed to work. Otherwise, why couldn't she move her damned arms and legs?

"Sit down, Sara."

She did, floating back into her seat with the loose joints and feather weightlessness of a defective puppet, rudely aware of just how vulnerable and fragile her body was and wanting above all to keep that body intact and alive, even if it was the aging and malfunctioning thing she sometimes saw in her mirror.

Another voice pleaded inside her, and she hoped it

was the real reason she had not simply cut and run like a madwoman. The voice insisted that Lucas was her problem, that she was responsible. It demanded she engineer some solution while her puppet-flimsy body was shirking its duties.

All this galloped through her mind in two seconds or less. Time really *was* screwed sideways.

"Don't worry, Sara." He was talking to her but not looking at her. "Let it happen."

The wild lights of police flashbars illuminated Claremont Street. Tires crooned on the street outside. Somewhere a guttural motor revved and rumbled, distantly.

The all-over chill she felt might have been blowing through the tiny window by the front door. But that was crazy, too.

Bang!

Another brown and brittle boneyard fence divided itself around the prow of the Charger, and the tilting confusion of tombstones and plot markers jounced in the front windshield like the waiting maze of a particularly hairy pinball machine. Stannard corrected course, arms bulging as he cranked the doughnut steering wheel, holding the car to his chosen path by muscle and will. The tow-bar-style front bumper began picking off marble slabs, five or six, and chalky debris scattered across the hood with a hailstorm noise and was lost. They were regaining speed in spite of the crappy ground. The left headlight went dead with a crunch as it met the crossarm of a crucifix-shaped gravestone and turned it to chalk dust. Horus' hands jumped up to shield his face, but he was otherwise nonchalant.

Stannard downshifted and dug out, vaulting the Charger through the far fence of the cemetery. After a few bouncing seconds of wiping out foliage in both directions, he fixed on the twin track of mud ruts he had described to Horus as a goat path. It was slick and messy, but the car fit, and it provided an adequate way to sneak up on Claremont Street from behind . . . a totally unanticipatable direction.

He was thankful for the hairy police chase, for the concentration needed to ramrod the Charger through the muck ahead, for all the obstacles cluttering the complicated road that led to Dr. Sara Windsor. His mind was occupied and kept at bay from the real question of just what the fuck he thought he was doing. Horus would not nail him with that one; neither would Cannibal Rex, for different reasons. Horus wanted to do what was needed, to be there for Stannard if the situation got overwhelming, beyond his capacity to cope. Cannibal wanted to hang out, in hopes of some serious mayhem. For Stannard, thinking too hard about what he intended to do tonight could abort everything. He knew this, and so programmed his mind to be other places, thinking other things.

He already knew he did not want the climax of this whole movie bursting out with him offstage.

He was aware that for perhaps the first time, he had to play the *part* of Gabriel Stannard, to become the Stannard of the sleeve copy and rock articles and promo hype, and to do it without the safety nets that were usually in place for the monied and noteworthy. Money and power had a way of insulating you, of pampering you into a warm stupor of self-security and surface passions. All the insulation in Beverly Hills, however, could not save him from the things Lucas Ellington was capable of doing to his mind.

The cops doubtlessly thought he was some kind of fuzzy-minded jukebox hero, as stupid as the airheaded teenagers who plonked down their drug money to buy his albums. That made Stannard bristle. No way his moment was going to be usurped by some overweight Maalox junkie who probably kept a framed picture of Jack Webb on his bathroom wall, no fucking way, dudes.

In the flash department, the cops were losers. Without their hardware they were nothing. While he, Gabriel Stannard, was . . .

Was. He *was*.

Nobody manhandled a microphone better. Nobody gave a more outrageous interview. Nobody could have succeeded in running the wild gauntlet he was now completing, besting it to invade the stage and perform the way he wanted.

Tented open on the Danish leather sofa in his bedroom next to the TV and tape trolley was a screenplay entitled *Shakedown*. Sertha had also read it. The plot involved the efforts of a group of high-tech thieves to rip off the gate receipts of a Woodstock-style rock festival. Lots of violence, chases, gunfire, and gadgets. A production floor of $30 million, they estimated, *if* Gabriel Stannard could be convinced to play the part of the main rock 'n' roller—the inside man who choreographs the heist, the prime target in the ensuing pursuit. He eats it during a climactic shoot-out on the Golden Gate Bridge, Stannard recalled. A meaty role, fair portions of good dialogue, and a spectacular death scene.

The casting genius who had proposed Stannard for the role had opened up a big and enticing door. Parts for rock stars were nothing to write *Variety* about; it happened a lot. But most were one-shots. David Bowie had been one of the rare exceptions. Tonight, a hero scene in Dos Piedras against a basket case would cinch his movie career and deliver him unto his entire future. Bad boys aged badly, he knew . . . unless they were versatile enough to switch hit, to shift gears, to ride the breakers of change.

It could be the perfect melding of fantasy with real life, after which the public would not bother trying to distinguish the difference. To stick his neck up to the knife this way was a fearsome gamble. He felt the physical ache of bluff and bluster versus sinew and gristle. Audiences never believed performers were real people. But tonight the Gabriel Stannard everyone saw on MTV could come to life by daring the old Reaper to do his worst and pulling off a typically audacious Stannard stunt. He would become immortal. Archaeologists would dig up his records and recognize him instantly.

Yes, he wanted this risk. The kickback would be as staggering as the danger. Past this event, he could relax from proving himself. The words of *Hollywood Weekend Wrap-Up*'s Mardi Grassley taunted him: Was Gabriel Stannard sizzle or steak? He promised himself that if he prevailed tonight, he'd toast Mardi Grassley with some ultrafine Taittinger in the back of a limousine. Then he'd charm her clothes off. Then he'd kick her smug rump out into the middle of the intersection of Doheny and Sunset Boulevard on a Friday night. He wondered how tough it would be to have a camera crew waiting there in readiness.

What he was about to do could pave the road to bigger and better lies for all and enough media attention to get supremely drunk on. He could ride the afterglow for a decade. If he won.

He shoved all this from his head. Get ice, as Jackson Knox used to say constantly. Get control.

"Too bad there aren't any decent rock stations in this neck o' the swamp," he said, pointing at the Charger's dashboard radio. Now that he had located the hillside path, he would arrive at his destination in less time than it took to listen to one of his own hit singles.

Reflectors winked just ahead in mirrored crimson. Everybody steeled for impact, but Stannard decided to slow down. A car was parked on the path. The single headlight revealed that it was unoccupied. It was a metallic-brown, mud-splattered Bronco, pulled over with its port wheels in one of the road ruts, leaning against the rise of the hill at an angle that barely permitted passage on the right side.

"Be a shame to get traffic jammed now," Stannard grumped. Horus craned to peer inside the Bronco as they passed. In the backseat, Cannibal Rex snapped the action on the Auto Nag again. He loved doing that; it sounded so *bad*.

The door handles of the two vehicles whispered within two inches of each other. "Probably teenyboppers," said Horus. "Fucking or doping."

"My *fans*!" Stannard hollered. "My boys, my girls, my lovely leather ladies. Hope they're banging each other to 'Maneater.' "

Just ahead was a barrier of posts twined with barbed wire. A rusty NO TRESPASSING sign hung from one corner. Beyond that was a brief drop to the dead end of Claremont. The street was quiet, utterly suburban . . . except for the sheriff's car and the two uniforms hunkered down behind it.

"Aww, *shit*." Stannard seemed let down and pumped up at the same time. He geared the Charger into reverse and backed up, killing his single headlight. "Cannibal, let's do it."

Cannibal Rex laid the Auto Mag on the seat beside him and opened up the black duffel, handing Horus the laser-sighted American 180 plus an extra clip. Horus checked it swiftly and professionally. He preferred a light rapid-fire weapon if it had to come down to guns. Cannibal withdrew the SPAS-12 riot gun and began slotting rounds of number-three buckshot into the magazine. Then he chambered the first shell and handed the gun over the seat. Stannard tucked it barrel down between the door and the bucket he was sitting in. Cannibal hooked a few of the flash-pop stun grenades into the button holes on his fatigue jacket. Then he handed over something small and heavy Horus had not seen before. The dark man's eyebrows went up.

Stannard unzipped his jeans and rummaged around

inside his leopard panties, nesting some small and deadly failsafe right next door to his notorious penis. Then he buttoned up, and Cannibal handed over an inhaler from which Stannard took several long, deep draws.

"Rocket fuel," Stannard said, exhaling slowly, feeling his bloodstream run through the high RPMs. "Okay, we got cops. Don't kill anybody. But let me get to the house."

"Let's do some crimes," Cannibal muttered, anxious to get on with it.

"That's it?" said Horus.

"That's it." Stannard grinned. They all sat unmoving for a beat, idling; then, with all the power his rockstar vocal chords and deep-dish diaphragm could expel, he screamed:

"Banzai!!"

and with a brain-rattling roar the Charger sucked up the slack on the trail, plowed through the fence, and crashed down onto North Claremont Street in a landslide of bushes, rocks, and mud-fill, accumulating speed in a crank-spiked flurry, ass-whipping right to left, smoke billowing from the wheel wells, long whiskers of barbed wire streaming backward from the car's chromium teeth.

The cops less than a block away were already pulling their iron as Stannard floored it and the opposite end of the street filled up with speeding police cars.

32

CHRIS CARPENTER HAD NEVER SEEN his dad's buddy K. C. Dew move his fat old ass so fast in his life.

The ululation of approaching sirens had suddenly been flooded out by the crash of splintering timber and the screech of bumper steel scratching sparks on blacktop. Chris looked up, and a lone headlight like the demon eyeball of the Hellbound Train lit his face, a fiery meteor coming at them full speed from the dead end of Claremont Street.

"Jesus *H.*," yelled K. C., sounding as though a manure truck had just unloaded into his swimming pool. "What the *christ* have we got here?"

Then the fanfare of engines drowned him out.

K. C. put the flat of his hand in the center of Chris' chest and shoved, wresting away the riot gun in the younger man's grip. Chris sprawled buttwise in the rainwater as the single headlight nailed them, trailing sparks, singing THE END.

K. C. rolled and brought up the shotgun, allowing that critical quarter-second to verify intent, a deadly eyeblink of calm reserved for the violently baptized. When there was no mistaking the lethal trajectory of the Charger, he pumped and discharged 2 three-inch rounds right down its throat in less than a second. The car went nose first into the street, collapsing onto its front rims and yawing wildly around to the left. One wheel disengaged and rolled off into the brush. K. C. was already loping toward it as it completed its one eighty and ground to a stop, leaving its parts in a trail behind it. A mag wheel bent into a potato-chip shape spun on the street like a fat silver dollar, clanging. Smoke rose from the rims, and the perforated radiator pissed steam into the wet night air. The phantom sniper in the front window of 7764 North Claremont had been momentarily upstaged, and as K. C. approached the crippled Charger, the far end of the street became clogged with a convoy of police cars. Chris was still sitting on his ass in a puddle.

Then everything lit up.

The men in the car ducked and covered as the flash-pop stun grenade dropped out the window by Cannibal Rex did its blinding trick. Chris Carpenter got his head slapped against his cruiser by the concussion and slid into unconsciousness with supernovae blotting out his vision. K. C. was lifted into the air, arms swanning, and landed spreadeagled in the street. When he was still, blood began to trickle out of his ears.

The final treat out of Cannibal Rex's goodie bag was Stannard's standby Magnum revolver. Stannard gripped it in one hand and the SPAS-12 riot gun in the other, kicked back his door, and began to sprint for the front lawn while everyone was still reeling.

Horus and Cannibal Rex piled out of the far side of the wrecked Charger and brought their weapons to bear just as the police convoys shrieked in, nose-to, in defensive slide stops. Officers hurried into position; weapons were aimed back.

Stannard dodged around the front of K. C. Dew's cruiser, his biceps feeling dumbbell stress from the hardware he was lugging while trying to run. He paid no attention to the voice that now barked at him through a bullhorn. It told him to stop. Jesus, how pat could you get?

Then it told him to drop his weapon, and he did. As he passed the front grille, the short barrel of the riot gun whanged crookedly off one of the ram bumpers and spun beneath the car. There was no time to scoop it up. Stannard did not break speed; half the front lawn was gone now, and he still had his trusty Magnum. The bullhorn told him that the lawn was dangerous. No gun-waving cops tried to intercept him even though the odds were tilted and he was wide open.

Providence could be questioned later. For now, he ran—building to a full-bore fullback charge, his muscular legs gnawing the distance down to nothing, the leather thongs on his deerskin shirt whipping his face.

The cops already had a million problems. They had to secure the street, to protect residents and themselves from the firepower in the hands of Horus and Cannibal Rex as well as Lucas Ellington. Would they blow him down on the lawn, a moving target in the dark?

Apparently not. The bullhorn wailed on, echoing in the rain, but he no longer found it intelligible. He took the porch steps two at a time, hit the planks, and rolled, his boots crashing into the wall and rattling the front door. He crouched below the porch rail, between the windows, where the cops would not be able to pick him off if they changed their tiny minds.

As he was fond of saying to his concert audiences, it looked a lot like it was showtime.

"What do you think?" Horus said.

"Mexican standoff," said Cannibal Rex, grinning like a person who has truly lost his mind. His wraparounds captured the strobelight glare of the police flashbars, and his deformed picking hand now caressed the trigger of the Auto Mag. He wanted to play a killer solo in the worst way.

From his crouch near the wheelless right front well of the Charger, Horus knew the police could see his laser spot dancing around on their cars. The rain and atmospheric conditions might hamper the sight; fog was murder on lasers. He also saw the bright blue flashbar of an ambulance, riding higher than those of the police cruisers, pull up and stop far to the rear. Major badness was slowly forming out of the storm, taking a shape, making ready to do violence. "No shooting," he admonished the coke-snorting maniac next to him. "Not unless we have to. Our job is to hold them back, keep them from interfering—that's all."

"He made it to the front porch," Cannibal whined. "He's got his piece. What the fuck. Let's rock 'n' roll." The bone earring caught random light as he mock-sighted the big pistol.

In Horus' brain, the options had already been weighed. Stannard had burdened him with Cannibal as backup. Cannibal was too hyper, not reliable, but Horus would do what Stannard asked. He was therefore a free agent to render Cannibal expendable if he proved to be a hindrance. The adrenalated jabber coming at him was not a good sign. If Cannibal Rex wanted to play bad guy, Horus would see it in his eyes, in the slight jump of his finger on a steel trigger. There was plenty of time to kill Cannibal Rex with a head blow before he got the chance to hurt someone.

Oblivious to everything but his gun and the game, Cannibal Rex emptied his inhaler into his skull and tossed it away. It clicked and rolled on the street.

"That's littering," said Horus.

"Aw, another law broken. Damned shame."

Then the music started, and everybody on both

sides shut their traps. It was loud and distorted, the bass notes penetrating the rainfall, and it was blasting out of Sara Windsor's house.

The singing voice was Gabriel Stannard's, and the song was "Riptide," Whip Hand's first hit single.

Raindrops rolled forward off the gray sedan as it stopped sharply, its headlights inches from the rear of a van-type ambulance. The sniper saw two paramedics in orange jerseys leaning against the port side of their unit, smokes in hand. They seemed unconcerned, wanting nothing to do with gunfire or blocking strays. They were here only to plug up the bleeding or body-bag the dead and so turned their backs on the standoff to stare into the empty field on the far side of Claremont.

The sniper sniffed trouble up at the point, the head of the cluster of law enforcement vehicles. If he ventured forward to scope things out, the locals would involve him . . . and he might not get to do his job. The paramedics saw him and decided to squat down to continue their conversation. Past that, they gave him no notice as he stepped off the pavement and was swallowed up by the rain-sprinkled darkness of the open field.

His boots grabbed the mulch, and the ground soon began to slope away and become pocky. No fun, to blunder into a chuckhole out here and maybe turn an ankle.

So many deadly weapons had come out into the chill night air. It was time for him to unsheath his own, in the name of civil good.

He fixed on Sara Windsor's house. He'd scanned the available maps and diagrams. He made his way toward his predetermined optimum vantage, unshouldering his waterproof case.

Most police tactical teams favored bolt-action Remingtons in the 800 series for sniper duty, but modern firearms technology was working to unseat bolt guns and forward thinking was important to the sniper. Most sniping ops, he knew, were within a hundred yards of the target, and his weapon of choice was a nightmare of accuracy for three times that distance. He unsleeved it with practiced-in-the-dark precision, careful not to snag the premounted opticals.

The sniper was an adept. He knew his job, and he respected history.

Once upon a time, in the late 1950s, a team of designers under Eugene Stoner fabricated a rifle-and-cartridge combination and pushed it hard at a government anxious to provide its dog soldiers with a weapon more modern than the standard field issue of the Second World War. The gun was designated AR-15, and used high-velocity .22-caliber ammo. The Air Force Security Police used it to replace a variety of rifles and submachine guns, and the army followed suit by ordering the guns for use by Special Forces trainers. In Indochina they achieved the status of legend. The Viet Cong offered rewards in gold to anyone who captured one of the fabled Black Rifles. The mythos was pumped by horror stories of the buzz-saw damage the AR-15's whirling slugs could wreack on a human body. President Kennedy kept one of the guns on his yacht, for shooting sharks. As the war escalated and Indochina began to be called Vietnam by the news personalities, the military's need for a smaller and more manipulable infantry weapon caused the AR-15 to be tagged for service use under the new designation M-16.

For the Dos Piedras assignment, the sniper had chosen a customized Insight Systems AR-I. It was based on the AR-15. Its power was guaranteed by the heavier 7.62-millimeter cartridges it fired; its accuracy, by the sniper's personal hot-rodding. He had replaced the "vanilla" plastic stock with one of glass-filled, injection-molded polymer. It was padded by a thick neoprene collar that could warm his cheek and make the whole package less slippery. He had covered the front grip with a steel-backed National Match handguard of dense, shock-absorbing foam. The position and terrain denied him the use of the Harris bipod, his "crutch." This shot would have to be made from a free-standing position.

He flicked on his optics and test-sighted the Windsor front porch. The gridwork of the Thompson Contender scope came alive in red—another personal modification. His line of fire bisected the no man's land currently in force between the crippled Charger and the barricade of police cars thirty yards away. At this range, the sniper could have turned Cannibal Rex's bald head into lasagna with a single shot. But that was not what he had come for.

He tracked the reticle across the front windows, right to left. All were shaded. A shadow scared briefly across the one nearest the front door.

He saw Gabriel Stannard move.

The shooting gloves kept his hands warm and his fingers free. Just as the sprinkles of rain began to get more ambitious, he shouldered the AR-I, maneuvered his toothpick around to the far edge of his mouth, and sighted.

God, he thought, *I love my job.*

Lucas knew a Gabriel Stannard entrance when he saw one.

Pinning the two sheriffs down behind their own cruiser had been simple. While one end of the street choked up with blinking gumball lights, the opposite end had filled up with the furor of Stannard's arrival. Mild surprise was Lucas' only reaction as he watched the jacked-up, overpowered street machine vault from nowhere, from the place of graves, to touch down in his field of fire. Guessing who was at its helm was no quiz. He felt sorry for the cops—those poor suckers were caught in the eye of a shitstorm they could comprehend only in the broadest procedural terms. They would not care about his back-story or the neat fit of the events about to happen. Now they were faced off by Stannard's own assault force, two men holding twenty-five at bay. Lucas had factored the police into his scenario, and it looked like Stannard had, too. The authorities were not stupid . . . they just had no idea of how it was supposed to go.

Lucas kept shy of the windows to avoid possible sharpshooters. The police had information, and none had dared to intercept Stannard on the front lawn because they were aware that at Lucas' Point Pitt cabin a man had bought the farm courtesy of a land mine, and they had seen how Jackson Knox had died. None of them would be eager to step down hard on turf that had not yet been swept for explosives.

There were no mines salted into Sara's front yard.

The older sheriff had been a man with a considerable bag of *cojones*. Lucas had watched him face down the oncoming Charger with the steady cool of a toreador dispatching an uppity bull. Through the Nitefinder scope, Lucas had seen K. C. Dew's tongue protruding from his lips in concentration as he gunned down the vehicle, tearing away its front tires with his second expert shot. Then Claremont Street had come alive with cop cars.

Sara was still mute in her chair by the fireplace. Soon her fear would kick over into anger, and he would not be able to cow her. She would attack.

Several times she had started to speak, then fallen silent. She was still mustering strength. He did not want to kill her.

The brilliant phosphorous white-out of the flash-pop had frozen everybody. Stannard's men were well packed, and Stannard had come upon the house with the speed of a Fury . . . but almost no weaponry. Lucas' eyes had recovered from the grenade burn in time to see him drop the shotgun. Soon he would be without his six-gun as well.

More sirens, distantly. Backup; maybe the fire department.

He ripped open a black Velcroed flap pocket on his pants leg and produced a cassette. It was time to get down to it.

Stannard's cheek was almost admirable; he'd made it, the crazy son of a bitch.

The phone in the hallway began to ring again, and Sara's now-sunken eyes sought it each time it made noise. Lucas walked over to where she sat.

"That'll be the police, outside," he said. "They want to know if you're all right, what I want, all that good B-movie stuff. Let's give them a little easy listening instead." He handed her the cassette. "Play it loud."

She reached, then snatched her hand back to reinforce her falling towel. Then she slotted the tape into her stereo, notched up the volume, and hit Play.

There was a huge piece of smoky quartz on the glass shelf next to the cassette deck. It was a hexagonal chunk with bubbles inside of it. It would make an awkward weapon, and Sara estimated she would get halfway across the room before Lucas chopped her down with his unstoppable Teflon slugs.

Lucas was nearly gone from the world, totally removed. A changeling had been substituted, a malign, alien creature that looked like Lucas and had his voice . . . but one that found more joy in the passion play about to enact than any salvation she might offer. It was Lucas with his emotions deleted, or, more to the point, Lucas with his emotional equipment reduced to the level of tools, used to get what he wanted. Needed, now.

She wanted to say no, to say that it had to stop now. But the stereo emitted an abrasive opening riff, and

Gabriel Stannard began to screech about getting caught in the riptide.

She knew what her mind was doing. It was converting Lucas into an enemy so she could goose herself into action and dispose of him. It was converting him into something she would not mind eliminating. Deep love relationships frequently evoked a similar pattern. Broken lovers circumvented trauma and the depression of loss by redefining the former partner in the most repulsive terms possible—not exactly a healing process so much as a survival mechanism. Her mind whittled away at him inexorably, changing him as much as he was changing himself. It was like a steadily brightening light. Soon it would be blinding.

Surrender would accomplish Lucas nothing. The police were obviously girded for a massacre; they wanted shooting to start, because it would simplify their options. There was no leniency in the face of a SWAT madman. At this point Lucas was armed, dangerous, homicidal. The only reason the police had not stormed her house was because they needed to know if she was alive; that was why the phone had started ringing. Their need for her to be alive would diminish as time ground onward.

Even if Lucas got what he wanted, he could never escape. Why was he stamping PAID IN FULL on his death certificate this way?

Lucas had mentioned cycles closing. He had no plan beyond what was to transpire here in her house, tonight. Unless . . .

Stannard came juggernauting in to impact with the wall opposite the porch balustrade outside. Lucas hurried to crack a shade and take a peek.

. . . unless Lucas survived, and was hospitalized, so the cycle could start all over again.

She realized, abruptly and defenselessly, what

would have befallen her if she and Lucas had gotten together in Los Angeles, "gotten to know each other better," as the lie went, gone to bed together at the time she had craved it, made love at the moment she needed tactile reassurance worse than any ache she had ever felt. She would not be breathing now.

He raised his voice to penetrate the raucous Whip Hand tune and beckoned her to the door. The rifle came up. "The man of the hour is at your front door, Sara. Why don't you let him in?"

33

THE DOOR OPENED TO A slit of light, and Gabriel Stannard saw a nude lady. Already things inside him were fighting to jump their hinges.

"What you want to do," said a voice, "is to crawl inside slowly, on your hands and knees. Push the gun ahead of you with the knuckles of your hand. Any frills, and I'll blow your spine out your asshole. Stick your head up any farther, and the cops down there will probably do the same."

A hot animal odor pulsed from him, the smell of lions on the sedge coming right out of his pores. Astrologically, he was a Leo; Sertha had told him that one day he would have to live up to it. The audiences did not know Gabriel Stannard was for real. Now he could feel how real his blood was. Cannibal Rex's dope charge fizzed away in his veins like champagne.

Conscious that the eyes watching him were wired to a trigger finger, he set the Magnum down uncocked and scooted through the doorway as instructed.

Hard, stringy, seesaw guitar riffs cranked hard into

the night. Behind them, his own voice, seven years younger. His heart had begun its own manic drum solo, and his system throbbed with the onrushing intoxication he felt in concert, where he controlled his audiences, got them to *show their hands* and jump up and down. When he exhorted the ladies down front to toss him their underwear, by christ, they stripped down and *did* it.

The naked lady shut the door, and before he could ask what kind of weird fucking scene *this* was, the M-16 was sniffing the bridge of his nose.

The woman, the doctor, had a look about her that said she had seen two autopsy films too many. There was a fire going in the hearth. And towering above him, armed and all in black, was the man who had given him the permanent scar through his right eyebrow.

The moment was perfect for him to tuck his elbow, roll, pluck up the Magnum, and blow the psycho's gray matter all over the foyer. The drugs, twanging and rippling through his muscle tissue, cut loose.

At the instant Stannard's body moved, Lucas stomped down hard on his other hand, anchoring him to the polished wood floor and arresting any hope of momentum. The muzzle of the M-16 swung away as a booted foot shot around to shut Stannard's face with a thud and the click of chipping dental work.

The singer fell back onto his butt, both hands clamped over his mouth and muffling a guttural noise of rage. His eyes shone at Lucas in the firelight, a bright, glazed blue. Lucas' eyes assessed him in turn and found no threat.

He stooped and easily retrieved the revolver. At the sight of his own blood oozing between his fingers, Stannard made another inarticulate growl and almost charged. The M-16 kept him right where he was, huddled against the front door. After a second he searched his gums with his fingers and came up with a chunk of broken tooth. He stared at it as though it were a sliver of ice from Saturn's rings.

"You shouldn't swear with your mouth full," said Lucas, motioning with the gun. "Over by the fireplace, back to the wall. And stay on your hands and knees. Now."

The bass beat from the stereo made the floor buzz. Stannard was aware that as he crawled, he was almost able to sneak his hand down into the crotch of his jeans. Almost.

"I expected more," Lucas half shouted, enunciating so his voice penetrated the instrumental bridge of the song. "Don't you have a speech? Something more flamboyant?"

Stannard's jaw felt like broken concrete. He slid around, backed against the warm bricks near the fireplace. With effort, he said, "You saw the video. Or you wouldn't be here. You're the same way. . . ."

More of his cockiness leaked away when the expression in Lucas' eyes told him that he had not seen "Maneater."

C'mon, bad man—take me down if you can.

The message had gone unreceived.

"You're totally in the dark, aren't you?" Lucas said. "You're so self-involved you don't even know why you're here. Is this the persona, the phony image, the lie you foist on children that makes them die?"

Stannard knew that explaining his movie deal and his need to maintain his record as the singer with the most covers in the history of *Circus* magazine would not serve. Behind that, a thought that chilled him like a shot of liquid nitrogen—the thought that this was *not* the man who had accosted him on the steps of the Beverly Hills Courthouse. This was a different guy who only looked like Lucas Ellington, and the image of the man Stannard had come prepared to call out started to flake at the edges.

"You're going to die in the dark," Lucas said.

Stannard had a cold flash of Jackal Reichmann as he had looked in intensive care, his stare fixed, his lungs filling and emptying rhythmically, as though his respirator were wired into a drum machine. The woman wearing the towel wore the same blank, zomboid expression. Now, as his backbone went clammy against the bricks in preparation to catch a bullet, the woman came to life and moved forward, nearer the fire, to protest.

"No," said Sara. "The dying, the killing—it stops, and it stops *now*, Lucas. Listen to me. You and I can go back. We can fix everything that went wrong. We can obliterate all of this. Look at me. I know what I'm dealing with now. This poor son of a bitch can't help you. His dying can't help you. See? He doesn't even know what's going on. . . ."

She stopped talking when the muzzle of the M-16 rose to zero in on Stannard's forehead. The singer tried to take the only opening he could see.

"Uh . . . better listen to her, Lucas . . . I mean, I can help get you out of this mess, man—maybe she 'n' me are the only people who can help you now." Sweat trickled freely from beneath the white-blond hair. Blood slicked his chin. The scar splitting his eyebrow stood out, bloodlessly pale against his tan.

Lucas aimed at the scar, the mark he had placed on Stannard so long ago, and thought about the greasy attorney Whip Hand's management had sent to buy him off with a settlement. "You're going to tell me about trials, and media coverage. Devices by which I am supposed to attain leniency and freedom in return for sparing your life now." He shook his head with the helpless grin parents reserve for excessively stupid children. To Sara, he added, "I've brought my entire life together, right here in this room. I need no further help. I've woven the threads just fine, and to my own satisfaction. Now I must hurry. This moment cannot hold."

Sara thought the only thing Lucas had woven together was a quilt of total insanity. Yes, he *had* achieved his various purposes—he'd gotten wife and daughter back in a multiform configuration. He'd reconstructed the past so it came out with an apocalyptic punchline.

A banshee wail from Stannard—the Stannard on the tape, wrapping up "Riptide"—cut them all off. Lucas quickly checked the front windows. The next song on the tape commenced.

"Recognize it?" said Lucas.

Stannard knew Jackson Knox's badass intro to "Hit Man" by heart. They'd banged out the tune together, with Brion Hardin contributing lyrics. The hit man of the title was Stannard, who onstage would prance through his King of the Hit Singles routine. The song was always a spike point of their live show; they built toward it, working the crowd, making them wet for it; then Whip Hand would deliver with a bang.

About a hundred newspapers had recorded with fact-mad fervor that "Hit Man" had been the song performed by Whip Hand at the moment the Los Angeles riot broke out and people started dying.

"Sara—get on your knees, please, and face him. Now."

"What?"

"You have to be looking up at him. And you, songbird, Mister Hit Man, you have to sing now. Sing for your life. Sing along with yourself. That should appeal to someone with an ego as huge as yours. Perform. You are here to perform for everyone, to show off. So do it. Don't laugh, because your life really *does* depend on your performance now."

"Go ahead," Stannard said quickly to Sara. "Get down just in case he fries a gasket and pulls the trigger."

She wanted to object, but her heart threatened to burst from her chest if she did not comply. She got onto her knees before the rock god.

"Maybe you could toss the audience a moon," said Lucas, savoring it now. "Drop your pants in public, like your buddy."

Stannard knew of Tim Fozzetto's ass-bearing routine for 'Gasm. That brought the rage surging back.

"Timmy's dead meat because of you."

"If I were you, I'd worry about my ass instead of his."

"And Jackal Reichmann's a vegetable! You really are one berserk motherfucker. You need a vet to put you to sleep."

"Can't hear you." Stannard's "Hit Man" vocals buffered the three of them from the outside world. "Come on, superstar. Gyrate. Entice the women in the audience. Touch your crotch."

Stannard's mouth stalled, but only for an instant. His mind shifted gears behind the ice-blue irises. "Sure. Whatever you want. Just don't hurt the lady, okay? Be cool with that piece, and you'll get whatever—"

"I already know that," Lucas said, finger whitening on the trigger. The females in the audience did not have to fear him. *He* was not the danger.

"Watch this." A lascivious stage smile cut across the singer's face. He had assumed his serpentlike concert masque. Slowly, methodically, with a practiced hand dance he had executed hundreds of times in hundreds of bedrooms, the ex–front man for Whip Hand opened up his pants. The yellow and orange and black of his leopard bikini briefs radiated from the V of his jeans.

Sara tensed, shutting her eyes, shaking. The gun barrel hovered too far behind her to grab. She was the no man's land between the two antagonists.

She could not see Lucas' face as he said, "Perfect—hold it right there." And fired.

Certain she was hit and killed, she yelped and hugged the floor. Certain she had felt the bullet hurtle past her face close enough to skin her nose, she stayed down.

Stannard screamed, drowning out his recorded self as the bullet shattered his right kneecap. He toppled to the left, his hand in his pants, with a grunt. His head knocked over the iron rack of fireplace tools, and a poker clattered on the hearth. Every particle of his Tarzan persona evaporated in that instant; Lucas saw it leave the singer's expression like a fleeing ghost, like a corrupt soul abandoning a drained corpus.

Lucas took one step closer, flipping the M-16 from single to rapid fire. From waltz to rock and roll.

Stannard's taped voice pealed into high screech, telling millions that he was the hit man, baby . . .

The wounded man jerked his hand out of his groin, and Lucas caught a fast flash of black onyx in Stannard's fist. Sara, who had recovered hands and knees and was trying to scrabble out of the way, saw the singer wince as the thing in his hand made a flat bang—*spack!*—and unleashed a flash of light.

The slug from the three-and-a-half-inch Magnum derringer, the fail-safe Stannard had tucked into his pants back on the goat path, took Lucas low in the left side of the neck and failed to erupt from the far side. He made a watery strangling noise that went unheard past the music and absorbed the momentum of the bullet with four anvil-heavy backward steps. His eyes squeezed shut in pain, then opened in time to see Stannard making for the .44 Magnum, which Lucas had discarded on the sofa a safe distance from Sara's reach.

Lucas clamped his hand tight around the pistol grip of the M-16, and the hammering din of the clip emptying itself obliterated all other sounds. The muzzle kicked up and up as a jagged, zigzag path of Teflon slugs tracked from the floor between Stannard's legs, through him, and up the wall above his head, finishing with four holes blown out of the ceiling. The light kick of the gun was enough to steal what remained of Lucas' balance, and he went backward through one of the front windows in a shower of glass, his throat gushing fresh blood.

The Whip Hand tape went dead between songs, and in the moment of abrupt silence Lucas' hand released the M-16. It clattered to the floor. He hung, seesawing on the window frame. Shards dropped from him and clinked.

Then Cannibal Rex snapped his own trigger, and all hell busted loose outside.

Gravity arranged Lucas, sliding him back into the room. His body settled into a slack sitting position, eyes opaque, his head lolling to the right like an infant's, exposing the pumping carnage of his torn carotid.

Sara opened her eyes and saw Gabriel Stannard curled into a fetal ball on the floor, soot from the shovel and poker blackening his face in streaks. A puddle of his own blood was widening around him. His hand twitched without instructions; he groaned. It was all he could manage. She could not tell how many times he had been hit.

She crawled naked to the window as "Killer Guitars" commenced with a rattling Jackal Reichmann snare drum flourish. Glass splinters stuck into her knees and the balls of her feet as she reached to Lucas and got spattered when he exhaled. Her hands came away thickly coated, crimson.

He was still alive. But there was no more of Lucas in his eyes. Lucas had been all used up.

She closed her eyes and tried to hold without breaking. Outside, people were still firing guns. It seemed noisy and furious.

Very deliberately, she got up and walked to the bathroom on bleeding feet to fetch her robe. That was important. It felt wonderful on her skin, drinking up her nervous sweat. She bent over the motionless but living form of Gabriel Stannard to upright the tool rack and arrange shovel, whisk brush, and poker into position. Above the mantel, the melodramatic eyes of the women in "Girl's Portrait" watched. They looked like nothing human. The Japanese painted for different values; there were almost no Oriental photorealists. *Jesus god,* she thought, *I'm going into shock now; I've lost my mind, and I'm losing time. . . .*

She stepped over to the sofa and lifted Stannard's .44 Magnum. It was much heavier than her Colt Diamondback. She checked the cylinder to verify the gun was loaded while Stannard's voice sang of the glories of the killer six-string, the electric axe, the fretmaster, the guitar hero. The new Pantheon. The shooting outside had stopped, and people wearing body armor and toting shotguns were running doubletime up her front walk.

She pulled the hammer of the Magnum back to full cock and aimed at Stannard's right ear. The weight of the gun caused the muzzle to waver, so she took two steps closer until it was impossible to miss. It felt correct now. Stannard had helped remove Lucas from the world; the Lucas she knew was gone. Her hopes had been erased, her work had been destroyed, and her chance for redemption by setting things right had been stolen. Lucas had wanted Stannard dead, and Stannard was still hanging on.

Now it was Sara who wanted to backtrack into the past, to change it around. Tears blurred her aim.

Pieces of the front door and frame exploded inward as the police kicked it down and piled into the foyer. Somebody shouted *no*; somebody shouted *stop* just as her finger applied pressure to the trigger. The safety was off. Her father had taught her how to shoot.

She wiped her face with her free sleeve and resumed bracing the gun with both hands. There was no way she could explain anything to these strangers. One overzealous cop raised his weapon to sight on her and was ordered to back off.

Sara turned, sighted, and fired. To her the motions were like swimming or riding a bicycle, unforgettable.

Three feet away the cassette deck sprang off the glass shelf, tried to spin, and crashed against the wall, scattering broken chunks of metal and plastic. The shelf held. Gabriel Stannard's voice was severed in an instant, and the component's blue digital meters faded out like dying eyes.

34

LIKE AN INSULT FROM HEAVEN, the rain got heavier and wetter and more miserable. The sniper spat his toothpick out onto the dark ground. Cheated of his moment, he felt fatigued and impotent, as though the plug had been pulled on his stamina.

Through his crimson-illuminated reticle, he had seen his target come crashing through the front window, obviously shot, obviously unmoving, no threat and nothing to deal with. The sniper's work had been done for him, usurped by some amateur. He wanted nothing to do with the cleanup phase; it was not his mess.

In Arizona, Lucas had isolated a similar target in his own sights and had the moment stolen from him as well. His response had been a sense of relief, of freedom. In Dos Piedras, the killer himself became the new bullseye, framed by a new scope, a better shooter, and the moment had again been purloined. The sniper felt no sense of burden lifted. He was pissed off that he had mushed out here in the rain for nothing.

He had seen every cop movie it was possible to rent on videotape. They never got it right; they were always out to lunch when it came to the challenge of portraying police procedure the way it really was. Good and bad guys meet; both draw their awesome high-tech shooting irons simultaneously, both are such expert shots that they blow their guns out of each other's hands. Or die in the moment of discharge. Or, sometimes, a SWAT sharpshooter was brought in to terminate the danger with the skill of a surgeon excising a malignancy. Irresistible force meets even more irresistible force. King Kong versus Godzilla. The good force was supposed to prevail. It wasn't over unless good triumphed. If good got its ass kicked, then there was usually a sequel to set things right. Now that the sniper thought about it, he liked those predictable cinema finishes better than this.

That was the way the world was supposed to work. You eliminated the misfit, and society could go chugging happily onward.

He saw the media trucks and jeeps begin to hamper traffic down at the point. Video bar lights clicked on, and harsh shadows capered on the wet pavement.

As it turned out, not landing the chopper in the open field had been an excellent decision.

Keeping snipers clear of the press was the golden rule of SWAT operations. There was a phenomenon called "post-shoot trauma." To protect the integrity of the team, each team member's exposure to media attention had to be minimized. The news bloodsuckers would not care that he had done no shooting and in fact felt bad about that. They would only be interested in getting the guy with the long rifle case on camera.

To get himself clear of Dos Piedras tonight, the sniper realized, he would have to proceed as though he *had* actually shot someone. The evasive escape tactics would be the same. That put him back into a context in which he could function. He sleeved the AR-I and twisted his ballcap around so the wide bill would keep the increased rain off his glasses. It might be possible to walk back to Vista View Park from here without being seen at all.

He turned his back on the scene and walked away, across the field, feeling a little better already.

35

"I DON'T KNOW WHY IT took so long to call," Sertha said. "Call it failure of nerve. People who are upset can waste so much time."

"Don't apologize; it's natural." The voice on the other end of the line was deep, succoring, almost the tone of an analyst. It was comforting to her, and knowledgeable, and so much more grown-up than Gabriel Stannard's.

The voice was all the encouragement she needed to pry herself loose. It was for her own good. If she felt no more than a tug at the thought of leaving, then she knew a tug was not strong enough to hold her. She saw her reflection in the glass-topped table that held the base unit for the telephone. She looked regal. Every hair was in place. The illusion was perfect.

"There were reporters swarming all over the house," she said. "We needed a private army to fight our way to the front gates. The hospital is even worse. I have no idea what they want."

"I saw the news, read the papers. They're like all carrion eaters."

"I've been alone here, and have had a lot of time to think. I thought about what Gabriel needs, and what I need. We never really connected, I think. I know that sounds like a cruel thing to say when I've spent so long with him, but it is true more and more. We never intertwined. Sometimes we ran parallel to each other; it looked like we were in sync. But I see him now in the hospital, and he looks at me as though I've come to sell him a magazine subscription. He's angry and frightened, and treats me dismissively. There is nothing I can do to help him except to be there for him . . . and he does not want me there. I do not think it is a front, false bravery. He truly does not want me there."

"You remind him of what happened to him—of what he was, as opposed to what he has become. You're not at fault. But you're going to be the one who pays if you permit this to continue."

"I know." At first the sanctuary of Stannard's estate had been a warm blanket against a cold, insectile world. Here she could be anonymous, and cleave to another human being, and build, because there was time. Lately the hounds were at the gates, and her privacy had become the victim of Stannard's newsworthiness. The sole advantage to staying was that she had the house all to herself. Stannard would inevitably be returned, and what would happen then was something from which her body urged her to flee, *now*.

If she remained, she would be finished. Emptied. She was sensitive to the one-way flux of energy from her to Stannard. Perhaps it had taken the extreme of his gruesome hunting sortie for her to recognize it, but she was smart enough to disengage before she was drained to a husk. Physically, she had become irrelevant to his existence, and later in the hospital his touch put her in mind of leeches, of ticks trying to thieve lifeblood as unobtrusively as they could. So she had choked off the conduit, pulling away to save herself . . . and she saw that he hated her, if only on the level of instinct, for not being more self-sacrificing.

Her looks were on the mend. First, the sclera of her eyes cleared, returning to veinless white. The flush of blood mellowed her lips and shaded her flesh. Her cracked and ravaged cuticles repaired themselves; the long nails were on their way back. She could walk out to the pool without feeling as though she had been used as a sandbag during a flood. On the worst of her days, she still had the power to turn heads, but only within the last few weeks had she stored enough surplus beauty to enable her to *radiate*. It was an effect that could only be gauged by the reactions of strangers; in a way, her own kind of feeding. To get this, she had to reenter the world. It was not too late, but what Robert had just told her was true: if she tarried here, paying the bill that would accrue would make her evaporate.

Two phone calls to New York City was all it had taken. The Objet d'Art perfume account, which had given up on securing Sertha Valich, proved more than eager to grant an eleventh-hour reprieve. "Actually," Joanna Traxson, the firm's head, had confided, "this is more like eleven fifty-nine and forty-five seconds, Sertha love, but for *you* . . ."

The second call had been to Robert, because beyond the work Sertha needed a friend, and there was no time to make new ones when her personal battery was critically low. She did not want to step off a plane at JFK and be alone. She had been with Stannard, and alone, for too long.

Now that it was done, Stannard was like a blown dynamo, circuits fused by one glorious overload. It was the way his eyes roamed over her and saw nothing that hurt the most.

Her luggage, all matched top-grain hides, was ranked and filed in the front hallway. The limousine would wait just as long as she wanted. This call might have been more expediently made from the mobile phone tucked into the vehicle, but Sertha purposefully wanted a more positive sense of disconnection. This was the final call she would ever make from this house, making up her next bed totally before jumping into it.

"Horus is coming back here today," she said. "He can handle this place with much more panache than I." It was time to divert Robert. "And it will be so nice to see you again. Since the new times are nothing to talk about, we'll talk about old times . . . and dinner, at least the first one, will have to be on your Gold Card."

"Platinum Card," he corrected proudly. "Ever see one? They issue merchants a booklet of special instructions on how to treat anyone who hands over a Platinum Card. It's quite outrageous. Yes, by all means, take advantage."

It was his tone she needed more than his words. He had assured her that he was still there for her, and beyond that it was all cute upper-crust banter, a social whirl she could dance in her sleep. What they had once shared had stayed with her, not growing cold and dead, but glowing with a minuscule core of heat that had been the cause for many pleasant reflections through several years. Now that she fanned the memory, she was just as pleased to see it respond, and warm. Realizing that people just did not fade out when you were done with them was new to her, and frightening. But now she was also willing—and that will sustained her.

"It's settled, then." He sounded glad. "I'll send my car to collect you when you arrive at JFK."

She cut directly to the goodbyes, but with an honest smile on her face. Before the tears could fill her eyes again and meddle with her thoughts, before unsaid words and regret could foul her logic and make her tarry one more day in a string of added days, and kill her that much more, she hung up the phone, closed the ornate double doors of the manse behind her, and walked out into the light, into the next chapter of her life.

36

IT WAS WEDNESDAY, AND IT was raining.

The TV set in Sara Windsor's Olive Grove office broadcast dazzling rainbow snow and the steady, soothing hiss of off-the-air static. The rain had returned, after two days unbroken by sunlight. She needed no special permission to be here this late at night, with her thoughts zeroed in on the flickering flame of the votive candle on her desk.

Staying home was too much of an ordeal.

The police had taken their time, enjoying themselves in their analysis of her living room. They excitedly compared bullet hole evaluations, and strung their trajectory wires, and dusted for prints, and their calm methodology nearly drove her into a screaming fit. Her home had been raped, in a way, and now the cops were getting their jollies by feeling it up instead of giving her healing time.

Holing up in an anonymous hotel room somewhere would be inspirational enough to make her use her Colt Diamondback revolver on herself. No, thanks. Faceless rooms reminded her of too many assignations with faceless men who drove expensive, faceless cars.

The most tempting possibility was to sell the house and move on. Her ex-hubby, Spence, had done it; career-obsessed Dr. Christopher Rosenberg had done it; and, in the most extreme fashion possible, Lucas had done it—and in so doing, had betrayed her.

The same ambulance had removed both Lucas and Stannard from the premises; how was that for a black little irony. By the time the stretchers were slotted into the waiting van, the two paramedics were besmirched to the elbows in thick, gelid blood. Two types.

Lucas' throat wound, though messy and serious, was not automatically fatal. The carotid artery is nearly as big around as a Magic Marker, and there had been enormous loss of blood complicated by secondary hemorrhage from the posterior branches of the artery. Quick incisions were made so that ligatures could be tied around the external carotid. Lucas was pronounced dead on arrival with the ligatures still professionally in place.

Lucas should not have died, and did. Stannard, who had absorbed more bullets than a being of meat and bone and blood had any right to, had survived.

She had seen it in Lucas' eyes, at the window. With his blood on her hands, she saw that the Lucas Ellington she knew had died long before Stannard had fired his surprise shot.

The deal makers in New York and Hollywood had sleuthed out her home number, but not the office number at Olive Grove. For the time being, she found sanctuary from the battering-ram siege of book and movie offers. "Based on a true story"—now there was a magical phrase. People would swallow anything prefaced with it. What difference did it make, when they were incapable of distinguishing between fiction and reality in the first place?

Across the room, on the TV, reality had signed off until the farm report, at five A.M.

The thing Gabriel Stannard had been packing in his crotch, the police had informed her, was a High Standard hammerless two-shot derringer. Then followed the jokes about concealed weapons, ho, ho, phallic symbols, yuk, yuk. Lucas had been dispatched—as they say in Victorian detective stories—by a tiny, ridiculous-looking thing that would be decorative adorning a Mississippi riverboat gambler's vest pocket.

Claremont Street was just as aversive. Men and women in official cars picked apart the dead end, the "goat path," the Grace Methodist cemetery, and the spot in the street where a man had died. There was plenty of paper for Sara to read if she wished. One preliminary report described the way in which a guitarist named Cannibal Rex—real name, Martin Killough Beecher—had been killed.

It had happened while Sara was hugging the floor in her towel. Just as Lucas' M-16 chopped apart Stannard and the living room wall, Cannibal Rex opened fire with his Auto Mag. The gunfire in the house had touched him off like a bomb, and the heavyweight slugs began to punch spectacular holes in the flanks of the foremost police cars as a general firefight erupted. The Charger began to come apart a chunk at a time as the cops brought their own firepower to bear. When Cannibal ducked down to change clips, a stiff-fingered blow from one of Horus' schooled, lethal hands had caused his brain to burst. Horus had not been held in custody very long.

The rounds from Lucas' gun had also perforated a switchplate for the ceiling light fixture, a china vase sitting on the mantel, and a framed photograph of Sara with her parents at graduation. The center geisha in the Takamatsuzuka reproduction, the one in the orange kimono, had a bullet hole in her exposed left hand.

A lot of the paper Sara saw concerned the cabin up at Point Pitt and the dead people discovered there.

Burt Kroeger's wife, Diana, had insisted on cremation, followed by a scattering of ashes in the Pacific Ocean. Sara supposed that meeting Diana was inevitable. She had no idea what to say to her.

In one pocket of Lucas' garrison belt, investigators had discovered a string of crystal beads, the kind that caught the light and divided it up into rainbow hues. No one could figure out their significance.

In Tucson, Arizona, the machines monitoring the life functions of Jackal Reichmann went steady and shrill. Eldon Quantrill lost his entertainment value and went to trial for triple homicide.

In San Francisco, Ralph "Sandjock" Trope, manager of the Rockhound nightspot, bagged himself another headline by positively identifying a photograph of Lucas Ellington as the mystery roadie with the diamond eyepatch he'd spoken with on the day guitarist Jackson Knox died. Ralph could not actually match the roadie's face with Lucas', but he could read the papers and knew a promotional opportunity when he saw one.

Since no positive proof against Lucas Ellington had been unearthed in the Denver murder of keyboardist Brion Hardin, he was blamed anyway. He had become convenient.

The news media gained a full nelson on the legend of Lucas Ellington, the rockstar assassin. The police earnestly plugged their forthright protection of innocent bystanders in Dos Piedras. It would be irrelevant to point out that the two men who died were the only ones who would have died under any circumstances.

Now, sitting in her darkened office, toying with desk knickknacks and staring at televisual snow, Sara realized that Lucas had forced her to do nothing. It had been his plan. Her only part had been to play yet another surrogate Kristen in the presence of Stannard, to complete

Lucas' reenactment of his nightmare.

She had not thought herself a killer, yet she had picked up the pistol and certainly would have shot Stannard in the head had the police not bashed through her door at that moment. She was not a killer, yet hadn't she killed Lucas by failing him, by not seeing the gun in Stannard's pants? She had surely spent aeons watching the singer draw and fire.

The ways in which normal people were compelled to kill was a mainstay of her field of study. The yellow legal pad was on the desk in the pool of dim light, mostly doodles.

Would Lucas have killed her?

Would she have killed?

And if so, what was the difference between them?

Lucas represented what could almost be termed another evolutionary step—Psychopathic Man, possessing the mechanisms to cope with what living has become, to survive in this world. That capacity was present in everyone. The difference was that the mechanisms finally turned on him and consumed him. But those mechanisms could not be scoured out of the human psyche; they were part of our genetic makeup. And despite the nasty implications of being surrounded by a sidewalk full of latent killers, Sara thought, we'd better be thankful for those mechanisms. Someday, they might mean our survival.

Nevertheless, she would go to her grave thinking that she had created a monster. In a way she had, but the monster was not Lucas Ellington, who was dead and gone. The monster was her.

And now there were so many new graves. . . .

Sara toed off her shoes and left them on the carpeted floor. Eventually she dozed off on the narrow sofa she kept in her office for the purpose, pulling a knit afghan around herself as her body temperature dropped. The candle burned down and extinguished, sending aromatic smoke curling into the air and flavoring away the harsher smell of the dead Salem 100s butted in the ashtray. Outside, the rain poured down with a vengeance, as though trying to drown the whole state.

When she was fast asleep, she had a nightmare about Stannard, and Lucas, and the events she might have changed. It was the first.

37

GABRIEL STANNARD POISED THE MUZZLE of the automatic riot shotgun on a thick cable brown with rust and fired round after round until the magazine was exhausted. His laugh was victorious and slightly mad. Strong sea winds knocked his hair about and rippled his clothing. Beyond his perch on the high steel, the night was shot through with stars like sharply defined gemstones. Snaky golden reflections from the water far below writhed across his face. He reached around to a back pocket. No more ammo.

Slugs panged off the cables and girders around him, and he flinched. High-velocity death was throwing itself at him. The shooters below had him targeted now. This high up, it was difficult to spring from one perch to another. He was trapped, and he knew it. Imminent death showed in the tension in his jaws, the bulge of his muscles, the glaze in his eyes. He hoisted his shotgun aloft like a bannerless standard and shouted that rock 'n' roll would never die.

In response, a hot slug ripped through his shoulder,

spattering the ironwork behind him with blood.

"Cut, cut, cut, *cut*!" shouted Logan McCabe from the stage floor. His expression was designed to inform his crew he was forcing himself to be tolerant. The special effects honcho, Jake Morrison of Firepower Unlimited, ambled over to pow-wow. The charges designed to scratch white ricochet trails off the simulated metal behind Stannard's head were so brilliant that they lit up the sky cyclorama behind him and cast shadows, revealing that the backdrop of sea and starry sky was fake. McCabe cocked back his baseball cap. Since the advent of Spielberg, all directors who desired success made sure to wear their baseball caps. McCabe's bore a Dr. Pepper logo. He decided to deemphasize the background by adding more fog—this *was* supposed to be San Francisco, after all, and every time McCabe had seen the Golden Gate Bridge for real at night it had been shrouded in thick mist.

McCabe's first AD, Louis Katz, called for new setups in twenty minutes. Time was burning up too fast to track.

Stannard rode a cherry-picker arm twenty feet down to the stage floor, where a grip handed him his cane. It was a dark hickory walking stick with a gold lion's head. By now, he had gotten pretty good with it. His limp was obvious but not overt, and he attracted no gratuitous notice as he moved to his slingback chair, the one with which McCabe had gifted him during the *Maneater* shoot. This where the star enthroned himself. The golden words on the canvas chairback said so.

A cold glass of Sweetouchnee tea found its way into his hand, and Stannard looked up into the eyes of Aki Blair.

She bent at the waist to peck him on the cheek. Her passage across the set attracted much more notice than Stannard's. Aki was lately notorious for a series of Levi's 501 jeans ads. She was leggy, curvy, almond-eyed, with very long, straight, glossy black hair. Her attentions to Stannard were designed to be seen. She was being well paid to pretend to be his lady.

The oil-based special effects fog was acrid and tended to settle in the back of the throat with a taste like cigarette ashes. Stannard drank half the tea and plucked out a pulpy-wet lime wedge to suck on. His icy-blue eyes assessed Aki. Quite a piece. Look but don't touch.

He decided not to be kind. He was in no mood.

"I'd appreciate it, love, if you weren't so fucking obvious," he said just as she turned to wave at one of the gaffers, a beefy dude Stannard knew as Blackie.

She jerked around as if on a leash, eyebrows up. "Just flirting," she said innocently.

"That's not what I'm talking about. I mean you and McCabe."

"Hm?" Her face, her manner, were so smooth and plastic that he suddenly wanted to smash her skull in.

Lowering his voice, he rasped, "You were fucking McCabe last night. You can't."

A shot of pain, like internal gas, bit him inside and made him grimace. His pipework was intact, but tender, delicate, and heavily scarred. A lot of healing had occurred since the debacle on Claremont Street, and none of it had gone fast or easily. The Teflon bullets from Lucas Ellington's M-16 had caused a hairy blood-poisoning problem. Then came massive trauma, blood loss, heavy shock. The artificial kneecap would allow him to regain about 50 percent of his right leg's flexibility. Of the five slugs he had stopped, one had lodged deep in his pelvis. One had punctured his left lung after splintering through a rib strut. One had chewed a four-ounce hunk out of his left triceps, near the armpit. The skin graft to replace it had been sliced from his once cute ass. Another bullet had skinned his neck, biting the tissue hard and opening up a lot of capillaries. The blood had flown. And the remaining bullet, the first one to hit . . . number one with a bullet, as they proclaimed on

KAFC's venerable *Heavy Metal Hour of Power* . . .

He watched Aki, head to toe, as she pretended to register indignation at his accusation. Jesus, he thought, every move she makes, she pretends there's a goddamn camera right there, eating up her image. Like McCabe had been eating her up last night. He imagined her hooking her slim, graceful hands around her knees and spreading wide so McCabe could gobble her. Her clitoris was large and medium sensitive; it was a lot of worthwhile work to bring her off. Stannard's tongue had done some time at that post, and although she could be played like a violin orally, those skills alone would not suffice, so she had assumed a variety of fascinating and not-very-photogenic positions for Logan McCabe, now the driving creative force behind *Shakedown*, coming soon to a theater near you. Stannard knew about the positions because Joshua Knopf, ace detective for hire, had done a bit of filmmaking himself. What it lacked in style it made up for in content, and Josh had supplied glossies faster than any commercial lab.

Aki continued to smile at him. They watched the crew swarm over the mocked-up portion of the top of the Golden Gate Bridge, working their antlike tasks and preparing for a second take of the climactic shootout scene. Stannard's contract specified that his scenes were to be completed first. He was no longer capable of doing the rock 'n' roll stage acrobatics himself. Gymnasts would be used for long shots in the concert scenes, to be filmed later. Two physical doubles had been hired, and good makeup rendered them into acceptable matches. All Stannard got were the close-ups. From the waist up he could still fake being formidable.

Stannard sighed and tried a stab at honesty. "Aki—fucking this director at this particular time is not going to advance your career one degree. You're already doing well; why keep adding stuff? You'll overload."

"So?" Clearly she was another one who thought she could handle too much.

"*So* . . . we need a little discretion, love. I can't have the crew laughing at me behind my back."

At last, in her eyes, he saw the flash of flame he wanted to see. "Are you telling me who I can and cannot sleep with?" She held the sweet bogus smile firmly in place. She had learned to be extremely camera conscious. She could hold that smile even if a flaming arrow thunked into the back of her head. She possessed a skill, if not a talent.

In that moment he knew Horus would have to be instructed to audition a new girl, a new arm doily for the public Gabriel Stannard. Aki was not going to work out. If she was simply cashiered, she might shoot off to anyone who would listen, to the film crew, to the magazines. No good. Perhaps she could be cornered into signing some sort of document.

Documents, he thought. Coverage. Endless contingencies, ceaseless paranoia. A suffocation of clauses and conditions. This was not Gabriel Stannard's way of doing things. His anger and frustration slammed into high heat, a bubbling pot of rage finally boiling over. The cobra kill sheen settled into his gaze, and he returned her so-sweet smile sweetly.

"Aki, my dear . . ." he said. Then he whacked her as hard as he could in the temple with the butt of his cane.

With a cry more of surprise than pain, she flailed backward and swept clean a metal tray of coffee and doughnuts, landing on her taut butt with a wet smack. Her hand clutched at her forehead, and when she saw blood she began to howl. The stage fell silent, and after a shock lull workers jumped to assist her. She made small squeaking noises as she imagined the damage to her photogenic features. Then she started shrieking. The cameramen and munchkins crawling around the bridge set continued their work with smiles of indulgence. Hollywood could be so weird.

In an hour, her eye would be satisfyingly hollow and black. Let the makeup guys try to conceal *that* little brand, Stannard thought.

"You son of a bitch!" she wailed, struggling ungracefully to stand up, wobbling and crying when she did. "Fucking *eunuch*!" Her tiny fist hauled back to paste the singer, and a huge, dark hand enclosed it fully and arrested its swing.

"That's enough," Horus said in a tone low enough to silence her. It was a guarantee of no bullshit.

"Escort her out," said Stannard. "Explain some fiscal realities to her."

Horus nodded and complied, his eyes half closing in his usual subtle and dignified way. The problem would be resolved. Aki had to be made aware that in this age of drug testing for employees, her lucrative Levi's deal could be made to evaporate with one strategic mention of her childlike propensity for controlled substances.

"Christ on a *hose*, Gabe, gimme a fucking *break*." McCabe appeared at his shoulder, watching without interest as Aki was led outside. "You two kids have a tiff? This sorta shit ain't good for crew morale, man, especially when we're behind the shooting schedule. It's too early in the film to have personality problems."

"Yeah. Right." Stannard nodded civilly, swigging his thick tea. "Logan? One item, between you and me as friends and buddies; director to actor. Jam your wick in some other hidey-hole, or I'll have my black Fury rip it off and hand it back to you in a hot-dog bun with extra onions."

Whatever instruction was headed out of McCabe's mouth dissolved into an incoherent mush noise. *Hhwwaaahh*. His complexion went the color of mozzarella cheese, and he cleared his throat without needing to.

Don't alienate McCabe, too, Stannard's new imp of conscience cautioned. "Logan—people in the throes of passion can be dangerously free with embarrassing information."

"Uh." He pulled the visor of his Dr. Pepper ballcap low over his eyes. "Uh, yeah, absolutely. Uh . . . we'll, er, be ready for you in five. Jake needs to wire up your blood squib again." To be honest, McCabe recovered admirably. Stannard sensed that he might. Aki would be dismissed from the director's cognizance since she no longer had anything to do with getting footage into the can this afternoon.

The blood squib was tucked beneath a flap of flesh-colored foam on Stannard's shoulderblade. There was a square pad against his skin that protected him from a possible burn. The little capsule, like a fat tick, was installed tantalizingly close to where he had caught a real live bullet. The anchors and foam were not fancy. The camera angle would not see the setup taped to his back, so special makeup to blend it in was not required. It was electronically detonated. When Stannard felt the *paff* and slight impact, he was supposed to react as though shot. That, he knew how to do from painful experience.

The deal with the studio for *Shakedown* had gone smoothly. What Stannard craved now, more than the work, was the visibility. The film would insist that he was still a driving force in the universe of rock. His fans would see that he was okay, that he still had all of his limbs, that he was still a functioning maximal badass. If your audience thought you were a cripple, they would abandon you.

The money was good but not necessary. His stock portfolio insured that his mansion of many televisions would endure. There was enough cash flow to purchase a whole stable of Aki Blairs, so he did not mourn her loss. He had but to snap his fingers and call, "Next."

Sertha Valich had gone. Dumped him. To hell with her. He could no longer do his thing in concert. But if this film could be efficiently faked, then so could a new video. He still had his voice.

Jake Morrison finished wiring in the fresh squib. Alligator-clamped leads dangled down Stannard's back. McCabe gave him the high sign from aboard the big Panavision dolly. The stage was growing unbearably dense with the stinking fog. If they all could keep breathing, it would look terrific in dailies.

Stannard rode the cherry picker back up to his perch on the bridge, and the picker pilot reminded him with a shout to be sure to attach his safety line snap ring to the U-bolt secured out of camera range. A twenty-foot drop to the stage could break a shitload of bones.

From up here, the picker pilot and most of the crew were invisible, smothering in phony fog. He heard Louis, the assistant director, hollering for *quiet* on the set, please, then McCabe's voice, softer and leaking none of the agitation of a moment earlier, telling everyone to please *settle*.

He told himself over and over that he still had his voice. He wondered just how far that talent would take him.

Below, McCabe called for action, and the shooting started all over again.